Land Of Hope

Briddon

LAND OF HOPE AND GLOREY

BRIDDON GIBBS

Book designed and produced by Starrydog.co.uk
Cover Design and Illustration © Starrydog.co.uk

Visit **www.briddongibbs.net** *for information about forthcoming books and locations of the places and landmarks mentioned in Land Of Hope And Glorey.*

Contents

The Whore of Babylon 11

Magpie Mine 62

Tinker Frith's Fish 176

I have used the landscape of Derbyshire as though it were a stage setting for a theatre performance. The fields and rivers, towns and villages, moorlands and hills, roads and railways are scenery for a series of stories beginning with the death of Queen Victoria. The stories are entirely fictional and have no links to persons living or dead. Just as I have used the old packways, or the wild flowers so I have sometimes used the old Derbyshire surnames such as my own. They are an integral part of the scenery. If by using any of these names I have given offence I humbly apologise. It was entirely unintentional.

Briddon Gibbs 2013

Land of Hope and Glorey
They're bobbies in our town
Nobody's as fat as Glorey
Hope plods up and down
Wider still and fatter
Glorey gets each year
Hope's feet are getting flatter
Soon they'll disappear. . .
(the skipping rope is turned faster and faster)
Slam the door of the Clink!
Turn the key of the door!
Knot the hangman's noose!
And-out-goes-she!

Skipping Rhyme that appeared in the school playground of the town c.1912

(The children in the school had been fortunate in that the headmaster was a fine musician and taught the children modern music. The skipping rhyme was based on the patriotic tune and music that many still revere today.)

THE WHORE OF BABYLON

The first snowflake settled on the engine and melted as the coal train eased into the goods sidings at three o' clock on a black January morning. The snowflake was extinguished as quickly as the life of the engine driver's victim within the next five hours. The night superintendent of the Midland Railway waited by a solitary gas lamp where the chain to the ignition swung in the rising south east wind.

"I've just heard something that's made me feel sick," he said to the engine driver. "They are saying the Queen's dead." The engine driver said nothing. He did not care a fart for Queen Victoria. Instead he saw his chance to kill his fireman, something he had planned for three weeks.

His trucks full of coal from the Pinxton Coalfield were uncoupled and he shunted the engine to couple half a mile of empty coal trucks for the return journey. Already the coal he had brought for the fires of Buxton was turning white in the trucks under the night sky.

The driver, Ernest Fox, was a small man with a ferret face and a thin red beard. He was called 'Foxey' because of his red whiskers, his face and his surname. Behind his sharp face was an obsessive personality. Jealousy ran through his conscious mind like a vein of molten lava destroying compassion and rational thought. His mate and fireman on the train with him that morning, Will Jackson, had been making eyes at Mrs. Fox. Fox knew that Will had a way with women and it was only a matter of time before he had his way with his wife. The only way the jealousy could be quenched was by killing Jackson and this was just the morning. He had planned it for several days but he saw that the death of the old Queen would facilitate matters. Folk, he thought, would think of nothing but the dead Queen.

Fifteen minutes into the return journey Fox picked up a shovel when the train rattled over the viaduct above the Wye in Monsal Dale. Light was creeping into the sky and the black line of the river far below was like Indian ink between the snow furred trees. As the train entered into the Headstones Tunnel Fox brought down the flat of his shovel on Jackson's skull. Jackson swayed as consciousness left him. Quick as a snake Fox leaned the body and sprawled it over the coal tender as though Jackson was reaching out to bring coal forward to ease shoveling it into the firebox.

When the train emerged into the open Jackson was leaning over the coals just as Fox had planned. He pressed levers and gathered speed. There was a downhill gradient now and all the signals would be for him. He knew that he was driving the train between the two slow early trains to Derby and they wanted everyone out of the way so the Pullman from Manchester Central to St. Pancras could take its load of rich passengers to London. He could now speed through stations and by signal boxes too fast to allow anyone to see Jackson was immobile.

Six miles further down the track and through three stations he passed over a small viaduct spanning a deserted lane that led to a gypsy encampment and applied the brakes, even though the distance signal told him to proceed. Here there was a long curve in the track amidst a private woodland of a large estate. He was out of sight of the guard in the guards van at the end of the train and the woodlands were always empty. He checked Jackson and thought he was still breathing. He selected a massive lump of coal and battered Jackson about his head. There was more blood than he had expected and the coal dripped blood on his boot. Swearing, he opened the fire door but the coal would not fit.

He had stopped the engine on a small bridge over a woodland stream and he threw the coal down into the water. He did this with six other lumps. His blows became fiercer and more vicious and an emotion gripped Fox of power and elation something his closed and watchful mind had never felt. Jackson was now surely dead. For a few seconds Fox remained still, breathing heavily. The release he felt was pleasurable to the obsessive man. The trickles of red blood in the sombre snow world excited him. The snow and steam hissed softly and he saw the light snow smoking through the trees. The alarm calls of the pheasants died away after the splashes and the stream diluted the blood until it vanished. Fox started the engine and in the next tunnel felt Jackson's pulse. He was dead. Coming out of the tunnel Fox sounded the whistle, a foolish thing to do as Lord John, owner of the estate had requested the Midland Railway not to disturb his game.

Fox's feeling of control and euphoria stayed with him until he reached the goods sidings at Rowsley where for some reason he felt a great feeling of unease as though some powerful sentinel was watching him. Glancing to his right he saw the stark and watchful tower on Stanton Moor, Stanton Stand, black and snow capped in the January light and Fox froze. A gripping premonition of what might happen seized him. They (and 'they' always lurked in his consciousness) could capture him and take him to prison…

He was transported back to the late 60's of the last century when he had been a boy in Derby.

His family life had been crowded and miserable and his brothers and sisters bullied and picked on him. They persecuted their pale unsmiling little brother with his vulpine face. At school it was worse. He was bullied almost to the point of losing endurance.

One hot July day in 1869 the older pupils were taken on a school 'treat' by the not unprogressive headmaster. He had arranged for these children from the back streets of Derby to visit the countryside. Mr. Thornhill of Stanton Hall had invited these 'children of the poor' to visit Stanton Stand, a tower for viewing the panorama of the Derbyshire countryside. The Thornhill family had erected the Stand to celebrate the great Electoral Reform Act of 1832 when the admired Whig politician Gray had passed a parliamentary bill giving a vote to the middle and lower middle classes.

Thornhill was to provide a picnic and a talk to the children about how the vote would soon be available to all men in Great Britain, thanks to the Prime Minister Mr. Disraeli who had just introduced his new Bill. Fresh air, history and a picnic in the garden of the hall. It was considered ideal.

They had got off the train at Darley Dale and began a long two mile uphill trudge to the Stand. The teachers strode ahead and at the back Ernest White and Jack Dalton played their usual game of 'putting Foxey in a trap' or 'hunting the fox'. This consisted of shoving Fox's head between gaps in walls or gateposts or chasing him back along the road where the hounds 'killed' him beating him with sticks or biting him. At one stage the Headmaster had indicated a roadside spring and horse trough where sweet cold water gushed and gurgled. He had said it was safe to drink and the grateful children did so. When they had all finished and it was Fox's turn they had held his head under the water saying they were drowning a vermin fox cub.

At the Stand they had gazed uncaring at the views of the Derwent Valley and the endless moorlands and Mr. Smedley's new castle perched on its hill above his kingdom at Matlock. Coming down the stone stairs past the narrow windows Ernest had forced Fox's hand between one of the light slits.

"Foxy's prison!" they had mocked. "You'll be kept here till you die! You're in the condemned man's cell waiting to swing!"

Fox had thought it may be true. His hand was wedged in the cruciform slit as securely as being fastened to a ring in a cell wall. He was a long time freeing his hand and the small platform on the stone stairs was like a prison where he would die…

Fox turned away from the January snow scene of Stanton Moor and kicked Jackson several times and some of his earlier feelings of power returned.

The train went on at the rate of a fast passenger train until Matlock where it slid through the station by a little used shadowy platform. Reducing speed still further in the cutting after the station Fox pushed out the body on to some limestone boulders at the side of the track. Then he stopped the train and got out and shouted that his fireman had fallen from the cab. Snow on the track side cleaned his boots.

It had been the perfect murder. Everyone believed it was an accident, another human tragedy in a grim world where the Queen had breathed her last. Fox had to work hard not to let a smile stretch his thin lips. Lord John wrote to the Directors of the Midland Railway. The letter was filed and an apology sent. The Directors, now they had the line built through the estate ignored the noble Lord and nobody bothered to find the offending driver. Life continued as if nothing, except the death of the Queen, had happened. Mrs. Fox felt weary with the seemingly endless interference, as she called it, from Mr. Fox during the Empire's mourning. The sense of power that Fox had felt in the snow filled woods translated itself into sexual energy. Only Mrs. Fox was aware of a subtle change and she did not share this intimate fact with anybody.

James Fitzwilliam Ball D.D. (Oxon.) on that snow choked Monday morning in 1901 of Queen Victoria's death, saw, in the corner of his bedchamber, the most exquisite gypsy girl he had ever imagined. Her long legs were curled beneath her and her dark eyes sparkled. And later, sitting at table in the morning room of the Vicarage, with his double solid-silver egg cup in the shape of a Viking helmet before him, he announced she had stolen his gold Geneva pocket watch.

Of course the police must be summoned at once. Sergeant Glorey, no less, must wait upon him as soon as possible. One of the maids must go without delay and summon that guardian of the law. James Fitzwilliam Ball took the top off the second egg.

Sergeant Glorey behind the pine fortification of his desk was not pleased. News of the Queen's death had come to him on the Station telephone, one of the few in the town. He had looked forward to spreading the news with doom and gloom throughout the town and making arrangements for crepe arm bands and drapes and police presence at dignified assemblies of grief. He had not planned a walk in the snow to the Vicarage. But he was pleased to see the maid.

"Take off your cloak, my dear, warm yourself before the stove before you go." Before putting on his outdoor cape he absorbed the curves of the servant girl as she warmed her hands at the fiery furnace of the little door into the Tortoise stove. His eyes, pale and bulbous as the dead Queen's Saxe-Coburg-Gotha eye, concealed an inner life as hot as the stove's.

Sergeant Glorey roared for Constable Hope to accompany him to the Vicarage. It was Constable Hope's first morning in the town; as soon as Glorey had inspected the new man at 6 a.m. that morning in the whirling snowflakes of the yard, he had taken a dislike to the young man.

Sergeant and Constable walked up South Church Street, the wind flapping their capes so they resembled two crawling bats under the snow-laced lime trees. Neither man spoke and they walked up the carriage drive to the snow tufted gothic pinnacles of the Vicarage.

The two officers were shown into the morning room where a fire blazed and the maids were clearing the remains of the reverend doctor's breakfast. Dr. Ball was staring out of the window. They were welcomed by one of the curates, Herbert Jones, his black hair flopping over a face as white as a church candle. He had been keeping watch with a mother and a young baby expected to die of measles that was scourging the poor in the town. Jones was also anxious about Dr. Ball. The town doctor had diagnosed 'softening of the brain.' The softening seemed to provide Dr. Ball with frequent hallucinations of girls, angels and the occasional demon. Jones wearily prayed that this one had worn clothes. After the last vision the Reverend Doctor had needed opiate sedation.

Dr. Ball had clearly forgotten the purpose of the visit. He stared out at the two acres of garden and muttered 'fairyland' to himself. The garden had always thrilled him. He had come to the town forty years earlier as an Oxford greek scholar, Canon of Lichfield cathedral. Awarded this rich Derbyshire living, he had been greatly disturbed at the time by the building of the railway. He had used his own money to purchase land and plant a small wood to hide an ugly viaduct over a deserted lane ruining his view from the vicarage. As the wood grew it also hid a gypsy camp that distressed the Canon. Gypsies had always haunted his mind. His eyes absorbed the view with his little wood and beyond that the great estates of the Hall. He did not know and would not care that soon in this fairyland life would finally be battered out of a man.

He suddenly turned round and stared at the two policemen.

"Aha!" he said to Glorey. "Don Quixote has found Sancho Panza!"

Jones, his eyes smarting from fatigue wondered at this flash of apt wit from a decaying brain.

"Dr. Ball fears there was an intruder this morning and she has stolen his watch."

"Can you describe her Canon Ball?" asked Glorey taking out his notebook and reluctantly removing his gaze from the servant girls at the table. Jones sucked on his breath angrily. If there was a blunder to be made Glorey would achieve it. He knew the schoolchildren relished the name of Canon Ball and he had been tirelessly getting the town to call their vicar Dr. Ball. The new young policeman saved the situation.

"Sir, could I ask you to feel in your top waistcoat pocket?" Dr. Ball did as he was asked and pulled out the shining gold of the Geneva watch.

"Well!" said he. "The cunning little vixen. The girl has made fools of all of you!"

Back in the Station Glorey thundered out his rage at the new recruit. "You'll not last long in this town if you question your elders and betters like that. You've a mighty lot to learn my lad. If you think we are going to let this drop you can think again. You can get yourself off to them gypsies and let them know we are watching them. I'll wager one of them varmints had broken into the vicarage. Ask a few questions. Go over the bridge and turn right down the lane. After half an hour you'll reach a three arched railway viaduct with a private wood to the right. Go under the bridge and after another twenty minutes you'll see the caravans. It would not surprise me if one had not been in the vicarage but you and your mouth have spoiled the evidence. Now bugger off Constable before I kick you out."

Hope set out knowing the walk was a punishment and quite pointless. Yet on that first morning he learned that no walk was ever wasted. It was something he never forgot. He was used to teachers and higher officials blowing hot and cold and shouting.

That was the way of the world he thought then.

Hope walked on, a dark figure in miles of snow filled countryside. His boots made a soft squeak in the deep snow. To his left rose a three mile long wooded ridge crested with snow tipped pines and the lower slopes a tangle of snow-feathered oaks and beeches above the railway. Before him the lane stretched white and untrodden to the viaduct and the gypsies. To his right endless fields sheeted with snow concealed the river. The winter silence was broken only by the slowing beat of a coal train somewhere far behind him.

Two rooks passed silently in the orange grey cloud of a snow day and he heard the distant bell of the church. He turned and saw the spire now a mile away above the smoke of the town chimneys.

"Shangri La John!" his mother used to say when they came on the train from Derby to the picturesque market town. His father was a well paid brass foundry worker at the Derby Midland railway workshops; a morose man who barely spoke to his youngest son. His main pleasure in life was Friday night when he became totally drunk, sometimes crawling home.

Final collapse came in the front room of the terraced house where the door led out to the street. The four boys and two girls accepted that Friday night would be taken up by their mother getting their father up the stairs. He was never violent but oaths and loose coins fell in all directions.

The mother never returned the coins she picked up on Friday nights. On Saturday morning the father handed over the rest to his wife for household needs. He was sober and silent until the following Friday. The mother used the coins to escape with her youngest son for trips out and picnics. If half a sovereign had fallen his mother bought a five shilling cheap return on the railway to this same town. She would pack hard boiled eggs in greaseproof paper with a twist of salt, a fresh loaf, cold meat, tomatoes and a pop bottle of cold tea. She would lean against the wall by the river and he would watch the swallows dart under the bridge, feed the ducks from the loaf she had brought and he would think how grey her face was and how old she was, for she was already showing signs of mortal illness.

She would turn her eyes and smile at him, the sun on her worn out face. "Shangri La, John. This place is heaven on earth. Just imagine, John, getting a job and working here!" She would smile and close her eyes.

And here he was. On a snowy winter's day at the beginning of his life and century. She had always favoured him above his other brothers who were much older than himself. She had allowed him to stay at school to ensure his reading and writing were good enough to get an office job. She had sent him to church and Sunday School and he had played in their football team and learned boxing. It was the Vicar of the church that had suggested he join the Derbyshire Police and then used his influence to ensure he was accepted, assisted with the endless references and medical and educational tests. Then he helped him apply for this post here.

If only his mother were alive to see him as constable in Shangri La . . . He had thought that last night. He had been glad to leave Derby. His sister in the next street cooked and washed for his father and himself after his mother died, but he knew she resented it. He knew his silent father wanted him out of the house so he could begin a new life with Widow Tweed who seemed to turn on lights in his face that his mother never had.

Hope was suddenly pulled out of his introspection and the silence of the snow was torn by a long coal train coming to a halt. Truck couplings squealed, waggons jostled as the train came to a shuddering halt. The primeval silence of the valley was broken. Hope stared with half attention, his inner life quickly regaining his attention.

Nobody had seen him off on the 3.20 from Derby the day before. Repairs to the line diverted the train by Nottingham and by Ambergate it was one and half hours late. It was dark when

Matlock was reached. A servant girl selected his compartment and rested her chin on a black tin trunk with the letters MF crudely painted on it. She had black curls and black eyes and she kept her sparkling eyes on him as the train threaded its way to Darley Dale and Rowsley. She got out at his station, determined to walk in front of him down the long hill from the station to the town, aware of her supple body shown off to full advantage in a well-tailored winter coat with black fur collar and trim boots with pearl buttons.

The church bells were ringing down in a wild clamour, already there were needles of frozen vapour like ghostly gnats dancing round the gas lamps as Hope crossed the bridge to his new life. The girl vanished in a swirl of coat and tight leather shod ankles and flash of eye, down the service road to the row of houses by the Bridge. Hope's face relaxed when he was alone in the Sunday streets.

Again the train imposed on his thoughts. The excitement of his new life had overwhelmed his consciousness. But now the coal train was absolutely still and silent. No steam, no whistles, no voices. Hope stared another moment then climbed back into his inner life and his new digs and landlady Mrs. Harryson.

He had walked down gaslit empty streets with gusts of bells and one distant horse and carriage and soon found the cottage in Water Lane where he was to lodge. He had knocked.

Nothing had prepared him for what followed. Mrs. Harryson, not much older than himself, had opened the door and welcomed him. The room he entered was unusually large with a fierce hot fire blazing. Warmth and light took him in. Two big and battered leather armchairs were either side the blaze of the fire. Two candles burned calmly on the mantelpiece undisturbed by airs or draughts in the room, burning in fine Sheffield silverplated sticks. The candlesticks were streaked with gold where the brass showed through the worn plate and they looked as if they had been kicked around at some time. In the middle of the mantelshelf was a good eighteenth century carriage clock its brass case deeply scratched.

Above this the astonished Hope saw a gilt framed picture of a regency buck of a hundred years earlier. The man looked as if he too had received a direct fist on his mouth at some time, as the canvas was cracked and dented, giving the mouth a twisted smile.

Against a wall was a solid oak bureau with a gas lamp on the wall above it. The gas was not lit.

The bewildered Hope just stared. The room was curiously masculine and very upper class despite the stressed articles. Once Hope had played in a football tournament organised by the church at Lichfield, followed by a tea. Hope had got lost in the maze of corridors at one point and found himself looking into the Bishop's study. This room was a shabby replica of the Bishop's room. There was even a bookcase, more books even than the Bishop.

But it was the picture that absorbed Hope. The man in the frame was clearly a negro or part negro, thought Hope, using the word he had been given in a vocabulary list in the Top Standard Class of his school.

He had looked almost helplessly at Mrs. Harryson. Almost as tall as he was she was, dressed in a bodice of white with a decoration of dark green buttons and beads to match the long green velvet skirt in the fashion of the times. Her honey coloured hair was piled in braids on her head and two drops at her ears were diamonds, Hope was convinced. Her dark brown eyes watched him, almost mocking him, but her lips - Hope was convinced he could detect negro influences there - were full and smiling. After her first words of welcome and introduction, she had said nothing as though she knew the room and picture would arouse any man's curiosity.

Hope finally was able to look at a massive table covered with a dazzling white Sunday cloth, where a meal was prepared for two. A large oil lamp turned high, radiated a powerful light through a shade decorated with wreaths of iris. He expected her to suggest they sit down for she had taken his coat, but she did not.

"You'll want to wash your hands Mr. Hope," said Mrs. Harryson.

"The Midland Railway always gives you a free helping of soot with your ticket."

Hope glanced at his hands that did not appear very dirty. At home in Derby they had only washed hands when the grime became apparent to the naked eye. But Mrs. Harryson was holding open one of several doors around the room and Hope obediently followed her.

This room was larger than any at home. It had a herringbone tiled floor with grooves that led to a brass drain in the floor's centre. A massive copper simmered over a small and fiery furnace as hot and bright as Nebuchadnezzar's, thought the bemused Hope, who knew the Bible but little else, it seemed tonight. Three baths were hung on the walls. Firewood was stacked neatly. On a cracked marble sideboard of seventy years ago was a brass bowl of steaming water, a white towel and a square of flannel and a cake of Pears soap.

Mrs. Harryson took the latch off another door and told him that was the lavatory and then she left him.

Hope washed his hands and was amazed at the muck that came off. He did the same with his face which he only usually did in the mornings and was likewise interested in the accumulated dirt. He opened the other door and went in the lavatory where a scrubbed seat displayed two circular holes, big and small, that opened into a deep and apparently bottomless pit, as Hope was to learn four years later. Hope pissed into the big hole careful not to leave drops on the immaculate seat. It was some time before he discovered the seat had a hinge to help him achieve this.

Back in the room she invited him to sit down. Hope's mouth watered at the biggest joint of sirloin he had seen in his life. Mrs. Harryson carved thick slices and Hope could not help staring. He had not seen a woman carve meat before. She gave him a huge square of Yorkshire Pudding crisp on the outside a hot savoury pudding in the middle. Parsnips in a creamy sauce, buttered sprouts were served. She brought out roast potatoes salted and crisp outside floury within. She put a large two pint white jug before him and poured ale into a silver tankard.

"It's from Mrs. Peters at The Anchor" she said. "She does the best brew in the town." Hope had not dared to disagree but did not need to. It was the best ale he had drunk.

Yet once again he had been puzzled. The rich silver tankard he was drinking from was dented heavily. The dinner plates and dishes and jugs were beautiful, with some kind of Chinese design but they all had chips. His own plate had a big piece missing so you could see the grey baked clay beneath.

After the meal Mrs. Harryson had invited him to finish his beer in the armchair to the right of the fire. Hope had stretched out his long legs before the fire. For a time he could not say much, the room astonished him. And Mrs. Harryson amazed him in so many ways.

They talked after a few minutes had passed until the carriage clock sent out nine repeated silver bell notes. Mrs. Harryson suggested that Hope may like to see his room as he had an early start tomorrow for his new job as constable. Once more she led him to the room with the copper and poured a basin of hot water and Hope realised he was supposed to wash, something he never did before bed at home. She also poured out a cup of cold water from a large jug of well water. The cup, an early Josiah Wedgwood had no handle. "For your teeth, Mr. Hope," said she. Hope looked blank. This was something else he had not bothered with.

She realised the problem. "I'll get you a toothbrush from Mrs. Swift the chemist tomorrow. You've fine teeth, Mr. Hope and you should look after them." She closed the door and Hope dutifully washed and pissed out the beer into the black hole. Returning he found her bent over the fire which was now a heap of red hot cinders.

She turned and indicated two candles waiting on her bureau. "Will you light the way Mr. Hope?" Hope lit two candles, both in silver bedroom chamber sticks, one with no handle and one with no snuffer but fashioned of heavy silver. At home, as here, there was no gas in bedrooms except for the rich. His mother had bought half a dozen penny tin candlesticks every September.

She filled a warming pan with the red cinders and held out the brass pan on its long handle and nodded at a door. Hope opened it and holding the candles high to light her, climbed a surprisingly elegant oak stairway to the upper floor. She led the way to his room in which a low fire burned. Hope had not seen a fire in a bedroom except when his mother was dying. The room had a low beamed ceiling which almost grazed his head.

"I haven't had lodgers before Mr. Hope. This room has not been used for years so I lit a fire to air it, but it is over the copper so it will always be warm."

She pulled back the patchwork quilt and inserted the warming pan between the sheets; sliding it up and down the bed several times until the room was fragrant with the smell of hot linen sheets and lavender. Mrs. Harryson had then wished him goodnight telling him she would call him at five for breakfast.

Hope slowly undressed and sorted his clothes and put on his nightshirt and climbed into the goose feather bed and blew out his candle. Warmth, comfort and youth plunged him into a deep sleep.

The alarm call of pheasants brought him back to present reality. His lodgings had been such a contrast with home, that he needed to think and process the events of last night over and over again. But now it was back to the January morning and the train. The pheasants in the woodland to his right were filling the cold morning with their alarm. Suddenly Hope's sharp eyes detected movement at last. He could see the guard at the rear of the train leaning out from the guards van, attempting to see why the driver had halted the train but the curve in the line hid signal and engine. The train had been stationary for so long that the iron stove pipe from the guards van had painted a vertical streak of blue grey on the black and white engraving of the valley.

Hope had thought the valley deserted and was free to internalise Mrs. Harryson and her digs. A slight sound made him turn. He saw a man dressed in thornproof tweeds of browns and blacks and greens, matching deerstalker hat with the blue and gold flash of a trout fly in its band, a gun under his arm and the heavy silver watch chain of a superior servant. He made no attempt at introducing himself plunging straight into the matter of the moment.

"In all my twenty years as a keeper here, I've never seen that coal train stop before. The signals for him I've checked with my glasses," he tapped the brass binoculars round his neck "and it's upset my birds."

Once the man's professional worries were discharged he remembered his manners.

"I'm Daniel Hornton, Constable, Head Keeper to Lord John whose estate stretches as far as your eye can see to the right of the lane." The two men shook hands.

When Hope had trained with Sergeant Dalby in Derby he used to send Hope out with a notebook and tell him not to return until he had written down ten things that were just a little out of the ordinary. Someone staring in a shop window for a long time, an open door when the house appeared empty, a man or a boy running at speed . . . So Hope felt the stationary train would be the first entry in his new police notebook.

He took out the cedar wood indelible pencil shoved at him that morning by Glorey, and pulled out his silver penknife, a final gift from his mother. He sharpened his pencil and wrote in his notebook. He pulled out his gunmetal pocket watch likewise grudgingly given by Glorey on its stainless steel chain. As he wrote a snowflake settled on the word 'coal' and turned the indelible pencil a livid purple.

Daniel Hornton watched him intently. The constable was a good six foot in height with a fine set of blond whiskers. Hornton noted his broad shoulders and big fists. He noted that the constable, despite his big hands, was writing in a good clear handwriting. Hornton breathed out a sigh. This man might be some good in catching poachers from the town and there were many. Hornton had always had nothing but contempt for the fat and idle Glorey.

The trucks suddenly gave out a convulsive shudder and the two men heard the sound of steam blasts from the engine. Huge bubbles of black smoke and steam appeared over the acres of woodland. The train gathered speed surprisingly quickly on the downhill gradient and vanished like an escaping snake. The men watched in silence and then there was total silence again as the train entered the tunnel that hid the railway from the Hall. They heard a shrill whistle as the train emerged nearly two miles away. Hornton snorted in anger.

"It was a sad day when Lord John's father allowed them to build the railway through his estate. The birds have never been the same."

Hornton seemed inclined to talk. For a time he discussed his poaching problems and then suddenly said "It's a wicked godless town you've come to, Constable Hope. Vice, drinking, fornication, I often look across the fields to it and think of those Cities of the Plain the Old Testament."

Hope looked at the town with its spire across the wintry water meadows and groups of hedgerow trees. To him the town looked nothing like the pictures of Sodom and Gomorrah that he had seen in the Bible on Sunday afternoons. He glanced at the gamekeeper. The man was what his mother would have called a 'ranter' from the Baptists or primitive Methodists. Brought up in a high Anglican local church Hope did not judge people or live by the Bible as the gamekeeper probably did.

And while the gamekeeper had been ranting he thought he had seen a figure on the railway embankment. At first he had thought it was a bent old woman carrying a bundle of sticks wearing some sort of white cloak. Then he thought it was his imagination. The snow was dazzling and played tricks. What he thought was a woman was a bush. Then it seemed to move and Hope found himself thinking the next bush was the bent old woman.

An explosion of snapping twigs and disturbance of last year's old vegetation, made both men turn round at once. Out of a track through the woods erupted a wild figure in an ancient flapping coat, her hair streaming out in dirty strands as she tried to push a battered old pram out on to the lane. Seeing the two men added panic to her attempts, and soon she was on the lane running for her life back to the town. Hope could see that the pram contained massive lumps of engine coal that gleamed with water as though polished. She rocked from side to side in tandem with the sway and squeak of the old pram, her hair flying in the snow wind.

"That is Maisie Frith," said Hornton. "And that explains why the train was stopped. That wanton little judy would be enticing the engine driver with her bodily wares in exchange for that steam coal." he sniffed with contempt. "She's well known in the town Constable. I liken her to the Whore of Babylon."

The Whore of Babylon was now a fast receding figure but at least, thought Hope, the problem of the stationary train was solved.

He said goodbye to the gamekeeper, glad to get away. Strongly expressed religion always embarrassed him. The walk to the gypsies took him another twenty minutes and when he arrived at the camp he made no attempt to visit the caravans. All doors were closed and there was no sign of life, apart from one wildly barking dog straining on its chain. Hope could see there were no marks in the snow that had finished falling soon after six. He noted this in his book.

Two ancient magpies, side by side in the warm ivy climbing up an oak, watched Hope return. They were the only two magpies for many miles, as Hornton pursued their kind relentlessly. Many of the two birds' offspring were nailed to a board by the keepers cottage. Secure in their ivy they watched Hope return quicker than he came. They leaned forward a little, like two medieval orelates, as he turned a corner. They took no notice of the pullman express from Manchester Central to St. Pancras as it suddenly roared by, full of dutifully grim faces mourning the Queen, as they gazed over the fast moving wintry fields. The two old birds opened their beaks a fraction as Hope walked under the viaduct, for he was still young enough to whistle to the archway to see if it had an echo.

Emerging from under the viaduct the whistle continued until some subconscious impulse made him turn to the wooded hillside to his right. A movement caught his attention. Surely, he thought, there was the old woman again, this time nearly on the sky edge of the woods. But as he stared she seemed to fade into the snow and trees, and once more he wondered if she were a figment of his imagination created from trees and snow.

At six o' clock Glorey dismissed Hope for the day with a sourness that reflected the national day of mourning, and anger that the new constable had spotted the gold watch. As for Hope, he looked forward to the comfort of his digs and Mrs. Harryson's cooking and warm fire and easy chair. He whistled under his breath as he walked the short distance from the Police Station to Mrs. Harryson's.

Darkness had fallen on the town. The market had been a subdued affair because of the Queen's death and the only sound Hope heard down the gaslit streets was the bleat of a sheep from the sheep pens in the market. Just as he reached the gate of Mrs. Harryson's small front garden, he heard the sound of running feet and saw the girl he had seen earlier with the pram, scuttling down an opening between buildings.

Entering what appeared to be a narrow alley, he saw the girl that the gamekeeper had described as 'The Whore of Babylon' push desperately at a door. The door grated open unwillingly and as Hope approached he heard her struggling to close it which she finally did with a slam.

Hope was at the door in a few strides. He heard the scrabble of a fleeing rat as he prepared to knock. The door was fitfully lit by a faulty gas lamp in the middle of the alley, that belched and leaked gas. Hope noticed by its light that the door was crudely made of planks, and the only window had two intact panes the rest were stuffed with rags and paper. Hope gave a sharp knock on the planks.

Silence. Only the bubble of the lamp and some snow melting from a roof disturbed the icy air. Hope knocked again, this time with great force adding the words "Open up! Police business!" The words gave him pleasure. It was the first time he had used them and it made him feel part of the police force and the keeping of law and order for the new King Edward and the Empire.

He heard activity within and fumblings at the door, which eventually was dragged open with squeals and groans, as the warped wood grated on the stone floor.

Hope stared at the figure that Hornton had called the Whore of Babylon. A shawl was wrapped round her thin body and fastened with a clothes peg. Below that was a skirt that had once been coarse black woollen stuff but was now a rusty brown. She was wearing a pair of men's boots. The sole of the left one was parting company with the boot. Her face was white and pinched and shadowed with poverty. Strands of matted blond hair hung in dirty rats tails round the white face. Yet, from this face, Hope was transfixed by her eyes that were as open and as blue as the sky. The girl held him for some seconds in this wide open stare until Hope broke the stare and looked beyond her into her single room.

The smell of extreme poverty entered Hope's nostrils. He instinctively edged back a little. In his life in Derby he had not seen anything like this. This tiny slum within the picture postcard town was as more wretched than anything nearby Sheffield, Derby or Manchester could show.

The hot fetid dampness breathed on Hope's face. He could see the damp on the walls gleaming like snail trails. The air stank of candle fat, stale fried bacon and boiled cabbage and the inevitable overtones of piss and shit. A haze of down draughted coal smoke hung from the ceiling and the upper rungs of a ladder that led to the single room above.

In the stagnant air of the room a fire blazed, as bright as the sun, in what had once been a handsome eighteenth century cast iron fireplace. Hope knew at once, from the fierceness of the fire, that the girl was burning the top quality steam coal from Wales that the Midland Railway fired its engines with. And there was the pram in the corner revealing its gleaming cargo of coal and still nearly full. The girl's eyes never dropped their gaze from Hope's face but he was unmoved by it.

He took put his notebook and pencil.

"I am going to report you to the Midland Railway Company in Derby. It is an offence to trespass on their property and pick up coal. I must warn you the Company is likely to prosecute you and you may well be fined up to forty shillings for your theft. Name please."

The girl's thin anaemic lips whispered something.

"Can you say it louder?"

Hope was quite unaware of the blue eyes that now seemed to silently plead, offer something that Hope was not in tune with. He felt exultation in his new power and even gripping the notebook was a pleasure.

"Maisie Frith."

Hope solemnly wrote it in his official notebook.

"And your address?"

"One Diamond Court."

Hope wrote it and snapped the notebook closed. It had been a successful day. He took one last glance in the room, to check the facts and suddenly noticed he was being observed by a filthy toddler kneeling up in a cardboard box by the side of the fierce fire. Obviously the child had hidden or been asleep earlier in the interview. The dirty face had the same eyes as the girl.

Hope frowned a little as he backed away. He knew that the Anglican Church in Derby had seen to it that he would never endure poverty like this. The Church had overseen his education, given him a job. He had been part of that Church since a small boy and his head was stuffed with anecdotes and religious tales. He recalled how Pope Gregory had seen the Anglo Saxon slaves in Rome, and looking at their eyes, had said 'Not Angles but angels!' and had resolved to convert them to the faith. For some reason the recall of this story sucked some of the pleasure of discovering the crime away from him. He made his way with heavier tread to Mrs. Harryson's. Then the thought of what was awaiting him cheered him. He knocked and entered her room and was at once taken in by light and warmth and fragrance of cooking and a log fire.

Hope hung his cape and tunic on a nail in the large room where the copper burned. Then without being invited, he sat down at the place set for him where he had sat the previous evening. It being a weekday there was no tablecloth, but the wood of the table was a scrubbed pleasing sight. Again there was a tankard of ale and a jug. Mrs. Harryson, supple and deft in weekday white blouse and grey skirt, brought in a large earthenware dish and began to ladle out liver and onions. She nodded at a bowl of creamy white mash. Hope helped himself and began to eat. The liver was sweetened with herbs and as tender as fine steak, the gravy luscious and thick. Hope recalled the liver his mother had cooked which his brothers and sisters had joked was shoe leather. He could taste the cream and butter in the mash of potatoes. He took a sip of the good ale. He realised that Mrs. Harryson had not spoken and while his mouth was full looked across at her.

She stared him full in the face. The almost mocking pleasant smile of the night before had gone and had been replaced by a look that verged on contempt.

"I thought I saw you knocking on Maisie Frith's door, Mr. Hope. In Diamond Court. I hope the poor girl was not in trouble."

With a certain amount of pride Hope recounted his day and how it had ended with Maisie Frith being caught in possession of stolen coal.

Mrs. Harryson then said a great deal. Her opinion of Hornton the gamekeeper was caustic.

"That bible thumping ranter. He lives and breathes the Bible and yet he would cheerfully see half this town burn in hell. So much for the message of Jesus Christ's love and forgiveness. He'd certainly burn me as a witch if he could. He uses his religion just to torment others." She snorted.

Hope looked at her in amazement. There was more to come.

"I wish you had spoken to me before you charged poor Maisie. That girl has enough to put up with. Half the men in the town tup with her when they can't find a woman to satisfy their itch. So do her own brothers for that matter. I have long thought that little Jacob is her own brother's son by her. You probably saw the poor little mite when you were laying down the law of England."

Hope was shocked. It was new to him to hear a woman talk so crudely and he was deeply shocked by her criticism of his carrying out the law and order he was paid to do. But mostly he was dumbstruck that a woman could talk like this. The meal proceeded in silence even over the cold apple pie and clotted cream. Hope moved into the fireside chair, bewildered and miserable. Mrs. Harryson vanished and Hope heard a door slam.

After an hour she returned.

"Maisie has put her fire out and taken the pram God knows where. The poor thing is out of her wits with what you have done."

More bewildered than ever Hope stared helplessly as she gathered sticks and logs. She disappeared again, only to reappear with a coal bucket. She left without saying a word.

Hope sat by the warm fire in perplexed misery. When the battered clock repeated its nine silvery bell notes, he dutifully went to bed, but that night without the comfort of the warming pan. He did not see Mrs. Harryson till breakfast the following day.

He knew that he needed to report the crime of Maisie to the Superintendent of the Station, who was responsible for crimes that involved authorities outside the town; Sergeant Glorey was only in charge of the town's affairs.

Glorey pounced on Hope and Constable Allen as soon as they had been inspected the following morning. A bull had been seen in Matlock Road wandering about and they were to investigate. As it turned out that took all the morning. Hope was secretly a little scared of facing a bull, but Allen, a few years older than Hope, seemed to know what to do. Hope could feel his confidence draining away. The bull scared him. Allen, who had none of the malice of Glorey, sensed this and put Hope in charge of a traffic jam that had built up. The narrow old turnpike road was already jammed with people coming to the town to buy black crepe and curtains and arm bands for the death of the Queen. Normally Hope would have been thrilled to direct the carriages and pony traps and broughams and a steam car, but he kept glancing out of the corner of his eye for the bull.

At noon Glorey victimised him again. Riding over Fillyford Bridge two miles south of the town Mrs. Stone had reported seeing a body floating in the river. Ignoring the fact the woman was notoriously short sighted, Glorey saw yet another chance to discomfit Hope.

"Probably only a tramp or gypsy," he had wheezed. "But you'd better investigate." He insisted Hope take a long heavy iron pole, with a hook on the end, to retrieve the body. Hope struggled the two miles in slush and snow carrying the pole only to discover the 'body' was a half empty white sack of corn that had fermented and inflated in the reeds near the bridge.

When he returned to his digs, he had not seen Superintendent Lomas to report Maisie's crime. He felt miserable and his body ached from trudging in the snow and his shoulders burned from carrying the iron pole. He was exhausted and depressed and began to regret ever leaving Derby. He entered the warmth and light of Mrs. Harryson's, more than a little apprehensive of the atmosphere of the previous evening. He found a repeat performance.

The oil lamp radiated light. There were prime pork sausages, crammed full of meat from the best pork butcher in the town, buttered carrots sprinkled with parsley and Mrs. Harryson's usual creamed mash, onion gravy and the excellent ale. And the cold silence. As the meal ended, Hope moved to the armchair and thought he had rarely been so miserable in so much comfort. Mrs. Harryson vanished and appeared again in her outdoor coat. Another mystery; the coat was fine quality; most women of her class wore shawls for outdoor walking. The door clicked behind her, and Hope was left in the light and warmth with his darkness within himself.

She returned as the dinted clock repeated seven notes. Hope turned and stared in disbelief and discomfort. She was holding the hand of Jacob, Maisie's small son, and Maisie herself was hesitating on the threshold.

"Come right in, Maisie," said Mrs. Harryson. "Ye've nothing to be afraid of." Hope noticed she spoke to the girl in the distinctive dialect of the town. Then, yet again, he was dumbfounded by this woman Harryson. She came over to his armchair and smiled sweetly at him.

"You must have had a hard day Constable Hope," said she. "What with that bull in Matlock Street and that long walk to Fillyford." (How did she know that?) "Those boots and feet must be wet through. Let me take your boots off. You'll be so much more comfortable." To his horror she knelt down in front of him, and expertly unlaced his boots and pulled them off. She placed them where they would dry. Hope looked down at his grey woollen socks, darned with various colours of wool by his mother and sister. His big toe was protruding where a new hole had worn through.

She brought Jacob a small china beaker with a duck on it. Hope could smell the fragrance of soup in it.

"Now Maisie." said she. "Let's get you warm and clean and comfortable while Jacob drinks his soup, then we can talk to Constable Hope." She led Maisie away to the wash room with its heat from the copper.

Jacob remained curled in the opposite chair, with the lethargy of malnourishment and poverty. He took a sip of his soup with the care of a little old man. After each sip he raised his blue eyes, and stared at Hope with the innocence and lack of judgement of a baby. Hope shifted uneasily in his own chair. When the soup was finished he stared at Hope with an unblinking blue stare until Hope could endure it no longer.

Standing up, he reached down one of the Sheffield Plate candlesticks, and then slid his hands along the mantelshelf in search of matches. He found a silver box, encrusted with what looked like precious stones, and empty holes where stones had once been. In an oval frame set in the box was a miniature, a finely painted picture of the negro in the picture that had fascinated him on the first evening. After staring, he took out six match sticks and lit them and blew them out. The china blue eyes stared at him, as though the boy were a doll. Hope dipped the matchsticks in the molten wax of the lighted candle to make a fast setting adhesive, and made two goal posts at each end of the table, one by his chair the other by Jacob's. He felt in his pocket for a clay marble he had picked from the snow earlier, and showed Jacob how to play matchstick football, a game Hope and his brothers had played endlessly.

Jacob picked up the idea, but after every shot his round blue stare returned to look at Hope. Hope was relieved when the wash house door opened and Maisie and Mrs. Harryson reappeared in a cloud of steam, and the scent of Pears soap. Mrs. Harryson opened a corner cupboard, with a key from a bunch at her belt, and put a steel comb back on a shelf. Hope at once recognised it as a comb for removing hair nits from the scalp.

"Well Maisie, I've been a nurse in this town for five years or more but I've never seen so many!"

But Hope was staring at Maisie Frith. She was transformed. Her hair had been washed and now was heaped on her head in coils of old gold. The heat from the bath and copper had brought a flush to her pale skin and colour to her lips. Hope thought she looked like one of the adverts for Pears soap he had seen in the chemist at Derby.

"Now, sit ye here," said Mrs. Harryson and she pulled a chair from the table for her and one for herself next to Hope. Jacob kept his unblinking stare on Hope.

Mrs. Harryson took one of Maisie's hands in hers and held it.

"Now Maisie," she said "I want you to tell Constable Hope here, everything you've told me. He won't hurt you or harm you." Hope saw her look down at his big toe poking out from his sock.

"I weren't even on railway bank," whispered Maisie.

"Now don't get upset Maisie," soothed Mrs. Harryson. "Just tell him the whole story, like you told me."

"Oo killed 'im. I seed'n ," whispered Maisie, and once again Hope had difficulty in following the language of the town.

"Now begin at the beginning," said Mrs. Harryson. "That is the end of your tale."

"Oo were dead because I seed t'owd woman."

Hope sensed Mrs. Harryson's impatience. Obviously patience was not one of her strengths of character. She turned to Hope and spoke to him, almost as friendly as she had on the Sunday night of his arrival.

"Sorry Mr. Hope. There's an old superstition in the town, that just before you die you see an old woman dressed all in white, with a hood and a bundle of sticks. Or bones. Folk know it for miles around. A very old legend. I'll tell you the full version one night when we're by the fire. Amazing in these modern times! It's strange how the belief is still talked about in the new twentieth century." She dismissed the old belief with a shrug.

Hope felt a shiver creep up his back, despite the heat of the room. He had seen a figure of an old crone creeping along the railway embankment, he was sure of it. A white figure, at one with the white landscape and bare trees of the wood that partly hid the viaduct and embankment. Carrying sticks . . . or bones.

Mrs. Harryson smiled at him. He decided to say nothing about the strange apparition creeping and crawling along the railway embankment . . . He did not want that chill disapproval to settle in the room again. Obviously he was forgiven, although he was not sure what for. And anyway, he was certain he did not believe in spirits or ghosts or premonitions of death . . . or witches or whatever it was. And yet . . . He made himself sit upright in his deep chair.

"Come on Maisie," Mrs. Harryson squeezed her hand. And Maisie began.

"Our Jacob's been right badly wi' measles and he's still got a cough. It's cold in our house and I wanted some coal. The best place is by the railway bridge just on that big bend, because coal falls off trucks when they go round it, and it rolls down. It's not on railway bank. It rolls down."

She looked at Hope and Jacob looked at Hope. Hope put his foot with the sock hole behind the other. A silence descended. Hope heard the whisper of the logs burning, the hiss of the oil lamp and the ticking of the carriage clock. He heard Maisie take in a deep breath.

"Our Jacob's cough were bad in the night, so I sets off when it was still dark. Jacob were asleep in his box. I had to go early because that Hornton is allus watching me. I don't like him looking at me, and when he ses me he gets hold of my arm and says bits from the Bible . . . There's some holly trees and a stream that leads to railway bank, and I've made a shelter in a holly tree where I can wait and hide."

Mrs. Harryson patted Maisie's hand to encourage her.

I stayed there a bit as I saw Old Hornton in the wood. It were a long time before he went. Then this big goods train came down the line and stopped just by the stream. And then the feller that were driving it, took a great big lump of coal and hit this other feller in the train on the head. Then he threw the coal into the stream and there were blood. I seed it. Then he kept doing it and this other feller did not move and the man looked pleased and he kept throwing coal in the stream and it were all bloody. I seed it. And then he started the train and it went. I heard it whistle in the tunnel."

"Bless ye" Maisie, said Mrs. Harryson. She got up and went out and came back with three ancient greenish wine glasses, a bottle of home brewed wine and some biscuits. She gave a biscuit to Jacob and she poured three glasses of sparkling wine.

"My elderflower champagne, Mr. Hope. I think you'll like it."

"I 'an't finished yet," announced Maisie after three sips of the champagne. Hope thought the pale straw-coloured sparkling wine was delicious. It exploded on his tongue with bubbles of flowery sweetness. His mother had bought sherry and port and ginger wine at Christmas and he had disliked the taste intensely. He began to feel much better. Mrs. Harryson smiled her smile.

"I saw Old Hornton go before the train came, so I got the coal out of the stream and carried it to the cart in another bush by the way into wood. It were a shame to waste it."

She sipped the wine from what, had she known it, was scratched and chipped eighteenth century Venetian glass.

"When I came out of t' wood I saw thee and Hornton. And I runned for my life." She tipped the greenish glass, that had a crack in the stem, and made sure she had not left any of the wine.

After Mrs. Harryson had seen Jacob and Maisie back home, she had asked Hope to light the candles for upstairs, as she filled the warming pan to place in Hope's bed. And later, Hope, lying in bed and listening to the thump of the winter wind, made plans on what he would tell Superintendent Lomas in the morning. Warmth and confidence soon brought sleep, deep and restorative after Mrs. Harryson's brew.

Nevertheless it was the Thursday after Queen Victoria's death, before Sergeant Glorey ran out of ideas to torment Hope.

Hope had been on the early beat, walking the road between the town and Edensor to the east. The church clock was striking eleven when he returned to the Station and entered the large downstairs area that was Glorey's kingdom.

Already Hope disliked this part of the Station. In the middle was a huge tortoise stove that leaked coke fumes and irritated the throat. The fumes did not disguise the strong body odour that Glorey was unaware of. There was a hint of leaking gas from the gas lamps above the counter behind which Glorey directed affairs. The varnished pine of this great barrier between Glorey and his public also gave out a sickly odour of resin and viscous varnish. Lurking in this strong bouquet was a hint of vomit from the market day drunks who were brought in every week.

Hope noticed that the Sergeant had his back to him and made his way to the staircase that led upstairs to the Superintendent's office.

Glorey did not hear him. He knew that Thursday was the day

when the women and girls of the town, who wanted to earn a few pennies, came to pick vegetables from the market garden next to the Station. The high class grocer's shop in the Market Square owned the garden, and would want the winter vegetables in the shop for tomorrow when Sunday roasts would be planned by the housewives and cooks of the town. Glorey knew this.

He watched work begin. Some girls and women were bending over sprout plants, their backs to his gaze, their skirts tightening as they did so. Others forked out celery and parsnips or turnips, the east wind exposing calves and ankles and providing Glorey's eye a chance for speculative views. His pale eye was moist with lust and imagination.

Hope knocked on the Superintendent's door and was told to enter. The room was a copy of the space below but very different in aspect. Superintendent Lomas was responsible for a large area of central Derbyshire, roughly twelve miles or more in diameter with the town in the centre of the uneven circle. It was a well paid and prestigious job, and Lomas supervised the policing of it with care and expertise. It pained him that he had to pass his orders to Glorey to give to the constables. As far as he was concerned Glorey was a waste of time and space, but as a good Methodist he was too much of a Christian man to say so directly. However, he knew Glorey's every weakness and there were many. "Constable Hope," said he looking up. He had briefly welcomed Hope on the first day.

He kept the Constable standing for a time as he enquired his business then told him to pull up a chair before his desk.

Hope felt much more at ease up here than downstairs. The Superintendent's desk was big but lower and seemed less of a barrier. The air was pleasant with the lavender shaving soap John Lomas favoured and the smell of his pipe tobacco; Lomas enjoyed a particular blend that included a Balkan leaf that permeated the room. A coke fire glowed ruby red in a severely functional fireplace. Lomas had his back to the window from where the pickers could be viewed working. A gleam of tin coloured sun came into the room from another south facing window.

Concisely, and handing over his notebook, Hope told of the stationary train that had stopped for no apparent reason, Maisie's coal theft and her story of the killing. Lomas read the notebook through a pair of perfectly circular gold rimmed glasses. He removed them and looked at Hope.

"You've the makings of a fine police officer, Constable Hope. Your notes and the way you tell of events are first class. But we have a serious dilemma here, Hope. To understand it I shall have to tell you about the Frith family, to which the girl Maisie belongs."

He lit his pipe, the ritual taking several minutes. Hope did not mind. The praise had pleased him. It was a different world up here compared to Glorey's. He did not realise that Lomas's attitude to Maisie would be as bewildering as his landlady's.

"Did you learn about the Black Death in your school in Derby, Constable?"

Hope was puzzled. He wanted to say '1349' but did not dare, in case he was wrong; he was also a little uncertain between that and the Plague of London.

Lomas pressed the smouldering tobacco in his pipe with a yellow finger.

"Memories are long in a town like this, Constable. Stories are passed down the generations and repeated. Many in this town would tell you that the Frith family appeared at the time of the Black Death and simply took over some land that might have belonged to victims and settled there. The cottage the family live in is certainly old. It is said that they just appeared out of the old hunting forests to the north of the county. 'Frith' is an old word for forest. Folk used to fear those wolf filled wastelands with their wolves and wild outlaws. The Friths were no exception. And they have terrorised the town ever since. The present set of Frith brothers are the bane of my life. They are varmints."

Hope nodded but he could hardly see where the story was going.

"There's a round half dozen of them. It's the men, Gerry and Bert and Horace you must watch. There are three girls, Maisie being the youngest. And believe me, Maisie can be a naughty girl as you have found out and no doubt Mrs. Harryson and Mr. Hornton have told you the rest, and they will have not told you lies."

The pipe was relit and fragrance ascended.

"Now, let us assume two things, Constable. That Maisie Frith is taken to court for theft of coal, and found guilty. She would be unable to pay the fine, and would face a prison sentence that might do her a bit of good. I doubt her brothers would help her out and pay the fine, if there was nothing in it for them."

The pipe crackled fiercely and the coke settled in its basket.

"Now, let us assume the engine driver is tried for murder with our Maisie as the key witness. Let us say she is serving six months in prison, and is brought to the Derby Assizes. She tells her tale. Now, Constable, the railwaymen of Derby are a powerful force. They are respected working men, and there are many liberal and radical solicitors in that town who would help the accused railwayman for free. And it would not take any solicitor or barrister long to find out what a naughty girl our Maisie has been. And they would say, quite convincingly, that the girl had made the story up, so the Court would recommend her sentence would be shortened. Or she could be pardoned for assisting the Crown prosecution. It has been known."

He looked at Hope solemnly through the blue haze.

"So, the worse crime of the two us dismissed. What I am saying, Constable, is that I shall not be charging Maisie Frith with the theft of the coal, if I find out there is substance in this tale of murder."

Hope stared and nodded. This was the second time his arrest of Maisie had been questioned, and he found himself all at sea. What he thought had been a simple case of right and wrong, was more complicated than he had imagined. But he followed Lomas' reasoning.

"I am glad you agree, Constable," said Superintendent Lomas coolly, "because I need you to assist me in the first stages of this case."

He reached for the phone mouthpiece, fastened to the wall behind him, and when the operator replied he shouted "Put me through to the Hall please."

He informed the unseen person loudly that he would like to consult with the gamekeeper Mr. Hornton, at noon today, by the railway viaduct. Then Lomas struggled into his great coat, that Hope thought was very smart and the two men clattered down the stairs.

Glorey was suddenly aware someone was coming. He sat down hurriedly. He certainly did not want Lomas to know where his thoughts had been.

"I need Constable Hope here, for the morning. Order my trap Sergeant. We are going down to the railway viaduct."

"Certainly sir. Gypsies causing problems again sir?"

Lomas ignored him and the two men went out to the stable yard. Glorey, red and sweating, waited for his thoughts and body to subside.

Hope fetched his cape, and then stood watching as the pony and trap were made ready. He was greatly impressed by such a smart outfit. The brass on the trap gleamed, and the seats were of a dark blue corded material. Lomas climbed in and the white pony whinnied and turned her head, and Lomas patted her affectionately on her rump and took the whip. Hope noticed two things. The badge of the Derbyshire police force that was painted on the outside if the trap was also repeated inside the vehicle. And there was a large bunch of snowdrops surrounded by ivy leaves fastened to the headboard. Lomas saw him looking and nodded at him to climb aboard.

"From my garden, Constable. In memory of the Queen. And do you know what they mean in the language of flowers?"

Hope had no idea.

Lomas' command, of what seemed to him school knowledge, made him nervous again.

"They mean 'hope'. I have hope for our new King Edward and Hope for our new constable." He clicked his tongue and the pony and trap clattered through the stable entrance and into the street, Hope a little out of his depth with the Superintendent's conversation. Lomas brought the trap to a halt outside the entrance to Diamond Court and asked Hope to fetch Maisie

"Now Maisie," said Lomas "I want you to be a good girl and we'll try and sort a way out of you thieving coal. So I want you to tell Ma Roland you will give her three pence (he held up a silver threepenny bit gleaming between his nicotine dyed fingers) if she looks after Jacob for a couple of hours, while you come with us and show us where you saw the engine driver doing what he did."

Maisie held out a very dirty hand for the money.

"No Maisie. I will give it Ma Roland. Now fetch her."

Mrs. Roland was fetched, paid and despatched and without waiting to be asked, Maisie climbed into the trap and fastened her large blue eyes on Hope as though she were offering him something. Today the eyes were flecked with white, reflected from the snow that still remained on nearby roofs. Hope noticed her hair was still fairly clean, but her face was smudged with dirt and ash and her hands filthy. The pony took the gradient of the bridge over the river with vigour, and Lomas stroked her with the whip gently tugging the reins, so she followed the lane that Hope had taken on his first morning. Today the landscape seemed to fly by and they were soon at the railway viaduct.

Hornton appeared out of a thicket of hazel where the young catkins were rigid and tight against the cold. The head gamekeeper shook hands with Lomas and nodded at Hope and looked at the girl he called the Whore of Babylon, as though she were a foul miasma from some heathen swamps of biblical Egypt.

"Maisie Frith is helping us with an inquiry," said Lomas, after polite exchanges had ceased. "She might have witnessed a criminal act on railway property that runs through your coverts."

"Aye, I bet she has," sneered Hornton drily. Whores of Babylon were capable of one crime only in his perception.

"So with your permission, Mr. Hornton, we will enter the private property of his Lordship."

Hornton nodded and a silent procession was led by Maisie. She squeezed her way through a gap in the thorn hedge.

"Cheeky little judy," growled Hornton, angry he had never discovered Maisie's illegal entry.

"I put pram in there," said Maisie nodding to a holly bush conical as a tent. The snow had grown old but it was possible to see the enlarged footprints and wide wheel tracks to validate her story. They followed the enlarged prints for half an hour or more until a tiny stream was reached, that flowed under the railway through a small arched culvert. She turned to Lomas.

"That's where the mester were clouting the other mester wi' lumps of coal. Then he threw it down into water. I seed it. I took it."

She looked insolently at Hornton who snorted. Superintendent Lomas stared at the scene for several minutes and Hope could hear Hornton muttering and sighing. Hope remembered that he had said Maisie 'gave favours' to the engine drivers. As he had walked along the side of the railway he had noted to himself that the trail Maisie would have taken had many difficulties for someone climbing the embankment to offer 'favours'; brambles, massive rough boulders, nettles, thistles, ditches and a pile of broken blue Bedfordshire clay bricks.

"Constable Hope," said Lomas suddenly. "Look in that stream and see if you can see any remaining fragments of the coal that Maisie Frith says was thrown from the engine."

Hope pushed through the undergrowth, following the giant thawed footprints and knelt on the bank. In the cold water he fished out several flakes of the high quality steam coal the Midland Railway fired its engine boilers with.

Lomas nodded. "That's it. Now Mr. Hornton, escort us off his Lordship's land if you please."

Hornton did so and Hope could sense his anger. Hornton's body seemed rigid as a winter tree. When they reached the pony and trap he finally exploded.

"That little wanton is fooling you Superintendent, trying to get out of stealing railway coal. I know her godless tricks and that of her brothers. You should not give in to the heathen and Jezebels of your sinful town."

Maisie once again climbed into the trap without invitation, and sat and looked at Hornton with what Hope could only say was a smirk. The timidity of her bath night at Mrs. Harryson's had evaporated. Lomas took out his pipe and carefully filled it.

"Thank you for giving us access to his Lordship's estates Mr. Hornton. I must tell you that you may not discuss our visit with anybody. If you do, you may find yourself on the wrong side of the law in a serious trial. I know you will respect that. And I shall endeavour to keep the law in my town just as you keep the game in your woods. God has given us all a task in this life and sometimes they are best kept separate from each other." He clicked his tongue and with the softest stroke of the whip the pony and trap clattered away back to the town. Lomas held the whip aloft in salute. "Good day to ye Hornton!"

Maisie's blue eyes settled again on Constable Hope.

Lomas informed Sergeant Glorey that he needed the assistance of Constable Hope for a few days. He did not reveal his plans to the Sergeant.

There followed for Hope several days of sheer pleasure. He had found his first week in the town daunting. His digs, however luxurious, were unconventional and John Hope had been educated in a conventional way and Mrs. Harryson disturbed his equilibrium. Then there had been the affair of Maisie Frith when the Superintendent and Mrs. Harryson seemed to interfere in criminal culpability. In Hope's view you had either committed a crime or you had not. If you had, the law would punish you. It was like his view of Heaven and Hell. There were only two possibilities.

Then there was Glorey, whose hatred for him grew daily. Glorey's area of responsibility was the town but Superintendent Lomas frequently passed on minor incidents to him, some incidents occurring six miles distant from the town. He expected Glorey to inform the constables, so as they patrolled the beat they would 'keep their eyes open.' Glorey used these incidents to torment Hope. Eggs stolen at a farm near Taddington was an excuse to send Hope, the six miles there and back, to 'report' on the affair. Likewise someone stealing flowers from Monyash churchyard was an excuse to send Hope along the slushy roads a ten mile walk there and back to 'report'. Glorey should have shared out these long walks and beats with the other men, but he was determined to rid the force of Hope. The thought of Hope spotting the shape of Canon Ball's gold watch disturbed his sleep as much as the thoughts of the women sprout pickers. Besides, Hope was everything Glorey was not. The fat middle aged Sergeant simmered with jealousy.

To sit with Superintendent Lomas in the trap was pure pleasure.

The snows on the Derbyshire hills had melted. For some reason which Hope did not fully understand the Superintendent was checking up on the Midland Railway that ran through the middle of his territory connecting St. Pancras with Manchester Central.

So the first Monday they visited a signal box in Monsal Dale. As they trotted along the roads larks were rising in the fields and plovers swept over them with a sad call, that disturbed Hope, but he later came to love. It was not until Wednesday when Hope discovered what Lomas was about and learned more in one afternoon than he had in a year in Derby about talking to the public.

It was only a short journey, hardly two miles to the signal box at Hassop Station. They climbed the steps to the Box and were welcomed in. Bells tinkled and the telegraph chattered and big levers were pulled but the signalman insisted on making them tea in white enamel mugs with red handles, and the badge of the London Midland railway.

"And how's the wife and kids?" Lomas asked his introductory question. After a lengthy reply, Lomas steered the talk to Frank's indigestion and how fried onions brought forth fearful wind and heartburning vulcanicity in the stomach. Sipping his tea with apparent relish, Lomas asked about the Station and the last time the Duchess used the Station. A fast passenger train rattled by.

"You deserve every penny you earn here Frank," said Lomas, from behind a cloud of tobacco smoke. "I'll bet you don't earn half the money the engine men earn."

That released pent up frustrations. The engine drivers pay was criticised and their lifestyle and habits. The firemen and stokers came in for Frank's criticism.

"I'll tell you something Superintendent. I'd just started my shift, taking over from Harry on the morning the Queen died. There's a coal train comes down the line before the passengers start. He came down as usual, but I could hear he was going at a fair old rate. But not too fast for me to spot what was going on. The driver were shovelling coal and the fireman was laid across the coals as drunk as a lord." He sipped his tea. "Dead drunk. In fact he looked half dead. They say he fell out at Matlock and were killed."

Hope noticed that Lomas made no reaction to this relevant fact. He sipped his tea and smoked his pipe and let the conversation drift where it would and then got up.

"Well I'm glad you're here keeping an eye on things Frank," said he.

It was back in the station yard by the coal merchant's office when he said "Right Constable. You write that down in your pocket book about the coal train." He watched Hope sharpen his pencil and write the details and cursed inwardly that he was saddled with that fool Glorey.

It was Friday when they found a similar story, this time from the Rowsley signal box. Albert Barber, the signal man was a hypochondriac and the conversation quickly turned to health. Albert had an irregular heartbeat, the Doctor had told him.

"Mind you, Superintendent, there are a lot of poorly folk about. Did you hear about the fireman who fell from his train on the morning of Her Majesty's passing? Well, I happened to be looking out as the train passed. The driver had sounded his whistle as he came out of the tunnel, and his Lordship has told them not to. So I wondered what was up, so I kept my eyes skinned in case there was something. When they passed, the driver were looking out, real worried he were and the fireman was sprawled over the coals. Probably been sick or felt badly. Anyway, he fell from cab at Matlock. Just shows you never know what's round the next corner."

Again Lomas showed no reaction until they were back in the trap.

Hope was not involved in Lomas' next moves, his visits to Matlock and Derby and a chat with Jackson's widow. It was a month later that Lomas summoned Hope and told him Fox had been taken into custody and that Hope should be prepared to appear at Derby Assizes in the next few months as part of the Crown Prosecution.

In the first week of October Hope was sitting in a second class compartment of the early train to Derby. He had been summoned to appear at Fox's trial. Sitting in his full uniform he could not help but feel satisfied with himself as the train gathered speed over the viaduct he had walked under on his first morning. Golden foliage of hazel and sycamore hid from view Maisie Frith's holly tree shelter. Hope now felt he was a man in his own right. His pale urban face now glowed with a light tan and good food. Mrs. Harryson's food was excellent and he was better nourished than he had been in Derby. His whole frame had broadened and his posture improved. Glorey's endless orders sending him on long beats had increased his strength and fitness. Walking out of the station in Derby he received second and third glances from women in the street.

On the same train in another second class compartment was Mrs. Harryson and Maisie who had been summoned as a witness. Maisie had been terrified, but under the care of Mrs. Harryson she was now ready. Mrs. Harryson had washed her hair and bought Maisie a bodice of blue silk with pearl buttons and a serge skirt of a darker hue giving Maisie a virginal air of a Madonna. The outfit had calmed Maisie more than anything could and in the first tunnel she had been entranced with her own reflection in the window glass, and wriggled with pleasure on the red plush cushions of the carriage. She had walked with unusual confidence on the station forecourt which was crowded with various law officials who had just emerged from the first class carriages of the London train.

Hope waited on the steps of the Court where the first assize of the new Michaelmas Term would soon begin to try Fox for murder.

He had arranged to meet Lomas and Maisie for a few minutes here. He waited for them, again aware of his own status and self-satisfaction at the progress he had made since he left Derby. A few russet coloured leaves, that had lost their way in the Derby streets, blew around his highly glossed boots. He kicked at them. The leaves blew away in the breeze, their dull red shapes soon to expire and turn to dust and death.

The Court was packed tight, as it always was when there was a murder trial that would end in hanging. Fox cowered in the dock. He was utterly defeated, wizened, shrunken and white with fear of his coming sentence.

Lord Goodfellow-Whyte was sitting and the Court looked forward to a death sentence as he was not known for his lenience. Edward Cholmondley K.C. who was conducting the prosecution for the Crown, noted with satisfaction how the Judge had glared at Fox with ill-concealed contempt at such a wretched specimen from the lower orders. Cholmondley had smiled. With luck he should be back in Hampstead for dinner.

Conducting the Trial as though he were in the presence of a bad smell, his Lordship only showed signs of humanity when Constable Hope read from his notebook.

His Lordship congratulated this tall upright young man (who looked more like someone from the Army Officer class than a rural police constable) on his 'concise and detailed observations.' His Lordship confided in the Court that too often the constabularies provided notes 'that were little better than twaddle'. Mr. Cholmondley smiled under his wig and thought of dinner in his airy comfortable dining room. Smiling, he rose to begin his manipulation of the prime witness Miss Frith.

Maisie's blue eyes focused on Mr. Cholmondley and he gave her a warm smile. He was partial to girls of this class and had used a great many of them in the past. Maisie, sensing this, allowed herself to be used and manipulated and whispered all the right things to him. During the whole interrogation neither Maisie nor Edward lost eye contact. The twelve men of the Jury were impressed by her maidenly shy stance and fearless courageous look. His Lordship looked at her golden hair and felt that there was hope for the lower orders after all.

Fox's Defence team had prepared their case with infinite care. As Lomas had predicted, a local evangelical organisation of railway workers had found a solicitor ready to work for free. In his turn he had provided a barrister who would be paid from local chapel charities. He had read all the information carefully. The solicitor and his team had visited the town and found out a great deal about Maisie Frith. James Bedford, barrister, aimed to reduce Frith into insignificance within minutes.

"You have lived in the town all your life?"

Maisie said she had. She found she could not get eye contact with this stern man who reminded her of her arch-enemy Hornton.

"And you would say that you are well known by everybody in the town?"

"Yes." whispered Maisie disconcerted that this man would not look at her as men usually did.

"Very well known Miss Frith?"

"Don't repeat yourself, Mr. Bedford," said his Lordship. "It is tedious and we do not have all day."

"No my Lod." Bedford was meek. He knew judicial fury would soon crash down on him but he knew it would be worth it.

"Yes," said Maisie softly, but to whom her confused mind was uncertain, And now she could hardly be heard.

"And yet, Miss Frith, there are many of these people who know you well, call you 'The Whore of Babylon'."

There was a gasp of horror, mixed with surprise and latent pleasure from the Court. His Lordship intervened with anger.

"Mr. Bedford, Mr. Bedford! That will not do. Apologise to the witness at once. I will not have small provincial town tittle-tattle noised abroad in my court, and used as evidence. Apologise or stand down Mr. Bedford."

Mr. Bedford had known this would happen, and smoothly apologised and withdrew the fact he had suggested the witness was known in the town by such a biblical, but vulgar term. He had planned to damage the key witness beyond repair. The words were said. The damage was done however many apologies were made.

And for a few moments his ploy had worked. But he had not taken into account Maisie Frith. She had blushed. She looked terrified. She looked beseechingly in the direction of Mrs. Harryson. Huge tears welled up in her eyes. Her head drooped. She would say no more. She stared at the floorboards, her eyes downcast and two tears trickled down her flushed cheeks. After five minutes his Lordship told her to stand down. The men of the Jury had forgotten the character assassination. All that was imprinted in their minds was a young girl dressed in sober blue, like a renaissance picture, weeping at an insult. All the men in the Court were transfixed.

The Defence crumpled before the lunchtime adjournment.

One of the first men out of the Court was Hornton. His face was rigid with suppressed rage fuelled by self-righteous beliefs. He had been summoned by the defence and the prosecution. He had been told by Bedford to be prepared for more character assassination of Maisie, but when he was summoned Bedford seemed to have lost interest knowing he had lost the case.

Nevertheless, Hornton strode through the streets of Derby with grim determination that the Whore of Babylon would get her just sentence.

Mrs. Harryson took Maisie to a pie shop but Maisie was ill at ease with her beef pie. She had seen herself in her new outfit as a heroine, but after the first nice man in the wig and gown had finished looking into her eyes, she had felt everything had gone arseyversey as she put it to herself . . . After the pie and Mrs. Harryson's assurances she felt better and they returned to the Court.

It was hot in the Court and Mrs. Harryson felt her mind wandering as various technicalities and details of the law were being discussed. She kept slipping a humbug to Maisie who had now regained her confidence and was stroking her skirt and wriggling her feet in the new boots Mrs. Harryson had provided for the occasion.

Mrs. Harryson stared at the wretched Fox. She felt profoundly sad for him. Stunted and badly fed as a child, with no proper education, she thought; the man had no chance. Of course, she thought, he needed punishing but not by what was coming. She shook her head slightly. She was involved with the growing women's movement but she could clearly see the working men still had a lot to struggle for.

Hope was back in the box on some detail of the law. She smiled to herself. Her plans were working out very well. She had known within the first hour of meeting him that he was just what she wanted for her plans. And looking at him she could see what a better education could do for a man. She knew Hope had only a limited schooling but she sensed it was superior to Fox's. Hope had been educated well by the church. Her food was doing the rest, turning Hope into what she wanted. It was all working out far better than she had planned. And she quite liked the man, even though in her view, he was far less intelligent than her. But she liked him . . .

She looked at the Judge and frowned a little. It angered her that this privileged and upper class fool was going to have Fox murdered. The frown was replaced by a smile. If only the Court knew about her own family . . . if only Hope knew about her family! He would probably pack his suitcase and leave if he did. She dreamily counted how many of her family had escaped being sentenced to death in this same court . . . If not hanged then certainly put away for robbery and worse. She wondered if she would ever tell John Hope the truth . . . It would take a long time she thought . . . perhaps at least ten years before she could be certain of her plans . . .

She jumped suddenly. She saw a clergyman in full frock by the side of the Judge. And how she hated the clergy. The old fool of the Judge had put on the black cap and was sentencing the sad little man to be hanged by the neck until he was dead. She shivered at the words and took Maisie's hand in her own and stroked it. 'Bastard law', she thought and 'bastard Judge'. Maisie looked at her as she squeezed her hand.

Mrs. Harryson suddenly thought of the man she had admired most, Professor Stockwell and his story of the shipwrecked sailor who knew he had reached a civilised country because he could see a gallows on the cliff top.

Her eyes full of tears and her hand still gripping Maisie she left the fetid courtroom. She wanted air, fresh air and to be away from all these men who thought they ruled the world.

Still holding Maisie's hand Mrs. Harryson took in deep breaths of the coal smoke tainted air of Derby. It was better than the Court Room saturated with men's odours and stale out-breathings.

A young man in a clerk's formal suit bustled up to Maisie.

"Are you Maisie Frith?"

Maisie turned luminous eyes on him, her faith in herself quite restored. She said she was before Mrs. Harryson suddenly realised what this was about. The man pressed a document in Maisie's hand which she instinctively took and he left her bewildered, once more looking to Mrs. Harryson for support.

Mrs. Harryson almost snatched it and quickly read the official summons from the Midland Railway Company lawyers ordering Maisie to Pay a *Fine of Forty Two Shillings for Trespass and theft on the property of the railway company.* Failure to do so, read the document, would lead to the case being handed over to the civil police.

Mrs. Harryson snorted with anger and exasperation. She knew very well who had reported Maisie. Still holding Maisie's hand she dragged her away at some speed.

"What's up?" stammered Maisie, alarmed by the force of her propulsion and Mrs. Harryson's face.

"Nothing for you to worry yourself over," said Mrs. Harryson and nothing more was said as the couple headed at speed to the headquarters of the Midland Railway by the Station.

Mrs. Harryson steered the puzzled Maisie to the grand entrance and pulled her up a flight of steps to the main area, where a big mahogany counter stood surrounded by potted palms and much red velvet above the thick maroon carpet, decorated at intervals with the coat of arms of the great Company. A smooth young man glided out grey of suit and face under sleeked hair.

"Madam?"

"I want you to tell me where I can pay this Fine," Mrs. Harryson brusquely announced.

The smooth face under the oiled gloss of black hair became irregular with ill concealed contempt and anger. His first thought had been here was a chance to ingratiate himself with a partner's wife and daughter. The woman in her brown coat trimmed with velvet and fur had seemed a lady. His voice became dismissive.

"Go out of here and turn right and-"

"I am not going out of this building," said Mrs. Harryson. "You will kindly show me the way and it will not be down the steps we have just climbed." She took off a glove and revealed a large antique diamond ring.

The man acquiesced. The woman was obviously a lady, perhaps one of those crazy radical women, who busied themselves with do-gooding in the poorer classes; whatever the case he could not ignore such a presence.

He led them down increasingly dingy and sooty corridors until they reached a chocolate brown door, with a brass plate that had the engraved legend of SENIOR LEGAL CLERK engraved on the highly polished metal.

The smooth official knocked and they entered and were quickly abandoned.

A man behind a desk under a hissing gas lamp raised his eyes.

You have an appointment? I do not recollect-"

"You will see me now. You have no others in this room."

The Clerk opened his mouth to protest but Mrs. Harryson slapped down the Summons in front of him and peeled off her other glove. The Clerk noticed a very heavy emerald ring on one hand and a diamond on the other. They were not new. This was not new money. The woman was obviously a lady of some class, even lesser aristocracy and certainly gentry. He decided to cooperate. The woman could be Somebody.

"I wish to pay this Fine," said Mrs. Harryson. "Two guineas I believe." She took out a brown satin purse and banged down two gold sovereigns and two silver shillings.

The Clerk read the Summons fussily, moving his glasses up and down his nose to focus on the smaller print. This done, he removed the gold glasses, and with a bunch of keys attached to a silver chain which were retrieved from his trouser pocket, he opened a desk drawer and withdrew a pink form. The drawer was locked and the keys reinserted into the striped trouser pocket. Mrs. Harryson remained standing as there were no chairs. Maisie felt her hand being crushed in Mrs. Harryson's.

The Clerk stood up and turned up the gas to a more threatening hiss. He selected a pen, lifted the brass lid of his inkwell, shook the pen slightly over a blotter and with a flourish began to write.

"Name, please, if the payee is different from the indicted."

"Fanny Arsehole." said Mrs. Harryson, who was by now at screaming point with the little man after the afternoon in Court.

Maisie's free hand fluttered to her mouth to stifle a giggle.

"I beg pardon madam?" The little Clerk's tea and tobacco stained moustache bristled with disbelieving horror. The pen shook. The gas flared.

"Annie Harryson," said Mrs. Harryson. "It is easy enough to register. Would you like me to spell it out for you?"

The Clerk, awash with fiery red blushes, sweated for the first time in his legal office.

Towards half past five on the following Friday Sergeant Glorey took up a position under the gas lamp, just lit by the lamplighter and outside the stationer and printer who sold newspapers to the town. Many of the townsfolk were hurrying to the shop for the week's edition of The Derbyshire Times or The High Peak News, which contained full details of the murder on the railway line so close to the town.

As they emerged from the shop and into the early twilight of an autumnal fog they were accosted by the Sergeant.

He was an imposing figure, his cape silvered and dusted with drizzle and the gas light gilding the helmet and silver badge. His sensuous lips gleamed in the gloom. Under the polished boots the dull red of fallen horse chestnut leaves were already turning to pulp. Each customer received a prepared speech from him.

"Good evening to ye. I see you've bought a paper to read about the Murder. I knew in my bones there were something afoot that morning so I sent young Hope down to see what he could sniff out. And I was right, you see. He did sniff something out and I was able to get things moving."

By seven o'clock, as curtains were pulled and suppers started, the town felt at ease that they were so competently guarded by such stalwarts of the Law.

Hope had been sent on one of Glorey's malicious wild goose chases. Some mischievous children had blocked a roadside culvert and managed to flood part of the village street in Ashford. This had been remedied by the local road mender but just before the distribution of the murder edition at four in the afternoon, Glorey had sent Hope the two mile walk 'to see everything is as it should be.' This kept Hope out of the town till seven and the end of his shift of beats. Glorey feared the congratulations would be directed at Hope instead of himself. Hope thought no more about it. Mrs. Harryson had served him one of the fine pork pies of the town, warm pork, a surrounding salty jelly and golden hot-water pastry. She had served it with some tomato chutney given to her by one of the grateful town women. This had been followed by Mrs. Harryson's blackberry pie and a jug of cream and the usual jug of ale fetched from The Anchor Inn.

Hope stretched before the fire and was content. He still saw the world in black and white contrasts. If you were a criminal you were punished. The hanging sentence for Fox bothered him not at all. Fox had killed another man and now the law would hang him. It all fitted into his Sunday School philosophy of either Heaven or Hell.

And he was privately glad Maisie Frith had been arrested even if Mrs. Harryson had paid the fine. That, too, fitted in with his simple view of life. He was well content and soon the comfort of the fire and the leather chair and the exercise and good food made him doze and then sleep.

Mrs. Harryson watched him for a moment. A mood of satisfaction registered on her face. Things were going well. She lifted off the oil lamp from the table and set it on the much stressed oak bureau. She unlocked the lid and settled herself at the desk. From one of the drawers she took out her most prized possession, an engraved silver Waterman fountain pen. It was one of her most cherished possessions and unlike so much else in the house was in pristine condition.

Soon the only sounds in the room were the soft scratch of the nib, Hope's snores, the snap of burning logs and a wind blowing the soft drizzle on the window.

MAGPIE MINE

God smote Ruth Bagley, in front of the whole congregation of All Saints Church, on Easter Day 1904. She fell to the floor, weeping. God knew she had killed her mother. She knew He knew she had connived with Annie Harryson and together they had murdered Liza Bagley.

All the town thought Ruth a saint. Now middle-aged, she had left her job as housekeeper to the Matlock gentry and come home to look after Mother. She had no alternative; as the only girl from a family of three brothers, it was her duty to look after her infirm mother. But God knew she had wanted Mother dead. That is why He hammered and thundered on her silk and muslin hat (bought in 1897 in Regents Street when her employers were in London just before she was called home). The now yellowing and sad hat was destroyed by God in front of the whole congregation.

Mrs. Liza Bagley had a minor stroke that left her weak and palsied and she had fallen and broken her leg in the November of 1897. Ruth resigned her post and came to look after her. There was nobody else and it was either Ruth did her Duty or Mother would have to go to the Workhouse Infirmary and Ruth did not want the shame and humiliation of the town - or Matlock - knowing Mrs. Bagley was in the Spike. But Ruth had wept bitterly at Fate for she loved her job in the Matlock mansion, and her own room with a fire and her account books and a bunch of keys to every lock in the house and control over thirty women servants.

She had sent for Dr. Bagehot, one of the two town doctors a year last November. Dr. Bagehot had examined Mrs. Bagley and had declared there was nothing he could do. He was very sorry. But now things had become impossible; Ruth was at her wits end. She was now down to her last sovereign and God alone knew how she was going to cope if Mother lived . . . True, her brothers sent a little money that bought food and coal but she had to keep dipping in her savings for emergencies and the Doctor's bill. Ruth could hardly cope with what was coming. And she needed the Doctor again.

Mother's bowels had gone awry last winter with increasing bouts of diarrhoea. Ruth had consulted Annie Harryson who was a trained Nurse and ministered privately in the town. Mrs. Harryson had given her some meadowsweet tea and other infusions and refused any payment as she frequently did when helping the poorer people. That had rankled with Ruth. She was glad Annie Harryson had not charged her but she was angry that the Nurse thought she, Ruth Bagley, Housekeeper, was a pauper. Still, as springtime came Mother recovered a little only to go downhill as the nights drew in and autumn came. Annie Harryson had said she must consult with Dr. Bagehot. But the Doctor had said he could do nothing for the extensive lumps now revealing themselves on Mother's stomach.

At Christmas the swelling in Mother's lower abdomen erupted and burst out. The stench was appalling throughout the tiny terraced cottage and Ruth was terrified lest the smell seeped into the neighbours houses.

Yesterday, Saturday 24th of February, she had called out Dr. Bagehot and she had to break into the last sovereign to prepare for the Doctor's fee. She sent Jack Harding, the neighbour's son, to fetch the Doctor and she had to give him a penny for that. Dr. Bagehot had come and had not even wrinkled his nose at the stinking wound or the erupting faeces. Instead he had told Ruth she must get help from Nurse Harryson. He would see her Monday and give the Nurse the details and then Annie Harryson would help Ruth manage her mother's nursing. He refused a fee and Ruth had been shamed that the Doctor thought her a case for his charity. And she knew exactly what it meant if Nurse Harryson was coming. All the women in the town knew what Nurse Harryson did with the dying.

Between the Doctor's visit and the Sunday evening of that weekend of ice and snow, Ruth changed Mother's sheets and night shift ten times. The fire under the copper never went out in the kitchen, the soiled washing bubbled and boiled itself to sparkling white cleanliness. As a Housekeeper to the Gentry Ruth had standards and by the Sunday night she was exhausted. Outside the pavements were iced and now and again a fine snow fell. The windows of the cottage ran with condensation. Just after six that evening, Ruth opened the back door to visit the privy across the yard. Mother was asleep and peaceful. Dr. Bagehot had sent up a large bottle of corrugated green glass of medicine with a red label announcing THE MIXTURE *for the sole use of the patient Mrs. Liza Bagley. This bottle when empty or otherwise must be returned to Dr. Charles Bagehot MD No. 1 Castle Street.*

It had worked like magic on Mother. She had slept for the first time in weeks. But the Doctor had not charged her and Ruth was relieved and annoyed. Concentrating on her shame Ruth slipped on the ice and fell against the privy step banging her shin and head. She began to sob.

Above the icy yard, a cold first quarter moon shone down on her. Two planets, one liquid silver the other a baleful red, showed through the trees of Chantry House garden like cold uncaring eyes. The church bells were ringing down, icicle sharp in the cold air, and hearing them Ruth sobbed even more bitterly.

Mother's illness had stopped her only pleasure since she had returned home, the pleasure of going to church with her school friend Betty Howard, and watching the gentry and the fine folk come into church. Betty and Ruth spent hours criticising and evaluating the Sunday rig-outs of the privileged. And now even that pleasure was denied her. And she wished Mother would hurry and die.

The thought entered her soul before she could stop it and she prayed then and there under the cold heavens for God to forgive her. But He would not forget.

She prayed again when she returned to the steamy kitchen but she knew God knew. And He knew she, Ruth Bagley would let Mrs. Harryson do her usual. She cried some more as she looked at the hole the fall had made in her Sunday stockings. Everything was past repair.

Monday was a sparkling frosty day and Dr. Bagehot, his rounds complete, found Mrs. Harryson standing in the sunshine with a broom in her hand supposedly sweeping the path but enjoying the sun.

"Good morning to you Nurse."

Annie Harryson gave him one of her warmest smiles. They were old acquaintances. They had both been at the Infirmary at Derby, he as a doctor she as a nurse. Both had been glad to return to the town and for the same reasons. He raised his hat to her.

"Mrs. Bagley is in a bad way Nurse. I need to talk to you about her. Can you come to the surgery tomorrow at noon? You'll be able to do that between feeding and watering that splendid young fellow who lodges with you?"

He gave Mrs. Harryson a broad wink.

The next day Mrs. Harryson was sitting outside Dr. Bagehot's French windows on his south facing terrace, sipping from a glass of what the Doctor called 'Rhenish wine'. Annie Harryson looked totally relaxed. Dr. Bagehot was possibly the only man in the town that kindled any affection or friendship within her. He treated her as an intellectual equal.

"Bombus terrestris is out about her business of collecting food," said the Doctor watching the bumble bees in the pool of lilac crocus by the flagged terrace. He knew Annie Harryson liked this sort of comment. He was aware she was the most intellectual woman in the town and had she been a man may well have been sitting with him as a fellow doctor.

"It is a pity the human world is not as merciful as the world of the Bombus. When those bees become weak they will die naturally and quickly and decently . . . Mrs. Bagley has several large tumours in her bowel and one has now ruptured the intestine and stomach wall and is spilling the contents of the bowel out of her body. Not a pretty sight Nurse. Ruth Bagley is exhausted with it all, but she is a proud woman and a religious one and will not complain because she believes it is God's will."

He sipped the golden wine with relish and held the glass to the sun for a moment, then offered Mrs. Harryson a sugar biscuit from a silver tray.

"You and I, Nurse, think differently."

He lit his pipe. Old friends as they were, he did not ask her permission to smoke. He sipped his wine.

"I suggest a nutritious liquid diet to minimise the eruptions of faeces. That will weaken her of course, but it will add dignity. You and Ruth are expert cooks and I can think of worse ways of exiting this world than sipping your soup in a clean bed."

He replenished their glasses from the slender brown bottle.

"I have prescribed the usual Mixture. Send down for as much as it takes. You know what to do Nurse. I'll call in now and again, but it grates on Ruth Bagley's nerves not to be able to pay me. You know what to do."

They looked at each other for a moment and then both sipped their wine appreciating the floral bouquet and the gentle February sunshine that lit their faces, and shone in the room behind them to reveal a chaos of books and faded carpet of Bagehot's bachelor den.

The following Thursday Annie Harryson and Ruth Bagley were together in Ruth's front parlour which she had never used since Mother fell ill. Ruth wanted Mrs. Harryson to see that she was not in the house of a pauper. A small fire burned in the grate and an Ashford Marble clock ticked on the mantelshelf, but the little window looking into North Church Street was coated in ice.

They talked generally for a while, Ruth perched tense and unsmiling on a horse hair chair, her thin hands to the mean fire.

"You will have quite enough, Ruth, seeing to the bed linen and nightdresses," said Annie equably. "I am happy to make the soups and jellies your mother needs to help her through this time of her life. And please do not worry about money, Ruth." Annie held up her hand as Ruth made a ritual protest that she did not need charity. Both women knew that Ruth did need charity. "I've plenty of bones and meat left over from cooking for my lodger Constable Hope. And I like to help anybody in trouble. Do not worry yourself about money. You have enough to do and think about."

Ruth managed to thank her, but her throat was tight with rage and shame and it made the thanks sound grudging and shrill.

So the two women worked unceasingly together. Mrs. Harryson was as good as her word. She brought nourishing soups devoid of any solids that would cause the horrific extrusions. She brought beef jelly she had made. She brought an endless supply of fruit jellies that she made with syrups she had made in the summer from strawberries, raspberries and blackberries. From her own moneys Annie brought cream flavoured and whipped with these fruit syrups. She made the old woman syllabubs with lemon and cream and white wine. When the pain was intense she dosed Mrs. Bagley with the Mixture from the green corrugated bottle and continued until Mrs. Bagley sank back into sleep.

Mrs. Bagley wasted away daily on this liquid diet. The nourishment nevertheless kept her optimistic and the medicine made her sleep. She was lucid and her sons agreed Mother was coping with her last illness very well. Everybody was resigned to what was coming and they were glad Nurse Harryson was doing such a good job. Except Ruth.

Ruth fumed with rage as she stirred the soiled linen in the boiling copper or as she ironed Mother's nightdresses ready for the next change. Ruth knew exactly what Nurse Harryson was doing. She was flouting God's Will. God, in His Wisdom, thought Ruth, had decided to try Mother with this torture before He judged her and admitted her to Heaven. It was what God had ordained. And Nurse Harryson with her herb teas and soups and jellies and secret syrups and that big bottle of medicine with the red label, was trying to ease Mother's pain and, what was worse, was hastening her death by withdrawal of solids. Oh yes, Ruth muttered over the boiling linen, she knew exactly what Annie Harryson was doing.

And yet she could not bring herself to stop her. She did not know exactly why this was, but she could not. She knew God would punish her for assistance in thwarting His Will for Mother.

She had no excuse for ignoring the facts, Ruth told herself as she ironed Mother's sheets to a perfection that made her so popular with the gentry. There was always talk about Nurse Harryson amongst the women of the town. Annie Harryson never went near Church or Chapel. Ruth shook her head over the iron and placed it back on the fire. Ruth herself had seen Annie Harryson, before she went to Derby to be a Nurse, coming out of the cottage of old Mrs. Trotter the town's ancient Wise Woman. That ancient old crone had left all her books about herbs and potions and possibly magic spells to Annie. Ruth sniffed and took the iron off the fire, tested the heat by spitting on it as genteelly as she could and put on the steel shoe over the base of the iron and began to iron again. She nearly made a patch of iron mould, a scorch, as she recalled Granny Goodwin, her mother's mother, telling her that old Mrs. Trotter's mother was a witch back in King George's time. Ruth knew Annie was poisoning Mother with those soups and jellies with herbs the witches had used.

The women in the town found Annie Harryson a constant source of tittle tattle. Mostly it was praise. Annie had remedies for everything a woman suffered or needed, and some said she went too far for women in trouble. They said that the only reason she had taken in that handsome Constable Hope was to cover up these misdeeds. Ruth nearly burned another hole thinking of what the Nurse and Constable might get up to. That was a scandal in itself. Ruth sniffed again. But like God's anger with her, the Nurse and Constable's cavorting (as she put it) kept intruding in her mind, possibly put there by the Devil, Ruth thought.

She put the iron back on the fire to repeat the process of heating the iron again. And all of the women in the town knew that Dr. Bagehot and Nurse Harryson were as 'thick as thieves.' Dr. Cole the other town doctor would have nothing to do with Nurse

Harryson. He liked to keep women in their place and would have nothing to do with women except as servants or wives. Yet the women in the town, even the gentry, used Mrs. Harryson. And now she, Ruth Bagley was doing the same. God would strike her down she knew it.

At the heart of Ruth's belief that Mrs. Harryson killed Mother was her belief in the Devil and the Powers of Darkness, as Dr. Ball had called them in a sermon before his brain softened. Ruth's family had always lived in Derbyshire. Her father, grandfather and his father and beyond had been lead miners at Magpie Mine two miles to the north west of the town in the limestone uplands. Ruth had heard stories of 'T'Owd Man', or 'The Knocker', a presence that lived deep underground, and had to be pacified with gifts of food and ale left by the miners. She had heard stories of the terrifying Piper in nearby Great Shacklow Woods whose piping was a warning of coming personal disaster. Likewise the Fiddler, on nearby Fin Cop, across the valley from the Mine, who played in storms when the Devil was riding the thunder. Ruth had shivered as she heard of The Old Woman, a ghostly spectre in white, who haunted the scene of death or warned of impending doom. The local gods still made their presence felt, even though the Christian missionaries from Rome of a thousand years earlier had tried to destroy them; but the memories of their powers lived side by side with the Christian beliefs. It was only a small step for Ruth to associate Annie Harryson with these powers.

Annie Harryson killed Mother, Ruth believed, in the middle of March 1904.

A pool of mild Atlantic air seeped over frozen Derbyshire and covered the town in a blanket of thaw fog. A weak depression developed over the English Channel and the feeble breeze backed to the east. Cold moisture-laden air surged up the Don Valley from the German Ocean and crept over the moors to mix with the warmer air. This colder air was heavy with soot from the blast furnaces of the Don Valley that made battleship plate armour and would in ten years help to blow Hope and his world apart. Mixed in this easterly breeze were similar particles of soot from the German furnaces also preparing plate armour. On this Saturday night there was a blanket of the thickest fog the town had known. Ruth knew this fog was sent by the Devil to assist Mrs. Harryson as she put an end to Mother's life. The signs were all around. To Ruth's eternal shame she did nothing to stop Mrs. Harryson.

The trouble was Ruth just could not help herself. Something inside her, perhaps the Devil she thought, made her promote events. So on that Saturday night of The Great Fog, when Ruth had heard Mother's laboured breathing and soft moaning, she had run for Nurse Harryson. She could hardly make out the light from the gas lamps even as she was underneath one. Had she not known the town blindfold she would have lost her way. The Fog had created a silent deserted world where anything could happen. Mrs. Harryson returned with Ruth. Neither spoke as they climbed North Church Street. Ruth felt as if a demonic enchantment had enveloped her.

Annie quickly assessed Mrs. Bagley's condition. She decided there was no point in summoning Dr. Bagehot. Mrs. Bagley was past the aid of doctors and she knew the visit of the Doctor put Ruth in a rage that she could not pay. Annie descended the narrow stairs and saw Ruth standing in the cold parlour. Ruth refused to talk to Nurse Harryson in the warm kitchen that smelled of fresh ironing and lavender and soup. Ruth had kept up her standards as a Housekeeper to the Gentry.

"Your mother will die tonight," said Annie gently.

Ruth nodded. Internally she seethed with fury. How did Annie Harryson know God's Will? But she said and did nothing. There was silence in the cramped dank parlour. Neither woman spoke. Outside in the street, muffled and unreal, they both heard men laughing and voices.

“The Frith brothers setting out for a drunken Saturday night,” said Annie as much to herself as Ruth.

Instead of preventing Annie Harryson from carrying out her diabolical plans Ruth sublimated her internal anger.

“I wish I’d been born a man . . . no responsibilities . . .”

“No you don’t,” said Annie soothing the angry woman. “You are alright as you are. Women should have the same freedom as men.” That twentieth century wisdom was wasted on Ruth. She felt she had been enchanted by Annie.

Ruth shot Annie a venomous look at such godless talk. Then she turned her back on Annie and went in the kitchen knowing that Annie Harryson would climb the stairs and hasten Mother’s death, no doubt hoping the darkness without would hide her sinful deeds from God.

Alone in Annie Harryson’s house that Saturday evening, Hope felt a strange restlessness. It was an evening off duty and he had hoped to relax in the comfort of the leather chair with Mrs. Harryson opposite him. He had come to enjoy the relaxed comfort of these evenings off duty. He would read his Daily Mail and she would read her TIMES or read her book. Sometimes she would knit or darn. After three years Hope had come to value her local knowledge of the town and its families. The three years had passed quickly, for Glorey kept Hope busy and Hope enjoyed his work.

Yet there was a core of tension deep within Hope. Something was missing. He had felt this keenly when he had been invited to the Wedding of Constable Allen. The wedding had disturbed Hope. He was a conventional man and thought he ought to copy Jack Allen. Yet he did nothing about it.

At home in Derby he had hated his sisters’ endless talk of sweethearts and ‘walking out’. That made Hope nervous and uncomfortable and embarrassed to face up to what he thought was his own shyness in coming forward. He was grateful that Mrs.

Harryson never mentioned sweethearts or romance. She seemed much more interested in his work in the town and eager to advise him over affairs such as the Maisie Frith case. Hope was grateful for that.

He got out of the deep comfortable chair and glanced at the battered carriage clock and as he always did at the portrait of the regency buck above it. He would go out for a drink.

Putting the fireguard round the fire he felt in his pocket for coins. Money was no problem these days. He had never had so much. Mrs. Harryson charged a low rent for what she provided and Hope wondered why she needed a policeman as a lodger, with awkward hours and an enormous appetite for the fine food she prepared and presented.

Coming out of the door Hope was brought to a standstill. For a second he thought his eyes had failed but turning in the gloom he saw a blade of firelight shining through the shutters of Mrs. Harryson's room. He had not even seen in the coal smoke and low lying Derby, anything like the darkness and mist around him. It touched his face like a cold breath of something alive. It was uncanny. Hope was glad he was safe in the town and not trudging a lonely lane on one of Glorey's pointless errands. Hope shivered slightly. There was something disturbing that like his earlier feelings he could not crystallise into thoughts.

There were only four gas lamps between him and his destination The Anchor Inn. All Hope could see of the first one were the faint two pairs of eyes of the incandescent white hot gas mantles that normally spread a pool of radiance around the street lamp. Crossing Bridge Street to where he thought the second lamp should be he trod in what felt like a huge dollop of fresh horse muck. Hope swore under his breath. Treading carefully he found the second lamp and then made his way to the others and the door of the Inn. It had a large boot scraper set in the wall and Hope rubbed his boot on it for some time. Mrs. Peters the alewife kept a clean house and he respected that. He was glad to enter the large room. The night was unsettling.

The Anchor Inn had, seventy years ago, been a coaching inn for travellers who did not care for the grandeur of the The Whitehorse Inn that dominated the crossroads where the spacious market square was situated. Originally a farmhouse and an inn The Anchor had possessed an orchard and garden that travellers liked to take refreshment and a meal within its walled confines. This had been sold off for the building of the Post Office, a gothic building that now dwarfed the once elegant Queen Anne farmstead. Its town field had stables that had been sold (when the railway arrived in 1867, and the Age of Coaching finally withered away) for the building of the Grammar School that had dwarfed the Inn still more. Yet within was space and comfort.

Mrs. Peters, widowed early in her life had remained in what had been her husband's inn. She was the last of the ale wives, women who brewed their own ale. She was an efficient woman and kept a respectable house. She was a great friend of Annie Harryson and Annie enjoyed the ale she fetched for Hope. The ale was enjoyed in the kitchen of the Inn; not even Annie Harryson dared to enter the world of men in the comfortable taproom.

Hope entered it now with pleasure. Like Annie Harryson, Mrs. Peters kept to oil lamps and candles. Both women disliked the harshness of a gas light. The lamp was turned high and Hope blinked after the eerie blackness outdoors.

"Good evening Constable," said Mrs. Peters reaching down his mug and pipe. There was a murmur of greeting from the other men. It was more polite than welcoming. Hope was still regarded as a stranger by the other men.

Mrs. Peter's customers were the respectable tradesmen of the town, church goers and craftsmen and Hope enjoyed their talk although he rarely joined in or was invited to do so. Their talk of weather and crops and prices and politics gave him more than an insight into the town. He took his mug and his pipe and sat on a settle a little way from the other men but still within the warmth of the great fire.

He sipped his ale and felt better. The smell of the Inn always eased him. Tobacco smoke and wood smoke and the faint smell of ale and hops from the large brewhouse mixed with the smell of Mrs. Peter's bread ovens; she made a comfortable living from baking bread and charging a small rent for the excellent oven - for any wife wanting to cook in a reliable communal oven.

Hope stretched his legs out and relaxed. To his left a large clock was attached to the wall ticking a heart relaxing sixty loud ticks to the minute. This handsome clock had once kept what the town had called 'coach time' which had been half an hour earlier than the church clock time. The hills to the east of the town delayed sunrise and the local time had been later than the London time. Above Hope was a long and cruel whalebone whip used to lash the coach horses up the Derbyshire turnpike gradients. Above that was a gleaming brass coaching horn polished to perfection.

"It's a rum night out there," said Matt Barker the thatcher, "a grand night for mischief and devilry." There was a murmur of assent and light laughter. All the men had sensed the strangeness of the weather.

As if on some supernatural cue to those words the door opened and a gleaming figure entered, a man whom many in Derbyshire considered was a devil. It was Tinker Roland Frith, Maisie's father and father to the town gang of Friths. Hope heard Mrs. Peters take in a sharp intake of air. Tinker Frith was not one of her customers.

"A mug o' thy ale missus. My lads an' me are having a booze up tonight an' I thought I'd start with thee." he stared at her and she realised why so many women were in fear of this man in their lonely farm houses. He continued to stare at her as she drew the ale and when she handed it to him he paid and turned to look at Hope. There was a silence in the room. The other men were angry. It was an unwritten law in the town that decided where you drank your ale and this was not Tinker Frith's domain.

Hope stared back. In three years this was the first time he had confronted Tinker Frith although he had heard much about the head of the tribe of Friths.

It was Tinker's stare that Hope perceived most. It was his daughter Maisie's stare. Unabashed, questing for something, appraising and brimming with infinite cunning. He stared at Hope from head to boot, his eyes lingering as though examining a beast in the cattle market or a poached trout.

"Good evening to ye Constable."

And still he stared. Hope was struck by the similarity to Maisie's long stares. Tinker's eyes were dark and unfathomable but that was the only difference. Maisie's were the colour of a winter sky, Tinker Roland's the colour of dark moist earth.

Three years of policing had given Hope confidence and he sensed Mrs. Peter's need of protection. He stared back and did not reply, a subtle warning to Frith that Hope had him in his eye. Hope absorbed as much detail as he could - three years had encouraged him to develop this skill and instinct told Hope that this would be useful at some time in the future.

Tinker was of average height but he was lean and fit and exuded an animal strength. His iron coloured hair was cropped like a convict and flecks of red rust revealed his original colour. A silver ear ring shone in the lamplight. He wore a leather jerkin of uncertain age which might well have been his father's for Tinker Frith followed the trade of his father and grandfather; wandering tinkers repairing kettles and pans and selling scissors, cutlery and blades which he procured or stole from illegal Sheffield sources. Likewise they carried a compact supply of fine Macclesfield silk ribbons from the other side of their kingdom, useful tools in terrorisation of women in lonely farms. The trade Tinker Roland Frith practised was still good. Although the railway had destroyed the packhorse trading, Tinker still used the old lanes on his exploitations and abuses in Derbyshire.

Still looking at Hope he fumbled in his moleskin trousers seemingly for coins, but Hope was not certain. Then he put the mug down on the bar.

"Goodnight to ye missus . . . Constable . . . gents." This latter was uttered with heavy sarcasm.

"That'll be all tonight Tinker. I shall not serve you any more," said Mrs. Peters, her courage flowing back a little with a note of her usual crisp authority in her voice.

"Dunna thee worry, missus. I shanna be back." said Frith. He looked at her as though, she recounted to Mrs. Harryson the following Tuesday, "he was removing every stitch of my clothing."

Once more he stared at Hope. Then the door closed softly and he was gone.

"Well, salt my taters," said Jas Green the watch and clock maker of the town, a radical thinker and not easily intimidated. "What were all that about?"

Before a discussion could start the door opened again and this time Horace Frith the youngest son of Tinker entered. Pipes were removed from mouths in astonishment. This was the first time Horace had entered and he certainly was not welcome. As the youngest of the Friths he had been apprenticed to the blacksmith, who kicked him out after six months for pilfering. Horace then took over the job as town 'Lavender Man' collecting the accumulated weekly soil from the earth lavatories of many of the streets, which in 1904 had no sewage system. He looked as filthy as his trade and this time Hope saw Mrs. Peters step back for a different reason. Like his father Horace asked for a mug of ale and drank it down with some speed in the room that was now silent and watchful as the town blackbirds watching a hawk.

"Goodnight . . . Missus, Constable," said Horace, uncertain of the farewells in a drinking place he did not frequent, ignoring the other men. And the door clicked softly again.

"Which bugger'll be next?" asked Frank Shipley the butcher. Mrs.

Peters fired him a warning glance because she did not usually permit bad language in the house but tonight was a strange night and it was not going to plan.

Again the door opened and this time Bert Frith entered. The men watched as if they were attending a theatrical performance. Pipes had not been reinserted between lips. Bert Frith was the acceptable side of the Frith gang. One of the town's cobblers with a small shop in Church Alley, he wore a good polished pair of his own well made boots. He wore a decent clean jacket and corduroy trousers, the only sign of irregularity was an over heavy silver watch chain and fob that sparkled in the fire and lamplight. He only spoke to Mrs. Peters and was out quicker than Horace. He only nodded at Hope.

The men held their clay pipes poised in their hands ready for Gerald Frith, the flash man of the Frith gang to arrive. They were not disappointed. After ten seconds Gerald swaggered in. Hope noted he was as cleanly dressed as Bert but his jacket had a touch of style with fashionable lapels, a good shirt and thick silk tie revealed under it and he had a watch chain that appeared to be gold. Like the other Friths he asked for ale. This time Mrs. Peters seemed to square up to him like a boxer preparing his corner.

Gerald did not follow the previous performances. Instead he picked up his white pot mug and sauntered over to Hope and seated himself, very closely, next to Hope on the settle. Hope, disliking the man's proximity and contact instinctively edged away from Gerald's bodily contact and the stare that was so similar to Tinker's and Maisie's. Hope could smell the wet wool of the jacket that was dusted with the vapour of the fog and the faint pungency of soot that the fog contained. Hope could also detect the sweet smell of a quantity of drink that Gerald must have absorbed in the other ale houses and inns of the town.

"And how's thy landlady this foggy night?" asked Gerald Frith with mock concern. "Helping some poor old soul to get to heaven quicker than she should?"

Hope was to forget what he thought at that precise moment. It was a strange remark. What happened next wiped it clear away from his memory. Gerald once more slid towards Hope on the wooden settle in a way Hope recoiled from once more.

He suddenly spread out his hand and Hope thought with anger that he was going to place it on his knee, but he did not. He wanted to show Hope a gold ring he was wearing.

"Do you like my gold ring Constable? I bet your landlady could buy you one like this. They say she's got her Grandfather's loot stacked away in a cave under her copper. That's why she never lets her fire out." He grinned at Hope with the innuendo and Hope realised he was more drunk than he thought and certainly more inebriated than his father or brothers.

Gerald Frith thrust the ring virtually under Hope's nose and Hope was forced to look at the ring. It certainly looked like gold and not pinchbeck as many were at that time. Looking closer he was startled and then disgusted. At first sight the ring had appeared to be a thick band of gold with an inset stone of red glass, but as Hope stared it was probably an Indian ruby. There were two bulbous studs of gold at the top of the ring and Hope had seen rings like this in Derby, knuckle dusters for dirty fights between rival groups in the town. The studs could rip an opponent's face to shreds and were typical of a gang leader. The red stone next to the studs gave it status.

Except Hope realised, the ring was a circular gold phallus, beginning at the large gold testicles and, rounding Frith's finger, it entered a wrought gold vagina, accentuated by the ruby that was cut expertly to mimic the female organ. Gerald Frith laughed a beer and whiskey laden laugh. The ring obviously gave the wearer great pleasure.

"Dost like it Constable? Ask Annie Harryson for one next time ye've got her cold witch's tits between your teeth. Just before you tup her. She'd give thee owt just then."

There was a murmur of anger round the room. The whole

company was outraged at such talk and in front of Mrs. Peters too.

Hope felt his head turn giddy with fury. Then he felt his stomach turn over as it did as a child when the swing boats at the Fair nearly turned full circle. His face began to burn. He knew he would have to knock Frith into the street and Frith was a powerful man, drunk and aggressive and virtually the same size as Hope. Hope had taken boxing lessons when he joined the Derby force but had never been in a situation quite as outrageous as this. Hope stood up and yanked Frith to his feet pulling at the lapels of the jacket.

The cloth though fancy was thin and not designed for such force. There was the sound of ripping cloth and flying buttons. The table with the beer mugs tipped over and the mugs fell, one cracking in two the other rolling away. There was a silence for a few seconds as Hope held Frith upright, and the ticking of the Coaching Clock seemed to increase in volume.

"Get out before I kick you out," said Hope finding his breathing had suddenly become more restricted. "Now!" He shook Frith a little and let go. "Get out before I arrest you for that filthy mouth of yours and a breach of the peace of this Inn. Out! Now!"

Frith stared at him for two seconds with that stare of the Friths. Then he lowered his gaze and saw Hope's fists clenched and ready for action.

What happened next was to puzzle Hope for months to come although by Christmas of 1904 he realised why Frith did what he did. Frith backed away.

"Beg pardon Constable," said he and head down made his way to the door.

"Go on. Out!" roared Hope with a strength of voice he did not know he possessed. He felt as if it were coming from another man. "And you're banned from this Inn. D' ye hear?" The voice that did not seem to be his own had unconsciously lapsed into the unique dialect of the north Derbyshire town. "Set foot in here with your foul mouth and you'll be accountable to me and the Law!"

The door closed as softly as it had when the other Frith brothers left.

Then all was relaxed tension. Mrs Peters rushed up trembling and saying she thanked God Hope had been present when the Friths had arrived and the men examined the table and Don Simpson, a carpenter, promised to mend it. The mug's remains were swept up and Hope was, for the first time, offered ale and tobacco by the other men.

That foggy night saw Hope, after three years, finally accepted by the working men of the town.

Annie Harryson moved quietly around the room and laid a fire in the tiny iron grate that had not seen a fire since Ruth Bagley had been born to Mrs. Bagley in this room in 1861. When Annie lit the fire the chimney smoked horribly, and Annie thrust open the window to create a draught up the chimney and keep the smoke away from the dying woman.

The fire soon blazed and Annie decided to keep the window open. She remained by the open window a little, because even the foggy air was preferable to the stale air of the sick room. And Mrs. Harryson smiled a little to herself. She had unwittingly carried on a tradition of the town that a dying person must have a window open so the soul could fly to Heaven.

She leaned out of the window. It would be her last breath of freedom for soon she must attend to Mrs. Bagley. The fog was as thick as it had been. Drips and taps came to her ears and several times she thought she heard a curious chuckling. Puzzled she listened for longer than she intended. The cottages were close by the Church and she could not rid her mind that some of the hideous gargoyles and carved devils on the church tower were laughing at human tragedy. Annie frowned at her own fantasies.

At eleven o' clock The Reverend Herbert Jones was brought upstairs by Ruth to assist the dying woman's last hours. Ruth had gone herself to fetch the Curate who was assiduous in his ministry.

When he and Ruth arrived in the tiny room the fire was red hot and the air fresh and cleansed. A candle burned steadily by Mrs. Bagley. She gave a low moan and Annie mixed a large dose of The Mixture from Dr. Bagehot's corrugated green bottle. The bottle had been refilled several times unknown to Ruth, although she realised later, thinking everything over, that this had been done. It was submerged knowledge such as this, that made God so angry with her on Easter Day.

Mrs. Harryson mixed the potion with some of her own blackberry syrup that the dying woman had come to relish in her last weeks of life.

The Reverend Herbert Jones looked on with mild distaste. He strongly disapproved of this Nurse Harryson who never visited a place of worship and deeply disturbed him. Jones believed the only way to live was through the Ways of Christ, and he had a fear that women such as this would spread disbelief through the town, and eventually that would reach the working people and then they would lose their morality, and terrible events would follow. He took long slow breaths to calm his fears. He did not speak to Nurse Harryson so strong was his disapproval of the woman.

"I shall leave you to your prayers," said Mrs. Harryson softly. "I shall be downstairs if you need me."

Neither Ruth or the Curate acknowledged her.

Jones was unswerving in his ministry and remained with Ruth and her mother until midnight, praying most of the time.

Returning to his house on Church Lane he passed the Church. The fog seemed denser than ever. He had to feel his way along the walls. He could hear taps and drips as the old snow melted on the church roof and now and again he heard a sound like demons laughing. Jones was of the evangelical school of thought and believed in the Devil and his works as described in the Bible. Despite his trust in God he shivered and almost crossed himself as Dr. Ball, a staunch high church Anglo-Catholic so often did these days, as his mind dwindled away. Jones felt a cold sensation ripple up his spine which did not entirely go until he had a hot cocoa before retiring.

Sitting by the open window Annie Harryson heard these fiendish gurglings more than once and told herself it was melt water in the gargoyle drain spouts below the spire.

Mrs. Bagley died peacefully at three in the morning when, Ruth noted, the fog was at its densest and the air full of strange noises that made her shudder as she thought of Mother's soul negotiating these demonic impediments as it made its way to Heaven and the waiting Arms of the Father God. Ruth had no doubt these demonic laughs belonged to devilish familiars of Witch Harryson.

Mrs. Harryson and Ruth worked in silence, preparing the dead body, washing and tending by the light of two candles above the fire.

At five the body was decent and Ruth shut the window with a bang. The wind had veered round to the west and the draught was making the candles gutter. At six Mrs. Harryson left with few words spoken. Standing at the open front door and glad to be rid of the woman she was sure was a witch, Ruth saw the sky had cleared and the fog had gone. A brisk wind was blowing the clouds to rags where a few stars shone through the tatters. Ruth could not help thinking Annie Harryson had called up the fog for her own dark purposes.

Walking down North Church Street Annie found herself turning to look back at the Church. The fiendish drips and taps of the thawing snow had unnerved her. She could not see the gargoyles, but the Church was still and black and deserted against the now flying clouds and tumbled stars.

By her gate Annie Harryson heard the scrape of an ill fitting door being opened and then men's voices, amongst them the voice of Tinker Frith. Annie instinctively tiptoed up her path and cowered by the door. She feared Tinker Frith more than anyone. She had heard countless stories of his abuse and foul actions. Annie shivered slightly. She knew Tinker. If he was so inclined he would do anything to her, without any fear of the law. She heard him again saying something to his daughter Maisie.

"You keep your bloody mouth shut about what's gone on in here tonight. What's gone on up them stairs is our family business. Do you hear me girl? One word and I'll shove something of mine down your throat that'll keep ye quiet for a year."

Annie opened her door with trembling hands. Tears filled her eyes for Maisie. God alone, if there was one, knew what those men had been doing with Maisie after their drinking bout. Annie had long thought Jacob, Maisie's son, was the result of an incestuous union with her father or Gerald, the two most devilish of the family.

Alone in her big room she leaned against the table. One reason she had wanted Hope as a lodger was to protect herself against these men, although it was not the main one. One day, thought Annie, all of the Friths will rot in gaol.

Ruth Bagley sensed Anger in the Easter Morning as she set off for church. Scudding clouds were blowing in from the Staffordshire moorlands, a stern reminder that a storm was imminent. Ruth did not like the look of it at all. It was a surly Easter Day. The children in the town had been disappointed not to see the sun dance as he rose over the horizon. That old belief still lingered here just as Ruth's beliefs had been passed down over the centuries.

A few drops of cold rain fell as Ruth made her way to Church. It was not far but it put her in a dilemma. Rain on the faded hat would decay it still further. On the other hand she dared not open her green silk umbrella bought in London, like the hat, when she had been 'Somebody'. Last time she had opened it she had heard the elfin sounds of small rippings and the frame was red rust. It would be easier to have gone through the north door of the church but Mother said it was unlucky. 'The Devil, the Choir and bad luck follow you through the north door,' she had said.

So Ruth dutifully, hand on faded hat, went round to the south door. Mrs. Turner the fishmonger's wife was shaking the rain from her umbrella.

"Not worth putting up my brolly for the short walk," said Ruth loudly, anxious not to appear foolish. Her voice sounded harsh above the clamour of the Easter morning bells.

"We've had no rain since that fog," shouted Mrs. Turner, "and now look at that sky."

Ruth did not look at the sky. It troubled her. She still felt God would punish her for not letting Mother's last illness run God's natural course. Life, thought Ruth, was a vale of tears and she had no right to meddle with God's will. She went down the steps into the Church, glad to turn her back on yet another reminder that God may bring down retribution on her.

On the whole Ruth was feeling better. She had received a nice letter from Matlock with a new reference to help her seek work. She had helped Mrs. Parker after that lady's cook had left without notice. She had taken in sewing and washing. Already there was a sovereign in her savings pot (a squat and ugly Toby Jug that had been Mother's proud possession). But she wished it had been a sunny sky.

Ruth made her way to the pew where Betty was waiting. Already the organ was rumbling and in the church the riot of the pealing bells was only a discreet humming and throbbing. The two spinsters sat in an unreserved pew; neither could afford the fee to reserve a pew for Sundays. But the whole congregation knew that pew was theirs.

It had been chosen with care. Just far enough to the back so the two women could swivel their eyes, but not their bodies, to watch the ladies enter through the south door. Their eyes could follow them and then watch them walk up the aisle to the reserved seats at the front of the church where the gentry worshipped. Both friends could remain rigid and reverent with only eye movement betraying a passionate interest in the elite of the town.

Ruth entered the pew and sank in prayer once more asking God to forgive her for letting Dr. Bagehot and Nurse Harryson interfere with Divine Will. She edged herself back on the pew her corsets creaking a little, in sympathy with her troubled brain. God did not appear impressed. Outside the stained glass the sky had darkened further and gusts of wind shook the ancient building.

Ruth tried to relax. She and Betty came early so nothing would be missed. They watched Fred Mellor begin to pump the organ faster as it voluntary increased in volume and complexity. They watched the servers finish lighting the altar and chancel candles until the chancel was a blaze of white and gold and candlelight. That cheered Ruth. Then she felt afraid again for another server was lighting the gas jets on the walls, a rare event at Matins. Ruth felt a chill.

The organist's Bach reached a climax of contrapuntal vigour and the bells were ringing down with festal fury. Betty's and Ruth's eyes swivelled as the gentry made their entrance. And there was no doubt about it. Lady Dalrymple looked the finest in a suit of spring green sailcloth, a small cream silk trilby trimmed with exquisite tiny ostrich feathers on her hair and waistcoat and cuffs of cream and yellow shot silk. Ruth's eyes at maximum swivel had seen her drop a primrose yellow umbrella gleaming with rain in the stand in the porch. Holding on to the arm of Sir George her ladyship made her way up to the front Dalrymple family pew, confident in her latest fashion statement. Betty and Ruth leaned back with a sigh to rest their eyes. When Betty arrived for tea on

Monday, carrying her usual treat of two penny iced buns, there would only be agreement on the finest Easter rig-out. Except that they would both forget Lady Dalrymple in what happened.

The organ ceased and Fred let go of the sticky pump handle and mopped his forehead. The five minute bell rang and Betty and Ruth viewed with scorn the late comers, flustered and embarrassed. Hailstones hurled themselves at the south windows. Now only late winter coughs and a rustling stirring and the tumult of the fury outside filled the air. Then Fred began to pump the bellows ready for the organist to couple the swell and great organ.

A loud chord warned the congregation. They rustled to their feet with accompanying coughs and the choir vestry door opened and the choir entered singing Jesus Christ is risen today. They were led by a server holding up a banner of gold and white. The boys passed Ruth who admired their scrubbed innocence. Then came the choirmen with Constable Hope clearly audible with his clear baritone voice. Despite what they said in the town about him and Mrs. Harryson, Ruth had to admire his fine head of hair and whiskers. Glistening red gold in the gaslight. It was rare to see him without a helmet. Everyone said he was singing Handel's *I Know that my Redeemer liveth* at some point in the morning worship. Despite Mrs. Harryson's association with Hope, Ruth and most of the female congregation looked forward to this solo.

Behind the choirmen came the two curates. On the left was Herbert Jones looking exhausted as always with his beliefs. In spite of all his efforts Jones always looked crumpled and worn in a procession, possibly because his heart was not in these high Anglican rituals. His Cambridge academic hood of white silk looked creased and soiled in the dim light of the rising storm. Jones was a Cambridge man and believed in carrying out the word of Christ by his deeds. Like many of his theological college he believed that Christianity was the only true way of life. His burning desire was to bring Christianity to the working people. He was certain if the mass of workers did not believe in God then the country would go to the Devil.

As soon as Jones learned that Hope had been 'rescued' and nurtured by the Church in Derby he had pounced on him and enlisted him to the Choir. Hope had a good voice and had been a choirboy in Derby and enjoyed singing and had been a willing and enthusiastic recruit. He had been taught in the Derby choir to read music and looked forward to practising his skills. As they proceeded up the aisle to the stalls Jones could hear Hope singing. 'A natural leader from the working class,' thought he, but his face remained strained with overwork.

On his left was the other curate Edward Runcorn almost bipolar in contrast. Runcorn, one day to be a bishop, was immaculate in his surplice and his Oxford M.A. hood glowing like a ruby. He upheld all Dr. Ball's Anglo-Catholic beliefs. Runcorn believed that the Anglican church was the heir in England of the Roman Catholic church and should therefore follow all its traditions if not its core beliefs. He accepted that Henry the Eighth had severed relations with the Pope and reforms had been made but the Anglican church was basically Catholic. It was Runcorn who saw to it that the altar was always a blaze of candles, that the choir bowed to the altar before entering the stalls and that the church music was of the highest quality. He had been delighted to receive Hope into the Choir but for totally different reasons. He knew Hope's voice would attract the ladies. Runcorn spent a great deal of time taking tea and cake with the ladies of the parish. He left the ministering of the poor to Jones.

It had not been easy to capture Hope for the service of God. Sergeant Glorey had told Jones that Hope was needed for duty every Wednesday evening, the Choir Practice night. "It's not possible your reverence," he had told a pleading Jones. Jones had arrived after christening a dying baby in Diamond Court, in the middle of the night, calling on his way home at seven in the morning. Jones appeared tattered and grubby. "And I need him every Sunday you see. There's more crime on a Sunday because the godless see their chances to sin" Glorey had inflated himself in the morning gaslight at what he thought was a masterstroke at preventing Hope from being welcomed into town life. And Glorey was a Methodist and anxious to restrict the work of the Church.

Moreover Glorey had seen Jones entering the homes of some of the most feckless and idle in the town and subconsciously he associated the clergyman with these dregs, scum, as Glorey thought of them. Jones, white and eye-bagged gave up. Glorey, red and sweating had leaned against the counter and watched him go with not a little satisfaction. He thought Jones could do with a new cassock, the backside of which was white and shiny with wear as Jones retreated.

The next day Edward Runcorn arrived in the Police Station. He carried his gold topped cane and did not remove his silk top hat when he entered. Runcorn wore an extremely well cut and tailored black clerical suit with a heavy gold watch chain with a diamond fob flashing across the black waistcoat. He half bowed to Glorey. Glorey struggled to his feet. He had seen Runcorn talking and laughing with Lady Dalrymple and one day the Duchess had stopped her coach to talk with the dashing young curate whose sermons were the talk of the ladies in Derbyshire,

"I understand, Sergeant, there is a problem with your duty rotas and you cannot arrange them so as to allow Constable Hope to attend my choral practices."

He fixed Glorey with a direct stare and Glorey seemed to shrink and deflate and a bead of sweat appeared on his forehead.

"I can sort that out for you sir," said Glorey meekly.

"I am greatly obliged Sergeant," said Runcorn smoothly and he raised his hat a fraction of an inch, inclined his head and left the Station, his nose wrinkling with disgust at the human odours that always lingered in Glorey's kingdom.

Hope was free and became a leading member of the Choir. The confrontation of the ejection of Gerald Frith in the Anchor Inn and the fact Hope sang in the Choir made him almost accepted in the town. It was a pity he lodged with Mrs. Harryson . . . the gossip flourished.

As the two curates processed by the side of Ruth, as always, Mrs.

Ball, the rector's wife, turned round from the front pew to see if her husband Dr. Ball was installed correctly in the procession.

Mrs. Ball, dressed in a flounced confection of daffodil yellow silk and white ermine trims watched her husband's progress. She refused to listen to any discussion about her husband's mental problems. She was determined to hold on to his position, and hers, at all costs. Dr. Cole had diagnosed 'softening of the brain' a diagnosis in tune with the medical knowledge of the times. Later in the century it would have been recognised as the early stages of a tragic combination of vascular dementia and Alzheimer's disease. Mrs. Ball refused to recognise any deterioration of the Rector's mental state.

"As fruit ripens it softens," she had told Dr. Cole "and that does not mean it is rotting!" she had said as she saw the doctor out of the rectory drawing room. And that was that. Even the fearless Dr. Cole was intimidated by Mrs. Ball's determination and unsafe logic.

The Bishop of Lichfield himself had journeyed to the town to see the situation for himself at the request of other clergy in the district. Mrs. Ball had allowed him to see nothing. His Grace returned to the station and was so shaken by Mrs. Ball that he had to take a double brandy at Derby station. Any mention of mental weakness of her husband by the curates was met with scalding rebukes. As it was, the two curates managed the parish extremely well, and Dr. Ball sat by the fire in his study, with an open book in front of him, occasionally writing a Greek or Hebrew letter in the margin with a gold pencil. Runcorn entertained the parish tea parties of the ladies by describing Mrs. Ball as the daughter of Mrs. Proudie from Barchester Towers. Laughter and teacups tinkled. And nothing was resolved.

Now Mrs. Ball checked her husband's progress with tigress' eyes. In the old days he had come at the end of the procession decked in ecclesiastical robes according to the church season. Today the Rector was in the middle of four altar boys. This was Runcorn's idea to ensure Dr. Ball tottered in a straight course to the stalls.

Two of the boys were Bert Frith's sons. That was Jones' idea desperate to involve the godless of the town in the church.

Jones had made Eddie and Bobby the two personal servers to Dr. Ball. They helped him into his robes and led him out. Eddie and Bobby also helped themselves to a great deal more.

Dr. Ball robed up in a private vestry that had originally, in pre-reformation times, been a chantry chapel. Ball, fascinated by the old Catholic traditions, had restored the chapel, put in an altar and made it his private vestry and chapel. Before losing his mind Ball had sunk in prayer before the altar before a service. There was also a chest of drawers containing treasures he had long forgotten existed. Ball had come to the town with a considerable fortune from his mother's family of Birmingham goldsmiths and had, in his Oxford days, hunted down relics from the monastic houses of the past before they were seized and nationalised by Henry VIII. Eddie and Bobby had picked the locks of the mahogany chest and already stolen a wafer box studded with emeralds that Ball believed had come from Welbeck Abbey. They had also taken a golden tube that was crusted in gems that Ball was convinced had come from nearby Beauchief Abbey and had once contained the little-finger bone of St. Filibert.

Bert Frith, their father, the most cunning and outwardly most conventional of the Frith Gang had a cobbler's shop. He also had a shelf of hats he sold to the working men of the town. These he bought from Stockport. He sold the treasures to a silversmith in Sheffield, known by his father Tinker Frith, and banked the proceeds in Stockport. Gerald's suit and gold ring had been bought from this fund of money managed and shared out by the cobbler Bert Frith.

Mrs. Ball watched her husband approach. She cocked an eye to the high lancet window as though challenging God over his choice of Easter weather. Her husband wandered by, kept in line by Bobby and Eddie who gently nudged the old man into a straight course. Looking on, Jones felt God's work was proceeding well. Ruth trembled a little at the back of the congregation.

The hymn ended, much to the sweating Fred's relief, and the congregation sank to their knees. Ruth found herself shaking like the church. There was something wrong. Runcorn prayed that Dr. Ball would keep his mouth shut. The old man now refused to wear clerical robes any more but wore his doctoral gown of red silk. He was now contentedly stroking the silk of the gown. Runcorn prayed fervently that the gown would distract him for the rest of the service.

Dr. Ball kept quiet most of the time. There had been two incidents this year. On Sexagesima Sunday Ball had suddenly said 'Let us pray for the departed moles of the parish.' The choirboys had stuffed their fists in their mouths. Runcorn with admirable smoothness had added 'And let us pray for all toiling men who have perished beneath the earth.' Jones had fixed the boys with a tragic desperate stare and their hands had fallen away. And on the first Sunday in Lent Ball had announced 'Blessed be the pancakes of this world.' Runcorn had rescued that, praying for the wives who cooked the meals and Lenten fare of the town.

"When the wicked man turneth away from his wickedness-" began Runcorn in his perfectly modulated voice; he was interrupted not by Dr. Ball but a woman's pitiful cry.

It was Ruth Bagley. God had smote her for her wickedness, His finger, cold and heavy was laid on her Sunday hat. The force of God's hand made her sway. He smote her a second time with a more terrible blow and she called out again and swayed on her Sunday boots that now lacked a pearl button. At the third blow from Heaven she fell to the marble floor and began to weep for forgiveness.

The kneeling congregation had begun to turn but soon forgot the cry for God's mercy from Ruth. The whole of the nave had become like a glass baroque chapel with spiral columns of crystal water pouring from the roof.

Runcorn strode down the aisle his fine leather boots already splashing in puddles, his surplice billowing like fat wings in his haste. He was followed by Jones. Ignoring the whimpering Ruth crying aloud for forgiveness, they unlocked the door to the west staircase and climbed the stairs to the church roof. When they reached the roof they stood on the cliff of the south wall in disbelief, like two agitated seabirds, the sleeves of their surplices flapping in the howling squall.

The nave roof had been totally stripped of its lead. The twelfth century oak timbers gleamed with the lashing rain, the first rain they had felt for seven hundred years. Tears and rain ran down Jones' face. Runcorn pulled his wet robes furiously around him and ran back down the steps to the uproar below.

At nine o' clock next day, Easter Monday, there was an official police meeting to review the theft. Of course Constable Hope, still wearing his choir robes, had climbed to the stripped roof and then informed Sergeant Glorey who was about to eat his Easter Sunday roast. Glorey listened to Hope with ill-concealed irritation. The thought of Hope being first on a scene of crime filled him with irrational annoyance, leading to a volcanic burst of heartburn resulting from his anger and a surfeit of roast beef fat. Glorey arranged a full investigation the next day.

On Easter Monday as requested Runcorn unlocked the door to the steps leading upwards to the roof. He kept the key because he frequently used the stairs in his enjoyment of the church. The steps were a relic of a lost kingdom. Built in the time of the Kingdom of Mercia in the eight century they had belonged to an abbey tower of some importance. The town had been on the marchlands between Mercia and Northumbria and the tower had been a watch tower as much as a decoration of a church. The tower had long vanished in the rebuilding of the church in the eleventh and twelfth century. Runcorn loved the history of the staircase but his handsome well-fed face was angry that morning, as he climbed the twisting Anglo-Saxon stairway. He wore a black cassock this morning, with a shining black belt, as he felt this was work, and work of some importance.

He was followed by Jones, similarly robed, but in a threadbare cassock. He was profoundly disturbed but for different reasons. He felt the desecration was a result of moral decay and a slipping of the world into a godless chaos.

Superintendent Lomas climbed the steps behind Jones, slowly and with care, smoking his pipe and not missing a detail, either of the stonework and its history or anything that could be relevant to the crime.

Sergeant Glorey followed still discomfited by the knowledge Hope had been first on the crime scene. Halfway up he was already physically distressed and breathless, his heart racing and his knee joints agony. A little further up the Sergeant became wedged on a sharp turn. He heaved and blustered and eventually scraped free, leaving a shading of limestone dust on the serge of his uniform.

Behind him climbed Constable Allen who was completely unshaken by the temporary blockage of the stairway by his superior. Allen thought Glorey a fool but was far more interested in his new wife and cottage and getting back to her. Glorey's antics had long ceased to bother him, and not having a great sense of humour mostly ignored Glorey and his foibles.

Constable Hope followed up the stairway which was now, as the five men were ascending, a symbolic medieval hierarchy of the climbers' places in society. Last of all camc Constable Fearne, a new recruit and was, as Allen had pointed out to his new wife, 'the biggest arsehole creeper in Derbyshire'.

By the time they were all on the roof Sergeant Glorey was totally winded. Sweat poured down his face and raced around the tracks of his chins. His breathing came in rhythmic wheezes and his giant legs trembled in his uniform. The curates tactfully averted their eyes. Jones prayed a little for God to reach the wickedness of the robbers. Runcorn fixed his eye with fury on a shattered stone cross that had topped the eastern end of the nave roof and was carved with a motif of the Blessed Virgin Mary. It had somehow survived the Reformation, but the robbers had knocked it down and it lay in pieces on a stone ledge. Runcorn fumed with rage. He had loved it up here. The church had been brutally restored by Flockton, a Sheffield architect seventy five years ago. The nave roof had been found to be almost in perfect repair and the roof and battlements were as they were in Henry III's time. The robbers had stripped away all the medieval lead which was not as secure as the early Victorian new lead on the other parts.

Looking down his nose at the perspiring Glorey leaning over the battlements, Runcorn did not deign to share this knowledge with the police. It required knowledge of the church fabric to strip the nave roof. And the medieval lead was thicker and purer. Runcorn, aloof and superior, said not a word.

Glorey leaned against the battlements and thought he would die. His heart hammered in his chest. Looking up he saw he had a jackdaw's eye view of the town and his panic-filled roving eye caught sight of Mrs. Davis in her backyard. Monday was washday and Mrs. Davis, believing she was unseen, had stripped down to her shift. She was a well-built woman and the shift clung to her curves. She was rotating the wooden handle of her dolly tub, a primitive washing machine. She had the tub full of the white washing and Mrs. Davis a powerful woman, rotated her body as she turned the handle to get her 'whites' sparkling clean. Her back was to Glorey although now and again he caught a side view. His physical malaise lifted as he concentrated on a sight that was to disturb his nights for months to come.

"When you have recovered yourself from the ascent, Sergeant, we will begin," said Lomas taking the pipe from his mouth and glaring at Glorey.

Glorey did not dare turn round to face the men. With reluctance he turned away from Mrs. Davis' gyrations and took deep breaths, but it was another minute before he had the confidence to face the others.

"Pardon me sirs," he said to the impassive curates. "I was a bit rushed. I had to attend to an irregularity in Constable Hope's uniform before I came to the church."

This was true. As usual Glorey had found fault with Hope and that morning it had been an imaginary smear on Hope's right boot.

"Then let us see what we need to do," said Lomas. Only a blink betrayed his concealed fury with his sergeant.

"It's as clear as day what's happened," said Glorey confidently. His pulse was lessening and he glowed from the pleasure of Mrs. Davis. "Clear as daylight to anyone with knowledge of local crime." He gave Hope a triumphant glare. "It'll be a gang of Sheffield cutlers that crept in on that Saturday night, under cover of that fog, you see. If not them then, some of them miners from Offerton. And likely …" He was about to say 'gypsies' but he suddenly recalled the last time he accused them, Hope had turned events to his own ends. Coal miners and cutlers loomed equally large in Glorey's mental catalogue of prejudices. He had served a year in Alfreton and the miners had scared him both physically and politically. And he had once attended a court case in Sheffield and returning to the town of Alfreton on a bicycle, he had passed a small cutlery works on the main road where the workers, resting on a bench had jeered and hooted at the sight of the plump young police officer pedalling by. The men in their brown paper caps and grimy faces and arms haunted Glorey as the epitome of lawless overpaid working men.

"Aye, us'll just have to keep us eyes open and us ears to the ground for they'll be back."

There was a silence from the men. Jones stared at the fat sergeant hoping he was wrong. Runcorn stared with scorn and did not even bother to reply. He would have a quiet word with Lomas some time about how he believed local criminals with pertinent knowledge were the culprits. Some local men knew this medieval lead was easily stripped away. The wind, warmer and sweeter this morning, tossed the jackdaws above them. They were busy with nesting and sexual quarrels in the spire above.

"Well, if that's your final word, sergeant, we will descend and keep our ears to the ground," said Superintendent Lomas lighting his pipe. Only Hope and Runcorn detected the icy fury and sarcasm in his utterance.

They descended the stairs in strict order of rank and class.

Outside in the graveyard Lomas said "One moment Constable Hope. I need a word with you."

Hope and Lomas stood together in the April morning while Glorey and Fearne descended the steps to South Church Street, Glorey lecturing all the while. "I've seen them cutlers swimming in a dam naked as the day they was born and they'll…" His voice faded and Hope only heard a blackbird from a garden and a thrush in the lime trees by North Church Street.

Lomas relit his pipe which took several minutes of packing, blowing, relighting and puffing. Hope watched the white spring clouds sail round the spire and watched a rainbow come and go. He saw that Lomas was watching Bobby Frith coming up the path to attend to some church tasks, that Herbert Jones felt would be good for his immortal soul caught in the coils of working class godlessness. As he was passing Lomas spoke loudly.

"So, as Sergeant Glorey was telling us, he says it is the work of cutlers, gypsies and coal miners." Bobby slowed down as he passed and Lomas repeated himself so the boy heard. Then he waited till he was well out of hearing.

"Right, Constable. Don't take any of that for granted. Just watch. Write down anything that strikes you as a bit out of the ordinary however small. Well, I don't need to tell you that, but I'll remind you just the same. You know just what I mean. And if you see or hear anything don't let on you've seen it. Write it down and think about it. And if you see something that is suspicious do the same. Whatever you do don't let them think you're on to something. Watch and wait and let them get in deeper and deeper and then- you've got them. Keep your views and thoughts to yourself. Not a word to me or the sergeant." He blew out several clouds of smoke and enjoyed a sprinkling of a warm April shower for a few seconds.

"Let them think we think it's someone else. Wait till you've enough to nail them. It's not as if they're murdering folks. We can wait. I can wait. Good hunting Constable. Together we'll sort it. But take your time. It would be a good Christmas present from you to the town if you can sort it. Right, back to your duties Constable."

Lomas waited for Bobby Frith to pass again. Bobby had been given sixpence by Herbert Jones to purchase some brass polish. Jones hoped polishing would brighten Bobby's tarnished view of the world.

"And keep your eyes skinned, Constable, for all those miners and cutlers that Sergeant Glorey was telling us about," Lomas called after Hope for the benefit of reinforcing Bobby's report back to the family.

He watched Hope go and then remained a little longer listening to a mistle thrush challenging the April weather on the topmost twig of a lime tree where the new leaves were as small as the flying raindrops.

After a tiring day on his beat round the town, and the Easter Monday Market where two cows had upended a cheese stall, and two drunks had knocked each other's teeth out, Hope was glad to sit down to his evening meal with Mrs. Harryson. He could see however that she was disturbed by some event in the day. She was unusually silent during the meal.

Hope ate his meal with the usual appetite. Annie Harryson had minced the remains of the corner cut of beef she had cooked for the Easter Sunday meal. She had mixed in turnip and onion, for at this time of the year there were few fresh vegetables to be bought. Then she had made the meat into a golden crusted pie and served it with a thick onion gravy with juices saved from the day before. Hope sipped at his usual pewter tankard of Mrs. Peter's ale. It seemed to taste better than ever since he had thrown out Gerald

Frith from her inn. He wondered if she had changed what she put in the jug that Mrs. Harryson collected from her back kitchen of the inn. The ale was good before but now it was excellent. He tried to make conversation when the ale had restored his spirits.

"We were up on the church roof this morning, or what is left of it. It's been stripped right down to the timbers. Somebody's going to make a mint of money selling that lot."

Annie Harryson sniffed and carried on eating her pie without much reaction. She saw that Hope had devoured half the dish of mushy peas that she prepared at this season until the fresh ones appeared. She offered him more and he piled them on his plate. Pie and peas such as Mrs. Harryson cooked was a favourite winter meal.

"Sergeant Glorey says he's sure it was cutlers from Sheffield or miners from Chesterfield or somewhere."

Annie Harryson's vitriolic annoyance took him aback.

"Well, that's really likely isn't it? The thickest fog I can ever remember and a gang of coal miners come in. Do they walk the twelve miles I ask myself? Or come by train a first class railway carriage, nine miles to Ambergate Junction and then change trains and come on the train another nine miles to here? Or did they come by cart, creeping into the town and creeping out again. That's a good idea. They would know their way in the fog and bring fifty foot ladders. Perhaps they brought the ladders on the train. What a clever man Sergeant Glorey is to think all that out. And the cutlers too. They could have used the same train. Mind you, Constable, what about the gypsies? Is he losing his touch not to think of them?"

She banged down the apple pie she had made. Hope did not reply. He hated it when she talked like this. He usually enjoyed the evenings spent with her. Three years as her lodger, he appreciated the comfort more and more. Part of him thought he ought to get out more and yet the comfort of her presence and her room and fire seemed to increase in value. He was more than happy to sit with her. He looked at her retreating back to the kitchen.

Yet despite all that, the restlessness that lurked deep within him surfaced. He envied Constable Allen with his cottage and wife and yet Mrs. Harryson's house and company suited him well. Even so, he thought, there was something not right in his life. Hope sighed and sank gratefully into the battered comfort of the deep winged chair. There was a sparkling fire and he luxuriated in it, stretching his long legs. The blue rainbow-day had given way to a cold clear night and there would be a frost later.

Mrs. Harryson appeared again with her coat on. She carried the remains of the pie under a white cloth in a basket and a jug of the steaming gravy. She was carrying a bucket of coals and sticks.

"I'm just going over the way to Maisie Frith's. God knows what's been going on there. If I was a believer I would ask God to tell me, so you could arrest those devil brothers of hers for unnatural acts."

Hope stared, shocked. He thought she was talking blasphemy and that registered more in his mind than the reference to the Friths' implied incestuous activities. He felt more ill at ease than ever.

"As I said, God alone knows what happened on that night of the fog. I know the devils spent the night drinking, because they were in every ale house in the town. You saw them in the Anchor and Gerald was sozzled when you threw him out. I think they went back to Maisie and, well, just did what they wanted with her. She's refused to go up the ladder to her bedroom. She's chopped it up for wood for the fire. The poor girl . . . as if blocking the way to her bed will stop anything . . ."

Hope, by the fire saw two things. That her eyes were filling with tears as she spoke, and he realised just how much she cared about the girl. And he thought he ought to offer comfort to her but he did not know what to do or even how to go about it. Back in Derby he had seen neither of his parents offering physical comfort to anyone in his family. Annie Harryson pulled herself together.

"Maisie's filled a sack with bracken and she's sleeping on that with a pile of old clothes in front of the fire. It's possibly an improvement on what she slept on, or was used on, upstairs. I've given her stuff for bed bugs, time and time again. And of course she says not a word, just stares at you with those big blue eyes. Not even torture would squeeze out a single word against her devil brothers and demon father. Ah well . . . Well, Constable, that's how the poor live in our fine country and Empire."

Hope was so dazed by these accusations, that he just watched her struggle with the door; then she was gone with a bang of the door.

Hope was more disturbed than ever. In all his life at the church school and in Derby he had not met or heard anyone talking like this. And a woman too, he thought, staring into the heart of the comforting fire.

After a while he calmed down. The ale, the blazing fire and the comfortable ticking of the carriage clock quieted his mind. He reached for his pencil and sharpened it to perfection, carefully directing the cedar wood shavings into the fire. He went over to his tunic and took out his notebook and wrote down what Mrs. Harryson had said.

Every Christmas Mrs. Harryson treated herself to a jigsaw and the two Christmases Hope had spent with her, had been enlivened by an expensive wooden jigsaw. Annie liked sailing ships and after the meal she had cleared the table and they had spread out the hundreds of pieces. Getting started was always a problem. Not until you were well into the puzzle did the first bits you had slotted together make sense. It was the same with Hope's notes. Not until he was well into the crime did the early notes he had made make sense. A chaotic Monday in June proved the point. The events, so meaningless in themselves, later proved vital to the case. It was to be four random notes he had made before Hope had a clear view of who had responsibility for the crime.

That Monday in June had begun innocently enough. It was Hope's turn to patrol the Bridge on that beautiful June Monday market day. Hope's turn seemed to come round every week. It was a difficult task. Herds of cattle and sheep converged on the Bridge from farms and the railway station. The traffic of horses and carts and some carriages had to be directed for there was only room for one vehicle at a time on the Bridge. Hope had made his way to the Bridge under the bluest of summer skies where the swifts circled almost unseen but clearly heard.

He found Dr. Ball likewise circling the Market Square and seeing Hope pointed excitedly to the church spire bathed in the strong gold light of June.

"Look upwards Sancho!" he had never forgotten his first name for Hope as a companion to Glorey whom he labelled Don Quixote. Hope obediently looked at the church spire where the reverend doctor directed his gaze. "Can you see Sancho? An angel, no less, sitting on top of the spire and curling her legs around my spire and all clad in green just as Dante described. Have you read Dante, Sancho?" Hope said he had not but promised he would soon and took hold firmly of Dr. Ball's arm.

"Come along sir. It's time for tea."

Hope was indebted to the generous minded Allen who had told him what to do when the Doctor escaped the feline guard of his wife.

"Tell the old bugger it's time for tea. It always works. Get hold of his arm and take him to the back door of the vicarage. The Cook is the only one in the house who can do anything with him. She'll sit him down and give him milk and biscuits. He usually gets out in the morning when old Mother Ball is getting dressed. Takes her an hour or more to get into her rigout. She uses a can opener to get into her corsets so they say."

Hope, ever grateful to Allen, had taken Ball back to the Cook and hurried to the Bridge. It seemed quiet. The swallows swooped under the arches, he could see the trout swimming around the water crowfoot that had small white globes of flowers with gold stamens gleaming at the centre. It was quiet enough to hear the cuckoo from the woods and the air was full of languid June blackbirds. Then chaos began.

He noticed Ruth Bagley, dressed in her faded Sunday best, almost cowering in one of the quoins of the Bridge built for pedestrians to step back from vehicles or animals. Following her troubled look he saw in the distance, thundering down the road from the station, a large herd of cattle. Ruth obviously had plans in that direction. He felt a tap on his shoulder. It was one of Ruth's brothers, Matthew, a quarryman.

Matt Bagley pushed a grubby brown envelope into his hand. "I'm glad I've seen ye Constable, I've been meaning to talk to ye for weeks. It's about my mam, like. You know 'oo died on that night of fog?" Hope nodded. It had taken three years to tune into the dialect of the town but he had the skill now. "Well, Constable, 'oo died happy. That Missus Harryson looked after her grand. Just afore 'oo died me mam says to me 'Tell Annie Harryson she's looked after me proud. Give her this when I've gone. It's a ring that old Lady Dalrymple gev her when she left 'er ladyship's service to marry my feyther. Will ye give it to Missus Harryson. It seems to mek it proper and lawful like if I give ye the ring to give to your missus." He nodded and was gone. Had he meant to say what he did at the end? Hope wondered.

Hope nodded and looking up saw two things. Firstly Ruth's furious stare. Her mother had been as proud as Ruth was, and had wanted to pay Annie Harryson for her care but Ruth had wanted that ring. Then Hope also saw that Sir George's Daimler, one of two cars in the town at that time, was chugging to mount the summit of the Bridge. It was closely followed by the herd of cattle.

The car shuddered and the engine died at the apex of the Bridge. The big herd of cows fragmented, snorting and bucking. One cow, udder swinging and bolder than the rest charged Hope.

The friendly Allen had advised Hope about cattle. "If a cow runs at you," he had said "whatever you do don't run away. It'll follow thee and you'll have one of its horns up your arse. Head straight for it. Run at the bugger. Wave your fists. And stand sodding still!"

The first time Hope had done that he had been terrified but it had worked and it worked now. The cow turned and dung splattered, some of it spraying the faded dress of Ruth, who screamed. The cow joined the herd that had now fragmented into three, one group racing up the Chesterfield Road, another down the road to the railway arches and another filing in the open gate to the garden of Mr. James the chemist's Georgian cottage.

Hope prioritised quickly. He and Sir George's chauffeur pushed the Daimler with all their force up over the hump of the Bridge where it free wheeled coughing and spluttering with Sir George at the wheel down towards the wider Bridge Street. A spirited cow followed with tail held high and crooked. Hope returned to the sobbing Ruth. The loss of the ring and the dung splattering had been the last straw. She wiped at the green brown smears with her best silk handkerchief.

A roar of fury clearly heard above the animal noises, made Hope look down to the meadow on the north side of the Bridge.

"Constable! Down here now if you please!" Looking he saw Hornton with the Water Bailiff standing by a small pyramid of dead trout they had found floating in the shallows.

"One moment sir," yelled Hope. "I have to escort this lady to safety."

Nothing but the word 'lady' could have mollified Ruth quicker. Hope offered her his arm and she clung to it. Despite the fact that the policeman was the 'fancy man' of that witch Annie Harryson, Ruth liked the sensation of holding on to the arm of the best looking man in the town.

"I'm going up to the Station, Constable, for the 11-23 to Millers Dale, do you think I'll make it?" Hope thought she might as it was only half past nine. “You see I’m starting my new work tomorrow. I’m to be a housekeepers assistant at the new hotel just built in Buxton. It’s called the Empire Hotel. Lady Dalrymple has stayed there to take the waters and her maid said they were looking for reliable assistants. I’ve got my own room and the wage is good. The Empire is very grand.”

Hope took her to safety and watched her to see there were no more cattle herds. He felt both distaste and dislike. The Sergeant at Derby had told him that feelings did not come into policing. “You’re there to see the law’s kept. Likes and dislikes do not enter into the law.”

Nevertheless Hope felt a distaste at this woman with her yellow skin and hard eyes and her sad faded clothes. Ruth Bagley had indeed landed herself a good job at the luxurious new Hotel, The Empire. But when the Empire fell on hard times in 1914 and Ruth returned to the town Hope was to discover why he had so disliked the woman, and even more in 1940 when she finally got her revenge on Annie over the ring.

Avoiding the splatters of dung on the Station Road that the terrified beasts had left, Hope was almost relieved to open the gate to the meadow and confront Hornton.

He walked along the field path towards a glowering Hornton, thinking how much he owed to Allen. Constable Allen, content with his wife and cottage and life felt no need to see his fellow men suffer. It had been Allen who had prevented Hope from making a fool of himself weeks after he had arrived in the town. On the beat on the road by a small wood he had heard a baby crying in distress, He had blown his whistle for Allen who was patrolling the town. Without laughter or ridicule Allen had explained it was an owl and stayed with Hope as the owl called so Hope would not make the same mistake again. Allen made no comment to Glorey. The town bred Hope never repeated the mistake. Thinking about Allen, Hope approached Hornton, and wishing that he could stop disliking people in the town such as Hornton and Miss Bagley. ‘I’ve no right to pass judgement,’ he told himself, but he could feel the irritation deep within him as he approached. Looking down to avoid Hornton's pious smug face, Hope saw his own boots and trouser bottoms were golden with buttercup pollen.

Hope noticed that Hornton had walked further up the meadow by the side of the river and had added more dead trout to the pile. Hope could see Hornton's arms folded in Old Testament judgement, awaiting his arrival. Hope also noticed Mrs. Harryson gathering waterside plants on the other side of the river and he watched her as he walked towards the impending judgements.

Annie was working in front of the garden walls guarding the Georgian terraced houses where Dr. Bagehot lived. There was an embankment here to protect he garden walls and silting produced a splendid crop of naturally irrigated flowers that grew better here than anywhere in the parish. Hope saw her busy under the last of the lilacs that frothed over the sandstone walls. He saw she was cutting the first flowers of a plant they had called 'mother-die' back in Derby. They said if you picked it your mother would die and it was deadly poison. Hope idly wondered what she needed it for. He could see her cutting water mint too. He knew what that was for - she had given him mint syrup once when he had overeaten the roast pork crackling she cooked so well. He could see red clover flower piled in her basket. She had given him a dose of those in syrup for a winter cough.

"You've taken your time Constable. I would have thought his lordship's business would have come before any other duties. If God has placed His Lordship in high estate, it is our earthly duty to follow His choice and serve his lordship as well as serve the Lord our God. And his lordship is being ill used in this Godless Babylon of a town."

"I had other duties sir, that were in line before your call," said Hope calmly. He knew this would be reported back to Glorey but he did not care. After three months he had given up trying to please the pig witted Glorey. His loyalty was to Lomas and the town. Hope knew Lomas would have helped Ruth Bagley just as he had before listening to Hornton's sermon.

The ranting sermon began.

"Look at these dead trout Constable. God's creatures put in water for the pleasure of His Chosen to live in high estate. And here they are, smote dead by the iniquity in this town. It is a great pity that his lordship's river has to flow through this vale of sin and fornication polluted and defiled by filth and wanton acts."

He paused for breath and glanced towards the distant figure of Annie Harryson amongst the flowers and then back to Constable Hope.

"It is one of the sons of Belial who have killed these fish!" roared Hornton with such a prophetical boom, that Annie, two hundred yards downstream, looked up.

"What he means," said Luke Smeaton the Water Bailiff, in the same employ to his lordship as Hornton, "is that some of the town shit has leaked out of Horace Frith's lavender yard on the other side of the river, and killed them fish."

Smeaton, as head water bailiff, was supposed to work in harmony with Hornton the head gamekeeper; but his hatred of his equal was possibly as venomous as Hope's for Glorey. The more Hornton used the language of the King James Bible, the more Smeaton employed basic, much earlier English words.

"It's not shit, Hornton. It looks more like salts of lead to me. When I worked at the Castle for the Arkwrights, there were a lead mine that flooded into the Derwent and killed the fish stone dead."

He bent down and picked up a dead trout and took out his pocket knife. The blade flashed in the sunshine as he expertly slit the trout. He held up a section of tissue from below the gill.

"See this?" he said as he waved it in Hornton's face and then under Hope's gaze. "That should be pink and it's got a purplish blue tinge. That's not shit. That's lead."

"And I tell thee these fish have been slain by the noisome waters from that spawn of Beelzebub, Horace Frith over there!" roared Hornton.

Hope knew all about Horace Frith. He collected all the contents of the town's lavatory pits in his cart, and took it to his field. The town was more euphemistic in its language than Smeaton. Horace was called the 'Lavender Man' and the field, which was on the opposite side of the river where he took the excrement, was called 'The Lavender Field'. Hope knew this, but had never been near the field where Horace apparently turned the town waste into less offensive manure that he sold at a good price to certain farmers who spread it on the land.

It was not the best way to spend a June morning but Hope could see that the only thing that would satisfy the righteous Hornton was a visit to the lavender field of Horace Frith.

"Well sir," he said to Hornton," we'd better go and see if we can see what has caused all this. So if you'd follow me sir, and you Mr. Smeaton, we'll take a look."

He made his way to a narrow iron bridge that spanned the river to a small island and then to a lane that led to the lavender field. Mrs. Harryson had told him the meadow and bridge had once been part of a small pleasure garden of the town that had long vanished, but the public path and bridge remained. Not for the first time he was grateful to Mrs. Harryson and her local knowledge. It gave him authority now to tell the two men to follow him over the bridge which he knew was a public way even if Horace put it about that it was his property.

This they did with Hornton inflated with evangelical certainty and Smeaton muttering the word 'shit' sotto voce like a spitting tomcat.

Their boots made a syncopated rattle on the Regency iron work, silver shards of June sun fell through the willows on to dark uniform and tweed suits. Below them, in the Wye, Hope noticed brown trout swimming and darting among the emerald green weed, crowfoot and glossed pebbles. It crossed his mind to suspect Hornton of bringing a basket of dead trout in order to deliver a sermon on the Sodom and Gomorrah he believed existed in the town.

Stepping off the bridge brought them into the fierce dusty white heat of the lane that led to the lavender field. It was bordered on both sides by a froth of Queen Anne's Lace. The wooden five barred gate to the field was wide open. The field was unlikely to attract crime.

It had been bought for Horace by the banker of the Frith Gang, Bert Frith, after the owner and long living lavender man, Nathaniel Matlock, had ceased his trade when he died at eighty years old. Bert had wanted to see his young brother settled. He was drifting into a life of petty crime. Bert believed in crime of a higher order.

His father, Tinker Frith, had stolen a candlestick from a lonely church in the Manifold Valley, twelve miles or more to the west, part of Tinker's western territory, where he terrorised farmers, their wives and a few young labourers. The candlestick, long thought to be brass by the Vicar and therefore not greatly missed, turned out to be thirteenth century gold. Tinker got a good price for it from his Sheffield contacts (In his turn Tinker was duped for the candlestick was later auctioned in London for ten times what he was given). Nevertheless Tinker handed most of the cash over to Bert, the only man in the world whom he was secretly scared of. Bert invested in the field for Horace.

It seemed an odd choice of a career for Horace. Perhaps Bert knew more about his brother's psyche than perhaps people guessed. At a time when Freud and the Viennese psychoanalysts were beginning to uncover the deep mysteries of the human mind, and discussing such terms as 'coprophilia', Bert had intuitively found an activity that suited Horace Frith.

Perhaps only one person in the town dimly suspected Horace's enthusiasm for his work. Dr. Bagehot, who slept badly, frequently smoked a cigar in the middle of the night, or took a brandy looking out of his bedroom windows; he watched the tawny owls in his moonlit garden from one window and from the other that looked into the street, he had seen Horace leading his midnight cartload to his field. Bagehot, well versed in German and medical writings may have pondered on Horace's unstinted conscientious collection of the town's 'lavender'.

However, all the town knew that Horace inspected the contents he collected with his lantern on full beam. The town knew that food refuse, rags or dead rats, cats or dogs would be fished out by Horace, with his pair of thick hide gloves, and placed on the doorstep of the offender. Only dung was accepted. Yet Horace knew exactly what he was doing as Hope soon was to discover.

The only sign of unpleasantness was Horace's cart by the gate that was now blue-black ebony with a coating of flies. Beyond were five acres of field with a stable of brick for the horse at the other end. Hope led the men along neat paths. One pit was open but there were no offensive odours. A sprinkling of lime, comfrey and young nettles and fresh grass cuttings that Horace sprinkled in layers on the pits ensured that. The other pits were grassed over as the worms and nature did their work. A pit that was mature and half empty, as Horace sold off the contents, gave off no odour at all and looked like a rich brown soil.

The place throbbed with bees attracted by the comfrey flowers that grew in beds alongside the nettles which also had luxuriant tassels of creamy stringy flowers. An acre of grass, growing to be mown, was full of clover and buttercups that likewise attracted bees. Later Horace would scythe and dry this for hay to add to his pits when there was no grass available in the winter months. This hay was fed to his horse. Horace's self-sufficiency would have enthralled William Cobbett.

It was not an unpleasant place. The three men said nothing but moved to the shade of a large beech tree. Horace added its autumn leaves to his pits to add extra sweetness and bulk. Hope could sense Hornton's disappointment. He had obviously expected channels of corruption snaking their way to the trout river. The pits were totally sealed. An embankment covered in nettles and comfrey kept the winter floods away.

Hornton suddenly strode towards the southern end of the bank silver and gold with buttercups and ox-eye daisies. The other men joined him, climbed the bank and trod the flowers and stared down to the river, where the trout seemed more plentiful in the shadow of the lavender field embankment, than anywhere else. Hornton fumed with righteous rage.

"Well Smeaton. Where are your salts of lead now?"

"I don't know do I?" said Smeaton then deliberately swearing to upset the gamekeeper. "Where's your leaking shit?"

Both men left Hope, arguing all the way along the lane, about the waste products of sin and salts of lead as killers of trout. Hope was left amidst the bees and flowers and the rustling beech and the whinny of the pony. Sharpening his pencil he made a note of the morning's events.

He held his breath as he passed the cart but otherwise the summer morning was as sweet here as on the bridge over the Wye.

Another incident occurred that did not make sense until weeks later.

One morning in early July, Hope was sheltering under a large hawthorn tree, on a lonely stretch of road on the limestone uplands.

It had been a beautiful start to the day, early brilliant sun blazing from a stainless blue. "Bright too early," Wallace the Ironmonger had commented to Hope at eight o' clock, as he brought the shop awning down over his window display. The pans and cheap tin ovenware in the window lost their sparkle as the shade gathered on the pavement under the awning. Hope nodded. It was a favourite weather saying in the town, protected in its bowl of hills, showers had a habit of lurking behind the uplands and then bursting into a blue sky.

Hope was on his way to record details of a chicken theft from a farm two miles to the west of the town. He would walk there and back. Glorey always found an excuse why the only bicycle of the police station was not available to Hope. In this high summer of 1904, Glorey had learned the North Western railway was improving its line between Buxton and Ashbourne and there were many gangs of navvies; they had replaced, for the summer, the gypsies and the miners and cutlers, as the source, in Glorey's simple brain, of all crime.

Hope whistled as he climbed from the valley on the lonely road to the uplands. He had been restless in the spring. Allen's domestic happiness unsettled him. He had felt depressed and shyly inadequate. The taunts of Glorey about courting and lady friends, often made daily, nagged him. As the spring tide waned so did Glorey's surge of renewed interest in sexual matters, although it was likely to rekindle at any time. And Hope was curiously content to sit by the fire with Mrs. Harryson.

The sun had burned down on his back as he walked and yet when he had reached the crest of the edgc of the high limestone plateau, he was aware of a plum and charcoal mass of cloud, furred with tarnished silver edges, that had silently boiled up from the Staffordshire moorlands. Hope cursed as heavy drops of rain began. He had not brought his cape. There was little shelter along the white road that proceeded for miles between drystone limestone walls. He managed to make it to a solitary thorn tree where an elder bush had grown with the thorn to provide some protection from the growing storm. Huddled against the trunk Hope saw another figure sheltering.

"It'll soon pass, Constable," said Jack Palfreyman. He was the road mender with responsibility for the six miles of highway between the town and Monyash. He looked at the cloud mass. "'Sink in the east it'll trouble ye least,' that's what my old dad used to say about these storms." There was a drum roll of thunder and the rain became a torrent. Hope said that he thought that was a cheerful thought.

Jack Palfreyman was a man taller even than Hope. His appearance was dominated by a massive pair of steel rimmed spectacles that supported two lenses of ten dioptres of concavity that resembled the base of pop bottles, and reduced his dark eyes to two black molluscs of wisdom. He knew, and loved, every inch of his road and the dots of his eyes now watched, with pleasure, as a milky torrent rushing down the road diverted itself into a well tended culvert, that would soak away in a spinney of blackthorn. When he was certain all was well he chatted amiably with Hope, glad of the company.

Within minutes the sun exploded from the clouds with midsummer brilliance and the uplands began to steam. Leaning on his shovel Palfreyman talked and Hope let him. He had taken Lomas' dictum to heart, that listening to talk and not commenting was the way to collect knowledge and information. The Superintendent had not wasted his time when he took Hope round all the signalmen in that winter of 1901. As they talked, a toiling figure wheeling a bicycle, was visible half a mile down the long hill. Palfreyman's lens flashed in the sparkling light.

"That's Horace Frith ye can see making heavy weather of his bike. He's taken to coming this way o' lately, since Eastertide. He works two days a week at Magpie Mine, he's the blacksmith there. Dost know Magpie Mine Constable? No, ye've no need I suppose. It's a lead mine two miles or less from where us is now. He'll turn rate when he's passed us. By gum, folk's'd think his bike were made of lead. Look at sweat. It's pouring off'n."

The road mender and Hope stared at the approach of Horace who was attracting a devilish halo of tormenting flies. His soaked clothes steamed and sweat glossed his face, which was a goblin parody of his sister Maisie's beauty.

"Seen enough Jack Palfreyman?" asked Horace, as he laboured by with malice in his voice.

"Middlin' thankye Horace," said Jack pleasantly, to neutralise the danger. Jack, like many in the town, avoided upsetting any of the Friths. Mysterious misfortunes could follow any hostility directed at the Friths. Jack cleared his throat and raised his voice so Horace could hear.

"Aye Constable. It's like I were saying. Horace works at Magpie Mine. It's easier this way on a bike than the shorter way by Sheldon. Very steep that way. Very steep." The second repetition boomed fortissimo in Jack's bass voice.

Hope felt there was something unsaid or implied but he was not quite sure what. As the last few drops of rain fell he took out his notebook. Jack watched him sharpen his pencil with interest and admiration.

Then he wrote down exactly what had happened unimportant as it seemed. After three years Hope had learned a great deal.

Drops of water fell from the tree as he wrote and tiny cream petals from the plates of elder blossom. The petals stuck to the page; it crossed Hope's mind that these single petals looked nothing like the blossom above. Things often seemed unconnected with their meaning in the world.

"Them drops are mucking up your book, Constable," said Jack admiring Hope's fast moving hand that ignored the petals and the purple blotches the indelible pencil made as it contacted the wet page.

"Not to worry Mr. Palfreyman," said Hope. "I'll be on my way now." He would go and see what Horace did at the lead mine. He had a feeling there was something he could not quite grasp and he would follow Lomas' principle of talking to people and see what happened. Glorey was always glad when Hope was away from the station tramping the lanes. Hope had all day to collect information; he would tell Glorey he had followed two navvies, who looked suspicious, and it had taken him all day and he was tired, and there had been nothing at the end of it. That would please Glorey. Hope's frustration was a major aim in Glorey's life.

Following Jack's idle chatter about Horace, Hope turned right. He had not told Jack Palfreyman where he was going. It was another of Superintendent Lomas' precepts. "Talk to people as much as you like. But never tell them what you're going to do or where you are going. You keep quiet about that."

But apart from Jack, there was nobody to tell, as Hope walked the white roads that webbed the limestone hills. Endless limestone drystone walls bordered the roads with wide grass verges now rivers of blue meadow cranesbill. Black and white cows grazed peaceably in the fields. A few fields had been mown for hay and they were lime green grass stubble under the now vivid blue midsummer sky. The lanes rose and fell on the plateau like gentle waves on the tropical sea that had once made this countryside's geology.

And Magpie Mine rose from this ocean of fields and walls and lanes like a silent sinister steam ship suddenly floating into Hope's perception. Two tall chimneys starkly watched him in silence. Even after three and a half years of tramping Derbyshire (which he was beginning to love with a passion that would never leave him) he still found certain aspects disturbing. The whistle of the wind on lonely starlit roads, the threatening hills crouching before a storm, the far off watchful chimneys of the lead mines' engine houses that seemed to be sentinels of some deeper spirit of the county. Hope felt it disturb him now as he reached the gate of the lane to the Mine.

He found the manager's office with no difficulty, knocked and walked in. The Manager, a squat toad of a man with polished oiled hair like two crow's wings, looked up in surprise. He got to his feet, his heavy silver watch chain swinging over a solid paunch. A sparkling expertly cut stone of a crystal mineral, found in the Mine, set in shining pinchbeck, dangled from his chain as bright as a diamond. Two lead miners sat on stools holding tin mugs of tea. They regarded Hope sullenly, their white faces showing no reaction.

Hope removed his helmet. His golden hair and tanned face, glowing with health from Mrs. Harryson's food, and Glorey's relentless errands that lasted for miles, made him appear, as Apollo might have shone at the gates of the Underworld.

"Just a call to see everything is alright." said Hope imitating Lomas as he introduced himself to the signal box men, and had his hand pumped by the Manager. "There's been some thefts around here, so I thought I'd see all was well." Hope chose his words carefully. Gossip in Derbyshire flourished and he knew Glorey would hear of the visit.

"Best tell Horace Frith to look out for his pigs," said one of the miners, not catching Hope's eye but staring into the corner of the room. He took a noisy slurp from his mug and belched softly, still expressionless as he studied a mouse hole.

The other miner gave a mirthless guffaw.

"Let me walk you round, Constable," said the Manager leading Hope out into the summer air much to the latter's relief. Not that he was surprised by the miners' attitude. He had discovered for himself that the gentry and the tradespeople in the town had a great respect for him, but the working men treated him with reserve and distance and even hostility as the miners had done.

"Aye," said the Manager who seemed to enjoy the chance of a fresh conversation. "Horace Frith is our blacksmith. Bit of a rum'un is our Horace, but he knows his stuff. He works here two or three days a week. The lead industry is not all it used to be Constable. Cheap ore from Spain you know. Anyhow, we keep going, we keep going. As I were saying Horace does two days or so here and he has a bit of a farm further up the road, Taddington way, a few pigs and hens and the likes. It's allus been a tradition up here that a miner keeps a few beasts on a bit o' land. And then there's Horace's work down in the town…" The Manager grinned. Nobody ever spoke without euphemisms about Horace's excremental activities. "What would we do without Horace?"

The Manager showed Hope the engine houses, the locked coal store, piles of waste and the winding gear and led him to Horace's smithy emphasising as he went, that the coal was locked up and the cash was in a safe in his house which he pointed to.

"Horace shoes the horses and now and again test-smelts any ore I'm unsure about. None of the ore is smelted here Constable. We've no furnaces for anything on a big scale. It was never the tradition for lead mines to smelt their own ore. No fuel you see on these hills. All the ore goes east to Chesterfield, Sheffield or thereabouts. Horace's crucible just does a sample if I need to test it." He pushed at the door which grated in an ill-fitting squeal as it opened.

Hope's stomach reeled at the smell of burned hoof, horse dung and Horace.

Horace ignored them both, busy with a horse's hoof. His forge glowed and Hope wondered how he worked in the heat and pungent air. A smaller forge was cold, next to the big forge. Hope could see the soot and white deposits of the lead crystals in the flu.

Hope was glad to walk down the lane in the fresh air. He did not like the place, the white faced men, the piles of mud and white spa and Horace's white dusted furnaces. It was not what he had expected. Two streets away from his boyhood home in Derby there had been a small iron foundry specialising in cast iron industrial goods. It had been one of Hope's pleasures to stand in the doorway, particularly in winter, and warm himself, while the small furnaces glowed red and white, while the workers shouted and directed flows of molten metal to moulds. Hope had admired the men and never tired of looking at the golden red scene with its friendly fumes of coke. But here all was sullen and run down, a shadow of its glory days in the Napoleonic Wars when lead was almost the price of silver, a sad ghost as white as the piles of fluorspar that were dumped all around. Even the soot on Horace's forge, thought Hope, was white and pallid. In the foundry the soot had glowed red hot and even when it was cold had a vibrant red hue.

When he was a mile away and walking down the steep hill to Ashford Hope began to whistle and wonder what Mrs. Harryson would serve for tea.

Thursday 4th of August 1904 was another entry into Hope's notebook that appeared irrelevant at the time, but yielded a vital piece of the crime when referred to in December of that year.

Although it was still early August, darkness was beginning to creep back at night. The Police Station remained open until ten o' clock, and Sergeant Glorey now began to light the gas in the blue lamp above the front entrance, that had the words POLICE inscribed on the dark glass.

The evenings were a worry to Glorey. As Sergeant he was expected to remain on duty behind his pine fortification for three evenings of the week. He always remained on duty on market day on the Monday. The rest was an anxiety to him. He had no problem leaving Constables Fearne or Allen behind his desk. But he hated to leave Hope in charge. He had to now and again for it was not fair on the other men but Glorey's nerves were taut and on edge as he ate his fried tea. Thinking of Hope sitting on his stool of power impaired his digestion of fried bread. Sunday night was a problem too, as he had to usually ask Allen or Fearne to do the duty as he was scared of the Reverend Runcorn who valued Hope in the choir at All Saints' choral evensong. It all caused an extra furrow in Glorey's florid plump face.

As for Hope it suited him to be on duty from six in the morning till six at night, walking the countryside and returning at night to Mrs. Harryson's cooking and her fireside chair. Evenings in

Glorey's downstairs kingdom left him indifferent.

On this particular Thursday Glorey could see no way out of telling Hope he was the duty officer for the evening. He left the Station at six, his appetite for his fried onions dulled by the sight of Hope behind his desk. Stepping out under the still unlit gas lamp, Glorey saw a large smudge of smoke on the land that belonged to Bow Cross Farm that looked down on the town from its high hill to the east of the town.

Had he not been such a leaden mountain of fat Glorey would have danced with joy. He saw the opportunity to send Hope to investigate what appeared to be a serious rick fire. At the same time he could put a notice on the Station door saying that all emergencies must be referred to Sergeant Glorey in his house adjoining the Police Station. It was forbidden by Superintendent Lomas to conduct duties in this way except in emergencies, but Superintendent Lomas could not criticise sending out the duty officer to investigate and Hope was out of the way. Glorey felt his appetite returning.

"Ye'll have to investigate Constable," said Glorey to Hope. Hope was sent and Glorey, his pale eyes moist with pleasure retrieved an Evans Throat Pastille tin, where he kept a supply of brass drawing pins. Wheezing slightly with satisfaction and effort Glorey wrote a card.

The duty officer Constable Hope has been called away on an investigation. All matters of importance should now be referred to Sergeant Glorey at the Station House.

"Aye," muttered Glorey as he pinned the notice to the door and locked it. His pleasure had overflowed into a vocalisation of supreme content.

"Good on ye to come up Constable," said Sam Walton the farmer. "It's either summer lightning or some tramp left his pipe in it after a sleep." Sam took him to the hilltop where the rick had been, taking a rake. They raked the still smouldering hay but found no pipe.

“Lightning maybe,” said Sam. He was unperturbed. There had been a good hay crop earlier and this was inferior surplus.

The summer of 1904 had been an indifferent one with a great deal of cloud. Today, however, was sultry and Hope had sweated as he made the half hour climb to the farm. As he climbed he had heard the rattle and grumble of thunder. Sam explained that now and again lightning could strike any metal left around the stack. “It only takes one metal peg left by the thatcher and it attracts it,” he explained.

“Come and have some tea,” invited Sam, glad of the company and a chance to talk. Hope readily agreed. Lomas encouraged talk and it was greatly preferential to sitting in Glorey’s office which reeked of Glorey’s body.

Hope enjoyed several cups of tea and slices of Connie Walton’s currant and seed cake and it was ten o’clock when he left - with nothing at that point to write in his notebook except the haystack incident.

As soon as he was out of the farmyard Hope sensed the strangeness of the evening. The perpetual twilight of the solstice weeks had ebbed away and dark night had settled. A lopsided moon, almost in its third quarter, lurched over the woods to his right of the lane and dappled the lane with faint light. A fetid hot wind blew from the east behind him and made him sweat. Sheet lightning from distant storms shivered from the western horizon.

“Ripening the corn,” Sam had explained as they had sat on the bench outside the back door of the farm drinking their tea.

The animals were as uneasy as Hope was. Sam’s two ponies in the next field were old friends of Hope’s as he passed them on his beat, or on Glorey’s pointless goose chases. He usually gave them one of his humbugs he kept in his pocket for his walks, for he had come to like the velvet feel of the horses’ lips as they took the offered sweet. Tonight they would have nothing from him. They watched him with their ears back, the whites of their eyes flashing at him. Jack and Bess the great carthorses were trotting restlessly at the other side of the field. Further down the lane Hope heard a sound that resembled thunder but was not, it was the stampeding sheep wild with something abroad in the stormy evening.

The distant hill of Fin Cop, the long whale back of Longstone Edge and the distant Stanton Moor seemed to leap at him as the lightning flickered. A cry of a rabbit caught by a weasel made Hope break out in a sweat again.

Nothing in his life had prepared him for this primeval aspect of rural Derbyshire. His school had taught him about Gentle Jesus meek and mild with an occasional reference to the works of the Devil. There was nothing in in his urban upbringing that could give Hope any reference points on this disturbed August night. He quickened his pace almost trotting down the steep lane. The alarm calls of roosting pheasants sent shivers up his now sweat wet back.

Marching down the lane Hope came to a section where a rift in the wooded valley allowed him a glimpse of the town below with its church spire and winding river. In daylight on one of Glorey's mad missions he would pause and look at the town that had so impressed his mother and was now becoming part of his life. Tonight he automatically glanced as he hurried along and was brought to an abrupt halt.

Far below in the river was a flash of condensed star and moonlight that seemed to leap from the dark river. Hope felt the sweat turn to ice down his back. The flash repeated itself. Hope was bewildered. He had noticed that there was a bright star close by the moon that slid in and out of the thundery clouds. He now had a mad idea that this star had fallen into the river far below. Tiny and black and static, the chimneys of Magpie Mine appeared in front of the shimmer of sheet lightning,

The Church school authorities had given Hope a proficiency in reading and writing and number. Rivers and seas of the World had been learned too. But the education givers had seen no reason for the urban pupils to learn the basics of astronomy. Hope had no idea that the star was the planet Jupiter, close to the Earth in the vastness of the galaxies, shining brightly in the far away stars of the constellation of Aries above an Earthly thunder cloud.

Common sense made him forget his crazy idea. However the sight had been an astonishing one and tired as he was he was determined to go and see where the star or whatever it was had fallen. He knew it was close by the Lavender Fields of Horace Frith.

Horace heard the unusually slow footsteps of Hope approaching over the iron bridge and dropped something carefully in the middle of a large patch of nettles. Then he slid behind his brick stable.

He saw Hope come and stand at his gate and survey the scene. Horace swore softly and with scatological fluency. His excremental interest permeated to all parts of his brain.

“Turd of hell from a shitty arsed swine,” growled Horace as low and venomous as a watching hyena. “Bugger off you arse faced devil . . . ” Horace swore with Rabelaisian ingenuity until he saw Hope walk away in the direction of Castle Street and the town centre.

As for Hope the apparent sight of the falling star had unnerved him. The river ran sweetly and coolly as he crossed it on the iron bridge. The moon had just climbed the willow trees on the river bank protecting Horace’s field and had flooded it with moonlight. By the river the air was cool and as usual the field emitted no odours. Hope looked at the beech tree shivering silver in the east wind and decided to go home to Mrs. Harryson. Glorey would neither expect or want to see him.

Dr. Bagehot heard Hope’s flagging footsteps that sounded unusually tired. Bagehot had been sitting on his small garden terrace with a jug of cold lemon and barley water made by his housekeeper and cold from the marble slab in the cellar. Bagehot also had a decanter of whisky and a jug of cold water. He had opened his garden door to the riverside path and the opposite one that led into Castle Street. The east wind blew over the river and cooled as it blew through Bagehot's garden. He had the freshest air in the town that evening. Bagehot made his way to the street door and watched Hope approach with weary steps.

"Good evening to you Constable. You're tired in this thundery weather. Step into the garden, man, have a glass of lemon and barley water."

Hope did as he was bid and with his back to the street gratefully drank three glasses of the lemon drink.

"Good for the kidneys," said the Doctor pouring himself another glass. Outside in the street Horace passed silent as the moving moon shadows from Bagehot's horse chestnut tree at the end of his garden.

Horace had followed Hope, in and out of moonlight and shadow and wavering light of the two street gas lamps. Now, with a footfall as light as a young rat, he made his way to the Queens Arms which he knew Hope would pass on his way to Witch Harryson's.

Horace ordered a brandy, still thinking of the "Witch" as many men in the town did, swilled it round his mouth, and moistened his lips and the stubble on his chin with the spirit. Then he took a pint of ale and stood in the doorway.

When he saw Hope approaching up Bridge Street in the wild light of the moon, gas and lightning, Horace began to sway. He lurched in front of Hope getting close to him so Hope would smell the drink on him.

"It's a stormy neet for thee Constable," he drawled, deliberately slurring his words. "And it's a grand night for witches." Horace laughed a mad laugh and what he hoped was a drunken one, and this laugh followed Hope until he turned down Water Lane to Mrs. Harryson's.

Hope ignored him but noted that Horace Frith was drunk after apparently spending the whole night in the Queens.

Horace finished his beer and returning to the Lavender Field over the iron bridge so that nosey old arse'ole Bagehot wouldn't spot him, returned to the nettle bed and his tasks.

Mrs. Harryson had the door wide open and the fire low. Hope walked in and shuffled his feet to announce his arrival. She was writing at her desk, and as usual, put everything away when he entered the room. Hope watched her, breathing deeply to counter his exhaustion. She always did this, concealing her writing. Not in haste, but with swift movements that clearly told Hope the writing was none of his concern. She closed the lid of the desk, which had a split in its eighteenth century oak. She had to lean against it to align the lock with its teeth. She turned the key.

"My word Mr. Hope. You look all in. There's water and towels in the bath house then sit yourself down. You'll be ready for some of Mrs. Peter's finest."

Sitting down a minute later Hope drained his tankard and Mrs. Harryson filled it again. His appetite returned when Mrs. Harryson put in front of a slice of cold rabbit pie and some fresh blackberries and whipped cream. Hope's fatigue and disquiet faded away.

When she could see him restored and had eaten herself Mrs. Harryson said "You looked flustered when you came in."

Stretching his arms and yawning with what was now a relaxed natural tiredness, Hope described his evening's activities, including the strangeness of the falling light and restless animals on the farm.

Annie Harryson gave one of her secretive smiles that intrigued Hope.

"It's a strange spot up on those hills," said she. "The old folk in the town are full of tales about it. It used to be the main coach road out of the town in the old days, and a new road was built soon after a coach crashed, after the coachman said he had seen the Devil."

And once more she gave her knowing almost superior smile.

"And have you seen that carved Stone in the churchyard with its iron railings?" Hope nodded. "Well, that used to stand on the crest of the hill above Sam Walton's farm. His Grandmother said she had seen the Devil by it and got Sam to help her dig it up and take it to the churchyard. They wheeled it through the town in a wheelbarrow. Folk talked of it for years."

Hope watched her intently, her face and half smiling full lips. This woman bewildered him. She had been visibly annoyed when Maisie Frith had spoken of seeing The Old Woman, who presaged a death if you caught sight of her face. And yet here she was talking of the Devil . . . And Hope's understanding of the Devil was limited to Satan tempting Christ, a story that he had never fully attended to in Sunday School class or church.

"My friend, Professor Stockwell, says that the Stone was an Anglo Saxon preaching cross, put up to scare away local gods or deities, when the missionaries came from Rome to convert us to Christianity." The half hidden smile again.

Hope was now thoroughly baffled. And who was this friend of hers, Professor Stockwell. An irritated scowl of jealousy shadowed his face for a second or two,

The carriage clock announced the half hour after eleven with its silvery bell.

"I'll write up my notes and then get to bed," said Hope a little abruptly. He was not sure what he would write yet but what he did write was of vital importance later in 1904.

Writing up his notes was a new strategy in Hope's guerilla war with Glorey. Glorey had boiled with jealousy when Hope had been congratulated over his notebook at the Derby Assizes at the Fox Murder Trial. Glorey planned revenge.

In January 1903 Hope had noted an empty brandy bottle by the second milestone out of the town on the Derby road. The bottle was freshly opened with the smell of the spirit still strong. Hope noted the same thing three times in February and March. A week after the third note he had written about the bottles, he overheard Mrs. Gill, the owner of a wine and spirit shop, complaining to Glorey that a bottle of brandy was stolen nearly every market day from her shop despite every vigilance and a locked cupboard. The following Monday Hope lay in wait behind the wall and saw Billy Jackson take out a bottle of brandy from a sack he was carrying and Hope watched him down the contents, as Billy, a farm labourer, rested against the milestone. Hope arrested Billy who appeared in the Police Court a week later.

Hope had made the notes right at the end of a notebook and the finished notebook had been locked in a cupboard in the cellar of the Police Station and Hope issued with a new book by Glorey with a sly smile. On the morning of the court appearance of Billy, Hope asked Glorey for the old notebook. Glorey said he had mislaid the key.

Hope and Glorey appeared in Court without the notes.

Major Bunyan J.P. who was presiding, was scathing. He poured scalding abuse on Hope for not being able to produce the original notes. Hope was red with shame.

"And you Sergeant Glorey," the Major had roared, "as senior officer, how the hell can you lose a key of such vital importance? Answer me man!"

Glorey kept his equilibrium. It was worth it to be castigated if Hope was tongue lashed like this in a public court.

"I'm sorry your honour," said Glorey passively. "Us'll have to be more careful like. But wi' Constable 'ope everything's at the last minute, allus rushing about the place. Ye'll have seen him no doubt dashing about the place. Everything at the last minute so I had no time to search for the key."

Bunyan brought down his fist with a 'Pah!' of exasperation and the hapless Billy received a sentence twice as severe as it should have been. It was several years before the ultra-military Bunyan acknowledged Hope when he met him.

Glorey was content, and simply burned the letter of anger, from the Chief Constable, in the Tortoise Stove. Hope had been chewed up and spat out by the major. The plan had worked well.

Hope had rarely felt so angry in his life and cheated. He took instant action. He knew from experience with teachers and superiors at Derby that superiors could never be challenged. That was the way of the World as Hope knew it.

On his next afternoon off he made his way up North Church Street to Frost the Stationer and Gift Shop. He asked to see what notebooks were in stock.

Mr. Frost took out his threepenny ones backed in thick card. He felt Hope wanted something better than the penny ones with coloured paper covers. Frost also showed Hope the sixpenny ones with thick board covers, tastefully covered with marbled paper and bound with blue on the spine. Ideal for the Constable, thought Mr. Frost, if he wanted something better.

Hope frowned. He was still sore from the Court appearance. He pointed to a row of black notebooks backed with a waterproof cover with swirling gold letters THE ALLWEATHER NOTEBOOK.

Frost did not want Hope to have one of these. They were half a crown each and he sold them to the master tradesmen, architect, plumber, builder and even to some local clergy to record botanical or geological interests. Mr. Taylor the lawyer kept one for taking notes on train journeys. Frost felt they were not suitable for a mere policeman. He covered the notebook Hope had asked to see with the sixpenny ones as he laid them out on the glass topped counter.

Hope would not be intimidated and bought two of the handsome notebooks. Mr. Frost wrapped them up with a face that looked as if he had eaten a stick of raw rhubarb. Frost wondered what the world was coming to with working men imitating their superiors. The next thing the constable would want would be the Moroccan leather bound notebooks, with gold edging for half a sovereign, that the Reverend Runcorn bought and Dr. Bagehot and Sir George. Or even a fountain pen, thought Frost gloomily.

"Good day to you Constable," he had said, his mouth tight with disapproval.

From that day on Hope wrote his own notes in the handsome All Weather books, as well as the official police notebook that was issued to him. He wrote his own notes sitting at Mrs. Harryson's table. He was fortunate that he was lodging with a woman who possessed a pen and ink, blotting paper and spare nibs, that she was more than willing to share with him. She emptied a drawer in the old desk, and gave him a key to lock the books away. The drawer was cracked but safe.

Three months later when Glorey attempted the same tactic Hope simply collected his own notebook from the drawer on his way to Court.

Glorey was still plotting his next move two years later, and could not think of a way, as Hope sat down to write down the strange events of that August night.

It was not easy. Hope had been taught to write and spell with great efficiency but not to express himself. Yet his notes turned out to be perfectly adequate when used in Court the following year.

Thursday August 4th 1904. Attended rick fire at Bow Cross Farm. Farmer Sam Walton suggested lightning as cause. Stormy evening, animals restless. Saw pools of flashing light in vicinity of Horace Frith's field. No apparent cause for this. Frith apparently drunk outside the Queens Arms after a heavy night of drinking.

The carriage clock sounded the midnight bells followed by the church clock and a closer growl of thunder. Hope locked the door, turned down the table lamp to extinguish the flame, lit his candle at the embers of the fire and contentedly climbed the stairs to his room.

The following morning, his boots shining with the thunder rain that still drenched the meadows, Smeaton the Water Bailiff walking by the Bridge discovered six dead trout, belly up in a quiet pool of the river. Swearing, but not as imaginatively as Horace, he took out his knife and examined the fish. This time there was no sign of lead ingestion. He decided not to report this to the Head Gamekeeper. Smeaton was not in the mood for a sermon linking fish deaths to the sins of Babylon.

The uncertain summer of 1904 came to a cool and cloudy coda in September. Thursday the 22nd of September however was an unsurpassable September day. The sluggish sun flooded the Market Square with light at nine and would set at six in a furnace of gold. Wallace the Ironmonger had filled his window with tin candlesticks. The townsfolk always bought new candlesticks for the winter on St. Matthew's day; some old Roman Catholic or pagan tradition was still stirring their minds at this time of year. Glorey was not impressed by the beauty of the day or the need to prepare for the coming of the dark.

He had had a 'bad night' tormented by unfulfilled longings and heartburn. He regarded Hope through puffy slits revealing pale eyeballs of malevolence.

"Stay here Constable. I need thee."

He chewed with distaste one of James the Chemist's magnesia lozenges and scowled at the healthy young man in front of the barricade of his desk.

"I've a job for thee. Aye, I have."

Glorey scratched his backside hoping that the pine fortification would hide this personal grooming from his most hated constable. Piles tormented Glorey at both equinoxes. His father had said the blood changed at these seasons, thickening for the winter, thinning for the summer; piles, he believed, were a symptom of this mysterious bodily change. Glorey's scowl deepened.

"I need thee to go along to the Waterloo." he regarded Hope with sour intensity. "Aye. There's a broken stable window there. Navvies very likely. By rights it's a job for Buxton but it's Mrs. Glorey's cousin who is the landlord and Superintendent Lomas says I can keep it in the family like. The only problem is, Constable, that it's a seven mile walk along the main road. Aye. Fourteen weary miles."

He studied Hope. Hope let his mouth droop. Three years of Glorey had made Hope a master of manipulation. There was nothing Hope wanted more than to walk the Derbyshire countryside this sparkling morning. There were people to talk to and things to see. But he must not show Glorey that the walk would give him great pleasure.

Glorey noted the sag in the young constable's mouth and warmed to his attack. "There's no bike either. Constable Allen needs that for a trip to Stanton."

Hope sighed and let his shoulders slump. He was always happier walking.

"Aye. Sorry about that but there it is." Both the entrance and the exit to Glorey's digestive apparatus felt better already, now he had wiped the morning smile off Hope's face. It never occurred to him that Hope was building up an impressive knowledge of the area in these endless walks, talking to all manner of people and accumulating a physical stamina that would serve him well.

"Aye, well. Bugger off, then."

Hope went out with dragging footsteps desperately trying to disguise the spring in his step. He knew Glorey would not care if he were out all day on the hills. Once on the main road he allowed himself to take deep breaths of the pure air, cold and clean as spring water.

Glorey had deliberately given him no directions or details but

Hope cared little for that. He assumed the Waterloo Inn was on the Buxton Road as Glorey had mentioned the Buxton Force. When he was safely round the big bend in the road, after the first milestone and out of sight of any of Glorey's cronies, (Glorey had many admirers in the town) Hope pulled out a map from his inside pocket.

This Bartholomew's Map of Derbyshire, scale one inch to the mile, printed on canvas in full colour was one of Hope's prized possessions. Seven shillings and sixpence from the railway Station bookstall at Derby, bought after a court case, Hope never tired of looking at it.

He had stretched in front of Mrs. Harryson's fire and followed the bright blue threads of rivers, black snakes of the railways and the shaded brown contours of the hills. Soon every place name of his area would be indelibly learned for the rest of his life. He soon found the Waterloo Inn a mile west of Taddington. He put the map away and whistled as he walked. It was a morning for exploring and discovery.

He had the road to himself. The railway took all the traffic and the cars had not yet made any significant appearance on any Derbyshire road. The blue of the sky deepened and the swallows were lined up on the single telephone wire to Ashford.

By the third milestone from the town, and a mile out of Ashford, Hope slowed down. The road took a sharp bend, here by Black Rock Corner, and Hope was happy to pause for a breather. As always, walking stimulated both mind and body, and as he paused, leaning against the wall, the thoughts still marched on. The usual ones. His eye rested on a stone archway on the opposite bank of the river. Smeaton had told him, when he met him here one day checking the Fish Ponds of his Lordship, that this was a sough that emptied the water from Magpie Mine, far away on the hill to the south west. Hope pondered a moment at the power of the subterranean waters, for he could hear the pounding discharge three hundred yards from where he was standing. The flash of a kingfisher, blue as a fragment of that morning sky, brought his thoughts back to Mrs. Harryson, as things so often did. That blue was like the silk bodice she wore for Sundays. The woman fascinated him totally; her secret smile, her great and polite reserve. Her endless supply of money - the rent from Hope was ridiculously low. That meant Hope had money for expensive maps. And then there were her sudden and always unexplained absences, sometimes for a week or more. When this happened a silent army of other women appeared and cooked his meals and ironed his uniform shirts. Annie Harryson seemed to command a silent regiment of women within the town.

He did not want to move from her comfortable house. Yet he felt he ought to, make some sort of move to lead a life like Constable Allen. And yet . . . it was as though the woman had some sort of hold over him. He looked away from the gush of the water from the deep, and began to walk again. The endless upsurge of water disquieted him.

Then there were the troubling and embarrassing dreams he had begun to have. Hope truly believed they were sent by the Devil and tried to banish them as he strode by Black Rock Corner. The Rock was the basalt, remnants of a volcano that had spouted lava in a tropical sea in the unimaginable past. Hope would one day learn that this geological outcrop had finally destroyed Annie Harryson's faith in God. She could not comprehend the great age of the earth and rocks with the Christian faith.

Lost in his guilt from images that bubbled up from his dream world and fascination with Annie Harryson, the sudden darkness took Hope by surprise after the white glare of the sunlit road. The massive Great Shacklow Wood spread its lengthening shadow far on to the road in September. Hope let his eyes adjust to the sudden shadow and watched a tiny bird in the river over the wall. As well as the map, he carried a slim pocket book of British Birds with black and white and coloured plates. The book had cost half a sovereign and was another indication of his low living costs with Mrs. Harryson. The wayside flowers did not interest him but the birds gave him great pleasure. He stayed watching the dipper for some time and enjoying the cold shade. He did not resume his walk until he heard the sound of an approaching cart. He walked on briskly. He never knew who might report back to Glorey.

"I can give thee a lift for a mile Constable," said the carter who was carting a load of straw. Hope climbed up, grateful for a rest and a talk. Lomas had trained him well. 'Just talk and then listen.'

"You'm new round here," said the carter. Hope explained he had been in the district for three years but he realised that to the carter that meant new.

With the arrival of the carter the world seemed to wake up. The woods in Taddington Dale were alive with the voices of women.

"We start nutting today," said the carter. "Allus on this day every year."

A whistle sounded faintly from the Monsal Dale viaduct round a bend in the river. Hope knew all about that from the Fox Murder trial and he knew it was a local beauty spot. Hope could see the piles of bottles and paper bags left by the trippers from Stockport and Manchester, who came every weekend on horse drawn conveyances or alighted from the Monsal Dale station.

"I've been to Blackpool on train," said the carter. Hope encouraged the subject of trains and journeys for several minutes. The carter, enjoying the company suddenly said "Dost know a bloke called 'orace Frith?"

"I've heard of him," said Hope feigning indifference. "Do those hazel nuts keep all winter those women are collecting?"

The carter ignored this. The fact the police officer did not seem interested in Horace Frith encouraged the topic as Hope knew it would.

"Horace Frith keeps his pigs yonder," said the carter jerking his head over his left shoulder. He said no more till he turned off the road up a farm track and Hope got off.

"We mun see thee again round here Constable," he said with a knowing grin and he jerked his head in the same direction of Horace's pig husbandry, as he had shrugged his shoulder.

Hope thanked him saying nothing but later he would write this in his own notebook, despite its apparent unimportance. As Lomas said, 'Folk let all manner of stuff slip out.'

Hope arrived at the Waterloo Inn soon after ten o' clock, and found Mrs. Glorey's cousin, the landlord, a quiet and efficient man, with none of the vinegar personality that Mrs. Glorey exhibited. He thanked Hope politely for coming and asked him to convey his thanks to Sergeant Glorey. He showed Hope the broken window, and said it was probably a tramp. "We get a lot of them," he explained. "Some of 'em have had enough when they've reached here. It's a long way to Chapel workhouse where they can get a bed for the night. Maybe one of 'em smashed this window desperate for a warm bed in the hay." This was a humane understanding compared to Glorey's thoughtless prejudices. Hope dutifully wrote this down. The whole episode had been a waste of police time by Glorey. But Hope was enjoying the day and there was more interest to come.

"I'll get a bite to eat for you Constable and a drink. Nothing strong as you're on duty. Make yourself comfortable on the bench outside. You'll find Old Feyther Mycock and Gaffer Thorpe out there already. They're two of my oldest customers. Old farmers. Old as the hills . . . Old Mycock can remember this coaching road being built and this inn . . . it's named after the Battle of Waterloo in 1815 . . . Old Mycock must be ninety or more . . . Well, I'll bring you some grub."

Hope joined the two old men on a bench pushed up to the whitewashed inn wall by the road side. The two old men blinked in the warm sun like two old dozing cats.

Hope introduced himself. The two old men stared at him, mouths wide open, toothless except for a single yellow tooth in the centre of Mycock's mouth.

Both old men were immaculate in snow white smocks gathered

and crimped and stitched with the local pattern of Chelmorton. Both wore brown broadcloth trousers tucked into gleaming tan leather leggings fastened round their calves with buckled straps above their boots. Both held on to shepherds crooks, while the other hand guarded a white pot mug of ale on the bench. Both men revealed a confidence based on prosperity. The expanding spa town of nearby Buxton had provided a good market for their milk, eggs, butter, local white Stilton-type cheese and bacon. The two old men were well content in a time of agricultural depression.

"Grand day," said Hope settling back in the golden warmth. Shadows of a wayside sycamore printed ink black dancing shadows on the white wall, a moving pattern, although Hope detected no wind on this perfect day.

The landlord appeared with a tray and a white cloth on it, relic of former coaching days. There was a blue rimmed plate with a generous wedge of pork pie with golden crust and gleaming jelly. A pot mug held cold frothing ginger beer.

The two old men watched Hope enjoy this food regarding him as if he were a rare species of migrant wildlife.

"You'm not from our parts." said Old Mycock in an accusatory tone. Hope explained he was from Derby, and the two mouths regarded him with open wonder. The mouths opened wider, as Sir George's Bentley appeared at the crest of the hill with a paroxysm of belches and coughs and snorts. It gathered speed down the hill, and passed them with a roar, Lady Dalrymple's veils streaming out like the tail of a passing comet, and Sir George saluting them through the white cloud of dust. They could leave their house soon after breakfast, and be at the Empire Hotel for coffee, providing there were no breakdowns. Twelve miles in one hour; no wonder Lady Dalrymple looked supremely content, if a little dusty. The new car was so superior to the fatigue of going for a train or the carriage . . .

The Bentley sped down the hill more with the pull of gravity than the thrust of gasoline. Hope watched the dust settle, heard the noise dwindle, saw the amethyst whale back of far off Kinder Scout loom out of the distant misted hills, heard the robins singing and thought he had never seen such a fair morning. The Bentley sounded its horn a mile away before plunging down the terrifying gradient of Topley Pike.

"Well. Salt my taters," said Old Mycock. And then-

"I bet yo' knows Horace Frith."

Hope dusted the bottom of his trousers pretending not to be interested. Mycock was nettled a little by the policeman's indifference and volunteered more. "Well, he keeps pigs round here."

This seemed to afford the old men a deal of amusement and two open mouths cackled and the yellow tooth did a sober vertical jig of glee. Hope carried on dusting.

By this time in 1904, Hope was beginning to learn an important fact. If a crime had been committed, men like Sir George or the Reverend Runcorn or Dr. Bagehot would tell you straight their suspicions, or describe a criminal to the last detail, or even their suspicions or prejudices, This openness applied to the tradesmen and the richer farmers.

It did not apply to the labourers or working men or even the older men like the two on the bench. If they suspected a crime then they dropped obtuse hints to the police, made sly comments or jokes. They were unwilling to help the police all they could. The police, they thought, ought to work as hard as they did for a living. And if a fellow workman was cheating the police and the police were too stupid to see it, then so be it. But they were willing to provide hints and subtle directions about a criminal. If the crime should go undetected a great deal would be said loudly in ale houses and inns and out on the field and inside the mines and quarries.

"Where does he keep pigs?" enquired Hope pretending to adjust a bootlace.

"Up on Jennet," said Gaffer Thorpe and they looked at Hope and laughed again and the tooth wagged its contempt.

"Right," said Hope. He recalled the engraved black letters on his prized map. "That's on the way to Magpie Mine. A bit windy for pigs up there?"

Hope could not have said anything better to gain respect. The local knowledge impressed them and the conversation sobered and the tooth retreated into respectful hiding.

The rest of the time was spent in the old men trying to impress Hope with their memories. Hope only half listened as they told him of the pack horses carrying lead ore down these local lanes, the coach of the Duke that used to stop here for a horse change as the Duke went to Buxton . . . Hope would find the exact spot on his map when he left the old men and look at Horace's pigs. He was now fully aware there was a rumour about Horace and he was being offered it as a puzzle to test police intelligence.

He said his farewells to the old men and they raised their hands. Hope was reminded of two bishops giving a blessing as they sat with their shepherds' crook.

Hope found where Horace Frith kept pigs. The long lanes were dotted with small buildings used by the lead miners as farm buildings as they supplemented their incomes from mining. But there was only one of these holdings that 'kept pigs'. Hope had been given a riddle and he was determined to solve it.

He had no doubt this croft was Horace Frith's. Hope stared at it looking for clues to the riddle of the morning. He counted seven scrawny pigs rooting in a field of about two acres. They had turned over all the grass and Hope suspected that when the winter rains came this would be a sea of mud. The door to the building was secured by one of the biggest padlocks Hope had seen. It was new. The little farm building was in excellent repair. There was a small chimney for the copper, which was common at that time, to boil up the mash for pigs and hens. There were three hens perched on the limestone wall which Hope supposed were Horace's. Yet there was nothing else to give him a clue. Nevertheless Hope stored it in his mind to write up later at Mrs. Harryson's table.

It was late afternoon when he returned to the Police Station. He had taken a long detour to avoid Magpie Mine. He did not want Horace to know he had been looking at his croft. Once more Hope thought what a perfect day it was, the gentle warmth of the sun, the air clear as wine, the hills misted with every shade of blue. When he approached the town he almost broke into a run and allowed the dust of the road to whiten his uniform. He arrived in Glorey's reception zone deliberately dusty and breathless.

Glorey was puffed up with importance as he watched Superintendent Lomas countersigning a document. It had been a good day. His digestive maladies had faded. At dinnertime Sally Winstanley, a domestic servant, had a picnic with a friend by the river; the friend had brought ale and Sally became 'merry' and had decided to paddle. She had fallen in a deep pool up to her waist and had become hysterical and had to be pulled out by Smeaton, who fortunately was in his waders further up river. She had been unable to stop screaming and had been bound over to the Police Station. Glorey had written down details as Sally stood before him, her wet skirts clinging to her legs. It had taken a long time for Glorey to process the details.

"Th'art back,"said Sergeant Glorey stating the obvious.

"I'm jiggered Sergeant. I've been round those lanes watching a band of navvies up to no good."

Lomas looked at Hope over his gold reading glasses and looked a long time but said nothing.

"Aye, well, ye've had a long day Constable. It's nearly five. Ye can bugger off home to thy landlady. Ye've had a long hard day."

Glorey swelled as he contemplated his own magnanimity. This show of humanity was purely for the benefit of Lomas who was not fooled for one second that Hope was being given an hour off duty. The only person who was fooled was Glorey. Even so, Hope was very happy to go.

"You're home early Mr. Hope," said Mrs. Harryson who had been reading in the last rays of the sun in a chair she had brought to her front door. "You'll have your bath before your tea."

Hope nodded. He wanted to sit in his bath and think things out.

Mrs. Harryson dragged out the tin bath, and filled it from the wash house copper. She threw in some herbs, putting out a clean towel to warm on the copper top, and checked the shelf to see if Mr. Hope had his clean under drawers ready. As she closed the door behind her she told Hope his meal would be ready when he was; she told him to take his time, as if she had a premonition that as he soaked in the warm water, he would solve the first part of the riddle about Horace.

He took off his uniform and hung it up on a nail. Then he put his under drawers and shirt in a basket for dirty laundry. He gave an involuntary sigh of pleasure as the warm water blessed his tired legs and feet.

He still wondered how he had been manipulated into these daily baths.

It had started within weeks of his arrival in 1901. There had been some heavy February rainstorms and Hope had received a soaking right through to his under garments. He had arrived for his evening meal and had stood before the blaze of the fire and steamed.

He had not seen the wrinkle of distaste on Annie Harryson's nose as the room filled with the pungent aroma of steaming wool cloth and other distasteful more personal smells from her new lodger. The last thing Mrs. Harryson wanted in her comfortable room were the emanations from an unwashed young man. Hope had sneezed.

"I'll get you a hot mustard bath now Mr. Hope. And get those clothes off. I don't want you with a bad chest. There's a lot about in this town with it being by the river." Hope had meekly obeyed. In Derby baths were a weekly event, usually on a Friday in front of the kitchen range. His mother would use the water in the bath, then his sisters and finally Hope got in with a top-up of hot water from the boiler. He could not recall his father having a bath. The bath was followed by a clean pair of under drawers. In winter the baths were suspended as Hope's mother liked him to keep his vest on all through the cold weather. Like many others she believed removing clothes in cold weather was 'asking for trouble'.

When Hope had had his mustard bath and changed into an old pair of trousers Mrs. Harryson continued her attack on the new Constable's personal habits and hygiene.

"Washing your under garments is going to be a problem Mr. Hope. There are days, sometimes a week, when I cannot wash them. I am often called away to help with births and deaths and nursing and you never know when that will be, and sometimes I have affairs and business in far away places. So the best thing is to change your undergarments every day. If you go to Mr. Clarke's, on Matlock Street, on your day off and get five new pairs and vests, that should see it alright. And there's always hot water so you can have a bath every day and a change. Then it won't matter how hot and sweaty or cold and wet you are. It's best for you. And me."

Hope was too astonished to protest. Only rich people had a bath every day. Nevertheless, he could not, and dared not argue. He wanted to say men did not do that sort of thing, but somehow the words dried in his throat. He went to Mr. Clarke who spread out the drawers on the counter for Hope's inspection. Mr. Clarke laid out the fine wool drawers with bone buttons on the fly. He did not show Hope the wool and silk mix or the Egyptian cotton ones the gentry wore. He did however suggest Hope should purchase a set of light linen or cheap American cotton for the summer and Hope did.

Hope was always puzzled by the fact there were always four clean pairs of drawers on the shelf, airing above the copper. Even if Mrs.

Harryson had been away for a week and someone else was washing and cooking for him, there were always plenty of under garments.

Ruth Bagley and Betty knew the reason. After an afternoon of gossip they always returned to Annie Harryson. "and you know Betty, she went to Clarke's and bought six, six, Betty, SIX pairs of gentlemen's . . . well, you know . . . Shameless she is Betty. Shameless." And mouths became tightly pursed and heads were shaken and eyes downcast before such gross immorality of a woman touching such things. "But Ruth, she went back a few weeks later for another SEVEN!" And their mouths became little cats' bottoms of tight prudery and delight in Annie's transgressions. It was 1914 before the town forgot Annie Harryson's visits to Mr. Clarke and what she brought out in a plain brown paper bag.

Yet Hope had come to luxuriate in the baths. He looked forward to them but was careful not to mention to any of the other men what he did every evening. He lay back now and watched the last of the sunlight on the whitewashed wall. Soon it would vanish and there would be no light from the little window until March as the sun crept out from behind the church spire on his way to midsummer pathways across the sky. Hope stared at the gold.

He thought of Miss Mountain the teacher who took the top standard class of his elementary school before he left at fourteen. He could see her now writing on the blackboard with a sharpened stick of chalk to accentuate the perfect copperplate writing she wrote on the board. "Thin strokes UP and press on DOWN John Hope." They had to write and copy in their books. The top standard was allowed paper instead of slates. Hope had kept the exercise book somewhere. He could remember every word of that lesson written on the board.

The Romans exported many metals from Britain. Bars of gold from Wales, Ingots of tin and silver from Cornwall and pigs of Lead from Derbyshire and -

Hope lurched violently in the bath and sloshed water over the rim. Pigs of Lead! Of course. Horace and possibly the Friths were involved in the theft of lead. He stared hard at the bar of gold on the whitewash and his mind began to race with possibilities as he relaxed again in the warm water.

As if on cue with his thoughts about the Friths he heard Mrs. Harryson's voice talking to another woman in her main room. Hope brought his train of thought to a halt. This was unusual. Mrs. Harryson saw a great many women of the town during each week. Many came seeking advice and simple medicines and nursing techniques. She usually took them into a room at the back of the house with a large cupboard and an oak table and chairs that all looked as if they had been in an explosion, so battered were they. Hope half listened to the conversation which Mrs. Harryson must know he would overhear.

"Try this ointment Lizzie. It's got celandine in it which should help your problem. Celandine is still called Pilewort in some places."

He heard Mrs. Clark whisper something like wind in old grass.

"Well Lizzie," said Annie Harryson, "you shouldn't let him. Never mind what he says."

More whispers rustled the air.

"Well, Lizzie I would not put up with that. It is not your duty to satisfy everything he wants you to do. I'll get you a mouthwash, with tincture of thyme in it, and it'll take the taste away. But it's not nice for you Lizzie. You should tell him."

More whispers and quieter than before. Suddenly the woman's voice turned up the volume.

"Clark's a good man Mrs. Harryson. He works all day, from six in a morning till six at night, in that quarry you know, and hands over all his money to me. I give him a bit for his Saturday drink at The Anchor and then . . ." The words became a whisper.

“That does not give him the right to do that,” said Annie. Then Hope heard Mrs. Clark raise her voice again.

“Well, he’s better than some in this town. Do you know, Annie, Mrs. Gill was telling me, them Friths go out on a booze-up every Sunday, Annie. God’s holy day, Annie. She says Gerald and Horace come round to her shop on a Saturday night, Annie, and spend a couple of sovereigns on booze and spirits. Six bottles of whisky sometimes. Between, let’s see, Horace, Bert, Gerald and that wicked old demon their father Tinker Roland. I’ve never heard the like. Never heard the like.”

“It still does not give Clark the right to do what he wants with you Lizzie. Anyway, where do they have this booze-up?”

“Well, that’s what’s foxing Ma Gill. She says they set off with all this booze on Gerald’s wagon on a Sunday morning about ten. If the weather’s alright. They don’t go if it rains. And all of them go. Tinker, Bert . . . the whole gang of them. Clark was talking to a bloke in The Anchor who knows a bloke in Baslow who knows a farmer at Curbar and they say them Friths make for The Peacock Inn at Owler Bar. That’s atop of a hill afore you go down into Sheffield. Every time. Clark says they’re as pissed as newts, if you’ll excuse his language Annie. You can hear ’em singing and ’ollering for miles around. Now what business have they there Annie? It’s seven miles away if it’s a foot. They’re up to no good Annie. How you can say my Clark’s a bad man after that I don’t know Annie. They drink more on a Sabbath Day than my poor Clark earns in a month.” Mrs. Clark paused for intake of air.

Hope, on full alert was sitting up in his tin bath.

“They’re up to no good Annie. My, but they’re a disgrace to this town. They want smoking out like the vermin they are.”

“I’m doing my best Lizzie. I’d like to see the whole damn lot behind bars. Now you must excuse my language. Right, Lizzie. I don’t know why I’ve kept you talking here. Come round the back and I’ll have a look down below and give you some stuff.”

"Bless you Annie," said Mrs. Clark and Hope heard their voices trail away and a door close.

Hope watched and waited. He wanted to see Horace's pigs again. There had been enough hints about them to warrant a second visit. He kept his face glum when Glorey asked him to visit Widow Turner in Sheldon, close by Magpie Mine. Widow T. had had a whole line of washing stolen in the night. Two linen sheets she had as wedding gifts, when she was married to a soldier in the Crimean War. She had left them in the moonlight to bleach and they had vanished. Glorey suspected gypsies, maybe navvies, regretted there was no bike available, and the weather was so bad . . . still, he could not help it. Hope was sent off into the countryside and forgotten about for another day.

Hope was pleased. The morning, early October, was dark with a thick weeping mist of early autumn. A perfect day for not being noticed. Hope had a plan.

When Widow Turner had been soothed, when Hope wrote down details in his notebook, and Hope had drunk a cup of tea from the pot that had been stewing on the fire for a week, he walked to the Jennet. It was a long walk but he had much on his mind. He had recalled the red chimney soot around the iron foundry forges in Derby, and the white dust and soot above Horace's forge at Magpie Mine. The colour was connected to the metal being worked, he reasoned to himself.

Hope stood for several minutes by Horace's farm building. The world was wrapped in autumn stillness. A distant cow calling . . . a drip of water from a sycamore . . . a robin singing...With sudden catlike speed Hope was on the wall and then the slate roof of the little farm building. The slate was deep purple with the drizzle and scattered with fallen sycamore leaves that could be slipped on. Carefully Hope edged up to the chimney and held it tight to steady himself. It had recently been pointed and was safe and secure, as were the Welsh slates that looked very new. Then with his penknife he scraped at the soot and deposits round the rim of the chimney. These he put in a brown paper bag he had been carrying around for days, waiting such an opportunity.

The drystone wall collapsed under his weight as he came off the roof and the sound seemed thunderous. Hope swore and fled into the mist where he listened for several minutes. He was wary of Horace but knew he would hear his approach on the rough lane with its loose stone chippings and puddles.

One stone at a time, then a pause for listening, Hope built up the wall as best he could. He had no idea of the skill involved in drystone walling but he hoped Horace would have his mind on other matters. When he had finished Hope retreated to return the long miles on the Buxton Road. He did not want anybody to know he had been snooping round. Thank goodness Glorey never questioned what he was doing when he had been sent on a fruitless chase such as a stolen washing line.

It was getting dark and the gas lamps were lit when he reached the town. He liked to see the lamplight on the wet pavements and the gentle hum of the town with the horses' hooves in the distance. He went straight to James the Chemist.

The smell of soap and medicines and the coke of the stove welcomed him when he had closed the door with its clanging bell, and wiped his boots on a door mat that said BEECHAMS PILLS on it.

"Could you test this sample, Sir, for lead?" Hope asked the Chemist.

"It will cost sixpence Constable. I have a form if you fill it in while I am doing the test, and you can get the cash back from Sergeant Glorey."

"This is nothing to do with that side of police work, sir," said Hope briskly. "This is a private matter and I will pay you the sixpence. And if you please sir, I do not want this test discussed with anybody else."

James, one of the higher middle class establishments in the town, bridled a little at the young constable's tone of authority. Then he smiled and nodded and disappeared round the back of his shop.

The fact was, after three years, Hope was getting a reputation. The townspeople liked this fresh young man, always smartly turned out, clean as a new pin with his open friendly face. Singing in the church choir and kicking out Gerald Frith from The Anchor helped too.

Hope stood in the shop idly reading the Latin names on a set of little drawers behind the counter and watching the play of gaslight on a huge flask of coloured water in the shop window. He heard James light the Bunsen burner and heard him reach for a jar of sugar crystals as he began the test. He returned quickly. He smiled at the young man. Hope somehow made him feel all was well in the world. He had seen him on his late beat turning the door handles of shops like his own, to see if they were secure for the night.

"It's a mix of carbon and pure lead, Constable." He could not resist a little patronisation however. "Carbon is the name we chemists give to soot. Now, I've written that out on my card, and the date you gave it me, should you" (and he emphasised the pronoun) "wish to use it for legal purposes. And not a word to the inimitable and inestimable Sergeant Glorey."

Hope was still young and fresh faced enough to blush very slightly. He did not know what the words meant but he sensed he had overstepped some invisible boundary.

Sergeant Glorey exercised his mind night and day for excuses to keep Hope out of Church on Sundays and managed it once a month. His fear of Runcorn prevented any more interference. When he had secured Hope for Sunday duty he was oily and paternal to Hope and on Sundays permitted Hope the use of the Station bicycle. So it was this particular Sunday in late October. A summons to appear at the Police Court needed to be delivered by hand to some railway navvies who lived right at the edge of the County at Totley. There had been a legal hitch but now Glorey had the Summons on Saturday for the men to appear in the Police Court in the town on Monday. Hope must deliver the summons by noon on Sunday.

Glorey beamed as he explained there was a Navvy camp just below Owler Bar on the Sheffield Road. Hope could have the bicycle. Glorey was sorry Hope would miss Church. But these navvies, said Glorey happily, were the cause of crime and drunkenness. So the Choir would have to do without Hope. A pity, but law and order came before warbling in church. Hope pursed his mouth and tried to look glum. It suited him perfectly to visit Owler Bar on a Sunday and see what the Friths were doing.

So Hope set off at eight o'clock in the morning of the 26th of October 1904 a date that yielded several pages of writing on his return that evening.

Eight o' clock was the time to commence Sunday Duty. Glorey was there and could not wait for Hope to leave the town so he could pin the notice to the Station door and walk with rapid tread for a fried breakfast of Sunday proportions.

There had been the first hard frost of the autumn. Mists filled the hollows of the white frosted fields but the sky was blue and the sun sparkled. Hope's bicycle wheels crunched on the white road before him, except where a roadside ash trees had shed their entire summer leaf in the overnight frost. Then his wheels were silent and he was aware of the total Sunday silence of the world, just the occasional cock crow and the sound of a falling signal, but no trains could be heard.

In Baslow the thatched rooftops steamed a golden haze in the sunlight above frost whitened gardens where the runner beans had blackened and wilted with the frost burn. The dahlias and nasturtiums had collapsed in the cold October night.

It was a three mile climb to the moorlands and Owler Bar, but Hope was content in the silence, with only a trickle of robin song here and there to keep him company. After Owler Bar he enjoyed a rush downhill to Totley and the Navvy Camp.

The Midland Railway had built a long tunnel there, ten years earlier, and were anxious to maintain the deep link to Manchester. A permanent camp had situated itself in a nearby field, and Hope soon found it. The men lived in old railway carriages, and were now sitting in the sun, washing and shaving, preparing for Mass six miles away in Sheffield. Hope accepted a mug of hot sweet tea from the overseer, after he had handed over the brown envelope addressed in Lomas' neat handwriting. Apart from Mrs. Harryson's carefully bought tea, it was the best mug of tea he had drunk for months. Refreshed by the drink and rest and the civilised air of Sunday in the camp, he departed to climb the hill again to the Peacock Inn at Owler Bar.

He had noted that the disused toll bar cottage close by the Inn was deserted and clearly nobody lived there. The orchard of stunted and wind blasted apple trees was overgrown. A perfect place to hide.

Concealing his bicycle Hope waded through the dew sodden grass to hide under a wall. He picked three rosy red apples and stretched his full length out of sight in the sun. He felt as if he were on holiday.

Apart from a man whistling at the Inn pump and a robin in the deserted garden, the silence was total. Now and again he heard the bells of Holmesfield and imagined now and again he discerned the fine bells from the twisted spire of Chesterfield. He had spotted the thorn of the crooked spire peering from the mists as he pedalled to the Inn an hour earlier.

He was half asleep in the sunshine when he heard them.

The Friths were obviously 'well oiled' as the neighbours in Derby had described Hope's father on a Friday and Saturday night. Mrs. Clark was right. They ought to be stopped. But Hope had learned that if he arrested them for disorderly conduct he would learn nothing of their greater crimes. Louder and louder. Then they rounded the last bend of the moorland road.

Hope thought it must be the old man, the father, Tinker Roland Frith, singing. He had a strong and musical voice and was serenading the morning with a song he had learned in the moorlands of the Derbyshire and Staffordshire borders. Hope's trained musical senses grudgingly admired the strength and melody in Tinker's voice if not the bawdy old song

"Wag a leg over leg, wag a leg under leg
Barbary Bell my Darling
With his cock straight up like a serving tup
Barbary Bell my darling . . ."

The chorus of Barbary Bell had been roared out by the three sons who had not inherited Tinker's grasp of song and melody; but as the wagon rumbled into the inn yard Hope heard Bert say "Shurrup feyther" and all went quiet. Hope noted how Bert seemed the leader of the thieves.

Food and more drink was brought out to them as they sat on a bench but Hope was too far away to hear what was being said. By noon he began to wonder, as did Mrs. Gill and Mrs. Clark, why they had come all this way. He began to feel tired and disappointed. The sun was now warm and had made him drowsy and irritable. Then he was alerted by a metallic crash.

"Gerrastride her then 'orace!" Hope heard the drunken and now unmusical bellow of Tinker. "Let's see ye ride the iron maiden! Get 'er between thy legs!"

Peering carefully, Hope saw Horace had brought his bike on the wagon. There was a panier on the front with a large sack in it. Whatever was in the sack was heavy, because Horace was having difficulty controlling the machine, and Hope could see his difficulty in handling the bike was not just caused by alcohol.

Then the Friths were silent and Horace wobbled away to the highway, where once there, he had gathered speed, and he gained more control. He sped by the tollbar cottage, down the hill to Totley. Hope waited a short time, then was after him, grateful for the bend in the road concealing him from the other Friths.

Hope had to pedal downhill to gain sight of Horace. At the bottom of the hill after two miles of daring speed for Hope, he saw Horace stop the bicycle at the very bottom of the hill by a Methodist chapel. Hope quickly concealed his own machine behind a hedge and watched Horace unsteadily wheeling the load down a lane on the right hand side to a mill and cottages. He saw Horace waiting by a clump of trees some distance and out of sight from the cottages. As silently as he could, Hope advanced and standing in a filthy ditch by a towering bed of nettles, he could see Horace. The ditch smelled worse than Horace's lavender cart, and clearly was a drain from the cottages. After a while a man in his Sunday best suit approached Horace.

Hope could not hear what was being said, but watched through a gap in the thorn hedge and saw Horace take out a brick of grey metal. Then another. He took out two dozen of these crude pigs of lead. Then he took out the last items and these caught the sun and in the dazzle Hope failed to see the silver boxes stolen from Dr. Ball's private vestry. The man appeared pleased with everything and put the lead back in the sack. Hope missed the more musical clink of the silver items. Then Hope heard and saw the clink of a quantity of gold sovereigns. The two men shook hands and after much talk and nodding Horace rode away with a good deal more certainty than he had come.

Hope waited some time and then went back a little way up the hill to his bicycle. His boots were soaked and stinking and he desperately tried to clean them in the grass of the field. He climbed on his saddle and rode down to the Chapel where he left the bicycle propped against the building and went and stood in the stream close by, to clean his boots. As he stood in the dappled shade below a cascading waterfall, he realised he would have to return a different way home. He must not be seen.

Sitting on a seat outside the Chapel he took out his map and located himself. He followed the road down from Owler Bar to the small village of Totley then down to the Chapel and the stream. And by the row of cottages he saw the words LEAD MILL.

He forgot his soaking wet feet and fatigue. He had already enough evidence to arrest Horace. A surge of energy rose in him. He found a path up to the village of Dore and another road home to the town. It was a long road but he had all the afternoon before him.

He wheeled the bicycle along a narrow path through a wood and came to the village of Dore. People were strolling in the sun of the Sunday afternoon, enjoying the last warm Sunday of the year. They looked curiously at the policeman they had not seen in the village before, despite the fact he wore the Derbyshire uniform badge. He nodded and spoke to them. One man nodded and then turned and called to a man working in the garden of a large cottage.

"Good afternoon Professor Stockwell. Clearing things up after the frost?"

Professor Stockwell stopped work, leaned on his spade and acknowledged the villager. Hope walked on but could not help staring.

This was the man Mrs. Harryson had mentioned when they were talking about the strange events of that evening last August. And once more Hope felt a curious wave of resentment that Mrs. Harryson should have other men friends. The more Hope looked, the more puzzled and annoyed he became and he noticed his own wet boots again as depression returned, based on hunger, jealousy and bewilderment.

Professor Stockwell's cottage was the first you approached on the path to the village. A large double fronted dwelling, it was more a house. The golden building stone of the Derbyshire village glowed in the sun. The garden was large and received the full sun. Professor Stockwell wore a shirt with no collar and his sleeves were rolled up. Hope could see his trousers were good cloth but he wore a belt like a working man and a stout pair of boots. Anything less like Hope's idea of a professor would have been hard to find; desperate to find fault, Hope thought that no gentleman would work on a Sunday afternoon. The man himself was tall and athletic with a sun tanned face and a neatly trimmed beard that was streaked with grey. Hope was disconcerted by the dislike he felt for the man.

It spoiled the ride home. Hope's greatest pleasure at that time was to sit in the deep chair opposite Mrs. Harryson, and make conversation by the fireside about the day's events and adventures. She was a good listener and Hope shared a great many of his thoughts and concerns with her. Sometimes she took her bicycle (another source of scandal for Ruth and Betty to delight in) on a Saturday, and rode away for the day. Hope was sure this was one of her destinations for she took the Sheffield Road out of the town. Sometimes she took the train and was away some days. But it was seeing this man that filled Hope with such a mixture of feelings that surprised him and took away the glory and earlier triumph of the autumn afternoon.

It was a steep climb out of the village to the alternative main road that would lead him back, and the main road itself turned out to be an arduous one as it approached the high moors. It was quite different to the morning's journey. This road led to a famous beauty spot, the Surprise View and Fox House, an inn that was popular with the townsfolk of Sheffield, for a trip in horse drawn charabancs, wagons or on foot. Three cars passed him as he pushed his machine up the road. His temper deteriorated further as he was passed by groups of girls in their Sunday finery. The Sheffield girls were bolder than his own town and Derby, and laughed and giggled as they walked by, 'eyeing up' the young policeman. Two asked for a kiss and three suggested various activities behind the roadside wall which made Hope blush and caused ecstatic glee in the groups.

Hope was asked the time by the gangs of Sheffield working men as they walked by, repeating the old music hall joke about policemen always having a watch they had kept from stolen property. Even when the road reached the plateau of the moors, and he was able to ride, the jeers and shouts continued; "Bobby Bingo on tin wheels", was apparently some local joke about policemen. Hope began to understand Glorey's fear of cutlers and Sheffield men.

He was glad when he had cycled by the Inn and the crowds of people, and began to ride downhill under the shade of golden leaved oaks where the chill and scent of autumn returned. He paused for a moment on Grindleford Bridge to admire the valley of the Derwent, then slowly returned home on the sun-gilded roads where the shadows were beginning to appear, long and dark from wayside trees. Still in a strange mood, he took off Glorey's notice from the door at four o' clock, and returned the key to Glorey. The Sergeant had obviously been sound asleep after a vast Sunday dinner, and received Hope in a pair of carpet slippers, to take the key. Hope said not a word about the Friths and Horace, but told Glorey he had had trouble with a gang of cutlers.

"Aye, ye would have," said Glorey closing the door on Hope with full fed satisfaction.

Back at his lodgings, Hope mused on Horace Frith. He knew Horace was melting down the lead to manageable 'pigs' at the Jennet and then selling it at Totley. But he wanted the whole story and he was determined to find out. Where was the lead from the Church roof being stored before Horace melted it? How did the other Friths help and what did they do? He wanted to indict the whole Gang. In the meantime, following Lomas' methodology he would watch and say nothing.

Hope found his resentment about Professor Stockwell still festered in him. Mrs. Harryson had cooked a joint of pork, roast potatoes crisp and gold and fluffy inside, with the last of the runner beans picked before the frost. Mrs. Harryson was constantly given gifts of fruit and vegetables from grateful patients but Hope wondered peevishly if these beans had come from the Professor's garden; she had cycled off on Wednesday up the Sheffield Road for the day. Mrs. Harryson smiled her smile as she passed the dish of apple sauce to him. There were stewed pears with whipped cream and chocolate and Hope had seen a pear tree in the Dore garden. Mrs. Harryson seemed not in the least bothered by Hope's sulk.

It was an unusually silent Sunday evening as they sat by the fire. Annie Harryson sewed with the gas lit behind her and the oil lamp turned high as she stitched something small and black with tiny stitches. She was also reading a book at the same time, something she seemed able to do. Hope, still nettled, caught sight of the words 'Rights of Women' and that upset him more. Why did she want to read stuff like that? He had read reports in the papers about women like that, wanting the vote and other strange ideas.

Annie Harryson, her face semi-shadowed and her full lips in her usual half smile, made no attempt to coax her lodger out of his mood. She never had patience with restless tomcats at the best of times and had been known to open her window and empty a jug of water at midnight on the sexual howlings of the town's toms.

The frost of that October Sunday had presaged winter and by the final week of November 1904 the weather turned cold and frosty with a little snow.

Hope walked down Castle Street one late afternoon, glad of his heavy warm uniform and looking forward to Mrs. Harryson's fireside that night. The cold was strengthening. A half-moon was already glittering with frost and he could hear the sound of sawing from Horace Frith's lavender field. Horace, with the aid of his brother Gerald's wagon, sold logs when the weather turned cold and the lavender pits froze over.

Suddenly Hope found his teeth were on edge and a shiver, not of cold, irritated his back. The sawing note had changed to a sound not unlike a fingernail on a slate or glass. Cautiously Hope approached the field and watched from behind an ivy festooned tree. Horace was no longer sawing wood. He was sawing a wide strip of lead into smaller strips which he carefully put under a sack on his bicycle basket. Then he sawed more wood for a time before sawing lead. Hope watched him for some time until he was doing it by the light of the moon, the lead catching the moonlight in dull silver flashes. When Horace appeared to have finished Hope made his way back as far as Dr. Bagehot's house and stood in front of it under Dr. Bagehot's gas lamp illuminating the word SURGERY.

Shortly after, Horace appeared wheeling his bike carefully on the icy road, the basket covered with a sack.

"It's rate cowd enough to freeze the bollocks off a lead statue," said Horace amiably as he passed. Hope said nothing. The arrogance and surety of the Friths astounded him.

Hope watched Horace for a week until the night of the full moon. He sawed logs most of the time but every now and again he took a metal saw and sawed lead. It was craftily done; any lead was concealed in logs should anybody approach the lavender field- which was unlikely.

At four in the afternoon, in the gathering dusk, with the rising November Moon massive behind the bare beech trees of Sam Walton's farm on the eastern hill, Hope saw Horace suddenly cease sawing. He made his way to what the more outspoken in the town called 'Horace's Shit Pits' and began to dig. Hope saw him tug out a long length of something rigid. This length was dragged by Horace to the bank that protected him from the river. There he left the dung encrusted strip, which Hope presumed was lead, barnacled with the remains of the town's waste. Then Hope had to scuttle to the lamp of Dr. Bagehot's house; only that night Horace did not speak to him; or he appeared not to see him.

Hope made a decision. He would watch Horace's field for as long as it took. He should have been off duty at six but he decided to stay out. He went back to his lodgings which was fragrant with the smell of an ox-tail stew and pear logs blazing in the hearth, scenting the air, a gift from a grateful woman from a farm near Rowsley.

"I need to keep an eye on something Mrs. Harryson," explained Hope standing in the doorway and flooding the room with cold fresh air. "Do you mind if I eat my supper when I get back? I might be late."

Annie Harryson gave him one of her warmer smiles. This was how she liked to see him, his still boyish face alert with intent and glowing with health and on the scent, she hoped, of some of the Friths or other men in the town up to no good. She noticed his side whiskers were frosted with ice crystals that were now melting into bright drops in the lamplight. His excited breath came in bursts of vapour in the icy freshness of the winter night. This was how she had planned things would develop.

"Take as long as you want, Mr. Hope. The ox-tail will only improve in the oven and I shall do the dumplings while you take your bath. It's a cold night and you'll be glad of both."

Hope nodded and looked at her for a while taking in the scene. She was in her own armchair and she was drinking from a very old and chipped glass goblet. She was drinking Burgundy. Hope was always puzzled and a little alarmed by the fact she drank wine. He knew half the wine would have gone in the stew. He wondered why she liked wine, why it went in the stew-you could never taste the wine in the thick savoury gravy. And it made him uncomfortable to see a woman drinking wine. She was reading again The Origin of Species.

Hope left the room discomfited as usual but fascinated, but soon forgot it. For the next three hours he patrolled the Sheffield Road, a long lane and the Bridge, all three in sight of the bank where Horace had left the lead. He knew Glorey, as long as he did not report back to the Station, could not care less where or what he was doing. Out of sight was out of mind for Glorey. He hated the sight of the young man and pushed him out of his mind as often as possible.

At seven o'clock, Constable Allen approached him. He was on late patrol and was surprised to see Hope in full uniform.

"What are you up to?" he asked Hope, but Hope was evasive. Allen knew him well enough not to ask too much and did not care anyway, his only aim was to get back home and to bed.

"You're a rum bugger, Hope!" said he and clapped him on the back. The two men chatted companionably for a while.

"The missus wants me to go to Matlock with her on Saturday and do some Christmas buying for the kids," said Allen. "But I'm on duty all day."

"I'll swap with you," said Hope. "But you arrange it or Glorey'll do the opposite of what I ask!" The two men laughed and Allen expressed his thanks.

"I thought of going in uniform with her," said Allen, "if the old cantankerous bugger said I could not change the rota, telling the fat bastard I'd seen a navvy man in Matlock wi' a Christmas tree wi' candles stuck up his arse, he'd have let me go to investigate!"

Allen went on his beat and his whistling died in the frosty silence. Never taking his eyes off the riverbank, Hope patrolled up and down. The great planet Jupiter rose in the east and Hope fancied it was the Christmas Star. Chimneys smoked up to the stars that had not been dimmed by the moon, and the gas lamps on the Bridge hissed and gurgled. Owls called incessantly from the woods by the Station, their steely cries floating up to the deepest blue sky. One horse drawn carriage went by and an hour later a cart and horse. Dogs barked. The moonlight became whiter as the frost hoared the riverside fields. It was a night of perfect stillness and tranquillity with the steely magic of midwinter.

Hope was to recall this glittering peace when, in 1940, on another identical night of a midwinter full moon, all hell broke loose around him. He did not know that night in 1904 that the world held horrors far worse than the Friths stealing the Church roof.

He heard a splash and became still. In the moonlight he saw the goblin form of Horace dipping the sheet of lead in the river. He submerged it . . . held it underwater . . . then pulled it out with a splash and a flash of white moonlight from the gleaming washed lead sheet. And Hope realised that is what he had seen four months ago on that stormy August evening.

He waited no longer. He would leave Horace to get on with what he was doing. He obviously had no idea Hope was closing in on him. He would continue to watch and wait. He wanted the whole of the Gang to be implicated. And he wanted to know why Horace was taking the trouble to process the lead into the crude pigs that he exchanged for money. Surely strips of lead that he sawed off would do as well as the pigs? He had the sudden pleasing feeling that if the Friths were caught it would be a Christmas Gift to Mrs. Harryson and to Lomas, two of the people he best wanted to please in the whole of the town.

Hope waited, although he was impatient to share his knowledge with Lomas. He waited a month till the next full moon, in the week before Christmas. Geese and turkeys were hanging outside the butchers and the big grocery shop even had a Christmas tree in the grand entrance by the glass door. Mr. Frost had a string of papier-mâché silver bells across his window with more decorative treasures inside and the sweet shops added pink and white sugar mice and gold chocolate coins to their displays. Hope sensed the excitement in the local children and in himself, although his was of a different nature.

Hope was relaxing in his armchair and had just lit his pipe. He had taken to smoking a pipe in imitation of Lomas and a lifelong love of tobacco was now beginning. Mrs. Harryson had told him she did not mind him smoking in the lodging as long as he kept to the finer cuts of Virginian leaf, and not some of the rough brands smoked by some in the town. Hope was glad to accommodate her; some of the cheaper tobaccos made his eyes water. A knock came at the door and Mrs. Harryson went to answer it. It was not unusual for people to knock for her help at any time of the day.

"Why, Tilly," Hope heard her say. He turned and saw Tilly Frith, the eldest daughter of the Frith family, standing in the moonlight of the doorway. Hope recalled a pantomime he had seen one Christmas, as a child, where the Dame in Dick Whittington looked not unlike Tilly Frith. Tilly had waist length hair the colour of old straw left under the sun, a sagging waistline and bosom and a pair of enormous steel rimmed glasses which enlarged her anxious and watchful eyes. She clutched a shawl around her, fastened with a clothes peg. Hope noticed she had a brown boot on one foot and a black one with missing pearl buttons on the other.

"Come in Tilly." said Mrs. Harryson; she had warmth in her voice for she felt Tilly had a raw deal in life. Viewed by the town as 'ninepence to the shilling,' with 'bats in her belfry,' and 'three sheets to the wind,' Annie suspected darker undercurrents that had formed Tilly's incapacities. The firstborn of Tinker and Mrs. Frith, Tilly had shared the large marriage bed of the Friths for three years and Annie, well aware of the sinister aspects that could develop in male sexual behaviour, had long thought Tilly's damaged mentality was based on some fearful interference when she was a baby and toddler.

"Sit down Tilly," said Annie. "What can I help you with?"

"It's mam's cough again," said Tilly. "She were badly all last neet and -"

Mrs. Harryson interrupted her.

"Why, Tilly!" she exclaimed. "Whatever's the matter with your right bosom?"

Hope looked and saw two lumps on the sagging stained bodice. He sensed Annie's alarm and consternation.

"Nowt!" said Tilly, pushing grey strands of hair away and adjusting the glasses and then the lumps. "It's the knobs off me drawer wi' m' treasure in. I tek knobs off afore I come out. I dunna want feyther looking in my drawers."

"I bet you don't Tilly," said Annie Harryson, sotto voce, with a depth of meaning that escaped Tilly but not Hope. The more he saw Tinker Roland Frith the more he sensed a depth of criminality of all types.

"Well, Tilly, I am sure Constable Hope won't mind being left on his own and I'll get my coat and some cough mixtures and syrups and come and look at your ma."

"Dunna thee come near us!" shrieked Tilly backing away. A sly expression flitted over her dirty face. "'orace and Gerry and feyther wunna like it. They've got pigs and nobody mun come near!"

"I'm not frit o' pigs Tilly!" said Annie brightly. "So I'll come and see your ma. I'll get the stuff." Hope noticed Mrs. Harryson spoke the dialect of the town to the poor woman. Tilly looked scared and then blinked her eyes.

"Aye. Mebbe you'll be alright. 'orace keeps the pigs in the old privy so us'll be safe."

Tilly writhed her fingers round the clothes peg as she waited for Mrs. Harryson. She leaned forward and moved her glasses to sharp focus to study Hope, and studied all aspects of him from head to toe as he sat in his chair.

"Constable 'ope looks a nice bloke," Hope heard her say to Mrs. Harryson as they set off under the light of the moon. Only 'orace says he's a lump of shit and he'd like to kick his arse all the way to Magpie Mine an' shove him down the shaft. But he looks alreet to me . . . do you keep pigs Mrs. 'arryson? . . . it's a grand neet . . . they say you love Constable Hope . . . do you Mrs. 'arryson?"

Hope heard their voices trail away in the deep silence of the midwinter night. He relit his pipe and could not stop himself from smiling even though he was alone in the firelit room.

Hope waited his chance taking a long time to begin his beat and was lucky. Widow Slater arrived with a tale for Sergeant Glorey about the disappearance of her cat. She had heard that gypsies stewed cats in their pots. This was music to the pre-judgemental ears of the Sergeant and added spice was given to the complaint, already pleasurable, because the Widow had a tight bodice over her comfortable and large bosom, covered with jet beads that expanded and shuddered with the emotion of the tale. Glorey was riveted to the spot, seeing or hearing nothing beyond the Widow's chest. Hope tiptoed up the stairs.

Hope was able to explain to Lomas most of the concealing and processing of the church roof lead. How the lavender field had been used for storage, then the lead was cleaned and cut up and stored in the privies of the Frith house. From there it was taken to the Jennet for more processing and made into pigs. Then they were taken back to the privies and once a month taken to the lead mill at Totley and sold.

Lomas was so pleased he shook Hope warmly by the hand; Hope had delivered the Christmas Gift to Lomas but it was not as Hope wanted. Hope was still puzzled. He could not understand why Horace Frith took so much trouble with the lead. Why not saw it into bits and take it straight to Totley? It was a day later when they all discovered the reason.

Superintendent Lomas descended the stairs followed by Hope. Glorey, still pink and sweating from the Widow, looked up irritably.

"I shall need Constable Hope and Allen this morning, Sergeant. You and Fearne will have to patrol the town."

Glorey agreed between clenched teeth.

"Certainly sir." He wiped his top lip with one of Mrs. Glorey's spotless white handkerchiefs boiled to sparkling perfection every Monday in her wash house.

Lomas took Hope and Allen in the horse and trap to the Jennet. It took over an hour to reach their destination with Hope and Allen walking up the steep hill from Ashford to spare the horse. The door of Horace's piggery was kicked in to reveal a small brick built furnace and a pile of coke and ash logs. In a pile were some crude pigs of lead. It was still a mystery to Lomas and Hope why this process was necessary. The furnace was a basic one and could only have half melted the lead causing it melt a little before making the crude brick-like pigs of lead.

Nevertheless Hope felt nothing but exultation as the horse and trap rattled back over the limestone uplands under a frosty blue sky. The hills were dusted with snow and the lines of sycamores marking the old lead rakes were finely veined against the sky. Christmas was in the air and Hope was triumphant and all seemed right with the world.

Back in the town they broke down the door of the old privy at the Frith's and found more of the curiously crude pigs.

Superintendent Lomas formally arrested Horace and Allen and Hope took him back to the Station handcuffed to them both. The Christmas shoppers in the town could not have asked for a better Street entertainment. A Frith in handcuffs being led past the hanging geese and poultry and holly wreaths, made it a Christmas to recall for many years after, until a more fearful Christmas of 1914 erased such pleasures.

Glorey, after his initial fury, had spent a stimulating morning harassing two gypsy girls in well-fitting bodices selling hot chestnuts from a brazier to the shoppers. One girl had a glossy red bodice and the other a holly green. The Sergeant had cautioned them three times and taken details in a notebook trying to write and look at the same time.

He followed Hope and Allen and Horace back to the Station with returning irritation. The last thing he wanted was for the shoppers to see Hope leading back a Frith to justice.

"Find a cell for Frith, Sergeant," said Lomas crisply. "He will remain here overnight and you will take personal responsibility for his detention. On no account is he to receive visitors. I shall arrange with the magistrate, Major Bunyan for a special session of the police court tomorrow even though it is Christmas Eve and a Saturday too. Thankyou Sergeant Glorey."

"Sir, he's a mucky bugg-I mean he's too mucky for one of my cells. He'd best stay in the stable and-"

"Sergeant, we are upholders of the law in the town. Sanitation and public health are the responsibility of the Sanitary Board of Health. Now do as I requested."

Constable Allen had to turn his face away.

Major Bunyan was only too pleased to convene an extraordinary Police Court for the theft of the church lead. Lomas requested that Hope should report to him at seven the next day to prepare for the Court.

Lomas prepared to climb the stairs that Christmas Eve morning at half past six, but he spotted a shovel propped up by Glorey's pinewood fortress. Glorey was guarding the cell key at his desk as vigilant as a dog with a bone.

"What is the shovel for Sergeant?"

Glorey inflated himself like a frosted crow.

"Well sir, I thought Constable Hope after the Court, could dig out the rest of the lead from Frith's shi-, er, pits."

"That is out of the question Sergeant. You have told me endlessly, and tirelessly, how untrustworthy Constable Hope is. It is far too important for Hope. No, Sergeant. Find another shovel and you and I will excavate the pits after the Court. It will give us an appetite for our Christmas dinner. Unless, Sergeant, you can find a band of navvies to do the job. I know you are an expert on navvy men and their ways and where they may be found."

By ten o'clock Glorey had persuaded a gang of men to dig for triple their normal pay.

The Court session was brisk. Major Bunyan sitting in a pool of winter sunshine cascading through the grimy windows and dimming the gas, had no mercy. Frith was remanded in custody unless bail for £25 could be offered. Such a sum was undreamed of by most in the town. It would have bought a freehold cottage and garden in the town.

Bert Frith stood up. He looked sober and scrubbed and subservient. Only Hope and Lomas sensed the sarcasm and hostility.

"Sir, I will stand bail. I will bring the cash to the Court within the hour."

It was a topic of conversation around all the Christmas dinners in the town.

"Damn and blast!" said Lomas when he and Hope returned to Lomas' office with their notebooks and papers. "Damn the Friths to Hell!" Hope stared at Lomas. This was strong language from such an upright and God fearing man.

"This means the Friths have all Christmas and the New Year to concoct a story. Damn their eyes! And God alone knows where Bert Frith has got that money from. And the Friths will have Christmas cheer and will eat drink and make merry with Horace and laugh at us and invent God knows what defence."

He followed Hope down the stairs to inspect the lead that had been retrieved from the Field.

It was propped up in the Yard, gleaming and wet after being

hosed down by the labourers.

And there was the answer to Hope's puzzle. The lead was embossed with motifs stamped into the medieval lead. Crosses, chalices, phrases from the scriptures in Latin, texts and crude images of the Saints were all stamped into the lead. It would have been so easy to trace unless Horace had softened the lead by heat and erased the tell-tale proof that this was church lead.

Lomas was fascinated. Not least by images of a bird, which he wondered was the holy dove or the medieval mark of Magpie Mine. Lomas enjoyed details of life and history such as these. Eventually he stood up to his usual straight tall self, and turned to Hope.

"I can't thank you enough for your work, Constable," said Lomas. "A happy Christmas to you!" He turned away and went back to his office. His Christmas was partially spoiled by Bert Frith standing surety. Hope was not to understand the implications till January when Lomas' forebodings proved correct.

As for Glorey, his Christmas was ruined. The town buzzed with the story of how Constable Hope had watched and waited and caught Horace Frith. Glorey felt liverish all Christmas and had to sip almost half a bottle of Milk of Magnesia after his Christmas dinner and the contents of a tin of Andrews Liver Salts over Boxing Day.

But Hope simply felt triumphant. And Mrs. Harryson seemed to join in with the rest of the town in her satisfaction with her lodger. After a splendid dinner of roast chicken and sage and thyme stuffing and plum pudding with rum sauce, they sat either side of a blazing fire.

"A good fire Mrs. Harryson," said Hope.

"Ash logs from a farm by Magpie Mine," said Mrs. Harryson. "What could be more appropriate? The farmer there had some trouble and I helped him with it, and he's brought me enough logs till Easter . . . You've given the town a grand gift Mr. Hope. And

I'd like to give you a little gift."

She handed Hope a small package of brown paper with a label embossed with holly.

TO John Hope. A Happy Christmas
FROM Annie Harryson

Wondering, and blushing slightly, Hope undid the paper and found a small black velvet pouch. He recognised it as something he had seen her working on once or twice. Carefully embroidered on the black, in white and silver, was the badge of the Derbyshire Police. And inside was a silver Geneva pocket watch, a silver replica of the gold one he had found for Dr. Ball on his first morning in the town.

He stammered his thanks. He had never expected to own such a watch.

"It was given to me by a grateful patient," she said. "it is of no use to me, but it will be to you. Look upon it as a gift from me and the town . . . now, wind it up and while you are doing that, I'll pour us a glass of port. Major Bunyan has sent us a bottle of good stuff, again as a token of thanks. You're as popular as Father Christmas it would seem. And that same farmer has sent me some young white cheese that will go with the port."

The New Year began for Hope and the town on a high note of optimism. Law and order was being forced on the Friths at last. When the Reverend Runcorn organised his usual Epiphany service accompanied with organ, bells and smells, he decided he would ask Hope to sing the part of Balthazar, one of the Wise Men from the east.

Runcorn knew that the fine baritone voice of Hope, now a hero, would cause a frisson of pleasure with the ladies of the Parish. He would turn down the gas and Hope and the other Wise Men would sing to the light of the candles only. He was impressed with Hope's musicianship and knew he could cope with an arrangement of Hope's verse in the minor key followed by the choirboys singing the chorus back in the major. ("And please, boys, don't shout Star of wonder, star of light, when you sing the chorus after Constable Hope's solo.")

So Hope sang at Evensong on the first Sunday of 1905.

Myrrh is mine a bitter perfume
Brings a life of gathering gloom
Sorrowing, sighing, bleeding, dying
Sealed in the cold stone tomb...

The candles guttered, the blackness of a January night had eclipsed the stained glass, Hope's face was half in shadow and the minor key lent a gothic touch. The congregation were lost in pleasurable admiration. They did not see the gathering shadows in the corners of the church waiting to creep out and eventually darken their lives.

True, Runcorn had been unable to find the gold and silver monastic relics that he knew Dr. Ball had collected at great cost, stored somewhere in the Vestry. Runcorn had hoped to use these in his theatrical Epiphany services. But the old man had now completely lost his reason and snarled and growled if the curates approached his Vestry; and Runcorn had other matters, ladies and the music of the services, so he thought no more of what he thought was Dr. Ball's memory lapse. He borrowed a gilt casket from the entrance hall of the Vicarage and that was carried on a purple cushion in the procession, to represent the treasures of the magi. Everyone was satisfied. Except Lomas who still suspected trouble in the Hilary Assize at Derby when the Friths would appear. They had been summoned at Lomas' request to appear, with Horace, as accessories to the crime of theft of church property.

Hope remained elated. He took his new watch to Jas. Green the town watchmaker and a man slightly feared for his radical liberal views, but respected for his craft.

"This is a fine watch, Constable. I will not repeat the music hall joke about asking the police the time from stolen watches." Hope would have liked to say it was a Christmas gift from Mrs. Harryson but was too embarrassed to say, and so he remained silent. Green put his jewellers' eye-glass down from his eye. "Kays of Worcester," he said reverently reading the black letters on the watch's face, "the watch has travelled a long way to Derbyshire . . . it is a fine Swiss watch . . . a rich jewelled mechanism . . . I will clean and oil it and regulate it and you will bring it me every new year for me to check it over and the watch will see us both out." He smiled. "It will cost you half a guinea Constable. If you own a good watch you have to pay for its upkeep. It's a gentleman's watch but I suspect the County do not pay you a gentleman's wage. A great pity. You are doing first rate sterling work ridding this town of bullies and pests. But it will be half a guinea. I have a living to make too . . . but it's a fine watch."

On a bright crisp morning the watch ticked in Hope's left breast pocket, next to his heart, as he sat in the Court at Derby. And as Lomas had predicted things could not have gone worse.

Unlike Hope, Lomas had spent a restless Christmas. He was furious that Bert Frith had paid for bail from the money made from the lead. There he was wrong. Bert had paid for the bail from money made from the filching of Dr. Ball's exotic collection of medieval and monastic gold and silver treasures. Bert Frith had employed a solicitor from Derby and a barrister. As Lomas had predicted they had concocted a story. All four, Tinker Roland the father, Bert, Gerry and Horace had new sober suits for the appearance. They looked respectable, subservient and hard working men. Only Gerry appeared on the verge of flash with his watch chain and ring.

But what horrified Hope was the callous way the family sacrificed Horace. And Horace seemed quite happy to be the sacrificial lamb grinning round the Court like a good natured hobgoblin from a Grimms' fairy tale.

Bert did the most talking, promoted by the barrister and solicitor as an honest and hard working man. Horace, Bert said, had stripped the church roof on the night of the fog, but the family had known nothing of it. He, Gerry and Tinker Roland had spent the Saturday night drinking. There were many witnesses. Constable Hope had seen them all. Yes, it was true Horace had been there too, but referring to Constable Hope he had arrived early, before his thieving . . . He kept leaving his thieving on the roof and coming 'to wet his whistle.' ('Silence in Court! This is not a music hall!') Yes. Said Bert, the family went to the Peacock every month. They liked to keep together as a family. They were a close knit family. And yes, they knew Horace cycled down to Totley. Tinker said he thought Horace had a lass in Totley. Tinker could not resist a slight emphasis on the word 'had'. Gerry said Horace told them he was 'off to see a man about a dog.' (Silence! SILENCE IN COURT!)

Hope had not seen Superintendent Lomas so enraged. 'They are making a fool of the law and us.' he said to Hope. Horace confessed to everything. Agreed to everything the family said. It was his crime and nothing to do with his brothers or his dear old dad. (Silence. SILENCE!) The Jury and Judge began to lose patience with the lack of evidence against the rest of the family. After all, they thought, the Constable had done a good job in tracking down Horace Frith so why complicate matters? In the end the Judge lost patience with the police case and the case against the rest of the Friths collapsed. Superintendent Lomas was castigated with judicial sarcasm regarding flimsy and spineless accusations.

It was irritability with the police that possibly made Mr. Justice Fenwick viciously harsh with Horace. His face reddened as he sentenced Horace before dismissing Lomas' charges on the rest of the Friths being complicit with the crime.

"Single handed and with not a thought of morality, you stripped the holy church of the town of its roofing, and thus defiling the temple of God. You have shown no remorse. You have smirked at the Court. You have shown dumb insolence to the Bench. You have traded base metal for your own base gain. I can think of nothing more calculated to defile God's Holy Place than you toiling like a detestable beetle upon its fabric in the dead of night... I shall make an example of you as a warning to others, that the fabric of the Church is untouchable. I sentence you to ten years hard labour."

Hope thought he saw Bert Frith smirk as the Case against them was dismissed.

Looking back Hope did not forget 1905. It was the year when, although he still loved the work he was doing, he began to have grave misgivings about the law. It was wrong that the Friths had cheated justice so blatantly. This feeling mixed with other emotions in 1905. He was still restless. He wanted to settle down like Constable Allen but seemed unable to make any moves to do so. Something in his mind seemed to place a barrier against such hopes. He began to have troublesome dreams that he believed were sent from the Devil. At this time his boyhood faith and Christianity had not been tested. He was deeply ashamed of these vivid and pleasurable, often nightly visitations. He prayed silently and fervently every Sunday he was in Church.

The distrust of the law was a start of a long process of understanding about life.

Hope never forgot Horace Frith. What he had done was wrong but there were others involved and they had escaped. Horace was a victim of his own family and legal system. In the 1920's Hope, directing traffic round the new War Memorial, would sometimes pause as the traffic eased, and look at the names on the Memorial and see HORACE FRITH.

Horace had been released in 1914 as part of a scheme that released prisoners near the end of their sentence into the Army. Horace had joined up and been mown down a year later by German machine guns.

Bert had sold the Lavender Field and it had become a stinking eyesore. Nobody understood it like Horace had. By 1915 the stench was so appalling that the town council had no alternative but to engineer a sewage system in the town and build new sewage works close by where Maisie Frith had witnessed the Fox murder.

Even in the 1930's Hope found Horace would trouble his mind. Walking in the woods with Annie on a summer evening hoping to catch the rare song of a nightingale, he would suddenly perceive the distant beam of the North Midland Artillery's War Memorial at Crich Stand, nine miles away, flashing its light in memory of the dead of the War. That little man, he thought, did not deserve what life gave him. Sharing his sadness with Annie in the darkening summer woods, she agreed. "Horace was like a beetle," she said, "as that old fool of a Judge said. But more like one of those humble dung beetles that rid the fields of dung and keep the world going and nobody knows or cares. Poor Horace. Nobody would have thought, except perhaps John Donne, that the world was made less when he was imprisoned and died." And Hope would look at her as usual, not knowing totally what she meant but knowing she was right.

So Hope in 1905 made a grim resolve. He would bring every one of those Friths to justice of some kind. He would uphold the law and beat it if necessary.

The town was unconcerned. They still thought Hope was the hero. A Frith sent to prison was just as it should be. All seemed right with the world. The Local History Society was thrilled by the motif of the magpie on the church lead and discovered a medieval bole hill to the west of the town where the lead had been smelted after it had been mined from the Magpie Mine. And life went on. Three more cars appeared. Nobody was aware, just as they had not been aware of the shadows in the corners of the church, that the Kaiser's provocative visit to Morocco in a gun boat was more sinister than they could have ever imagined. Only Hope sensed that all was not quite as it appeared in the land of hope and glory.

POSTSCRIPT, AUGUST BANK HOLIDAY 1969

Hope sat in the afternoon sunshine, an old man now, by Annie Harryson's lavenders. Or what was left of the lavender after the vicious winter of early 1963. Enough plants survived to attract the bees in the late afternoon sunshine. Hope was dozing a little. His leg, where he had been shot, still ached after all the years that had passed; his injured jaw also nagged with a dull ache. But Hope still enjoyed a pipe of tobacco.

He awoke suddenly as a shadow passed. He blinked in the warmth. The sky had cleared to full August blue scarred by a vapour trail leading to Manchester Airport. The roar of the bank Holiday traffic, through what had once been the market square, sounded like one great engine.

Jacob Frith, now a man in his sixties put down a plastic carrier bag in front of Hope.

"I've brought ye your shopping Mester Hope. It's bedlam out yonder. Traffic jam. I canna get used to that new supermarket being open on a Bank Holiday Monday, but there we are."

Hope nodded and offered Jacob his tobacco pouch and Jacob sat down and filled his own blackened pipe. Hope smiled to himself. He thought of the select grocer's shop that the supermarket had taken over. Self-service and clinical rows of packets and tins and jars to buy. Half living in the past, as Hope was these days of his old age, he suddenly remembered the Christmas of 1904 when he had arrested Jacob's Uncle Horace and led him by that shop where a great Christmas tree had been hung with silver bells. He blinked at Jacob through a cloud of tobacco smoke.

"Do you know, Jacob, I never knew how your Uncle Horace got all that lead single-handed to his lavender field . . . as your Uncles said in Court . . . were you too young to remember anything?"

Jacob removed his pipe and grinned

"No, I bloody weren't! They scared me to death, Gerry, Bert and me Grandfeyther Tinker."

Annie used to say Tinker was both father and grandfather to you, thought Hope, but kept his thought to himself.

"I bet you were," said Jacob to Hope, "after what Bert did to thee . . ." Jacob's voice trailed off and he shook his head in a mix of bewilderment at his own family's ways and the ways of humanity in general.

"Varmints they were, the whole lot. My mam, Maisie, were terrified… terrified of her own feyther and brothers. " And he fell silent again. After fifty years the terror still disturbed him.

"What happened to me was no worse than what the town did to you," said Hope angrily. "Anyway, how did Horace get the lead to the field? I'd like to sort it out before I die. I shan't lie easy in my box if I never know."

Jacob laughed. He broke into the town's dialect now virtually dead and a form of speech Hope still found difficult after sixty years.

"About midnight on that foggy night there were a knock on door, and me mam went. They were all there. Tinker, Gerry, Bert an' Horace. They pushed in and Bert started.

'Us'll bring some stuff in and ye'll sit and keep thy gob shut . . . ye'll sit there by fire, wi' babby, and say nowt. Dost understand madam?' Jacob slipped deeper into the dialect. "Oo sez it to me mam, then turns, an' Tinker comes up to 'er and oo sez the same, only he starts touchin' 'er where he shuddna and then cuffs 'er."

Hope was appalled but not surprised. Tinker Frith's sexual abuse was to fill 1905 with far reaching consequences, not least for himself and Annie. Jacob continued.

"All that neet they brought in lead and climbed ladder to us bedroom until it were full o' sheets o' lead. When it were done they chopped up the ladder and we had a blaze up in the fireplace and they were drinking an' Tinker were frying bacon and talkin' mucky to my mam, and laffin'. Then they went. Tinker gorr'old of me by the throat, and shook us, and touched me where he shuddna, and tells us If ye sez one word Jacob lad, I'll cut thy bobby-fish reet off and eat it mesen. And oo threatened me mam an'all an' she started crying."

Hope offered Jacob his pouch again. Jacob filled his pipe again and Hope noticed he was shaking and then Jacob carried on in a steadier voice.

"Anyhow, every Friday night, when lavender cart set off in the town, Horace called and he used to give me a bag of sweets. He was alright Horace, you know. It were cruel what happened to him."

"Yes," said Hope half to himself. "I've thought that for years."

"Anyhow, Horace used to bring a rope ladder and climb upstairs and bring down a sheet of lead and tek an' put it at the bottom of his lavender cart and then cover it up wi' muck he collected. Nobody saw him. He collected muck in the dead of night. And folks steered clear of the lavender cart! An' he'd tek it to the field. I've no need to tell ye the rest. Ye found it out for thysen!" He gave Hope a look of admiration that took Hope back to that Christmas of 1904 when everyone in the town seemed to greet him with that countenance.

Hope struggled to his feet grimacing at the old pain and the other old man helped him.

“We’ll have a tot of whisky Jacob. I’ve waited sixty years to find out what happened.”

“Well,” said Jacob swigging back the whisky and another that Hope poured, “they can’t touch us now. That’s why I can tell ye. And they all got their comeuppance in the end. Except . . .”

The two men became silent, their inner eye looking back to 1905 and the years before the Great War that changed everything for ever.

TINKER FRITH'S FISH

Roland Frith, 1850-1905. Known as Tinker Frith throughout North Derbyshire, Staffordshire and Cheshire owing to his expertise in repairing kettles and pans. It was inevitable he would be murdered; the fact he survived until 1905 is remarkable.

'Roland Frith 1860-1905,' it should have said on his tombstone if he had one. After his murder he was buried under the west wall of the churchyard with Bert Frith watching with an impassive face and the Reverend Herbert Jones officiating, convinced that another of his flock had descended into Hell and feeling responsible.

As was usual with unmarked burials Herbert Jones placed a cheap wooden cross on the mound of fresh earth. The following year the mound was covered in a glorious riot of buttercups, red clover and ox eye daisies. The next year nettles took over, and the lime trees against the west wall of the churchyard, dropped their nectar and raindrops and autumn leaves and by 1914 Tinker left no trace on the surface of the earth.

He lived in the memory of the town's children until 1940 when other terrors replaced the predatory Tinker Frith. After that date 'the skellington of Tinker's coming to get ye,' was forgotten.

It was inevitable Frith would be killed one day. By whom was not so certain so long was his list of victims who would have killed him if they dared or had chance.

Of his three daughters, two of whom he had routinely sexually abused, two would have killed him. Tilly, his eldest, had been reduced to such a wreck of self and body that she neither had the mind or stamina to kill him. Maisie certainly would, had the chance arisen. Molly, his youngest daughter, would have done likewise; she had fought the old devil off, but she knew his potential.

Beyond the family there was a cook in Wildboarclough whom he had raped on a dark night and she would cheerfully have emptied a cauldron of boiling water or fat over him. A young gamekeeper in Macclesfield Forest had been sexually assaulted by him and he would have strangled the old sod with rabbit snare wire if opportunity arose. A farmer's wife, seduced in a barn by Shutlinglow, thought of rat poison and how she could administer it to the tinker. And John Gratton, whose father had died when John was ten, and who farmed the farm below Sam Walton's, had been raped when he was twelve. John, as he cleared his fields on the edge of the wood to the east of the town, thought of Tinker Frith a great deal as he swung his axe removing sycamore saplings.

The catalogue of those harbouring murderous intent was endless and it was secret. Secret because the women thought their husbands would abandon them, or blame them, and none of them could imagine approaching Glorey or his equivalents in a police station. Men like Superintendent Lomas were too remote and austere, to report a rape to, or forced seduction. A few women, and only a very few, confessed to Annie Harryson and she was likewise restricted by being sworn to secrecy and the inaccessibility of the upholders of the law.

And the men and boy victims were even less likely to approach a police officer and explain their pain and humiliation. Thus it was inevitable that the law would be taken into an individual's hands.

Tinker Frith was seventeen years of age, and a Pedlar in his own right, as his ancestors had been, when the Midland Railway built a line through central Derbyshire from Ambergate to a Manchester link, thus introducing the inhabitants to the shops and goods of Derby, Matlock, Buxton and Manchester. The Age of Shopping was beginning. The Age of Pedlars was dead.

It was no problem to Tinker Frith. He had learned all he needed to know from his father, a Pedlar and a man more quietly sinister than Roland. Tinker Roland simply peddled his wares in west Derbyshire and the Staffordshire and Cheshire moorlands, where the moors and valleys, for the time being, discouraged the building of railways. And when the London and North Western Railway built a line between Ashbourne and Buxton through the heart of his territory, Tinker was beginning to feel his age and stayed at home to torment local people. And his daughters.

Nevertheless he continued his trade right up to his murder in 1905. Trips to the big towns were still a treat and a luxury and there were many women and wives who could not help being fascinated by Tinker's back pack of glittering wares, particularly if they lived in remote farms or hamlets.

For to be honest Tinker had an eye for quality goods and for thieving and bargaining. His pack was full of quality goods from the surrounding industrial towns, lightweight goods that he could carry easily. Small Sheffield silver plate bedroom candlesticks, small silver boxes and silver knives somehow extracted from Sheffield. Then there were small china boxes from Derby, possibly seconds or possibly ill gained, exquisite designs of blue and gold on the china. Likewise delicate blue china jewel boxes from The Potteries surrounding Stoke. A few rolls of muslins and the best cottons from Manchester mills with sprays of rosebuds and forget-me-nots. Fine cotton threads of glowing colours from the Stockport manufacturers; jewel colours for a penny a reel, or free if one allowed Tinker's ever seeking fingers a little licence. And a wonderful collection of vivid square yards of Macclesfield silks. Tinker liked silks; they were light to carry and he produced them with a flourish and some women could not resist them . . . and there were many ways to pay. To women trapped in a farmhouse miles from a railway station, with only a trip to the nearest market town for relief, from onerous toil, a visit from Tinker Frith could not be resisted.

At the bottom of his pack Tinker kept his solder and tools for kettle and pan repair. Despite Derbyshire now having two rail links in 1905, Tinker Frith made a good living and even in his fifties still caused a tremor of fear and pleasure when he made his appearance.

Tinker's father had died in 1867, but by then he had taught his son Roley, as he called him when he was being intimate with him, all the old pedlar ways. The Age of Turnpike Roads had made many old pedlar ways into macadam roads but many of the old trade routes remained, narrow lanes, deeply cut by three millennia of rains, for some of the trade routes had been in use since humans first colonised the county. Down these ways Tinker and his father made their way like weasels under the moon and stars or by sunshine when they were convinced they were unobserved. And Tinker used these ancient ways till the end of his days. Ownership or the law concerned him not at all. Two of the old packways through ducal estates had been stopped and closed a hundred or more years ago, but Tinker and his father followed the old ways evading keepers as adroitly as adders or magpies.

Tinker's father had taught Roland all he knew and this included sexual initiation as well as commercial expertise. The Frith family would have been of great interest to the new science of anthropology, for Tinker's father initiated Roland into some sexual practices unique to the family, that might well have had their roots in a past further back than even the Dark Ages and the coming of Christianity.

Had Freud, alive at the same time, known of the Friths he could well have modified his theories, for it was to be almost a century before lack of conscience, or empathy, was to be considered in personality disorders. Tinker and his father lacked both empathy or conscience and were totally free of sexual guilt.

Darwin and Mendel might have pondered over family traits in the Frith family. Certain dominant aggressive and sexual violent traits had persisted since their life in the wild forests. Yet their sexual adventures had kept their gene pool revitalised by new additions without diluting certain unique elements.

In 1868 Tinker had married Jane Milner. He had forced Jane, not totally unwillingly, into sex behind the Shambles in Sheffield Market. Jane became pregnant and Tinker met his match in her father, a Sheffield butcher, who went after Tinker with a knife and almost frightened him. Tinker was afraid of no other man in his life except his son Bert.

Jane went back to the town and the Frith house, a rambling collection of buildings and stables, animal houses and an unusual number of privies. As soon as one earth lavatory was full another was built and the old one sealed and used for anything convenient - such as pigs of lead.

The Frith dwelling, under a cliff in its own woodland, depressed Jane at once. When the baby was born, Tilly, she slowly declined. During that first year Tinker remained at home a great deal, and it was Annie Harryson's view that when Tinker tired of Jane and having no other outlet, he turned to abusing Tilly the toddler. Certainly something or somebody had damaged Tilly beyond repair.

Tinker resumed his pedlar life style soon after Tilly's third birthday, returning home at All Saints and Halloween, or pig killing time a week later. He remained at home until Lady Day in March, then he made his purchasing and thieving trips to the big towns and cities surrounding Derbyshire. By May Day he was away down the lanes cajoling, terrorising and fleecing women in remote localities and sometimes men with his pinchbeck cufflinks and collar studs and rings.

In the winter months he impregnated Jane with a dozen children of which five survived.

After Tilly, Gerald was the oldest boy and was abused into the family ways as Tinker had been by his father. Gerald accompanied his father in peddling for a time, but soon abandoned it and bought a wagon and horses and became the local carrier, as dangerous a man as his father.

Bert was his second son but Bert, like his sister Molly, seemed more aware of the wider environment. Molly and Bert had to attend the local school as education was now compulsory. Bert and Molly saw how others lived and perhaps something of their Sheffield grandfather made them fight Tinker off when he approached. Education threatened the Frith peculiarities more than anything had for a thousand years and that included the missionaries from Rome.

Maisie, his next child was putty in the hands of Tinker. Yet that did not mean she would not have stuck a knife between his shoulder blades if the chance arose and she could do it undetected.

Horace, Tinker's last surviving child, he left well alone. There was something in Horace that even Tinker could not approach or master.

Such was Tinker Frith's life in 1905. He expected to live and enjoy himself for a great many years more. His end was as sudden as an August thunderbolt.

It was strange that of all the people Tinker had terrorised and abused in the three counties, none feared him more than his second daughter Molly. Puzzling too, as Molly had never been seriously abused by her father although he had tried and certainly touched her in many inappropriate ways and situations; but there had been no sexual act or rape. Maybe Molly's high intelligence and fastidious nature made her keenly aware of her father's potential to harm.

Looking back in her years of solitude Molly could see how the tragedy of her life had developed. Her return to the town in 1901 was her first mistake. But the greatest mistake of all was seeking help from Constable Hope. That had been the turning point that led to everything going wrong.

Molly as a young child had been brave, alert and eager to learn about the world. She sensed, even at the age of four, her father was not of any advantage to her and that his attention was malevolent. At that age she could not have put into words what she felt. It was more of an instinct to avoid her father and not to be alone with him.

Jane Frith, Molly's mother, was certainly aware of her husband's sexual predations on her children; but Jane, like many others at the time, saw no alternative. If she left Tinker there was only the life on the roads or workhouse and the latter would have separated her from her children, particularly Molly, whom she loved dearly in her own inadequate manner.

So Jane Frith kept quiet when Tinker crept into the bed of Tilly or Gerald or Maisie. She simply got on with the one thing she could do, and that was to provide food for Tinker when he was at home in the winter and the children all the year round.

Money was always plentiful. Tinker always left her a tin of sovereigns when he went off on his summertime forays. And Jane, if she could do little else, could make stews with meat and vegetables and meat and potato pies or pasties. Her children even if filthy and abused, were well nourished and physically healthy, perhaps much better than some of the children in the town at that time.

Molly was glad to go to school when she was five. She sensed home was dangerous. The teachers were pleased and amazed at her quickness and aptitude. For the more liberal of the teachers, Molly seemed to be proof that compulsory education for the masses was the right thing.

But it was mixing with other children that saved Molly from her environment. She made friends quickly and some of the more relaxed mothers felt sorry for her, and encouraged her to spend time in their houses. Molly loved that, seeing how other fathers loved and played with their children, watching the mothers perform tasks that her mother never did.

It was when she was seven she began truly to see how different she was. One warm June day after a skipping game in the school yard, John Ramsey was behind her in the line returning to the class. He pinched his nose.

"Molly Frith's drawers are made of kippers," he announced to his friends and Molly was at once given the name of 'Fishcake' or 'Kippers'. Molly was deeply wounded and ashamed but knew the reason. Her mother Jane Frith did not do washing like she had seen other mothers do.

Molly was not the type to suffer in silence. She discussed her problem with Bert, her brother, who was very similar in temperament to her and closest in age. She asked Bert for money and Bert, who knew exactly where his father kept his money, gave her some. He distrusted his father as did Molly and watched him night and day to avoid him. He saw no wrong in robbing his father. Like Molly, he saw his father was a bad father, and that justified his stealing as a punishment. (Even at nine Bert took a great interest in money that persisted all his life. In 1905 he was already banker to the family's criminal income) Molly went to the Monday market and bought a quantity of underwear for herself and Bert. To the amusement and admiration of Mr. James the

Chemist she bought soap and face cloths and toothbrushes and some tins of Gibbs' tooth soap. Bert and herself were never called names again, (Cleanliness was not the main reason Bert was not mocked; he was feared in the playground for his calculated and deadly revenge for insults).

While she was wearing these new underclothes, Molly watched the mothers of her friends very closely on Mondays, which was the wash day in the town.

Bert helped her to collect firewood and they fired up a copper in one of the outhouses. Molly never bothered with ironing, but she saw to Bert's and her own washing.

She and Bert were very close friends. Bert was as keen at school as she was. When she was eight Bert and her discovered an old loft that had been used by a Frith ancestor for some craft purpose, possibly weaving and dyeing. They climbed through a trap door into the loft which had a long south facing window and a large hearth. There was a good oak floor. Molly and Bert made this their special place. Bert, like Molly had a deep instinct to keep distance from his father and saw this den as a retreat.

Eventually they brought sacks stuffed with clean hay and blankets and slept there. They lit fires. It was here they wallowed in books which they both loved. They bought cheap copies of ROBINSON CRUSOE, THE ARABIAN NIGHTS and books by Charles Dickens from the market. Molly liked to read aloud and 'do voices' and Bert could listen to a reading for hours and sometimes their reading went deep into the night.

They played endless games of pirates and desert islands and sailing ships and the loft was their ship. At night they pulled up their rope ladder pretending they were in a tree house in a jungle and they were keeping wild animals away. What they really kept away was their father creeping about in midwinter nights searching for his own sexual gratification.

Molly left school at twelve as did the majority of her school friends and was glad to escape Frith House and go as a scullery maid to a big Hall to the south of Matlock. She learned quickly and by the time she was sixteen she was Cook's and Housekeeper's most reliable maid. Molly could turn her hand to most things. And she had made sure she knew everything about washing and personal hygiene.

When the Cook had a stroke before a big dinner party, it was Molly Frith that took over. The dinner she planned and prepared was the talk of upstairs and not least by a young aristocrat belonging to the Bentinck family. He felt he could solve a problem that had been worrying him for a year or more.

His favourite aunt, Aunt Louisa, lived in the town where Molly had been brought up. He had spent holidays from school there while his parents ruled a province of Burma. The holidays had been his idea of heaven. Louisa Bentinck thought boys went off and had adventures and let him roam far and wide. His aristocratic connections greatly impressed Hornton, and he was allowed freedom of the woods, trout rivers, and fishing became a passion. Derbyshire and Aunt Louisa were the joys of his life.

But the last holiday, when he had come down from Oxford, he had noticed his aunt was beginning to 'lose it'. Talking to Bagehot had alarmed him. Bagehot was convinced that his aunt, like Dr. Ball, had softening of the brain. Bagehot had shocked and upset him greatly by showing him illustrated plates of brains that had 'softened' and shrunk to the detriment of the patient. As the brain 'softened' Bagehot explained, it seemed to develop a strange kind of 'mould'. Nothing could be done to alleviate it said the doctor.

Miss Bentinck's nephew asked to see Molly on the day after the dinner and interviewed her in the morning room after breakfast. His aunt, he explained, needed a young companion to be with her all day. She needed someone to keep an eye on her, organise everything and cook nourishing meals which they would both share. Aunt Louisa needed someone to read to her, help her with her needlework and painting and keep her brain going as long as possible. Bagehot had told him that would help.

The house was small, he said. A regency terrace. Molly knew it well, a double fronted gem of a house with glory roses climbing the wall and next door to Dr. Bagehot's.

Bentinck explained that she would be given a free hand with a monthly allowance and would employ town women to wash, scrub, clean; all Molly would do was to cook and eat with his aunt and read to his aunt, and watch over her. Molly would have a bedroom and a sitting room of her own. There was no room for any other servants but Molly could employ whoever she wanted and would do no menial tasks like washing up or washing clothes.

Molly had, to her own astonishment, missed the town, her friends, her mother and up to a point she missed Bert. She saw herself playing house, shopping in the town in all the smart shops and cooking delicious meals. Molly accepted the post as companion and cook.

She returned to the town in January 1901 on the same train as John Hope and sat in the same carriage.

Looking back Molly saw this was the first mistake. She should never have returned into the evil kingdom, as she called it, of her father.

Realisation of her mistake came over the first months of 1901. At first all went well, very well. She had a small sitting room that faced on to the sunny street, by the side of the front door. It had a carpet and a sofa, and Molly had never dreamed of such luxury. Likewise her bedroom above, this retreat also faced the street. Here she lit a fire every night to undress in warmth and comfort, and bathe by firelight, admiring the two candlesticks on the mantelpiece, and the pot dogs she had bought herself. She felt like a lady and the two rooms enabled her to organise and play at house. The comfort and upper middle class conventions made her think she had made her way in the world, after her peculiar childhood.

It was shopping that gave her the greatest pleasure. She would take a basket on her arm and visit the best shops; many of her friends worked in the shops, and she felt like a visiting lady. Sometimes she would go to Bloomer's Tea Room and have a quick pot of tea, and a vanilla slice brought by Susan Shawe, whom she had sat next to at school. The new life gave her the greatest pleasure. Susan had been one of the girls who had used the name 'Fishcake Frith'.

Of course there was gossip. Ruth Bagley said his Lordship must be crazy to employ a Frith. His Lordship was very well aware of the gossip and the Friths. He kept a close eye on Molly's accounts from the start and found nothing untoward. Moreover his aunt put on weight within weeks from Molly's cooking, and began to make conversation again at mealtimes. Miss Bentinck listened with enjoyment, but little comprehension, to Molly reading from The Times. She looked forward to a reading of Dickens or Thomas Hardy after the evening meal. His young lordship thought Molly the 'bees knees' and would have married her himself if she had come from a different class.

Most gratifying to Molly was meeting the Reverend Jones in the street. He raised his battered hat to her.

"Good morning Miss Frith."

"Good morning sir."

And Molly would walk on with an extra bounce to her already eye catching walk. And the Reverend Jones would smile, for here was Christian Society reforming the lower orders.

One market day in early March, after almost six weeks of bliss, Molly left Miss Bentinck beside a heaped fire in the little drawing room, that looked to the tiny garden, and through a wrought iron gate to the river and meadow. Miss Bentinck had a silver pot of coffee and a silver jug of cream, with chocolate shavings folded into it and a plate of chocolate covered Bath Olivers. The old lady beamed at Molly when she told her she was going shopping and marketing.

"But the rain my dear Lilian! Do take a brolly!"

Sometimes Molly was Molly and sometimes Susan and sometimes Mary but today she was Lilian.

Before going Molly checked that Maisie was scrubbing the kitchen floor properly, and that Mrs. Jackson had all she needed in the little wash house in the corner of the yard. Mrs. Thorpe was polishing silver and then she would clean and black lead the dining room grate for the fire, and Molly would cook a little steak for lunch with a glass of red wine, as Dr. Bagehot had prescribed. "Plenty of cream and red wine my dear. Her old body and brain needs encouragement!"

Rain was sweeping up the Wye valley in gusts on a southerly gale. It was the same pattern of weather that had drenched Constable Hope and enabled Mrs. Harryson to get him into a bath and clean undergarments.

Molly sheltered under a market stall, exchanging rather coarse banter with the cheese factor. His cheese was excellent so she put up with him; and Molly could certainly give as good as she got.

Then she saw her father watching her. He was by Deacons Bank wall sheltering, but she could see him clearly, his bright canine eyes on her, definitely watching. His battered old leather jerkin gleamed rat brown in the rain, and his sodden moleskin trousers added to his mammalian aspect. Even at this distance Molly felt a shiver. All the feelings of danger and fear she had felt as a child seeped back again.

It was the first time she had seen him. She had been to see her mother, taking her a bottle of brandy and a bunch of violets but there had been no sign of her father and she did not ask about him.

From that date she began to slide into a pit of fear that was not totally unjustified. Within a week she had the locks renewed on the back and front door as they were still the original eighteenth century ones, and could be easily picked, she thought.

That autumn of 1901 she began to fold the shutters over the windows at night, something that had not happened in the house for eighty years since the riots in Derby had scared the then occupants.

That winter she would look out of her bedroom window, at the dark street with its moving tree skeleton shadows in gaslight or moonlight, and imagine she could see those eager dog-bright eyes watching for her in the shadows. Most of the time it was her imagination; there were also nights when she perceived reality. Tinker was lurking and watching and waiting.

In the summer of 1902 she persuaded his Lordship they needed a new garden gate that opened on to the riverside path. Molly chose one that barred the entrance and would take a padlock and chain. She had seen the rat gleam of Tinker one stormy night outside the gate and that had not been imagination.

The problem was that she was on her own for much of the night. Miss Bentinck was ready for bed at eight after dinner, and fell asleep once enthroned in her pillows. Molly would retire to her sitting room with a book and try to relax in front of her fire, but was alert to every footfall in the street behind the shutters, every rattle of the shutter in the draught.

In 1904 she had the lock on her bedroom renewed. She had seen Tinker under Dr. Bagehot's lamp with his shining eyes looking up at her window.

By 1905 she was spending an unhealthy amount of time watching from her bedroom. The only comfort she had was on the nights when she saw Constable Hope, on his beat. Hope liked to stand under the horse chestnut tree, that spread its branches over the wall of Dr. Bagehot's garden. There he could see the comings and goings from The Castle Inn, the Queens Arms, traffic such as it was, approaching the Bridge, as well as a vista right into the Market Square, past The Wheatsheaf. It was the best vantage point in the town; watching and waiting as Lomas had taught him.

Molly began to watch and wait for him. His cape shining with rain in winter reflecting the gas lamp, or his face clearly visible in the long June twilights which certainly comforted her evenings. Molly found comfort in him. It never even occurred to her to tell him of her fear or what her father had done. Molly was no different to many women of that time - talking about sexual fears to a man, was undreamed of.

And in any case the shame that it was her own father haunting her, was another hindrance. Molly knew she was on her own with her fears and on her own if her father got to her. Nevertheless the presence of Hope in the street gave her the only true moments of peace in those years before the murder. She did not realise it but Constable Hope was the only man she had felt any flicker of emotion for, except, perhaps, a sisterly affection for Bert. Her father had driven out any thoughts of gaining comfort from a man. Constable John Hope seemed different as he stood under the great tree.

Despite her fear that was growing into terror, Molly did not actually have a confrontation with her father until a spring Thursday in 1905.

Once a month, like many servants at that time, Molly was allowed a day off. As a 'superior' servant she had a whole day instead of the usual afternoon. She usually spent part of it visiting Bert and his family. She used to take a gift to Eddie and Bobby, barley sugar, aniseed balls or humbugs or whips and tops. But it was Phyllis, Bert's five year old daughter, that she really went to see.

Phyllis, the favourite of Bert Frith and the love of his life, was a blonde curled and blue eyed child of the type that Charles Dickens, half a century earlier, would have instantly called an 'angel on earth'. Phyllis had the rosiest of cheeks, caused possibly because she had contracted tuberculosis. Dr. Bagehot had sadly diagnosed this as 'consumption' when Phyllis was three and the child did not recover properly from a bout of winter coughing. Phyllis had now been coughing blood flecks and Dr. Bagehot cursed Fate and inadequate medical knowledge, as the child had somehow contracted a virulent and rapid form of the disease. He sensed that when the child died it would flip Bert Frith into madness and violence that was always ready to erupt in the Friths.

Molly went for her tea on her holiday Thursday, and prepared the child something tempting to eat. Violet, Bert's wife was a competent cook, but it was Molly who had learned how to prepare food for flagging and delicate appetites, that seemed to afflict the rich.

Molly would call at Turners the fishmonger, and buy some Dover Sole. She would lightly fry the fish with some wafer thin crisp potato. She made a buttery sauce with cream and a little white wine left over from Miss Bentinck's previous dinner. Phyllis loved this and dipped in the potato crisps with zest, much to everybody's pleasure.

This particular April Thursday Molly was already on edge. Her brother, Horace, had been sentenced to a long prison sentence and her brothers had been in court. The local paper had reported the case in full. The town had buzzed with talk about it and how clever Constable Hope had been in, his detection of the theft of the church roof lead. Molly kept herself away from such goings-on but secretly wondered how much her father and brothers had been involved. She had never taken to Horace, her younger brother; he had been a child apart, rejecting any of Molly's attempts to mother him, or give him affection. Despite this, Molly felt Horace had taken full responsibility for something he was not totally guilty of. She had tried to tackle Maisie, as she scrubbed the floors, but Maisie had just looked dumb, her eyes wide and blue as the April weather.

Molly had sensed the town was talking about her, and she had lost a little bounce from her usual elegant walk. That morning she had gone on the train to Matlock, and made sure she had a compartment to herself, so nobody would meet or talk. Molly liked Matlock. She felt the shops there were superior, as they catered for the ladies who stayed at the Hydro. She returned with a sky blue bodice and blue skirt and boots and was soothed. After leaving these brown paper parcels in her sitting room she had made her way to Bert's. She was too late for the Dover Sole and bought roe which Phyllis liked too. She took a rather circuitous route to Bert's cottage to avoid being seen and arrived flushed. She told Violet breathlessly she had no Dover Sole.

"Dunna ye worry," said Violet who was fond of her sister in law. "Bert's gone and got some lovely trout and Phyllis loves it the way you do it. Will ye do it?"

Molly nodded but a cold liquid seemed to creep into her veins. Trout was a delicacy for the gentry and aristocracy and it was rarely for sale in the shops. Bert could have only got it by poaching. Poaching did not trouble Molly; it was a sort of game played by working men and the skill was not to be found out. But Molly knew about trout. When she saw the fish on the table she saw two splendid fish that could only have come from the River Dove. His Lordship had brought them many times to the Hall and to his Aunt Bentinck. His lordship was one of the elite who fished in the upper Dove valley.

There was only one man who could have poached these and that was her father. The fact Bert had been talking to her father filled her with foreboding. She had always seen Bert as a barrier against her father. And now he was talking to him. Possibly to get fish for Phyllis, but that made no difference. Molly could not face the idea that Bert was even talking to their father. She had always thought in the last resort; she could come to Bert for help . . . but if he was asking for Tinker's fish . . .

The whole town knew about Tinker's Fish. Tinker Roland would appear in April or October with an ancient leather satchel slung over his shoulder and offer the best trout in the world for sale. Everyone knew they were from the River Dove. Everyone knew they were poached. Yet he was never caught. How and where he caught these prime trout was a mystery. But in spring and autumn he would appear in a side street, in the shadows, and offer, at a price, the delicacy.

If you approached him he would open his bag and pull out the fish with a grin, and what the more sensitive knew was a semi-obscene flourish. Despite that, a few of the more well off paid the high price he demanded for these succulent fresh-water treats. Sir George's manservant bought them and served them to Sir George as a late supper with an imperial pint of champagne.

'Tinker's Fish' was a crude innuendo in the Kings Arms. This was a small inn, a low whitewashed building, tucked behind the houses on the main Manchester road. It was one of the older buildings in the town, and predated the turnpike road, and had existed in the age of pedlars and packhorses. The coming of the turnpike road with its coaching inns had pushed it into a side alley. Yet it flourished with a slightly suspect but loyal and large clientele. Lomas had it in his eye and told Hope to stand a while close by it and just keep his ears open. It attracted a customer that had somehow resisted the Methodist influence in the town and the Victorian prudery that had throttled sexual talk since Regency times. The talk here was often crude and coarse in the low smoke filled tap room. The atmosphere was very different from the farmers' talk in The Wheatsheaf or the good conversation in The Anchor or the radical talk in the Royal Oak led by Green the watchmaker.

"Did ye see Tinker wi' his fish?" would be asked and "Ye mun keep away from that. Ye duuna know where it's been!" Or "Ye dunna know where oo's pulled it out of!" and so on, each allusion filthier than the last. The landlord encouraged such talk. He did an under the counter trade in smutty cards and books.

It was the only inn that Tinker used for pleasure. He sensed maybe, that like him, it was a relic of an earlier age. The men in there knew the old language. Tinker always referred to his penis as his fish, a word dating from Tudor Derbyshire.

When Tinker was murdered, he was not mourned, but he was missed. "A rum bugger, old Tinker," they said, and smoked in silence, recalling his evenings spent with them in the Kings'.

Tinker was a born entertainer. After a few pints he would stand up and sing from a vast repertoire of lewd ballads, dating back hundreds of years. Here the men liked "When Fanny went a-marketing, her lips were sealed in prayer…" a ballad that lasted twenty minutes. NELL'S WELL was another strong favourite. Tinker also had a small leather vagina, a 'Pedlars' Friend' he called it, made from animal skin, with its ancestry dating back to the tribes that the King of Mercia found hard to convert to Christianity. Tinker worked this artefact with one hand, like a puppet. It moved to the music of a whistle made from a bird bone that he played with his mouth and the other hand. The music produced was both sensual and eerie, echoing from the time when modern men appeared after the ice in a tundra speckled hill country.

The men found these performances of Tinker both fascinating and aphrodisiac. Yet a few sensed an undercurrent of something else. Most of the men in the tap room had a great interest in sex and women, but their appetite and lust was mixed with other human emotions such as empathy or loyalty or affection and love. These emotions were unknown to Tinker and not a few of the men sensed the danger of Tinker Frith and his wild performances and appetites.

As did Molly. When she had put Phyllis to bed and told her a story, careful not to make her laugh too much and bring on coughing, Molly prepared to make her way back to Castle Street. Coming out of the cottage and walking down the hill, she saw Bert talking to her father.

Bert nodded to her and thanked her and said there would be some more trout next time. She faced her father, and could smell him and see his animal mask of a face, closer than she had for years. Tinker was triumphant. He had long feared his son Bert and had at last found a way to get into his good books. Tinker knew that Bert was the next leader of the Friths if he was not already. Tinker saw that he now had a little power over Bert, for Bert would do anything for Phyllis.

Molly could feel her father's leer and intention as she walked down Bath Street, and once again her body sagged and this time it was with fear.

For almost four weeks nothing did happen. Then one Monday night in May, Molly, hyper vigilant as she had become, was greatly alarmed.

Miss Bentinck liked Molly to read aloud after the dinner that Molly prepared every night. Molly quite enjoyed this. She had read to Bert when they slept in the loft, and enjoyed making a drama of a book with differing voices. Miss Bentinck had recently slipped back into her childhood tastes, and was working her way through Dickens with David Copperfield and now Oliver Twist. The latter had been a big favourite of Molly and she put a great deal of effort into the reading. There had been a cockney kitchen maid when Molly was a scullery maid and Molly had learned the accent and did the part of Nancy with such effect that Miss Bentinck was still wide awake and entranced at ten o' clock. Molly did not care - she preferred this to being alone with her thoughts and fears in her own little sitting room.

This particular evening, when Molly was in full flight with a savage rendering of Bill Sykes (spiced with her own father's breathing patterns), both her and Miss Bentinck became aware of a tapping deep under the house. Molly looked up from the book and saw that Miss Bentinck had heard the sound under the Turkey carpet.

Molly's first thought was that her father was underground and coming to get her. Before the days of main sewerage, the drains of the town, for the few privileged to be connected, were a great mystery. The poorer dwellings had their privies emptied by the now imprisoned Horace. Any other waste water was simply emptied into the gutter in the street; but the houses of the gentry had more mysterious arrangements. Mrs. Harryson's house had a large drain that took Hope's bathwater away to some deep unknown destination, as did the houses of Castle Street. Some said there was an ancient lead mine deep under the town where everything went. Others spoke of deep tunnels leading to some secret soak away. Certainly the old drains did not lead to the trout river which was clear and unpolluted. There was possibly a system of ancient tunnels beneath the town…

Molly knew this and instantly thought of her father tunnelling beneath the house like a questing sewer rat. Coming to get her . . . Molly had slid into irrational thought patterns like this and she trembled slightly. Miss Bentinck had other ideas.

"My dear Lilian," said she (Molly had been Lilian all that day) "my second cousin the Duke of Portland has reached me at last! He has been making tunnels, you know, for many years at Welbeck, and now the dear boy has reached me!"

Molly smiled wanly at this demented hope. She had heard of this eccentric Duke who lived underground sometime in the last century, and had spent his life constructing an underground network of tunnels beneath Welbeck. She smiled faintly at her employer. The spell was broken and some of her irrationality drained away, and she lit Miss Bentinck's candle and helped the old woman upstairs and prepared her for bed. Content with the thought that the long dead Duke was busy beneath her, Miss Bentinck was soon deeply asleep. Molly returned back to the drawing room. She stood listening. The grandmother clock with its rocking galleon that voyaged with the ticking seconds, made Molly jump violently as it announced the hour of ten. The tapping seemed more insistent and was right under the house, Molly was sure.

She turned down the lamp but left the gas on in the hall but was not quite sure why. Panic was attacking her in a way it had not done before. She went into her bedroom and looked out subconsciously searching for help.

In the days before the First World War and global world trade, the clocks stayed on sun and Greenwich time. It was almost dark but the perpetual twilight of northern England meant that Molly could still see the new horse chestnut leaves on Dr. Bagehot's tree, outlined against the faint light of a summer night. And there, standing beneath it, was Constable Hope.

Molly ran down the stairs lightly. She undid the two locks on the front door and ran out into the street. The gas lamp was lit and she saw Constable Hope turn towards her as he heard the sound of running feet.

"Constable, could you help? I'm the maid at Miss Bentinck's and we've been . . . we think there's someone under the house!"

Hope had been waiting for his beat to end at eleven and go back to bed. He had been on duty from six in the morning till six in the evening with a break for tea and his bath (Mrs. Harryson never failed to have it ready). Now he was on duty from eight to eleven, a day calculated by Glorey to produce maximum inconvenience to Hope. Nevertheless Glorey had some justification for this long day. It was a special May Market and Glorey had employed all his men on full duty. Drunkenness was not uncommon after these spring markets as well as fights for positions by drovers in the mornings. Very little had gone wrong this particular market day. Hope was glad of something to do and followed Molly.

He entered the house and wiped his feet which greatly impressed Molly. He closed the door quietly and stood under the gas and removed his helmet. Molly was even more taken with him. She had seen him when they had shared the same train compartment back in 1901, when they both came to the town, the Sunday before the Queen's death. But then, thought Molly, he had been a pale faced boy. Now he was a man that filled her with confidence and trust. The tapping came again.

Molly saw him give it his full attention and she relaxed a little. Men in the market, the coal man, the butcher's delivery man and her vile father, always looked at her as though they were seeing through her clothes. Hope was polite and obviously out to solve her problem. Molly felt more relaxed and confident with him than she had with any man except her brother Bert, and she had now lost her faith in him as a protector.

“Is there a cellar, Miss, in the house?” said Hope, after a while of careful attention. Molly said there were two, one you got to from the yard, but they never used because in winter river water got in it, and Miss B. had had the door bricked up, and the other one was a wine cellar which you reached from the kitchen.

“Can you take me in it Miss?”

Molly fetched a candle and importantly selected a key from the bunch round her waist and opened the wine cellar door. Holding the candle high, she led the way down a steep curving flight of stone steps until she reached the little wine cellar; just enough room for two people, but they would be touching.

The tapping began again. Louder and metallic. Molly had lost her fear and was just a young woman with a man she liked the look of. She watched him as he listened and looked and studied the floor, ceiling and wine shelves.

Molly had made labels with the help of Dr. Bagehot. “Open a bottle every day my dear. It’ll help her sleep. It will thin her blood and keep fat away from the brain which I fear is part of her condition. Red wine for red meat and white for white meat and fish. Reds for game. You can’t go wrong.”

After a minute or two pressed up to him, she sensed he was puzzled. She watched his every movement and liked what she saw. He was totally absorbed by the noise and seemingly unaware of her, but Molly liked this. She felt safe with him. Imagine if her father caught her or came up down here . . . she shivered.

The shiver made Hope look at her for a brief moment. She saw him take out a good silver Geneva watch. She knew all about gentlemen’s watches and she polished his Lordship’s when he came to stay. She was surprised an ordinary bobby had such a good silver watch.

She watched him take out his notebook and resting it on an empty shelf make a note of the time and date and noise. Molly admired his writing. There was also something else about him that reminded her of his Lordship and she was some minutes tracing it. Then she knew. It was his smell. The Constable smelled like his Lordship. Shaving soap, hair oil and soap from a bath and clean laundry. Again quite different from the men who usually pressed against her. Molly had been aware of smells and odours since that day at school the boys had called her 'fishcake'.

"Right Miss," said Hope. "It's a puzzle. But we'll keep an ear on it. Any trouble just come round to Mrs. Harryson's and I'll come."

Molly led the way back up the steps with a return to her usual latent sway and curve in her climbing, but Hope was taking a last look round the cellar. Molly let him out, thanked him and turned down the gas. The tapping had stopped. She went to double check the doors and windows and feeling more cheerful, went upstairs. She went to the box room that looked over the little yard and garden to the river. Through the wrought iron of the gate to the river bank she saw the shadowy form of Constable Hope. Molly slept more soundly that night than she had for months.

Hope settled himself on the cool grass riverside path outside Miss Bentinck's wrought iron gate. There was a big clump of yellow iris to conceal him. Hope could not help sighing as he made himself comfortable. It had been a long day. Despite this he wanted to solve the source of the mysterious noise. Fully alert he stared through the dark amethyst twilight. He was rewarded by two taps that carried over the faint chuckles and gurgles of the river. It was not from underground at all. It was from the iron bridge that led to the now increasingly chaotic lavender fields. Peering through the faint yellow lamps of the iris, he heard a man's low voice utter some angry words which he could not catch.

He saw a shadow move from the bridge and then all was left to the short simmer night, the night sounds of the coots and moorhens and ducks. Hope stayed on the grass until he heard the faint chimes of eleven from All Saints. Then he went home to bed after he had written up his usual notes.

Next morning he made it his business to walk across the bridge. Despite the fresh May morning there was already a whiff of excrement in the air. Bert had employed men to take over Horace's collection but they merely collected the night soil and left it in a pile.

Trying to concentrate on the bridge Hope could see absolutely nothing amiss. The bridge seemed its usual sturdy iron self. Trout swam in the emerald weed in the river where the white globe flowers of water crowfoot made the river more beautiful than ever. Swallows swooped around him. The gold of the buttercups on the river bank made his pupils retract almost painfully with the golden shimmer. There was nothing to reveal what the noises were, or why they were happening. Slightly annoyed that he had not spotted anything, Hope resumed other tasks.

It was not surprising that Hope could see nothing amiss. Tinker Roland was at work and Tinker was a match for any young constable.

Tinker Roland Frith, despite his sexual obsessions and violent lusts, was a man of great knowledge and skills. He had learned these from his father in the manner of all the generations of the Friths. It was a frustration to Tinker that he could not pass any of these skills to Gerald his eldest son. The railway and social change indicated these skills would die with Tinker. And Tinker mourned the passing of them.

Gerald had been a curious and willing participant in Tinker's sexual abuse and experimentation and initiations. But he had shown no interest in peddling, poaching, living off the land and cooking over a fire under moon and stars.

Tinker, certainly no fool, knew that it was no good approaching Bert. Bert made it perfectly clear he wanted nothing from his father. Except in the last weeks. Tinker saw that the way to Bert was through Phyllis. Phyllis needed delicacies usually reserved for the gentry. Tinker could provide any specialities such as trout that Phyllis fancied. So began a relationship between father and his second son, that Tinker was going to exploit to the utmost.

It was Molly's next Thursday visit that week, and Bert wanted trout. It was a month since Molly's last visit and Phyllis was off her food again and coughing and Bert hurt about this. Bert knew that Molly knew exactly how the gentry had their trout cooked and he wanted the trout cooked like that by Molly. Molly knew exactly how things should be. Tinker, however desperate for Bert's approval, knew that poaching in the Dove was right out of the question as high summer approached. The keepers guarded it night and day. Tinker considered another possibility. He thought Hornton and Smeaton fools, and in a way he was right. He felt, that for Bert, he would have a try at outwitting them. It was against his instincts to poach at this season, but to get the approval of Bert was important for him. Tinker knew these trout were not as fine as those from the Dove but he sensed the little girl would not discern the slightly inferior flavour. He was prepared to show Bert how he caught the trout, show his son a family secret that was generations old.

Tinker had sensed for a week or two that Bert would be wanting trout for the sickly Phyllis and thus told Bert that he could get her trout any time-and show Bert how to do this. So on a dark and windy night, Tinker had crept along the iron bridge to the Lavender Field lane like a cautious rat, and made wooden pegs to fit the ornamental holes, part of the pattern in the bridge. The bridge had a pattern of perforations as well as much rusted bolts and rivets weathered by over a hundred winters.

The following day Tinker made his way to Sheffield, twenty miles by the old lanes. He scorned the system of the turnpikes. Following the way his ancestors went he climbed through the woods to Walton's farm then down to Pilsley and Baslow by a sunken lane overarched with old trees. Climbing high on the moors above the modern road, he slipped along Fox Lane like a sinister swimming snake through the foam of Queen Anne's Lace, down to Millthorpe and up to Fanshawe Gate. He knew a farmer's wife here, fascinated and sympathetic to some of Tinker's appetites. She was disappointed that after tea and bread and bacon, he took what he wanted from her within three minutes standing behind the pig sty door. He was in Sheffield by noon calling in favours from a Little Mester on Castle Hill. The man made him some rivets to match the wooden ones Tinker had brought. Tinker made sure they used old iron to match the corroded iron of the bridge. He was back in the town by nightfall and spent the night in Maisie's bed.

Tinker had a vast store of skills and knowledge, but already the modern world was overtaking him. In the last week the weather had turned much colder and Tinker had not allowed for the contraction of metals. When he tried to hammer in the rivets to hold his trout net they would not fit.

Tinker was as agitated as a trapped stoat. Bert, who was with him, had lost his temper and had tried to hammer in the rivets for a long time against all his father's instincts. That was the sound that had resonated through the earth to funnel up in the cellar of Miss Bentinck, which seemed a natural amplifier for the tapping. Tinker danced and scuttled in the dusk on the bridge, out of sight, only his silver ear ring shining like a malevolent crescent on the willows.

"Leave it lad! Leave it! I'll get ye new'uns tomorrow. It's only Monday. I'll get ye some tomorrow and we'll have 'em in place tomorrow neet! Us'll get 'em Thursday morning early, ready for our Moll to cook for little Phyllis . . . Leave it lad!"

But Bert would not. He hammered and tapped for a long time. Hope, coming to crouch by the iris heard his final two attempts at hammering in the rivets. Tinker had long vanished into the shadows gibbering filthy oaths. Tinker never allowed his temper to foul his plans for anything.

Tinker was as good as his word and slipped along the lanes to Sheffield not even stopping for the specialities of the flesh that he so craved. It was cold north westerly air and Tinker wore his winter cap of rabbit skin. And on the Tuesday night Bert and Tinker were back on the bridge. Or at least Bert was, for Tinker hid in the willows.

Hope had returned, on several occasions, even if he were not on duty, at the same time to the iris, on the chance of hearing or seeing something. Molly had seen him and was glad. This time he saw Bert Frith hammer something into the bridge but this time with ease. The sounds were hardly audible.

Then he could not see what Bert was doing for the night was cloudy. Bert was lowering a net fastened to the rivets, but the dim light and Tinker's old magic meant Hope discerned nothing except Bert leaning over the river.

The trout net was ancient craft and magic. Tinker had spent time, cross legged in front of his camp fire and a midwinter blaze in Frith House, fashioning this net from the finest Macclesfield silk thread. The colours were interwoven to fool the casual observer, and even the skilled one. Gold and silver threads were intermingled with browns and greens and here and there a sparkle of blue and there a few knots of white for foam. The mingling of colours fooled the human eye as skilfully as a conjuror's manipulation. The net was made to imprison the larger fish letting the other ones escape. It was big enough to billow out in the river and keep the trout swimming within its confines, without panic. It had never failed.

Hope heard Bert mutter as though to himself "Thursday morning at two," but Hope could see nobody else, and when he was sitting at Mrs. Harryson's table with his notebook he wrote that down. He was not aware of the cunning Tinker merging with the willows' deeper twilight.

The next day, Wednesday, Hope had a twelve hour day in the town; Glorey considered Wednesday a quiet day, and not finding any long distance trails for Hope, was content to let him patrol the town.

Hope walked across the iron bridge several times but saw nothing. Tinker's rivets blended perfectly with the iron rivets of the bridge and staring down into the gold and silver sparkle of the water, Hope could see nothing different. A greater number of large trout were swimming around the emerald weed and brown and gold pebbles, but Hope saw no relevance there. Smeaton, seeing him looking came and joined him. He saw nothing untoward and was rather pleased at the number of trout swimming in the current downstream of the bridge. Hope said nothing. In his four years as a constable he had learned that other people, with the possible exception of Allen, just ruined investigations.

After his bath he announced to Mrs. Harryson he had business to attend to during the night. She never asked questions unless Hope discussed a problem with her; Hope gave her no indication of what he was about so she did not ask.

"Well, Mr. Hope, I shall still be up until early morning. I've letters to do. I'll get you coffee and a bacon sandwich before you go."

Hope wondered what she wrote about and to whom. He knew she wrote to a lot of women in London, he had seen the postmark on incoming letters for her and had posted sometimes ten or more letters at a time for her if he was passing the post office box. For some reason she liked her letters to be posted at the Post Office and not the small box in the street wall opposite the house.

Hope slept in his shirt and trousers in the deep chair until she awoke him at one. She fried bacon and put it between thick slices of her fresh bread. She ground some coffee beans and made a jug of coffee, the smell of the hot water poured on the fresh grounds was a smell Hope associated with Annie Harryson till he died.

She gave him a large cup and swirled in cream and then a generous measure of rum.

"The porters at Covent Garden in London have this to keep them going through their night," said she, smiling. "It'll do the same for you." Hope wondered how she knew about the market in London.

The coffee and rum revived him and by two he was by the iris clump just as light began to seep into a cold dawn. He was unprepared for what happened next. A robin in Miss Bentinck's plum tree began to sing. Then a thrush sang in Dr. Bagehot's damson tree with such power and force that Hope was astonished. Within five minutes a forceful chorus of hundreds of birds in the gardens was making the air shake. Although he kept his eyes on the bridge Hope was amazed. It was the first time he had heard the intensity of the birds' dawn chorus.

By four o'clock it was losing some of its volume and power and Hope heard the bell of All Saints' chime. And nothing had happened.

As the chorus dwindled so did Hope's expectations. When All Saints announced the fifth hour of the day Hope was glad he had involved nobody else. Yet he stayed. He began to think of going back and getting some breakfast. Usually if Mrs. Harryson heard him, she would come down and see what food he wanted.

At half past five by the Church bell he thought he heard angry voices. But this could mean nothing. Already he had heard two horse and carts setting off on early work. Then he saw Bert Frith on the bridge muttering to himself, in great anger it appeared.

"Ruddy stupid old arsehole . . . if he thought of our Phyllis he'd leave his cock alone and wake us up as he said."

What happened next put this vituperation out of Hope's mind and he did not write it down at the time, for Bert began hauling up leaping trout as if by magic. So astonished was Hope by this seeming trick, so hypnotised by the fish that seemed to leap and fly between the bridge and water, and yet were pulled ever higher by invisible forces, that Hope did nothing for several seconds.

Only when Bert Frith had a small pile of dead trout on the bridge did Hope rear up from behind the iris. And it was not without some fear in the pit of his stomach. He reached for his whistle but he was not sure who would help him so early in the day.

Bert Frith was not aware of Hope till he heard his boots on the bridge.

"Bert Frith, I'm arresting you for poaching and robbery of his Lordship's fish," said Hope. He marched towards him and was genuinely scared Frith would have him in the river. Hope could swim, it had been part of his training in Derby, but he knew Bert to be a strong man and there was nobody about. Frith could get him face down in the river and drown him and nobody would be wiser. Hope's body would be found later and Frith would have gone back with his fish. Hope's wildest fantasies could not have predicted Bert Frith's next move. The pupils of Hope's eyes were dilated as he anticipated a charge from Frith or a sudden blow.

"Ye can put them bloody things away," said Bert Frith, nodding at the handcuffs dangling from Hope's hand. "I'll come."

Bert was a long time sorting the net and putting the fish inside. Hope began to think he was being taken for a ride, but eventually Bert got to his feet looking Hope full in the face with such scorn and hatred, that Hope almost flinched. There was a strength in Bert Frith that made him the most unpredictable and successful of the Frith Gang. Not averting his own gaze, Hope felt the danger and realised this was the true power behind the Friths. Yet, as Hope confronted him with an aggression that masked a deep fear, he prayed Frith did not sense it, but he feared he did. It made Frith's attitude all the more sinister.

"You'll walk in front of me," said Hope, "with your hands clasped behind your back and you will accompany me to the Station by the way I tell you."

To his surprise Frith did this. Hope carried the net and fish, and the two men walked through the clover and buttercups to the gate and Hope directed him over the great stone Bridge and through the town market square, avoiding narrow streets and escape routes.

The town was stirring. For many it would be a six o' clock start. Girls and a few men walking to Arkwright's cotton mill, were greatly diverted by the sight of Bert Frith, hands behind back, followed by Hope with a seemingly invisible net of fish. Farm labourers on foot to farms outside the town saw the same enjoyable spectacle.

But it was a wagon load of quarrymen on their way to Darley Dale who began the cheering.

"Hey up Bert! Tha's met thy match wi' that bobby. Now he's got thy fish in his hands that's thee done for!" The wagon went on its way rocking over the market cobbles with ribald jeers about letting your fish fall into the hands of bobbies.

There were jeers and shouts around the Square after the quarrymen had set the example. This was a change in tempo and mood within the town. Two years ago nobody would have dared to shout at Bert Frith in such a situation. By nightfall all the town knew Hope had outwitted Bert Frith and Hope's stock rose considerably.

Yet . . . just as 1905 was the year the Kaiser began plotting events that would lead to Hell in 1914, so was Bert Frith so humiliated that, in that same year 1914, he would exact a long thought out revenge on Hope. But that was far away in the future… The summer sunlight arrived in the Square and flooded it with warm golden light.

Glorey usually entered the Station in blustering majesty at six. It was only a few minutes to six, and Hope, without revealing too much pleasure knocked loudly on Glorey's station house door. Glorey flung open the door with temper, flecks of shaving soap quivering on his jowls and his vast belt undone and waving round his legs like a black snake hovering with intent.

At that moment Lomas rounded the corner, majestic in formal cap and superintendent's great coat, earlier than usual, his focus on some letters that had been on his mind during the night. Glorey did not see him.

"Bloody hell, Hope. Couldn't it have bloody waited? Go and handcuff the bugger to Lomas's cart wheels until I'm ready." He handed Hope a key.

"Good morning Sergeant," said Lomas. "I hope I did not hear the instructions to the Constable I thought I heard. Suspected prisoners have their rights and dignity until proved guilty."

"Aye, er no, sir," said Glorey hoisting the errant serpentine belt and adjusting his massive trousers. "I just said, sir, Frith must cool his heels in the yard while I quickly get ready."

"Hurry up then Sergeant," said Lomas crisply. "I have much to do. And what are your plans for Constable Hope today?"

"Well sir, there was a break in at Rowsley Station so I was sending him there this morning . . . it's four miles . . . but he's used to doing it."

"I am sending Constable Hope back to his lodgings till noon. The man has clearly been up half the night. I have telephone calls to make once I have to write three letters and these can be done at your desk. I will take over your duties till noon and you will take over the Constable's. There is no bicycle available as I want Constable Allen to cycle to Matlock with a legal document. Dismiss Sergeant, and make yourself decent, man."

During this pantomime Bert Frith secreted two prime trout inside his jacket's inner pockets. Phyllis would not go without. And his plan seemed to be working.

"You have waited patiently, Mr. Frith," said Lomas. "I shall ring Major Bunyan to convene a special police court sitting this afternoon and I shall commend your acceptance of arrest and patience while the Force sorted out their routine affairs."

Bert looked at him with a face impassive as the stone carving of a demon gargoyle that emptied water from All Saints' spire. Hope led him to a cell for the morning. Glorey did the Rowsley walk which nearly killed him; and had not some gangers on the railway at the Station not given him a can of hot sweet tea the walk might well have finished him off. He returned with palpitations and rage.

The special sitting of the Police Court commenced at two in the afternoon. Lomas and Major Bunyan were anxious to convict Bert Frith before he had time to plan evasions and excuses. Both remembered how they had been outwitted by the theft of the Church lead. Both men were aware Bert Frith had been involved in the theft of the lead, but Horace had been made the scapegoat.

Bunyan regarded Frith as though he were a bad smell, as Lomas, punctilious and fair to the extreme, told the Court that Frith had accepted arrest, and had been compliant in his detention in the Station. Sunshine, made dusty by the Court windows, lay in molten slabs on the chocolate brown windowsills. Bluebottles circled the gas lights. Bunyan never relaxed his stare from the accused.

Frith pleaded guilty without reservation.

"Do you wish to say anything before we sentence you?" asked Major Bunyan even more short tempered than usual.

"Sir," said Frith, unctuous to the limit. "I know I have done wrong stealing from his Lordship's river, but you see, sir, I have a little lass back in my cottage, sir, that is suffering, sir, from an illness that will one day kill her, sir."

Frith stopped here with what appeared to be genuine emotion. Major Bunyan stared at him, intently, with that penetrating focus that his soldiers, when he served in Afghanistan in the 1880's knew so well.

Major Bunyan could spot trouble six miles away. What to some men had appeared as specks on the mountains, Bunyan knew to be rebels. Bunyan also used that gaze when listening to his soldiers. He had an ear for what he termed 'dumb indolence' and 'silent insubordination'. Bunyan detected several things now, as he regarded Bert Frith.

Bert Frith blew his nose loudly on a rag. Molly had taught him to do that when they were at school, and had learned it was better than your hand or sleeve, Tinker's method of nasal voiding. There was a long pause. The bluebottles took off from the gas lamps and dived and veered towards Frith. The two trout concealed in his inner pockets caused them to buzz in the heat, as loudly as the first planes were doing at that time. Crazed with heat and thirst and the odour of river fish, one bluebottle made an emergency landing in front of Bunyan, who swatted it with speed and accuracy. The bang from A GUIDE TO HER MAJESTY'S JUSTICES OF THE PEACE seemed to rouse Bert Frith from his possibly genuine emotions. He resumed.

"My Phyllis, sir, needs delicacies that I cannot afford, sir. I know that God has made me a poor man, sir, and I am not supposed sir, to have such things as trout, sir, but with my little girl coughing blood, sir, I forgot myself, sir, I forgot the station that God placed me in and took the trout for her . . ."

Major Bunyan had thought he detected lies, insubordination and insolence. Bunyan was a man who saw the world in simple rules and design, He was about to send Frith for a short sharp shock to Derby Gaol. He suspected Frith was mocking God and Society as well as the Court. But his own sister Fanny had died of consumption when Bunyan was ten. He had loved her as much as Frith loved Phyllis. He had watched this sister cough blood into a white lace handkerchief as they had played in the garden. Like Frith, when Phyllis died, a large part of his emotional corpus died when she did, and only a painful scar tissue remained. Bunyan could not even bear to think of the dead sister.

Bunyan snapped.

“I shall fine you fifty shillings. Next time you will be sent to prison. Fine to be paid in seven days. Dismiss.”

It was a hefty fine, two weeks wages to many in the town.

And Bunyan left the Bench. Lomas wondered at his facial expression. The Major looked almost tearful. Frith’s face registered nothing.

Molly had been to Matlock on her day off as usual, and on the red plush train seat beside her were the usual presents, including a doll for Phyllis. She looked out as the train approached the town. The town, set in its hills, always looked its best as the train approached it from the south, and Molly reflected that she was lucky to have such a good job in her favourite place in the world . . . if only her father were not around her . . .

She walked down the lane from the station with the hedgerows draped in may blossom, the field full of buttercups and a cuckoo shouting to her from the woods. Her spirits rose. Crossing the Bridge she saw Smeaton and Hornton in animated talk on the distant iron bridge. Entering Bridge Street she saw Ellie Slater who worked at the Mill.

“Moll . . . Moll!” she was breathless. “They’ve took your Bert! When us were going to work this morning, us saw Bert wi’ that big new bobby, tha knows the one that Annie Harryson keeps close by ’er,” (here a sly grin spread over Ellie’s face) “anyway, he had arrested your Bert an’ he’s been in Court.”

Molly said little, but hurried on pale faced. She hated this sort of gossip about her family and she was surprised at Bert. She could only think her father had been involved in some way. She knew nothing would come but trouble if Bert got friendly with their father.

At the cottage all seemed normal but there was a cold atmosphere. Molly did not ask Bert what had happened and he volunteered no details of his day. Both Bert and his wife watched Molly prepare the trout with more than usual interest. It became apparent why when Molly was preparing to leave.

"Don't bother coming again, Sis," said Bert, on her way out. "It's you and your big mouth that's got us in bother today. I know you've been sniffing round that fancy bobby, takin' him down into your cellar to listen . . . So dunna ye come again. Ye'll not be welcome."

Molly brushed by her father who was grinning at the gate of the little garden. Tears were smarting in her eyes. Bert was her only hope against her father.

Tinker Roland smiled to himself. He saw yet another chance to ingratiate himself with Bert. He would teach his daughter a lesson. She'd always been a little madam, a vixen and he'd teach her a thing or two. In the language of Tinker's crooked and malformed personality, teaching a woman a lesson meant a sexual assault. He'd sort her out for Bert.

On the last Sunday in May Tinker Frith padded down the riverside path to the garden door of Miss Bentinck's garden. He picked the lock with speed and efficiency and was in the back garden under the apple blossom. Molly had not been served well by the blacksmith and whitesmith's apprentices when they had fitted the new ornamental gate and lock. They had been more interested in Molly than locks and bolts.

Tinker stealthily approached the kitchen where Molly was working, preparing a roast leg of lamb for Sunday lunch. The kitchen was full of the aroma of roasting lamb, mint and rosemary. Molly was rubbing salt into the joint to crisp it when she looked up and saw her father at the door grinning his manic grin.

Molly began to make a soft noise like a sleeping dog having a bad dream. When the realisation of a nightmare is achieved, a paralysis of mind and body cripples the will. She felt her legs weaken almost to giving way and letting her crumple to the floor. She managed a hoarse "get out father." Tinker moved forward again with that idiotic grin that was peculiar to him alone. He undid the flap on his moleskin breeches and began exhibiting himself.

It was an oddly puerile and curiously pathetic action, although Molly, terrified, did not, of course, see the stunted child in her father, still showing off like some precocious boy obsessed by his infantile discovery of sex. Molly felt herself sway and her breakfast rise in her throat and she heaved and vomited at what she saw.

Tinker was content to let this demonstration of his sexuality continue for some minutes, for it had always been a black hole in his sexual approaches, that he thought if he showed himself off his victims would give in to his lusts. This lack of understanding saved Molly in this first attack.

With supreme effort she launched herself into action and picked up the razor sharp knife that she had been chopping mint with for the mint sauce. She slashed her father's cheek from under his eye over the cheekbone and down to the corner of his leering mouth.

He screamed like a trapped stoat with snare wire round its neck, and with the blood spurting on Molly's white scrubbed kitchen table, he picked up the roasting tin with its scalding fat and sizzling lamb and hurled it at his daughter. It missed but hit the dresser and burning fat sprayed Molly and her father.

Howling, Tinker ran from the kitchen. Blood rivulets ran down his leather jerkin and on to the daisies and plantains of the grassy waterside path. He raced round to the main street and hammered and kicked and screamed outside Dr. Bagehot's door as uninhibited as a four year old.

Winny McGuire Dr. Bagehot's housekeeper, opened the door and fainted. Bagehot, who had been enjoying coffee and THE LANCET came out and yelled for Treeton his new assistant.

Dr. Treeton revived Winny while Bagehot propelled Tinker into his surgery. Splashes of Tinker's blood punctuated the eighteenth century tiles leading to the surgery.

"Calm down man," said Bagehot, none too kindly. He had been told nothing good about Tinker by Annie Harryson, who had said she would poison the old devil, given chance, for all the unreported sexual attacks he was guilty of.

"Calm down damn you! . . . That'll need stitching. I charge a guinea."

This was possibly the first time in Bagehot's long years of practising medicine that he had announced he would expect payment before treatment.

Moaning, and much to Dr. Bagehot's later amusement, when he thought about it later over his whisky, Tinker took a sovereign from the depths of his blood spattered moleskins and gave it the Doctor. Bagehot noticed the front flap of his trousers was undone.

"Close yourself up man. How the hell did you come by this?" He asked Tinker this question approaching with wadding and a big brown bottle of carbolic acid. Tinker screamed like a pig being killed as the Doctor pressed the wad soaked with carbolic to his face. He tried to hold Frith still, but was unsuccessful. Tinker writhed like a trapped reptile.

"I fell into a blackberry bush catching rabbits!" he screamed.

Dr. Treeton came in. Winny was sipping brandy in the kitchen and much recovered. She was used to receiving bloodied and battered patients but the sight of the infamous Tinker Frith had been too much for her. Treeton held Tinker in the vice like grip of a young man and Bagehot staunched the blood and clipped the flap of flesh.

He did the first stitch without giving Tinker any pain relief. Dr. Treeton looked at him in amazement. He had only been with the Doctor for a month, but had come to respect him greatly, he had not expected such brutal lack of concern for a patient.

"Now I've started Treeton," he said "fetch me the ether and pads and the morphine."

Dr. Treeton knew better than to ask why there had been a delay and to ask why the patient had suffered.

After half an hour Tinker was out in the sunlit street with a scar on his cheek neatly stitched. He slunk off to the deep shade of a willow thicket near to Horace's abandoned lavender field, and spent the afternoon whimpering and scheming in the dappled shades.

It did not even enter Molly's head that she should complain of her father's attempt at raping her. She could not even begin to imagine explaining it to any man. She thought of the scandal it would cause if the incident was reported in the town. She did not even begin to think of reporting it to a court. If she had, the certainty that she would lose her job in the ensuing scandal would have prevented her from saying anything in public.

She locked the back door and drank some brandy that was kept in the kitchen for when she made Miss Bentinck her lemon syllabub.

After half an hour she began mechanically to resume her tasks. She picked up the lamb joint and salted the skin again. She piled coal on the fire of the range till it roared like a furnace to crisp the meat.

She cleared up her father's blood and was violently sick. After that she felt a little better.

Lunch was served precisely at one by the chime of the grandmother clock in the dining room. The lamb had recovered. The fresh peas were cooked to perfection and the new potatoes gleamed with mint flavoured butter and chives chopped with the knife that had cut her father's cheek to the bone. The white damask curtains of the little dining room were illuminated with the May sun and a gentle breeze wafted the lace curtains. A silver jug of lilies of the valley scented the warm air. Miss Bentinck sipped Burgundy with the contented smile of the unaware innocent.

For once Molly ate nothing and hardly spoke. Even the misted perception of Miss Bentinck discerned all was not well and she noticed the little red spots of burned skin on Molly's pale cheeks.

"Why my dear Mary," said she. "You have the measles and are not well. You must go round to Bagehot directly after the meal."

Usually Miss Bentinck forgot what she had said five minutes ago, but something stirred in her today and she insisted Molly went next door and even stood in the front door to see she did.

"I've splashed myself with hot fat, doctor," said Molly.

Dr. Bagehot examined her cheek or pretended to. He took her pulse. He felt the tremor and detected the harshness of her breath tainted with vomit and alcohol. He felt the tremor and saw the pale face. The usually radiant young women had suffered more than burning fat.

"Is that all Molly?" he said kindly. "Do you want to tell me anything else?" He repeated this in the most gentlest tones.

Molly shook her head and the Doctor could see there were tears in her eyes.

"Well," he lied. "I cannot really give you anything for those burns. You need to go round to Nurse Harryson. She has all sorts of wonderful salves and creams that will stop any scarring of that lovely clear skin of yours. Now, Molly, when you are feeling a bit better, promise me you will go round to Mrs. Harryson's and tell her exactly what happened with the fat. Winny will keep an eye on Miss B. Just tell her when you are going. And it must be today. "Promise?" he asked softly.

Molly nodded and Dr. Bagehot saw a tear run down her cheek. But it was after tea before Molly could face telling Annie Harryson what had happened.

The May sun had disappeared behind the hills to the west of the town and the streets were in shade before Molly could rouse herself. The quiet Sunday evening streets suited her mood. She did not wish to be observed.

Mrs. Harryson's door was ajar and Molly could see into the large room before she knocked. She saw Constable Hope stretched out in an armchair at one side of a freshly lit fire and Mrs. Harryson at the other. Both were laughing at some shared joke. She could see the Constable in his shirt sleeves after returning from Evensong at the Church. He had obviously been enjoying supper after his singing for which he was now noted throughout the town. There was a young white Derbyshire cheese on the table, crumbling where it had been cut, a jar of Mrs. Harryson's damson chutney, a pile of freshly baked teacakes speckled with currants and peel, and a butter dish with the deep golden butter of early summer. Hope had a half empty tankard of ale on the edge of the table near to his chair.

Molly at once felt a sense of loss and exclusion. What Ellie Slater had said was right. This man was Annie Harryson's. She knocked hesitantly.

Annie Harryson was out of her chair in an instant and by her side. She took one of Molly's hands.

"Why, Molly . . . whatever is the matter? Come right through, this way . . ."

And Hope heard the door click after them as Annie took Molly into the room at the back, a room she used for private discussions. And now it was Hope's turn to feel suddenly excluded from Annie Harryson's attention that he so deeply appreciated.

Molly told Annie everything.

Annie held both of Molly's hands in her own until the end of the story and then put her arms around Molly.

Molly, now relieved of the tension and repression began to sob wildly. Annie held her close.

"Molly . . . Molly . . . we've got to stop him . . . he's been up to this with women for years and even . . . well, never mind that now. Molly, let me bring in Constable Hope, he's such a kind and gentle man. Let us tell -"

Molly's shuddering shame and fear and pain flipped into hysteria.

"No Annie! No! No! . . . No! . . . I couldna bear it . . . the Court . . . you saw how that swine of a lawyer treated our Maisie . . . I dunna want to tell a soul . . . it was bad enough when our Maisie were up in court, folks laughing, and pointing, grinning behind my back . . . and then our Horace, No! Annie no!"

She began to gulp for air and her body shook. Annie tried stroking her hair and wrists but the hysteria grew.

"And before he threw the fat, some of his stuff went on my arm." Here Molly began a terrible dry retching, and Annie was afraid she was going to have a fit, or seizure, but she dare not leave her to fetch some sedative herb mixture.

"It's got in me through my skin . . . it'll make his baby -"

"No, love," said Annie cradling the shuddering Molly. "Babies are never made like that. Never in a thousand years."

But Molly would have none of it. The hysteria now took full control of Molly and she began to scream.

"But he's the Devil and not . . . like other men . . . get rid of it Annie! Get rid of it Annie! You know how! Get rid of it . . ."

The words were screamed over and over again.

Hope, stretched out before the fire, in the scent of wood smoke, and lilac from a jug on Annie's desk, heard these cries.

And he became very still, with a sudden realisation. Mrs. Harryson was like Mother Turner, who had lived three streets away from his home in Derby, and had been taken by the police and jailed for getting rid of unwanted babies.

Now it was Hope's turn to feel sick. Surely not . . . Not while she had a bobby living in the same house . . . unless that had been a plan . . . yet she was a respectable woman, a trained nurse, somebody had told him she had trained in the big hospital in Derby . . . and yet . . . Mother Turner had got rid of hundreds of unwanted babies . . . some women needed such services even if they were breaking the law.

But the screams continued.

A terrible dread clamped itself on Hope's well being and serenity. Surely not. God forbid . . . that would ruin everything in their lives.

Annie knew she should slap Molly but could not after all the girl had suffered. Instead she reached for a large pestle she used for her herbs and brought it down with a crash on the table.

It worked. Startled, Molly's screaming turned to quiet weeping.

Annie quickly mixed something out of a cupboard she unlocked and made Molly drink it. Within minutes Molly was breathing normally.

"Oh Annie . . . I am so tired, so very tired."

Annie took control as she always did with the problems of the women around her.

"I'm coming to stay with you for a time. I shall tell Miss B. you have measles. She said so herself! There's plenty of room in Number Two and no way are you going to be left alone while that madman swine of a father is in the town. We'll go back now, I'll get you some soup and a bath with some of my herbs in it to wash things away. Trust me, that's all it will need. I'll get some stuff that will give you a good night's sleep. Now, my love, come along."

"My word, Mr. Hope," said Annie, "you look as if someone has walked over your grave. Now, I'm staying with Molly for a bit. You'll get your own breakfast tomorrow but after that there'll be different women in to see to you as usual. You will not starve, Constable. You must be looked after. (Hope detected sarcasm but did not know how to respond) I don't know when I'll be back."

Hope stared at her, his dark imaginings suspended for a time. There was a chill in her voice and a cold anger that he had not seen in her before. Had he not been in his chair he would have backed away from her, so powerful was the cold fury.

This was the beginning of a change in Mrs. Harryson. Hope was looked after as usual in his lodgings but something had changed. When he did see Mrs. Harryson she was cold and made remarks about men and criminality he did not fully understand for many weeks until after the murder of Tinker Frith.

When they reached Castle Street Molly suddenly said "Annie, if I could poison the bastard I would. I would."

They stood in the deep shade of Dr. Bagehot's overhanging chestnut tree heavy with candles of blossom and looked at each other before making their way to Number Two.

In early June on a luminous night Tinker Roland Frith left the town. He had his pack on his back and was making his last foray and journey, the last of the Derbyshire pedlars, before his death. His face was like a puppet's, such as Mr. Punch, that had been ripped apart and hastily repaired. In the dim light of the June night he looked grim and damaged beyond repair,

Annie returned to her house next day with enigmatic remarks about men and crime and what they got away with. Hope was bewildered by these, and depressed by his own suspicions of her. It was an awkward time.

She bought a large pack of blank postcards and a sheet of halfpenny stamps and sat writing postcards at the table, in full view of Hope. She tore off the green stamps, the colour of the young summer leaves in the town, with such force as she stared at Hope, so that he could not help thinking she was tearing at him. Her angry brown eyes looked at him accusingly as she licked the stamps. Then the cards were posted and the atmosphere in the house was as tense as the diplomacy in embassies and closed rooms throughout Europe, as the men in control of Europe's destiny discussed what was to be done about the Kaiser's provocations and war mongering. But even there, the conversations were not as acidly vicious as they were in Mrs. Harryson's house.

The summer of 1905 made its usual stately progress over the Derbyshire hills and the birds fell silent as July approached, as if in sympathy to the cold silence that now reigned between Hope and Annie Harryson, the one suspicious of his landlady and the other gripped with a stultifying anger about mankind and men in general, their control and what they got away with.

Postcards addressed to Mrs. Annie Harryson began to arrive and were always propped against the candlesticks, so that Hope could not help but read them.

The first was from Adders Green, a village deep within the Staffordshire Moorlands.

Dear Annie

Tinker Frith arrived Tuesday tinkering with pans and kettles. He went Monday.

God bless you Annie

Hilda Webster

In the silence of the evenings Hope, well fed but miserable, took out his Bartholomews map to see where Tinker was at. The Roaches, then Flash. He had resolved to get Tinker for his abandoning Horace, but he also sensed Mrs. Harryson was eager to point the way for him, but too angry to say why.

Annie

Jack took us to Buxton market with cheese and saw Tinker on the Leek turnpike. Bob our shepherd says he's put a tent up by Washgate. The old devil's got a right cut down his chops which don't improve him.

I think of you a lot Annie and all the help you do folks

Bertha Winstanley

"What cut has Tinker got?" asked Hope after this postcard arrived, and was obviously displayed for his information. Annie was reading and sewing in the usual silence. Hope felt it was important he should know. As Lomas said, all sorts of things fitted together after a time. The force of Annie Harryson's tirade silenced him again.

"Why, Mr. Hope, he probably had a tangle with a blackberry bush while picking some early fruit for his pudding by his camp fire.

That is all it will be. Men like Tinker Frith never do anything wrong. He's a man, you see. They have the vote and the fear of all the women around them. What could they do amiss? Everything is on their side. No doubt we shall see Tinker soon for the government cannot last much longer and then Tinker can vote, while we women just go about our cooking and scrubbing with our mouths shut tight. Just a blackberry thorn that has ripped his cheek. Nothing for you, or Sergeant Glorey to give a second thought to. Carry on enjoying your map Mr. Hope. You will never find out about the cut."

Hope fell silent miserably. He had not forgotten his suspicions of abortions and now Mrs. Harryson sounded as if she supported those mad women who called themselves suffragettes. Hope could not understand it. He agreed with Constable Allen that things were alright as they were. Why alter things?

Postcards followed from Longnor and then High Needham and then Monyash. Tinker Frith was making his last journey along the old packways. Looking at the map Hope guessed correctly that Frith was slowly returning to the town.

The lime trees were in blossom around the Church, the last flowering tree of the year, that next year would drop their golden flowers on Tinker's grave beneath. Their sweet scent rolled down to the market square perfuming the usual acridity of flattened horse dung on the road. It heralded the arrival of the town fair.

For the market town and its surrounding farms, early July was the appropriate time for a summer fair which had taken place ever since the Friths peddled their wares in Derbyshire. The hay crop was in and the sheep had been sheared and taken to the sheep washes in the rivers. Now there was a pause before the oats were reaped in August and the barley, and what little wheat there was, was ripening in the fields.

A Fair arrived. The Arkwright cotton mill closed down for a week and the great boilers that powered the machinery became cold and awaited their annual de-clinkering. The mill workers, apart from the stokers, had a wakes week holiday. Trips were arranged to Blackpool and the fair was there all week.

Ellie Slater went round to the kitchen at Number two to chat to Molly.

"I'm going on a trip to Blackpool a-Tuesday. Excursion train leaves at seven. I'm rate excited. Then can I come wi' ye to Matlock a-Thursday? I shall be jiggered but I know ye can only go on Thursday. Then us'll go to Fair. Say ye will, Molly. You need a bit of fun Molly. Gerrout a bit. Ruby Smith says ye've looked rate pale for weeks. If I didna know better I'd be thinking ye'd been wi' that big bobby (Ellie smirked at her own admiration of her sexual innuendo) but Annie Harryson keeps that for herself!"

Molly smiled faintly at the mill girl's chatter. The mill workers were known for their crude talk and to shut her up Molly agreed with all she asked.

It was true anyway. Since that vile appearance of her father she had been lifeless and sad, despite Mrs. Harryson's kindness and tonics and talk. Nothing would ever erase that morning from her mind. She felt soiled, and life seemed to hold nothing for her. Bert's anger with her had wounded her more than she would have ever believed it could. She missed Phyllis and she missed Bert.

So they had a day in Matlock and a big high tea, and then as dusk fell they walked down from the Station to the Fair. Thursday night was always the wildest night for some reason and Ellie was going to enjoy herself and see that Molly did. Ellie had bought some bottled ale in Matlock and the two young women sat by the river and drank a bottle before making their way to the fair.

The usual uproar met the two women, and they linked arms and Molly felt the ale numbing her sadness, and they visited the Fat Woman's tent, and Ellie said she'd keep off the roly-poly puddings after seeing the mountain of flesh in her tent. They wondered at the calf with two heads, and laughed till their stomachs hurt in the tent of magic Mirrors. Ellie gave the man with the steam organ a penny to play If You Want to Know the Time ask a Policeman, and collapsed with helpless giggles, and Molly said it was really Ellie who fancied Constable Hope, as she was always going on about the biggest bobby in the town. More shrieks of fun. Then they went to the Swing Boats, which they had agreed on the train was the best thing ever.

The Fair was run by a Welsh company and the man in charge of the Swing Boats was Charlie Foster from Cardiff. Charlie's mother was Spanish and his father was from Trinidad and Charlie was six feet tall and his muscles well developed from working the boats. He was a striking figure of a man, not least in a Derbyshire town that had had no new strains of the human race since colonisation after the last Ice Age. Charlie was looked on with a mixture of wonder, admiration and jealous hostility by the farm labourers, lead miners, quarrymen and railway workers, who had come to enjoy the fair and whose families had lived in the district for generations. Some of the women and a few men covertly looked at Charlie with other thoughts.

Not least amongst the men who watched Charlie was Hope. Glorey had made certain that Hope was on patrol for this most difficult evening. Hope was, like the other men very much aware of the stranger and found himself walking around the swing boats more often than the roundabouts and shooting galleries and sideshows. There was something about Charlie that both intrigued him and puzzled him. The man's face struck a chord, reminded him of something, struck a resonance deep within him and confused him. There was a connection not made and Hope stared a great deal at him. As Lomas had said, connections of events could take years to fall into place. Just keep looking and watching.

Charlie for his part stared a great deal at Molly who was more and more under the influence of alcohol. Ellie was determined to give her a good time and they had visited the beer tent before lurching and giggling back to the swing boats.

Molly, as she soared up to the summer blue twilight, felt all caution and restraint lift. To hell with her father, she thought, as her stomach seemed to part company with the rest of her as the boat returned on its trajectory. Why should he ruin my life? And Bert could sod off too, she thought. The first stars came out and the big silver Vega seemed to smile down on her.

As the fair got ready to close Charlie made a suggestion to Molly.

Molly had always liked men who were big and tall, possibly as a subconscious protection against her father.

"Go on Moll!" said Ellie thickly. "Have a good time for a change!" Ellie, drunk but generous, for she genuinely believed her friend needed a good time, watched with only a hint of envy as Molly and Charlie wandered off into the darkness of the July night.

The fair closed down at ten and by eleven Hope was certain the town was quiet, just one drunk shouting his head off far away on the Monyash Road and two of the town dogs replying with barks and the church clock striking eleven. He was glad to return to his digs and looked forward to a warm bath and bed. The big chill, however, met him at the door.

"Good evening Mr. Hope," said Annie Harryson reading with the lamp turned high. "There is a nice crumbly young cheese from a farm near Longnor, just as you like it. And some of my potted beef and plenty of today's bread and some tomatoes from the Dalrymples' hothouse, given to me by Mrs. Slack the housekeeper. Help yourself Mr. Hope. There's a jug of your usual from Mrs. Peters."

Hope sat down and ate ravenously. Mrs. Harryson had delivered the menu in a voice as crisp and cold as a January morning. Hope was just beginning to feel sated when there was a sharp urgent knock at the door. Mrs. Gill, the beer and spirit seller walked in and sat down.

Annie Harryson regarded her coolly. Mrs. Gill was one of the few women in the town that she did not identify with. Edna Gill was too insensitive to sense the cool reception.

"Eh dear me, Annie Harryson. What a night! What a night! Mrs. Glorey and me, we thought we'd take a turn round the fair. My word, Annie, the world is getting common. Some of them girls is that brazen! That Ellie Slater and Molly Frith, behaving no better than they ought. Mind you, Jim Slater, her dad, was a drunkard as you know, and as for the Friths . . . well, no more need to be said. We walked about, but the best thing Annie, were them monkeys! Eh dear me! Dear me! It cost Mrs. Glorey and me a shilling, but it were worth it. There were these six monkeys dressed in frocks, and I shouldna say it in front of the man here, but they had little bloomers on wi' real lace under their skirts. Anyhow, there were this woman playing a Can-Can on piano, and them monkeys picked up their skirts and danced, an' kicked their little legs up! Laugh? Laugh! (She reduced her voice to a whisper.) We both wet oursens!" She paused and uttered a dry laugh, a faint echo of the merriment that she and Mrs. Glorey had enjoyed earlier.

"Anyhow, that's not what I've come about. It's business with the Constable." She turned her thin face to him, her eyes hard and accusing behind her steel glasses.

"There were a darky, Constable, working them swing boats wi' them shameless hussies screaming and looking at him. What they want a darky for in a fair I don't know. He should stay in Africa."

Hope was aware of Mrs. Harryson looking at Mrs. Gill with a contempt passing anything he had received.

"They're not to be trusted, Annie. I mean we dunna send missionaries out there to th'Empire for nothing do we? Their ways is not our ways. They need learning from us. Anyhow, he came in our shop this afternoon for some beer, and later I found two bottles of brandy gone. Jack Wright told me as I went home, he'd seen this darky and Molly Frith, going up Station Road after the fair wi' a bottle in each hand. Well, they weren't going to catch a train were they? Anyhow, Constable, I've come to report a theft from my shop by that darky. He gave me the creeps, Constable. They're nonna like us . . ."

Hope heard Mrs. Harryson taking a deep breath. She said

" 'If you prick us, do we not bleed? If you tickle us do we not laugh? If you poison us, do we not die? And if you wrong us will we not avenge'? "

"You what?" said Mrs. Gill.

"Nothing that you will worry over Mrs. Gill," said Annie icily. Hope saw her glance at the picture over the mantelpiece, of the Regency Buck, as though for help. "The Constable will investigate it for you. Goodnight Mrs. Gill."

She escorted her to the door. Hope stood up wearily.

Mrs. Harryson shut the door. "That woman is the greatest fool in the town. She has a spirits cupboard with the key in the lock the other side of her counter. When she goes round the back for beer any nimble man can hop over the counter. Oh dear, poor poor Molly. You'd better go Mr. Hope. If you don't she'll have the whole town and Glorey in uproar tomorrow after this poor man's blood. I'll stay up and see you have a warm tub on your return. Your feet must be killing you…"

Hope went feeling rejuvenated. She had spoken almost kindly to him. It was good to hear someone else getting the cold edge of her tongue.

Station Road was deserted, the gaslights making a phosphorescence on the white dusted hedges. As he walked up he heard a labouring coal train on its way to Buxton steaming up the gradient. He had a childish urge to race it before it got to the road bridge over the line by the Station and failed. He was tired. He waited until the long train of trucks filled with coal went through. The cool night air was filled with steam and sulphurous smoke billows. The train seemed endless with the trucks screaming and protesting as they rocked through the Station. It was some minutes before the air was clear enough for Hope to continue and cross on the bridge.

He knew where he must look. An ancient packway lane headed for the woods on the eastern hill. Before it did, it passed through some overgrown fields that had once grown grain in the Napoleonic Wars but were now a mass of broken walls, bracken and rabbit shorn turf, well known to courting couples in the town.

He was right. Although well past eleven o' clock the night was luminous with the northern horizon reflecting the light of the perpetual midsummer day of the far north. To the west a glittering silver crescent balanced on the hills with Venus sparkling close by like some cast aside celestial treasure.

By this light Hope saw two empty bottles silvered with dew on the ledge of a broken drystone wall. Below these came the unmistakable sound of a man and woman together.

Hope picked up the bottles and glanced at the bottles. He could see that they were from a Shrewsbury shop. He also saw that Molly and the 'negro gentleman' (as Hope wrote later) had removed most of their clothes, and to use the favourite phrase of Constable Allen 'were hard at it.'

Hope had witnessed and 'moved on' many acts of furtive sex in alley ways in Derby or against walls in the darkness of the town's night, but he had never witnessed anything as abandoned or as unashamed as this, and it troubled him deeply as he returned with the bottles. Firstly it made him aware he was twenty five and had nothing in his life like this. It also disturbed deeper levels of his being that would trouble his dreams for months to come. By the time he crossed the bridge over the quiet river he was in a temper with everything.

He strode through the market square and hammered loudly on Mrs. Gill's shop door and shouted 'Police!'

He watched while a faint glow indicated that the Gills had risen and lit a candle. Mr. Gill slid back the bolts and Mrs. Gill, in a nightcap and a rather grubby flannelette dressing gown, peered behind like a cautious elderly cat.

"Just to tell you, Mrs. Gill, that I apprehended the negro gentleman and took these bottles from him. You can see they are not from your stock, so you can now rest assured that nothing has been taken from your stock in trade. I thought you'd best know this. You'll sleep easier. I bid you goodnight, Mr. Gill, Mrs. Gill." And Hope took the bottles and was gone.

He knew, as he returned to Mrs. Harryson's, Glorey would make him suffer for this but he did not care.

Mrs. Harryson was waiting for him and he briefly told her what had happened before putting the bottles in the ash can outside her kitchen door. He could sense she was pleased that the 'African' had not taken anything from Edna Gill, but he could also see she was troubled, possibly by what Molly was doing. She had certainly thawed a little. She gave Hope a wan smile.

"Finish your supper and I'll fill a bath," said she.

Eating with renewed appetite as the battered clock chimed the half hour after midnight, Hope suddenly realised why Charlie Foster had stirred something in his consciousness. It was because his face was almost identical to that of the Regency buck that hung over Mrs. Harryson's fireplace. However, quickly writing his notes before his bath he did not write that down.

The summer of 1905 progressed with tensions in Europe and in Hope's world that would explode into unimaginable outcomes in 1914 both for Hope and Europe.

September arrived, the prelude of Tinker Roland Frith's murder. During the July Fair the weather had been warm and golden but from that date the clouds gathered and now September brought silver skies and chill winds.

Glorey had punished Hope in a variety of unsubtle ways for rousing his wife's friend at midnight. Silently aware of this and the value of Constable Hope, Superintendent Lomas every few weeks took Hope with him on his rounds. Such outings saved Hope's sanity, taught him a great deal and made his job seem worthwhile.

"I shall need Constable Hope all day, Sergeant," said Lomas one Friday in late September. "Please rearrange your duties."

"Yes sir," said Glorey, turning the colour of an infected lobster and inwardly cursing.

Hope and Lomas climbed into the pony trap and Lomas headed north for Hassop and Longstone. He talked incessantly, and Hope marvelled at this knowledge of farms and crops and agriculture. Who was late harvesting their barley, who had trouble with labourers, who had not paid rent, who kept their drystone walls and hedges in good condition or who stuck an old bedstead in the gap. They approached Hassop Station.

By talking and listening Hope often suggested solutions to local crimes. On the last trip Lomas had explained how Frank Bell, the Coal Merchant in Hassop Station Yard, had been aware of some hardly noticeable pilfering from his coal store. As the months went on the coal seemed to fall below the whitewashed markers quicker than it should.

Hope had mentioned, that on his very early morning beats that Glorey seemed to arrange for him much more than the other officers, he had met every time Andrew Price, the night porter of the Station, wheeling a barrow of manure. Hope had enquired why the manure was wheeled two miles to Price's cottage in the town; it seemed a lot of effort to cultivate cabbages and roses. Price had replied that he could not let the Station's horse muck go to waste. Hearing about the coal depletion Hope had challenged Price and discovered the wheelbarrow contained a veneer of horse dung from the Station sables, concealing Mr. Bell's stolen coal.

That Friday morning Lomas had driven into the Station Yard and checked with Bell that all was now well. The Coal Merchant thanked him and said it was; he was a staunch local Methodist preacher, and could not resist a dig at the Superintendent.

"I see you're still smoking your pipe, Superintendent. If God had intended you to smoke he would have given thee a chimney."

"Indeed Mr. Bell," said Lomas. "And He would have given me a fireplace to burn your expensive coal in winter as well. Good day sir!"

The pony trotted off on the old turnpike towards Longstone. Lomas pointed with his whip to a narrow lane leading back to the town between limestone walls. "One of the old packways, used long before these roads. And still are by the few, and Tinker Frith. Have a walk along this one day on your beats Constable. And see what you can see. Do not just walk the highroads. Go on footpaths and the old ways and lanes. Change your beat routines, watch and listen."

Hope nodded, little guessing he would be following the track of Annie Harryson along that old lane within days.

Lomas insisted Hope returned to his digs at three in the afternoon, again to Glorey's chagrin. Hope loved those days with Lomas and went into the house still euphoric. The house was silent and cool with no fire or sign of Annie Harryson. His spirits began to sag. He was becoming sick of the atmosphere that had hung over him since that night Molly Frith had come seeking help. It had worsened since the incident with Charlie Foster. For some reason Hope did not understand, that affair had made Annie Harryson angrier still.

There was a new postcard on the mantelpiece turned so Hope could red it without touching it. It was written in an educated and fluent hand.

Dear Annie

Tinker Frith was in our Park by the Hall as bold as brass last night. He persists in following the old packroad that was stopped a hundred years ago! His Lordship has threatened to shoot him if he trespasses again. Frith is truly a highly objectionable man. He told Tucker, the head gardener, he was returning to the town for winter.

The trouble I talked to you about last Michaelmas, has quite abated thanks to your ointment.

Sincerely yours

Clara Starbuck

Hope knew of Clara Starbuck, the housekeeper of the Hall and estate where the coal train murder had been committed. He did not know he was reading of Tinker Frith's last journey to his murder.

It was cold in the house. Hope though the might have been better in Lomas' office. He stared idly at the picture of the Regency buck that was so like Charlie Foster. The connection still puzzled him. A slight noise made him turn.

Coming down the stairs was Molly Firth, her face white and drained of all health.

"Sorry to disturb you Constable. I've been lying down upstairs after Mrs. Harryson gave me some medicine." And she passed through the door and was gone.

All of Hope's suspicions surged back. Without seeing Annie Harryson coming silently from the kitchen, he took the steps upstairs two at a time. She followed him silent as a hunting predator.

He went in the bedroom next to his, where he had never been

before. The bed was dented and warm where Molly had presumably been. The bed was untouched but the patchwork quilt of yellows and creams was still warm. The room smelled of lavender and there was a jug of glory roses on the windowsill from the bush that rampaged over the house wall. Hope looked under the bed, searching for buckets, chamber pots or implements. Mrs. Harryson watched from the landing. He opened and shut drawers. Coming out he did not see her pressed against an alcove made by a chimney stack, like a night shadow.

He went into her bedroom, a place he had not dared to think of entering before. It was fortunate he did not see the look of cold fury on Annie's face. Again he found nothing. The room as fresh with the breeze gently blowing the curtains. There was a jug of roses, this time by the wash stand and a smaller one by the bedside which had a pile of books too.

Hope crashed down the stairs not seeing the statuesque Annie at the end of the landing, her face as rigid as marble. He went into her private room at the back of the house where she saw patients, a puzzling rom, obviously an old part of the house with a Queen Anne fireplace, cupboards full of herbs and jars, but no tools of an abortionist. Hope returned to the main room after checking the kitchen. Mrs. Harryson was poised on the third stair up.

Hope tried to open the battered desk although he knew what was in it as he had often seen her writing there.

"Lost something Constable? Or hoping to find something?"

If her voice had been cold since the May incident with Molly, it now had the caustic sting of liquid air.

Hope blushed deeply like a naughty schoolboy. He said nothing.

"You and I, Constable, need a long long talk together," said she in a voice he dared not reply. Despite nearly ten years of policing and more since leaving school, being chastised by a woman left him tongue-tied; it was an event he was not prepared for. The last woman to harangue him had been a school teacher when he was in school.

"And we will have that talk on Sunday. You will come on a walk with me that will take all the day and we will put an end to all that is troubling you."

Hope feebly protested that he was singing an anthem at Matins.

"No," said Annie Harryson, "you are not. You will go to the Reverend Runcorn and tell him you are going on an investigation to Black Harry's House. It will take all day. Shall I tell him or will you?"

That last Sunday in September dawned with a blue perfection all the more exquisite after the leaden skies of that month. It was, thought Molly wearily, as she tidied Miss Bentinck's bedroom, like the old woman's sapphire ring that she wore on Sundays.

Molly remained at the bedroom window for some time. She heard the chimes of nine from the grandmother clock. Molly did a great deal of staring into the world. The meaning she once saw in it appeared to have vanished. The vile incident with her father had left her with a debilitating lassitude. The few hours of abandonment with Charlie had ended in pain; the next day Charlie had left the town and Molly felt more cheated and worthless than ever. She stared unseeing into the beauty of the day, she did not notice a cobweb sparkling with dewdrops outside the window.

Still she remained there. These days she had to drag herself from task to task; all pleasure in her work had drained away. But she suddenly noticed two figures striding out along the riverside path.

It was Constable Hope and Mrs. Harryson. Mrs. Harryson was a good two paces ahead and leading the way. She had a canvas knapsack on her back like a man and an old walking stick with a gold band round it. She was wearing a russet skirt with a woollen bodice like a farmer's wife. And the Constable too was wearing only a shirt with no collar, a pair of old trousers and his usual highly polished black boots. He too was using a stick that looked curiously old fashioned, but his had a silver band. He had a cap on like a workman but Molly could see his red gold hair and whiskers. Mrs. Harryson was wearing a scarf tied round her own fine hair like a gypsy. Molly stared in spite of her depressed spirits. Where were they going dressed like two common people?

Then two things happened. She was overcome by a grief that almost made her cry aloud. They were a striking couple and no doubt doing what the town gossiped they were doing. Ellie Slater was full of what she thought happened in Annie Harryson's bed when she took 'that big Bobby into it'. And Molly heard a noise above her that she thought was a pigeon. It was not. It was her father above her on the roof.

Roland Frith was on the roof above Molly, pressed between two tall chimney stacks like a gargoyle in the morning sunshine, quite still except for the small movement Molly had heard as he made himself comfortable for a long wait.

He was back in town after the summer. He had thought a great deal about Molly in his tent under luminous midsummer night skies. What had been denied him was now an obsession. He had encouraged himself to enjoy rape fantasies alone in his tent at night. He still believed Bert would thank him for 'sorting out' this daughter of his. Tinker Frith was a man who usually achieved his sexual wants.

In the September morning darkness he had climbed on to the roof and now sat and waited patiently. He watched that Witch and Bobby walk along the riverside, leaving black footprints in the cold silver dew. A smirk twisted his ruined face. He would like to sort both of them out too, preferably the Witch but he would not mind a go at Hope.

But Tinker was pleased two of the town's nuisances were walking out for the day, no doubt for a good tup out in the country. And his job for the day was Molly, and that made his task safer without those busybodies sticking their noses where they had no business. There was plenty of time, the chimney stack was warm from the Old Bat's fires below, and the sun was good. He blinked in the warmth and stretched again, and Molly once more thought there was a pigeon or starling in the roof.

Through the dew soaked fields marched Annie Harryson. Then up a steep bank by a wood dripping with dew and the oaks loud with jays devouring acorns. Across a wide field where the sun warmed Hope's back for the last time that year. Then the track entered between limestone walls for a time, then a vast field, then narrowed between walls again.

Not a word was uttered by Annie. Behind him, far away, Hope heard the bells begin their Sunday peal, golden and ethereal in that spring-water air of late September.

They reached a small gate where they could cross the railway tracks and Hope saw below the road where Lomas had driven the previous Friday.

Mrs. Harryson held up her hand imperiously as she listened for trains, but there were none. They walked under the humming telegraph wires and then were enveloped with the smell of tar from the sleepers as they crossed the rails

Still nothing was said.

Back in the town the air vibrated with the sound of the bells, punctuated only with the sound of the town's garden robins and the occasional horse and carriage. The church bells irritated Tinker and he shook his head like a cat with water in its ears. He could hear Molly's voice through the open French door of the little drawing room. Molly was encouraging Miss Bentinck to sit in a chair by the open window in the sunlight while she prepared her morning chocolate.

Miss Bentinck no longer attended matins. She had done so up to a year ago and had contentedly slept through the service, her gentle snores, soft as a purring cat rippling through the musty air of All Saints. Then one terrible morning Dr. Ball, hugging his doctoral red silk bonnet, had suddenly called out 'Cursed be them that rend the air of God's holy tabernacle with the trump of their snores!" The choirboys had dissolved in giggles, twittering and squeaking like swallows preparing their September flight to Africa. Molly and the Reverend Runcorn had both petitioned his Lordship that his Aunt Bentinck should be excused church attendance.

While Molly was arranging Miss Bentinck, Tinker uncoiled into life. He slithered down the heavy leaden drainpipe and was in the little yard outside the kitchen. He watched Molly prepare the coffee and chocolate through the kitchen window like a stoat watching a rabbit, only his head and bright eyes visible above the sill. Now and again he touched himself.

When Molly took the silver tray out of the kitchen Tinker moved silently to the kitchen door and gently turned the handle.

Mrs. Harryson had marched Hope along sheep pastures till they reached the village of Longstone. Here was the Sunday quiet and only the five minute bell of the church disturbing the air. Hope was beginning to feel the heat. It was one of those days in the decaying year that for a few hours mimics the heats of July. Hope, after over an hour of walking, although not fatigued, was hot and thirsty.

Annie Harryson sensed his distress.

"Drink from the water emptying into that horse trough. It's spring water. Have a good drink because the springs where I am taking you are not to be trusted."

Hope did as he was told and drank deeply and gratefully after she had done the same.

Then she led him from the main street into another lane. She led him ever upwards and they walked on for an hour.

The countryside became wilder and of a type Hope had not experienced on his beat. The limestone country around Magpie Mine and Monyash and Taddington where Glorey continually dispatched him on trivial errands, Hope had come to love. The rolling plateau with its birds and drystone walls and wild flowers had a stark but orderly beauty. This higher limestone countryside that frowned down on Hope's patrol, was malign, the pastures rougher, the trees stunted and the emptiness a threat rather than a solace.

They climbed a winding lane, on the giant south facing scarp of Longstone Edge, once the valley side of a long vanished river in a past geological epoch, now an abandoned giant scarp that dominated the town, and world, that Hope patrolled, always looming to the north of the parish, always visible, unless skulking behind mist and cloud. The pastures became even more rough with thistle clumps and strange weeds. Trees were sparse now, except for the occasional sycamore or crouching hawthorn immobile in the heat, and elder trees glossy with berries, black as beetles in leaves that had turned the colour of stale wine. The air buzzed and whirred with a million insects with a light percussion of crickets. Tiny blue butterflies fluttered over bleached grasses where here and there harebells grew or yarrows.

There was a feeling of desolation. Drystone walls were collapsed. Piles of earth showed where lead mining had been attempted. Now and again were meres covered with lurid green vegetation. And always the path wound upwards. The sun was merciless on Hope's back as he followed Annie, her skirt hem now heavy with a baroque ornamentation of white thistle down and burrs. Hope began to hate the place. The low bourdon note of the insects made it feel alive with brooding intent and a daytime waning moon hung in the west like a fossilised eye watching them toil upwards. Ever upwards.

It was almost midday when they reached the summit. Hope was now mentally and physically challenged. He had a tremendous thirst and he hated this place. It was completely cut away from his usual beats. Only the wind now softly hissed in the coarse rank grasses. He expected Mrs. Harryson to stop on the summit but she carried onwards for another half hour and then quite suddenly sat down on a flat rock.

"Sit down Mr. Hope, I am going no further with you."

Tinker had found the kitchen door locked. Since that fateful morning Molly never ventured out of the back door alone unless there was somebody else in the kitchen or laundry. She did not even go outside to shake a table cloth.

Tinker padded across to the laundry and entered. There were two rooms, one with sinks and a copper and a table, the other a small room with a water closet. Tinker sat on the lavatory bowl and relieved himself and emptied his bowels but made no attempt to use the flush. He opened the door a crack and found he could see what was happening in the kitchen and began to plan his assault. Now and again his eyes flickered to the gate into the little garden which he knew gave access through the french doors. He knew that was a way into the house and he knew that the mad old bat Bentinck would not notice if he crept by her. She did not feature in his mental entertainment that culminated in self gratification.

Hope sat obediently on a slab of outcrop limestone encrusted with fossils and felt aware of the sweat cooling in his armpits and back. Mrs. Harryson undid the buckles of the haversack and took out a brown earthenware bottle and a small cup. She poured out some drink into an earthenware cup and handed it to Hope.

"Drink this Mr. Hope. You look as though you need it." Hope did as he was bid.

It was Mrs. Harryson's own infusion of lemon, herbs and honey. It was still cold and the mixture revived Hope within a minute. He suddenly felt better in mind and body and handing the cup back with thanks, he looked at her expectantly. She said nothing but poured out a drink for herself and drank it more slowly than Hope had done. Then she turned to Hope.

"You see the farmhouse a half mile or more ahead? That is Black Harry House. You will no doubt find it on your Bartholomew's map when we return."

Hope thought, not for the first time, that this woman mocked him.

"Black Harry House. We will go no further because I do not wish to make the present owners be aware of my existence." This statement was followed by a long silence and Hope could hear the wind softly rattling a tuft of harebells by his left hand.

"My great, four times great grandfather came to this wild place nearly two hundred years ago, sometime in the 1720's. I do not know whether he built that place you see before you, or simply murdered the inhabitants in it and took it over. Anything could and did happen up here. It was beyond the King's law."

Another silence. She looked at him with what Hope could only think was an amused expression.

"I have often seen you looking at the oil painting above my fireplace. That was my Grandfather. The great grandson of the man who lived here. It will not have escaped your sharp powers of observation, Constable, that the man in the picture has negro blood in his veins. Or as the sweet Mrs. Gill says about me behind my back in the town, 'a touch of the tar brush.'

This time Hope noticed her face hardened. It was the same expression she had worn when Mrs. Gill had ranted against Charlie Foster the swing boat man.

"The man who came here in 1720 was called Black Harry. He had a woman with him. I have never been able to discover whether Black Harry was so called because of his dark skin, or because he blacked his face with charcoal as did many criminals in those days when they committed their crimes. I am sure your history lessons in the Police School in Derby taught you about the Black Acts of the 1720's. It is still almost a capital offence to blacken your face and commit a crime."

Again Hope almost squirmed with her superior tone and sarcasm.

"Whether Black Harry blacked his face or was a negro, nobody knows. Maybe he was an African slave who escaped from the Liverpool docks on his way to America or the West Indies. He might well have been a white man who, as I said, blacked his face. Or his woman might have been the African . . . One of them, or both might have been black. We are not so far from the port up here, unlikely as it seems. Anyway, African blood was in our family whoever put it there."

Hope could see that she was beginning to forget him as she described her family past.

"Black Harry was a highway man. Can you see that distant ridge of hills?"

"That is Hucklow Edge. In those days the main turnpike from Manchester and Buxton came over there heading for Sheffield. It was a hellish road. Over the hill is the Sir William Hill where my Grandfather said, his grandfather said, the coachman would flog the horses with whalebone whips to get them up the gradient. You could hear the horses scream from here. It was a fearful journey. And there, Black Harry would attack and hold up the coaches. It is said he murdered whole coachloads of people and divested them of their possessions. They say he stripped the Duchess of Devonshire of all her jewels. He took all his loot and treasure back to Black Harry House. The Redcoats could do nothing. He was king of this wild place. He had a gang of men with him and kept anyone out. It is said he murdered and shot nearly fifty soldiers in his lifetime, as they tried to impose law and order up here. They say the place was packed with gold and treasure and fine clothes and wine, yet he was the wildest, dirtiest, most ragged man ever seen, with a gang of men and women just as bad."

She stopped.

"You look perplexed Constable."

Hope was. In his Derby school there had been a small box of books that well behaved pupils were sometimes allowed to read. Hope had read about Dick Turpin and had seen a coloured illustration of a man dressed in a black coat, trimmed with silver lace, waving a silver pistol and wearing high boots. This image of Dick Turpin and his horse Bess did not match Annie Harryson's description of a wild man of this wilderness.

She read his thoughts.

"Did you ever read Robinson Crusoe Mr. Hope? You did? Well, its author, Daniel Defoe, travelled this way and called this part of Derbyshire 'a howling wilderness'. And so it was. Have a final look at Black Harry's kingdom, where murder and rape were monthly occurrences. Then we must retrace our steps a little, so I can tell you the next bit of my family history. And while I am telling you that I will give you your dinner."

Once again Hope almost flinched under the tone of her voice.

Tinker crept across the garden and into a small stone grotto where there was a bench and a stone table in the fashion of a hundred years earlier. Miss Bentinck liked to take her strawberries and cream in here on hot June afternoons. Tinker settled himself like a goblin in a cave and watched.

He watched the Old Bat drink her hot chocolate. He watched his daughter take it away. At twelve he saw her return with a decanter of Madeira wine and a sponge cake which the old woman liked as a snack to sustain her until lunchtime. Tinker watched Molly pour a glass of wine and cut a slice of cake, then leave the old woman alone. He saw the old woman lean back in her chair, saw her head loll and heard the snores that had penetrated the clouded mind of the Reverend Doctor Ball.

Tinker advanced. He stood before the old woman and sized her up with the cold merciless eye of a professional rapist. He picked up the whole cake and rammed it in his mouth devouring it whole. Then he picked up the cut glass Madeira decanter and put the neck to his lips and drank half of it.

Then he left the room and noiselessly climbed the stairs and went into Miss Bentinck's bedroom.

Molly, coming into the sunlit drawing room, looked in amazement at the empty cake plate and half empty decanter. Molly thought no more of it. Sometimes Miss B. was seized with spasms of childish greed. And these days Molly was so depressed, and drained of vitality, that she often did not know what she was doing, and wondered if she had put the cake in the pig swill bin while her mind was suddenly filled with the intrusive thoughts of her father. She shook her head. She must remember to bring Miss B. a full decanter of wine. She could not recall whether it was full or not. She awoke the old lady and gently took her into the dining room where a joint of roast pork made the old lady perk up.

"Roast pork, and then apple pie and vanilla iced cream my dear Sarah. My favourite luncheon!"

Molly poured out champagne. Dr. Bagehot had prescribed it for Sunday lunchtime to give Miss B. 'an appetite'. This, with the hot chocolate and Madeira, Bagehot hoped would nourish the atrophying brain.

Molly drank a whole glass before eating. It gave her an appetite too, for the world seemed a drab and pointless place to her after her father's attack and Charlie's departure.

The lemonade had revived Hope but he felt daunted by the climb back to the summit of the Edge and felt himself sweating again in the heat of the September sun that now beat on his face. He wondered at Mrs. Harryson's stamina. She had refused all offers of his to carry the knapsack. She seemed cool and unperturbed by the heat.

They reached a couple of slabs of limestone that seemed to make a natural table and resting place. Hope could see, spread before him, a vast panorama of central Derbyshire stretching into the infinite mists of the September day.

"Make yourself comfortable Constable," said Mrs. Harryson, as confident as if she were in her own parlour.

Hope watched with helpless interest as she assembled the lunch. She spread a white cloth over the stone and unpacked a game pie she had made.

Hope knew she received many presents of hares, rabbits, partridges, chickens and other food from grateful women who were her patients. He had often wondered how much of the produce was poached.

His misgivings were abandoned as he watched her cut the pie and hand him a generous slice. The meats gleamed in the sun, moist with jelly and the crust was as gold as that autumn day. Beginning to eat he thought food had never tasted better. Particularly tasty were some fragments of dark meat.

"It's grouse Mr. Hope," said Annie, "from Mrs. Watson, one of the keeper's wives on the East Moor. I performed a service for her that she was grateful for."

She was taunting him.

Hard boiled eggs were arranged in greaseproof paper alongside fragrant tomatoes.

"From Mrs. Turner. Grateful for my services."

Hope said nothing. The pie consumed his total consciousness. Delving into the depths of the knapsack she took out a brown bottle of Indian Ale and uncorked it.

"Not as good as Mrs. Peter's. Bought from the sweet Mrs. Gill. This is the stuff they send out to India so the soldiers can order the natives about more easily."

Hope had no idea why she spoke those words with such heavy irony. It seemed a normal fact to him; but he drank the pale ale with gratitude. It was just the thing with the game pie. And it suited the hot day which Hope was sure was as hot as India.

"I'll cut you another slice, Constable."

He noticed she was eating some ripe pear with her portion of pie and she was silent for several minutes as she ate her food. Then she started.

"Look down at that view Mr. Hope. It's quite something. There's the River Wye, winding its way, and our town with its thorn of a spire sticking out of the haze, where you will have been missed leading the singing, as the rich and confident thank God that he made them of high estate."

For the second time in a few minutes Hope was bewildered by her tone.

"You can just pick out Mr. Smedley's castle at Matlock. A great gewgaw in this lovely landscape and a monument to how money can be made from fools staying at his Hydro in Matlock."

Hope munched on, confused.

"It was on this exact spot that my Great Grandfather used to come as a boy, walking away from the den of thieves that was over the hill at Black Harry House. He hated that place. So he used to come here, as he said, to look at the world beyond his father's mad kingdom behind him. He used to stare down at the town where we live and dream of what might be there. Black Harry House was stuffed with books and newspapers because when the gang held up a coach they took everything, including, I am told, the women's clothes and more besides. So my Great Grandfather knew all about George the third and the loss of the American colonies and Mr. Pitt. And he wanted to explore the world. More pie Mr. Hope?"

Hope had now absorbed three quarters of the pie and a pile of tomatoes, three eggs and most of his ale. She took out another bottle.

"He was determined to escape. His father was, perhaps, the maddest of all the Black Harrys. It was told in the family he burned a coach load of passengers alive one foggy night in 1779. My Great Grandfather knew that things could not go on for ever like this. So he made his plans. There were two families of servants at Black Harry House who lived and thieved and bred with my family. One of these families had a son called Jack Derby, a man ten years older than my Great Grandfather, but the two were solid in their friendship and they began to plan their escape. It was surprisingly easy. Such was the chaos up here at Black Harry's that children ran riot and nobody cared what was going on. It never occurred to Black Harry that anybody would want to leave. After all, there were fine clothes, wine, the best food that money could buy, stolen from the length and breadth of the county. And books if you wanted to read. So why leave? There's a pear under the paper if you want it, Mr. Hope.

So Jack dressed himself in the most fashionable clothes that were all over Black Harry House and took a small fortune in gold, stolen of course, and suddenly appeared in the town below. Be careful Mr. Hope. There's a wasp on your pear. You will need my services if you get it in your mouth."

Hope smacked the wasp away and then carried on, semi-hypnotised by Annie Harryson.

"Jack said he was a gentleman's agent from London and was in the town to purchase land and property. Nobody said anything or suspected he was from that nest of vipers far away to the north of the town. He bought a portion of land with a small farmhouse on it, in the centre of town. In those days the farm houses were in the centre of the town, and the shared farmland was all around the edges of the town. The Enclosure Act in 1812 altered all that. Stand up Mr. Hope. There are ants advancing up your trouser leg."

Hope was now lost in confusion. He was not sure what the Enclosure Acts meant. The ants were frustrated in their intent.

"It was a small farmhouse Jack bought. It was to form the core of a new house that Jack would build. That is the house where I live today and you lodge. The first thing Jack did was to supervise the digging of deep cellars and a drain through them. It is still there today. Your bath water runs away down it, to where I have never found out. And of course the contents of our privy go there too; you may have noticed that we never needed the services of Horace Frith. Our waste just vanishes deep underground to some eighteenth century system. You might like to ponder on that next time you sit on the privy performing your business."

She watched Hope blush slightly and took out another pear for him.

"Little by little Jack built, or supervised the building of the house. Soon most of the old farm was absorbed. Only the room, where I see patients to administer my services, remained from the old farm. The town looked on with little interest. The new house was in the middle of a field then."

She ate a pear and was silent for a time. Above them a dragonfly rattled by as brilliant as any jewel that might have been in the Black Harry store.

"What the town did not see was that on dark misty nights, Jack Derby drove north on his cart and met my Great Grandfather at this very spot. My Great Grandfather came here every dark night with a small bag of treasure taken from Black Harry House, and often as not Jack was there. Then the sack would be hidden under a pile of stone and Jack would return to the town house. And he would hide the treasure and coinage under the sewer in the cellar. Jewels, coins, clocks, watches, Venetian glass . . . He took small sums of gold to the different banks in the town, again so as not to arouse any interest. All this took seven years or more. The Black Harry of that time, his father, had missed nothing, but a vast fortune had left Black Harry House. Every bit stolen, Constable. You have been lodging with stolen property."

Hope did not know how to respond.

"My Great Grandfather chose his clothes with care and one day in the 1780's a new gentleman took up residence in the town, a Mr. Jonathan Harryson. He took up residence in the new house and his Agent Mr. Jack Derby moved into a new house on Castle Street where Miss Bentinck now lives. The town was impressed with the new arrival and he was welcomed into the society of that time. He married a pretty young banker's daughter who was charmed with his tall dark good looks. They had a son and that is his picture that I often see you gazing at, Mr. Hope. Eat that last egg. There is some salt in that screw of paper."

Hope did so.

"Well, Mr. Jonathan Harryson had escaped in the nick of time. A new road was being built in the valley below Black Harry House. One windy snow filled night a troop of redcoats laid siege to Black Harry House. Within a month the inhabitants were in Derby Gaol and Black Harry was swinging on a gibbet at a new crossroads on the new turnpike road, just a mile below Black

Harry House, a warning to anybody who might want to follow in Black Harry's footsteps. The days of Black Harry had gone for good."

Hope continued in a bemused silence.

"So Mr. Harryson lived like a gentleman and when he needed more funds to support his pretty wife's lifestyle and parties he simply dug up a few coins from under the drain. Now, Mr. Hope, I have not finished yet, so have some of this cheese from a grateful farmer's wife in Hartington, young and crumbly as you like it. There is an apple from my tree to have with it. Now, all went well for ten years or more. Then times became troubled and everything fell apart. Is the cheese to your liking?"

Roland Frith was in Miss Bentinck's bedroom. He remained quite still for several minutes, his shadow black and grotesque on the rectangles of golden sunlight, falling on the rosebud sprigged regency wallpaper, wallpaper of the finest quality, bought by Mr. Jack Derby for his wife a century earlier.

Tinker silently moved to Miss Bentinck's dressing table and picked up her jewels. He examined them with interest but replaced them except for a pair of sapphire earrings which he put in his pocket.

He fingered the curtains with professional regard and looked at a drawer full of silk underwear and another full of silk stockings. He handled these with the intense perusal of a tradesman and a man possessed by a sexual fetish. He closed the drawer but kept in his hands a pair of silk drawers and a pair of silk stockings. He then felt under the bed for the chamber pot, a highly ornate vessel of fine Staffordshire bone china embellished with cabbage roses and forget-me-nots. Tinker pissed into the pot taking some time and handling himself with the usual affection for himself. He left the pot half showing under the bed.

Then he went out on to the landing and stood listening. He could hear the murmur of Miss Bentinck and his daughter. Molly, after a glass of champagne and some lunch felt a little better and was doing her best to engage Miss Bentinck in stimulating talk, before the old woman lapsed into her long afternoon sleep.

With an unerring instinct for violation, Tinker went straight into Molly's bedroom and lay on her bed. Arranging the silk garments he undid his trousers and masturbated.

"Well, Mr. Hope, as I said all went well for ten years or more. Then came the French Revolution and War against France. Times were hard. Food was short and rebellion was in the air. A band of lead miners from Eyam and Foolow, just north of Black Harry House had heard rumours that Black Harry's son was in the town with all the treasure that the Black Harrys had collected. They were hungry, they were resentful of their low wages so one day, armed with pickaxes and clubs they arrived in the town. They surrounded the house where we live and battered down the door. They dragged out and bound my Great Grandparents. My Grandfather was away at school or else they would have had him too. That saved him. You see, the Harryson's were behaving like the rich gentry, sending their son to Rugby School and eventually to Cambridge. More of that in a minute. More of the cheese? It's very good isn't it? All payments for my services Mr. Hope. Well, the miners and labourers stripped the house of everything. They took all the furniture into the market place and made a huge pile of it. By this time Jonathan had suffered a heart attack and was half dead, but that did not worry the rioters. They put him on top of the pile of furniture and were prepared to burn him alive. Another gang ripped up the floorboards in the house desperate for Black Harry's treasure. They discovered the cellars of course, and began to drink the wine. In one of the cellars an open drain full of waste water and piss and shit flowed. They did not think or care to look under that. You have had enough cheese Mr. Hope? Oh, I see the talk of effluent has made you pause."

She handed him a sip of the lemon and herb cordial and waited.

"Well, Jack and the other gentlemen were seriously alarmed. Indeed, there had been scenes like this in Paris and many felt such action could well spark a revolution here. After all, the King's coach had been upset in London and there were tales of Jacobin meetings in Sheffield. Revolution could easily have happened here. Jack and another man got the Justice to warn the men but they took little notice and the militia were called out. By now Jonathan was dead on the pile in the market square. One thing saved my Great Grandmother who was trussed up with him. Because they could not find the treasure they were reluctant to burn her. They thought she may know. She had no idea where the treasure was. She knew nothing about it. She had no idea she had married Black Harry's son. And the drink was flowing. All the port and claret had been opened and when the militia arrived the men fled or were arrested. It turned out to be easy as the rioters were dead drunk. Eventually Jack got all the stuff back in the house but all of it was damaged in some way. You might have noticed how battered all my stuff is, Mr. Hope. No more cheese? Anything else?"

Hope thanked her and she began carefully to repack her knapsack waving away any offers of help.

"My Great Grandmother refused to return to the house and went to live with a cousin in London. She felt all the town was talking about her and the fact she had married into Black Harry's family. Supplied with funds by Jack, my Grandfather, after finishing his degree returned here and loved the place. He was very popular in the town, as was my Grandmother. My Grandfather was a learned man and organised learned societies in the town. Of course he lived like a man of wealth and yet had the sense to keep the battered furniture to allay suspicion and any further burglary. Eventually the rumours died. Yet they were true Constable! Nowadays there is only that old bastard Tinker Frith and his sons who suspect I am living over a treasure trove. Now, lean back and relax Mr. Hope. There's just a bit more to tell. Why the Friths think you are cohabiting with a treasure hoarding witch."

Hope did not relax. He felt both his stomach and brain had taken in a load too much.

Molly took the pots and glass and silver into the kitchen. She felt better after her lunch. She stayed there about fifteen minutes arranging the pots and pans ready for Maisie to wash and sand and scour the next day after her scrubbing. Molly herself washed the plates and glass and silver and put it away. She looked round the kitchen to ensure it was tidy and then went into the drawing room and found Miss Bentinck fast asleep. She sighed. She had discussed this with Dr. Bagehot who said that as the brain softened more and more, Miss Bentinck would slip into a semi-comatose state. Molly did not like this idea. She had enjoyed reading the newspaper or a book aloud to the old lady after lunch. Molly covered the sleeper with a shawl for the sunshine had left the room, and was now westering and shining in the street at the front. Soon it would get dark.

Molly hesitated a moment in the hall. She thought of going into her sitting room and reading, but the stimulation of the champagne had now been replaced by drowsiness, and a dry mouth. She thought she may rest on her bed for an hour. She went back to the kitchen and poured herself a glass of lemon barley water she had made, that morning, for Miss Bentinck's 'water works' as Dr. Bagehot called the old woman's bladder function. She took the glass upstairs.

Opening her bedroom door she confronted her father sitting up on the bed, his trouser flap undone and exposing himself and grinning at her with all the threat of a nightmare.

Molly made a slight hiss in her throat. Her brain had directed her vocal chords to scream but her throat was so constricted with fear, that a hiss was all that happened. The glass fell from her hand and rolled down the three steps that led to her little room. After many seconds she backed away and her legs, as weak as if she had some debilitating nerve degeneration, she drunkenly half fell down the stairs. At the bottom she fell. For a few seconds she was unable to move as in the worst nightmares.

She crawled to the front door and opened it. Kneeling, she managed to lurch into the sunshine of the street.

Upstairs Tinker heard the front door open and then a faint scream. The dangerous grin was erased from his face and arranging himself and doing up his trouser flap he cautiously went to the top of the stairs.

Seeing the front door open and the sunshine flooding in, he lightly ran down the stairs and seeing nobody in the sunlight ran through the drawing room, past the snoring Miss Bentinck and into the little garden.

Then he climbed as fast as a scuttling spider up the lead pipe and was on the roof. He pressed against the chimney stack, his eyes hawk bright as he watched his prey Molly totter like a market drunk to the end of the street where she confronted Dr. Bagehot, bag in hand, returning after a difficult confinement.

Tinker swore and growled for several minutes.

"So, Mr. Hope, my family lived the life of comfortable gentry. And as I said, people forgot the rumours. After all, if the Harrysons had been rich, why did they not replace the battered furniture? Or move to a fine house? The field around us was disposed of in the Enclosure Act. Houses were built. It was hardly the place where a wealthy man would stay.

My Grandfather sent my father to Edinburgh to the university there to train as a doctor and he returned to the town to practice. He was the doctor here before Dr. Bagehot. I loved my father, Constable. He educated me himself to give me an education as good as any boy. I wanted to be a doctor myself but it is not easy for women. So I trained as a nurse at Derby, in your town. I did well. But as soon as I had completed my training my father became ill with a strange disease that slowly paralysed him and ended up choking him to death. To this day neither myself or Dr. Bagehot know what it was. At the same time my mother became swollen and ill with a tumour that grew in her womb. I nursed her, Constable, as my father wasted away. I did not want her to go to hospital. I had seen what happened in hospital. Chloroform and ether to make the patient unconscious, the tumour cut away, the patient stitched up. Then weeks of agony. A slight recovery and then the tumour returns with extra force. So I decided to ease my mother's pain and let her die a calm and dignified death. And I was helped by a wonderful old woman called Mrs. Trot. She was the daughter of the town's apothecary but was a scientist in her own way. The Wise Woman of the town. There was nothing she did not know about the human body or herbs. I would go as far as saying she knew more than my father or Dr. Bagehot. They both said so themselves. With her help I nursed my mother and father to go gently into their final sleep with care and dignity."

Hope noticed tears rolling down her cheeks and turned away embarrassed. There was silence, profound and deep on that high Edge. The insects had ceased their whirring and scraping now the sun was falling into the west. No bird sang. The railway was silent and they were too far away to hear any horse traffic. After a while Mrs. Harryson blew her nose.

"Of course the town knew Mrs. Trot was teaching me everything she knew. But because she was a woman they thought she was a witch. Many men in the town still do think wise women are witches as they do me, but they are glad of my help when they get a boil on their arse or they cannot piss when they are old."

Hope noticed grief had turned to anger.

"Well, Constable. After my mother and father had died I resolved on one thing. I would dedicate my life to easing pain and suffering in the town. I had the money. It's still there in the drain. I had the knowledge. I thought I would become some sort of Robin Hood. The money that the Black Harrys had stolen from the rich, I would give back to the poor. And I would make their lives more bearable with my skills and medical knowledge. And that is what I am about Mr. Hope. Will you arrest me?"

Hope did not know what to say or do. He blinked under her stare and eventually turned away. There was a silence that lasted for five minutes.

"You are a clever man Mr. Hope. You must have wondered why I am Mrs. Harryson?"

Hope had, but had never dared broach the topic.

"I'll tell you Mr. Hope. Then we must make our way back to the house above Black Harry's treasure before it gets dark. I take from your silence you are not going to handcuff me or put me in the custody of the amazingly stupid Sergeant Glorey"

Molly ignored Dr. Bagehot's greeting and he watched her with some concern as she walked unsteadily away. He knew about most of her troubles from Nurse Harryson who had told him her concerns in their confidential talks. He quickened his steps and opened his front door, threw in his black bag and roared for Winnie. Then he went next door and let himself in. He found all was tranquillity, with Miss Bentinck snoring delicately and snug beneath her shawl. He noticed a glass at the top of the stairs and climbed them. He noted the spilled barley water on the stair carpet and the dishevelled bed in Molly's room but did not investigate.

Returning downstairs he instructed Winny to stay with Miss Bentinck until Molly returned. He was aware the girl would return in her own time, and as Annie Harryson had told him, would refuse to talk. Winny told him that she would give him his dinner later, knowing the Doctor would be more than happy to take bread and cheese and wine in the sunshine until Molly returned.

In the street Dr. Bagehot saw Tinker sauntering up the street. The Doctor glowered at Tinker, for Annie had told him her suspicions but had told him on no account to break Molly's confidences.

"I have you in my eye Tinker!" growled the Doctor.

"And I'll have you up your fat arse!" muttered Roland under his breath as he gave the Doctor a sickly smile.

Molly, feeling faint, walked through the sunlit afternoon streets, where normal families were taking Sunday afternoon walks. She felt an outcast, soiled and unwanted, a victim of her mad father whom nobody could control and she flushed red with shame. By the time she reached Bert's cottage she was hysterical and sobbing wildly.

Bert had told her she was not welcome but she had nowhere else to go. She half fell into the kitchen where Bert and his wife were drinking a pot of tea.

Bert listened in silence, never taking his eyes off his sister. In truth he had half regretted his ban on her visiting. After all, Molly had cared for him as a boy and he felt he owed her a debt. Nevertheless he said nothing but quietly left the kitchen leaving his wife to soothe Molly with hot stewed sweet tea.

Bert found his father at the gate and smiling. Tinker genuinely believed he was doing right by Bert. He had a strong desire to keep the men in the family traditions and desperately wanted Bert to recognise the strength of the family, and its unique centuries old way of life.

"I've summat to show ye father," said Bert going into the brick coal house. Tinker gladly followed him hoping for a variety of expectations from sexual to poaching skills.

Bert shut the door and locked it and pocketed the key. His father looked at him with intelligent bright eyes that shone with primeval expectations.

Bert picked up a knobbly thorn stick that he used for cornering rats and gave his father the thrashing of his life, a beating that lasted for ten minutes and left Tinker unconscious and half dead in the coal dust.

Bert left him sprawled in the black dust and did not care if he lived or died. Bert went out leaving the door open.

Tinker lay there till two o'clock the following Monday morning when he crawled forth in the moonshine from a waning harvest moon. Slowly Tinker crept down the moon-silvered and deserted streets. He collected his tent and belongings and went to spend the remaining days, before his murder, in the woods to the east of the town.

"So, Mr. Hope the last thing you need to know about me. Take this."

She handed him a splendidly engraved silver telescope, a finely wrought eighteenth century spyglass. Hope recognised the coat of arms of the Duke of Norfolk on the silver and presumed it was from the Black Harry trove.

"Direct it to that far line of trees on the horizon Mr. Hope. It is a miles long belt of trees that marks an old Roman road. Locate it to the right of the trees. Take your time."

Hope brought the round image down through a sheet of sapphire and was suddenly amazed to see the craters and cheese-like face of the daylight moon as it was setting in the west.

"Now Constable. Search to the end of the trees and you will find a handsome farmhouse of two storeys, with a walled garden and orchard, solid limestone with a Welsh slate roof and Georgian windows . . . Yes? Good!"

Hope rested the telescope in a crook of his fingers.

"After I returned from Derby I nursed my parents until they died and then a number of people in the town. A man called Professor Stockwell had come to live in the house you are looking at. He had been a professor in Cambridge and was known to my father. His wife was stricken by lumps in her breast and these had spread to other parts of her body. She had been born in Derbyshire and Professor Stockwell bought the house, to let her end her days there in the peace and tranquillity of where she had spent her childhood. Neither he or his wife had much faith in hospitals, or the way surgeons carved and mutilated the body to very little purpose. He had heard about me and my nursing skills and he asked if I would move into the house and become their nurse. I became cook and nurse to the wife and of course, cook to Professor Stockwell. Of course the town knew where I had gone and what I was doing. The town had called me Nurse Harryson. But now they thought I was the Cook. And women who are cooks are always called 'Mrs'. The name has stuck. Most folk in the town call me 'Mrs. Harryson.'"

Hope pretended to study the house. For some reason the name of this man Stockwell filled him with resentful jealousy.

"Lily Stockwell survived for two years and during that time I was very happy. The Professor introduced me to so many books and ideas. He taught me German and we read the German philosophers. My father had taught me Greek and Latin. I often sat with Lily as she slept and I would read and, the next day we would discuss what I had read. It was a happy time. He also introduced me to socialism and the Fabians. I began to see for the first time how cruel and unjust our society is, how the rich and powerful take more than their share, how the poor suffer. How the land is unfairly distributed. How the capitalists that own the wealth exploit the workers. How intelligent men like you, Mr. Hope, are given a poor and narrow education in school. He introduced me to Edward Carpenter over at Millthorpe and I cycle there often to talk and join in talk about how to make the world a better place."

Hope was now totally at sea. He could see little wrong with the world and his place in it.

"When Lily died Professor Stockwell sold the house. He gave me the two leather chairs that I have by my fireside. They were from his college rooms in Cambridge. I know you find them comfortable Mr. Hope. Of course you met the Professor when you passed through Dore when you were chasing the Friths. You saw his cottage where he lives and grows his own food and writes his articles. He bought the cottage there so he could walk to Millthorpe and see his great friend Mr. Carpenter. And now we must return Constable for we need to be home before darkness falls. The days are short now."

It was a long walk back to the town, downhill, but Hope was exhausted. His mind buzzed with pointless intensity like the wasps nests that would soon be destroyed in the first frosts. The sky became a deeper blue, the shadows lengthened and the town was in shadow when they reached it, the chimneys contentedly smoking and the bells ringing for evensong, the lamplighter finishing his rounds. Hope collapsed into Professor Stockwell's chair, his body aching his mind exhausted by eighteenth century crime and the new socialism, neither of which he could cope with.

A bowl of creamy onion soup and Mrs. Harryson's bread and farm butter revived him and he sipped Mrs. Peter's ale and began to relax. He still did not know what to say or do or how to respond.

"When I heard we were to have a new constable in the town I was interested Mr. Hope. The police in this town have been lacking in their duty for many years. I thought I would see what the new constable was like and he could lodge with me. And now I have seen, Mr. Hope. You are a good man Constable Hope. A just and fair man, intelligent and thoughtful. It is men like you that can help to rid the town of some of the men who have made life miserable here, men like the Friths. Tinker Frith in particular. Perhaps you and I together can make a difference Mr. Hope. Me with my money and skills, you with your abilities in discovering crime. You are a good man Mr. Hope. A very good man."

She said no more. And after his bath Hope was so fatigued he climbed the stairs to bed, oddly happy with Annie Harryson's praise. He blew out his candle hoping to convince himself that it would be wrong to report Annie Harryson's stolen wealth from two hundred years ago, and at the same time try to come to terms with her socialism, which up to then he had vaguely understood to belong to people who rioted in Trafalgar Square.

He did neither. His mind had also glossed over his suspicions about her being an abortionist. Her praise and warmth towards him had been an opiate to his suspicions. He fell at once into a deep and restorative sleep and awoke the next day happier than he had been all that year of 1905.

Tinker remained in his tent for a week. His method of recovery from Bert's thrashing would have interested Annie Harryson had she known about what he was doing, and had she been able to overcome her revulsion for the man. Tinker collected a large quantity of the blackberries that had now been left to rot on the brambles since Michaelmas Day. There was a belief in the town below that the Devil pissed on blackberries at the end of September at Michaelmas, that the berries were unfit to eat. In a sense they were, but the change in the sugar content seemed to provide Tinker with a natural analgesic, something he had learned from his father and a knowledge that might well have reached back to before Roman times. He also drank a quantity of fresh warm rabbit blood. Tinker was an expert snarer. He drank vast quantities of fresh spring water and chewed constantly on hazel nuts. Whether or not these ancient remedies revived him, or whether Tinker was made of resilient material it was hard to tell.

For three days he remained in his skin and fur sleeping sack, sweating out his pain. On the fourth, although he remained in his tent, he opened the tent flap and regarded the autumn world which sparkled through this prism shaped aperture.

He saw the gold of the beeches, the yellow of the hazels, the deep emerald of the holly and ivy and he saw John Gratton. John and his mother worked the small acreage of a farm above the railway station, a farm at the edge of the woods that had been truncated by the Midland railway's land grab of thirty years earlier. In the Napoleonic Wars when grain prices were high the farm had been prosperous but now was surrounded by fields abandoned to bracken and scrub, made worse by the railway carve up. John was fourteen years of age. His father had died four years ago from a sudden onset of a fierce diabetes that the doctors and Annie Harryson were powerless to combat or understand. John had taken over the farm, left school and was now the much admired youngest farmer in the parish.

Tinker had raped the boy shortly after John's father's death, an act of such criminal pathos and brutality which was totally lost on Roland Frith. Tinker watched the young man through the triangle of tent aperture that was hidden in the woodland undergrowth, and thought he would repeat the action.

On the eighth day Tinker saw John working in the small secluded Acorn Field as his family had always called it, due to a constant uprising of oak saplings in the grass, from acorns buried by the jays.

It had always been a yawning chasm of emptiness in Tinker's percept of the world that his victims may not enjoy sex as he did. He expected his victims to enjoy what he did to them. Creeping up on John he placed his hand between his legs genuinely thinking this would encourage the boy to engage with him. John, turning with surprise and anger and then shame, saw Tinker grinning at him. John had never forgotten the shame and humiliation and feeling of pollution he had experienced at the hands of Tinker. He had kept his secret to himself.

However John had grown into a young man in four years. Work on the farm had given him power and strength. He swung his right fist and hit Tinker with such force that Frith was sent sprawling, his upper body falling into a tangle of saplings and hedge cuttings that John had been cutting. His legs and backside were available for attack and John spent five minutes kicking these with his heavy farm boots until he was exhausted and was somewhat purged of the shame of four years ago.

"Touch me again Tinker and I'll kill you," he said and there was murder in his eyes.

John had broken some of the small bones in Tinker's foot, so the rest of the day Tinker expertly bound his foot with herbs and strips of leather.

At three in the morning he made his way to the little farmhouse. He threw three rabbits to the farm dog as it emerged from the kennel. Tinker went into the farmhouse porch and filled John's boots with shit. At the end of each day John filled a beer bottle with the day's left over cold tea which he took with him to the field, finding the cold milkless tea a refreshing drink and stimulant. Tinker half drank the bottle and then pissed into it. Then he returned to the tent.

The following morning Annie Harryson was baking bread and pies when she heard a hammering at the door. It was John Gratton. He half fell into the room where Annie could see he was convulsed with dry retching. She sat him in Hope's arm chair and saw with alarm his face was white under his tan and filmed with a sheen of unhealthy sweat. His tongue kept protruding from his mouth in a prolonged attempt to vomit something that had been expelled or would not be rejected. Annie could see his stomach was empty although the retching racked John's body.

For five minutes Annie was bewildered. Then she suddenly had a suspicion. Mrs. Baker, the Station Master's wife and one of Annie's grateful admirers, had told her 'that varmint Frith was camping near to Gratton's farm behind the Station'. Annie knew a great deal about the sexual habits of Tinker Frith from confidential talks to Maisie. She likewise had a detailed knowledge of sexual acts gleaned from consultations with women in the town. It suddenly dawned on her what Frith might have made John Gratton do. She knew what certain men liked women to do to them and knowing Tinker she would not be surprised if he had made the young man do it to him.

"I think you've swallowed something evil," said she. "I've just the thing to cleanse your mouth and stomach of anything foul you've swallowed."

John said nothing but allowed her to mother him and eventually drink a variety of sedatives and mint and camomile. This was followed by brandy and fruit syrups and cordial and eventually John lay back in the chair exhausted but feeling his stomach relieved of the filth he had taken in from the bottle.

He said nothing to Mrs. Harryson and she did not expect him to, but there was murder in her eyes as there had been in John's.

John left Annie sixpence which she accepted knowing young men had their pride. Hope met John as he was returning for his dinner.

"Young Gratton looks badly," he remarked to Mrs. Harryson as he sat down to a steak and kidney pie stuffed with wild October mushrooms.

"Yes. But it'll not be him you'll find dead," said Annie and Hope detected some of the anger that had surrounded him for months and he had hoped the walk had dissipated.

Dr. Bagehot was walking along the edge of the woods to the east of the town. It was a golden afternoon in October with a sky as blue and translucent as medieval blue glass. The Doctor appreciated it to the full. His decision to take on a young assistant was paying him dividends. He had advertised for a newly qualified doctor who was eager to eventually move on to further study. Dr. Bagehot was thus able to discover the new trends in medicine from his assistant's new qualifications and current studies. And it freed him to enjoy the world and people around him.

Today he was absorbed by the adders that lived on this west facing woodland slope that opened out on to exposed rocks and eventually farm land. An admirer of Darwin he watched with pleasure the wood brown vipers with ink black zigzags on their backs, as they basked in the last of the warm sun. Bagehot was enraptured by the blend of colours of the adders on the warm slabs of millstone grit outcrops.

A little further on he saw the tent of Tinker Frith and was likewise entranced. It was like a romantic oil painting of rustic simplicity, although the Doctor knew all Annie suspected about Frith. Nevertheless the leather tent, Frith's kettle and iron pot hanging from a tripod of sticks over a crackling fire, pleased Bagehot. It was something from another century.

"Good afternoon Tinker. Do the vipers not bother you?"

"Not me sir," said Tinker. His eyes gleamed with intelligence when they were free of sexual predations. "They fear us humans sir. They hear through their bellies, my father told me. Tread heavily where they live and they'll move aside. And they'll seek the warmth of the sun sir, but never the heat of a human body. My father said they can tell the different heats through them forked tongues. He reckoned they could feel insects close to their tongues as well."

Doctor Bagehot went on his way musing at how much knowledge there was in the world outside the confines of the universities. Much further on he came across John Gratton with a forked stick catching the vipers and dropping them into a large canvas bag.

"Why rid the world of vipers John?"

"There's too many sir. A few dunna matter but these last years they've multiplied like rabbits. They dunna bother me but they'll take chicks and eggs and I've lost young lambs in spring when they're still sleepy. They'll bite a young lamb if it treads on one just coming out of its winter sleep, and it kills them."

Doctor Bagehot reached the lane and crossed the railway bridge after a London express had whistled by. He was content with his world and the golden October and was heartily glad he was not bound for London.

Constable John Hope was sitting with the farmer Sam Walton at Bow Cross farm. When Glorey left him alone to choose his own beat, he liked to walk up the lane from the town, check that all was well with the railway station, then continue through the woods and up to the farm, and calling in on Sam to see if all was well with the farmer. The farm was convenient to tramps and other wayfarers and Sam appreciated the constable keeping an eye on things. And at the back of Hope's mind was that August evening of a year ago when he had seen the flash of Horace's lead. You never knew what you may see up here. They sat under the farm wall with a mug of tea. Already a winter chill was in the air and the gold of the earlier days had been replaced by silvery clouds and cold mists.

"I'm glad ye called," said Sam Walton. "Only I'm getting a bit frazzled, like. I'll tell ye why."

Hope could sense by the way Sam had lapsed into the dialect of the town that something was bothering him. Sam offered a pipe and Hope smoked one with Sam. He listened with attention as the language of the town sometimes baffled him.

"Sithee, that old devil Tinker Frith's set up camp down yonder. An' there's been nowt but trouble. Last Sat'day your landlady were pickin' 'erbs and whatnot in t'woods an' oo started on Tinker like a ruddy fishwife, Constable. I've never 'eard owt like it. Oo were yelling at him, calling 'im all names under sun . . . stuff from bible, codomite, ye've never 'eard owt like it. Well, I got wind up, ye could 'ear it from up at farm . . . so I went down the lane . . . an' Annie Harryson, she were threatening Tinker wi' that silver knife oo uses for cutting stuff for 'er medicines. Well, I thought oo were goin' to kill the old devil . . ."

Hope could see that Sam was disturbed by this confrontation but he calmed down now he had told Hope the most embarrassing bit, the narration that was hardest to tell. He drank his tea and ate his wife's cake with satisfaction and, much to Hope's relief, reverted to more standard English.

"Well, soon after I heard shouting again. This time it were young Gratton, the young farmer just below us. A grand lad, Constable. Only fourteen, an' he's more idea about farming than some three times his age. Well, he were having a barney with Tinker again. "Come near me or my land and I'll kill ye!' Well, I stopped what I were doing again and went down and calmed him down. I could see he were right upset, but about what I couldn't tell. And that old devil were laughing at us from the woods. John were that mad. I could see he'd have gone for Tinker if I hadn't calmed things down. And there's worse to come."

Sam took a long and noisy slurp of tea and wiped his mouth.

"Aye. Next day Bert Frith arrives, yelling at Tinker at the top of his voice. Such language Constable. I know it's quarter of a mile down those woods but my Connie could hear everything as she hung her weshing out. 'I'll kick your so-and-so arse from here to Derby you so-and-so bloody old sod and I'll cut your so-and-so bollocks off before I do and your . . .' well, I canna go on Constable. It's not decent you know. My Connie weren't bothered she said, but that's not the point. And Bert Frith says to his father 'I'll see ye buried six foot under before I'm done!' "

Sam looked at Hope and drank more tea.

"There's them in the town that say you're the only one who can sort out them Friths. You're a big man Constable. Why dunna ye finish off Frith wi' your truncheon? Ye'd do the town a service!"

Hope said he would look into the matter.

It was late October and the world was darkening and Halloween approaching. Winter was waiting. Glorey was watching in the seven o'clock darkness for Hope to enter and receive the day's tasks. It was perhaps the most futile investigation Hope had been ordered to do and yet Hope was to think about this October day in 1905 for the rest of his life.

"Aye," said Glorey, dyspeptic, pale and bloated under the gas, expanding with satisfaction as the fuel of his malice invigorated him.

"Aye. It's a wet morning lad, but tha'll have to walk to Edensor and make a report. There's a lady there who knows the Duchess, and she says she's had all her geranium pots took. I want a detailed report by noon. Now bugger off."

Hope was too disgusted to say anything. On the other hand he would be dry under his cape, he could have a cup of hot sweet tea with Sam and a bacon sandwich from Connie Walton. There were worse ways to spend a morning so he let Glorey see his long face. Glorey watched him go, Hope pretending to be annoyed, Glorey sucking a sodamint with grim relish.

Returning to the town from Sam's, Hope had the feeling of unease that he had felt when he had first seen the flash of Horace Frith's lead sheet far below in the river. The day was dark, the mist thick. Sounds were confusing and his imagination began to race. There were rhythmic sounds that could have been heavy drops of moisture, or a woman running far below, or a goods train down at Rowsley sidings three miles away. And the wind blew the mist and turning round he thought he saw a figure following him, an old woman muffled in a shawl or cloak but he was not sure. His eyes could not separate mist and twigs from human form. The world seemed to be as fluid as the weather.

Then there was no doubt in Hope's perceptions. A stifled scream that certainly was not a jay or an animal, and a yell that betrayed human terror. Hope increased his pace down the lane and was aware of young Gratton, the farmer, crossing the lane a hundred yards ahead and almost running back in the direction of his farm. At least Hope thought it was Gratton, but the mists swirled and later, much later, he was not so sure; for as he stared he suddenly saw what appeared to be the figure of an old woman with a bundle of sticks entering the woods where Gratton had emerged from. But as he blinked she faded.

Hope came to a halt under the dripping branches of a great beech tree, where leaves fluttered down with the rain drops. He noticed two uprooted dandelions in the lane as though Annie Harryson had dropped them. Over the years he had seen Annie collecting such items, seen them drying in the wash house on trays by the copper boiler. Hope remained still for several minutes. Then he decided it would be a good time to order Frith out of the woods. It would be something positive to do on this morning of mists and imaginings of which Hope was rather ashamed. All this shouting and yelling was a threat to law and order, He had been thinking about this for a few days and had decided he would order Tinker from the parish under the Vagrancy laws. He hoped Tinker would obey this and move on. The problem was that Tinker was a householder and not a vagrant. In the eyes of the law he could not be moved on. Yet Hope was going to try it and back it up with some warnings about disturbing the peace with foul and abusive language. He knew Sam Walton and Annie would be thankful and he wanted their admiration and approval. And it was time he had a go at Tinker Frith. And he wanted to do something to dispel his imaginings in the mists and drippings around him.

The scent of cooking meat and wood smoke led him to Frith's tent by the side of the old abandoned hill road down into the town. The tent flap was shut and the fire was hissing with anger in the rain as it was slowly dulled. Hope strode forward and shouted

"Frith! I need a word with you!"

Nothing happened. The feeling of unease came over Hope. The world was curiously inimical in the falling rain. Hope caught in his outer visual field a movement of mist and light and suspected it was the figure of the old woman, but it vanished.

Hope pulled aside the flap. Tinker was sprawled across the dry bracken on the floor of his tent. His face was striped with blood and his mouth was open. Hope could hear his breathing, deep and powerful and yet not the normal respiration of a healthy man. Hope shook his shoulder and a trickle of blood oozed out of Frith's twisted lips. Hope got to his feet quickly. He noticed for the first time that there was a canvas bag on the bracken similar to the one John Gratton used for catching snakes.

Hope ran quickly down the old causeway till he reached the modern lane and ran to the railway bridge. He went through a small gate and then clattered down an iron footbridge to the Station platform and found Baker the Station Master. He explained the situation and Baker unlocked a door and with the help of two porters, brought out a stretcher and a blanket, stamped with the badge of the Midland Railway Company, ready for an emergency on the railway. Hope and a porter made their way back to the camp as fast as they could.

Together they lifted the unconscious old pedlar on to the stretcher and covered him with a blanket. Hope turned Tinker's head to one side and he vomited a little blood.

Hope led the way at the front of the stretcher and they returned. They placed the stretcher on the floor of the second class Waiting Room. Baker suggested that Tinker should be taken to the Workhouse Infirmary. Hope agreed and quickly entered the men's lavatory to rinse his hands of the bloody vomit that had trickled on to them. He saw Bert Frith washing his hands at the tap and basin on the wall. He noticed that Frith's hands were stained and the stain had not been removed by the water and bar of carbolic soap the Midland Railway provided in the second class urinal. Hope wondered at the stained hands but not too much at that moment. Bert was a bootmaker and often had tan and leather dye on his hands. However as they lifted Tinker's stretcher up, he asked if Frith were waiting for a train or had alighted from one. The Station Master said Frith had not bought a ticket and there had been no train to alight from for an hour. Baker had told Bert that his father was unconscious on a stretcher but he had shrugged his shoulders and turned away.

But when Hope and the porter brought out the stretcher from the waiting room, their boots loud on the boards in the silence, Bert Frith was on the platform too. He was talking to his sister Maisie.

Maisie scrubbed for the Station Master's wife two mornings a week. Maisie had gained a reputation in the town, along with less favourable suggestions, that she was a good scrubber. Something in scrubbing a floor seemed to satisfy Maisie, the vigorous cleaning with a stiff brush and a bar of red carbolic soap seemed to give her pleasure. Mr. Baker kept a tight hold of his wife's housekeeping money and Maisie had come to collect her sixpence from the Station Master for scrubbing the Bakers' kitchen and scullery floor. She looked at her father on the stretcher with as much concern as she would have shown for a dead rat by the river.

"Feyther wunna last," she said with the assurance of an oracle. "I've seed T'Owd Woman on the road, oo passed us when I were coming out from Missus' gate. Feyther wunna live."

Bert Frith said nothing. He had strolled out on to the platform, seemingly preoccupied. Hope thought how odd the Friths were and recalled how they had sacrificed Horace. It was as though his father did not exist.

Hope was appalled. The callous nature of the Friths sickened him. But something deeper disturbed his very being. He was sure he had seen the Old Woman too. Just as he had on the morning of the murder on the railway line. And it shook his religious and masculine foundations. That he should have the same perceptions as Maisie Frith angered and shamed him. He had been educated and brought up a good Christian and now he was seeing a spirit or a ghost, some old superstition in the town. They said that the Old Woman appeared when folk were close to death.

Hope said nothing except to give a command to lift the stretcher.

The solemn little procession crossed the station yard. Sam Walton had just entered it with his horse and cart and milk churns ready for the Derby train. He nodded at Hope with unconcealed satisfaction.

“Thank’ee Constable for sorting him out. The old bugger had it coming!” And after delivering his churns, Sam went down into the town, and by nightfall the whole town was full of the news that Constable Hope had ‘sorted out’ Tinker Frith once and for all.

Leading out of the station yard was a stile and a field path that led to the Workhouse and Infirmary two fields away. With the help of another porter they carried Tinker over the stile and then made their way to the Infirmary.

Tinker Frith was admitted into the grim building that was the men’s infirmary of the workhouse, the paupers of the parish last resting place. Matron, with a face as inexpressive as a hatchet, ordered two nurses to remove the clothes of Tinker and send them to the furnace. The unconscious Tinker was scrubbed with a solution of dilute carbolic acid and inserted into a clean bed of coarse boiled calico sheets.

This action alone, had Tinker been conscious, would have killed him. Dr. Bagehot was sent for but he was out of town and Dr. Treeton was attending a birth. Dr. Cole was busy with his afternoon surgery and rang the Workhouse to enquire why he was needed. On hearing it was only Tinker Frith waiting his attention, he went on with his consultations.

Tinker Frith never regained consciousness. For a man who had lived his life under the heat of the sun, or the frost fired stars of winter, it would have killed him if he had perceived he was prisoner in the workhouse hospital, The Bastille his father had called it when it was built. The long ward of the hospital, with its coke stove fumes, old men coughing their way to death and the gaslights, would have paralysed his will. As the dreary day ebbed away and rain dimpled and smeared the big high windows, Frith breathed his last.

Matron covered him with a clean sheet and he was taken to the mortuary.

Both Dr. Cole and Dr. Bagehot arrived at the Workhouse together, Bagehot on foot and Cole in his pony and trap. The October mists had cleared and there was a gash of crimson in the west and already the stars were glittering. It would be a frosty night. The two men made their way to the Mortuary. Neither spoke. They were both poles apart in political and medical views.

A porter unlocked the door of the Mortuary and they entered the gaslit whitewashed chill. Cole shivered theatrically. He made no attempt to remove his top hat or riding cloak. He whisked off the sheet that covered Tinker Frith and let it fall on the floor. He kicked it under the table where Tinker lay, and grunted. He stared for a moment at Tinker's naked corpse and made no attempt to disguise his disgust and contempt.

"Well, Bagehot, the town and county is well rid of this criminal specimen of humanity. Damn good riddance. I'm not going to soil m' hands by examining him. The world's better without him. It's fornicating men like him who drag down the stock of the general population of the working class. I'll get a form and sign it."

He went over to the roll topped desk and undid it and took out an official form. Bagehot did not speak. He had removed his hat in respect to the dead and held it to his chest. Cole took out his pince nez and dipped the pen in the ink and signed the form.

"Put what the hell you like Bagehot, as long as you do not

provoke an inquest. I don't want any part in such things. This man is vermin. I don't want a single second of my time wasting on him. He is of no more worth than a dead rat. If you want any investigation or inquest count me out, do you hear? Get a new form and sign it yourself with your new socialist assistant."

Bagehot took the form off Cole.

"I shall do an autopsy and make my report on Frith just as I would do for your friend the Duke. Frith was a human being, albeit of dubious morals and has every right to my attention, whether he was a pedlar or a prince, fornicating as our King is likely doing at this moment. I bid you goodnight Doctor. It will soon be your dinner time. Leave Frith to me if he is beneath your contempt."

Dr. Bagehot ripped up the form that Cole had signed and put it in the dustbin. Cole snorted and strode out.

Bagehot heard the porter say "Goodnight sir," and knew Cole would not reply. He stared down at the rigid corpse until he heard the irritable clatter of Cole's pony in the frosty night. Then he undid his bag of medical instruments.

He began with Tinker's head. He examined the mouth and noted that there was a curious blistering as though Frith had taken a poisonous herb. Bagehot frowned slightly. He had not expected that. He fetched a saw and a razor ready to open Tinker's skull. Before he did he noted that Tinker's hair was matted with blood, and he fetched some green soap and spirit and cleaned the head.

He noted two things. Firstly, a jagged wound possibly made by Frith hitting a stone on the ground. Or being hit with a stone, for Bagehot could see tiny grains of quartz when he looked through his magnifier, the tiny grains of quartz that were present in the millstone grit and sandstone of the rocks to the east of the town; rocks where the adders basked. Bagehot enjoyed geology as well as natural history.

The brain was engorged with blood, possibly from the fall or blow, but Bagehot was not totally sure of the cause. The brain was swollen and discoloured and once again he frowned, wondering if poison or toxins could be responsible. And Frith might well have had a stroke as well if he had died in acute fear of something or somebody.

Tinker's lungs were congested with blood and stomach contents that must have been ingested or inhaled after the fall or blow. Bagehot saw the stomach was healthy but inflamed and the liver was swollen. Once again Bagehot thought of poison or possibly Tinker had been treating himself with some herbs or plants as many of the older generation still did.

Bagehot lit a cigar and went to the door where the porter waited patiently. Bagehot knew him, a man who had been twisted by rheumatic disease and crippled by arthritis and who had no alternative but to come to the Workhouse, where he had been made to work as a porter.

"It's a frosty night, Matthew. And it won't do your joints any good standing there. Go inside, man."

"It's against rules sir, to go inside while doctors is here. Master says I mun wait here."

"It's not against the rules if you go in and I am out here with my cigar. Now go in Matt. Go on. I'll sort out the Master or Matron!"

Matthew went in the shed which was little warmer than the chill outside. He stood miserably just inside while a ghost of him reflected in the white glazed tiles watched Dr. Bagehot smoke.

Bagehot was annoyed. It was complicated. It could have been a fall, a blow to the head or even poison. He smoked his Havana and contemplated Orion and the star belt and felt better. He returned inside and Matthew scuttled out.

He sewed up Frith's corpse chewing on the butt of the cigar. Then he stood back contemplating. Frith had seemingly been in good health. The muscle tone for a man of his age was excellent. No wasting or atrophy and very little fat. The stomach had been as taut as that of a young man when Bagehot had opened it with his blade. His eyes wandered down to Frith's genitals and he suddenly peered closer. On the inside of the thigh next to his scrotum were three punctures. Examining them Bagehot found several more and realised they were marks where the fangs of a snake had entered. There was one on his penis too. Looking at his legs Bagehot found two more. Chewing his cigar he called for Matthew.

"Matt, I need assistance to turn the body." Matt groaned with the exertion and together they laid the corpse on its stomach. Matt fled out again.

Bagehot forgot the punctures and turned up the gas. Frith's back was striped like a zebra with old bruises from what looked like a severe beating administered some time ago. Yet there were three stripes, red and livid that looked as if they might have been done some hours before death. Bagehot was perplexed at this discovery. The beating would have been enough to kill another man less strong than Frith.

He noted several more punctures on the buttocks and on the ankles and calves. And his shins and lower legs were bruised as though kicked by heavy boots. The more he looked the more the blows of the beating seemed to belong to different time periods.

Bagehot stood back and surveyed Tinker for some time. He could not, in all honesty, attribute a single cause of death. He had not had to deal with such a complexity of causes before; each one was sufficient to be used as the cause of death, but which one?

"I've finished Matt. But I may return tomorrow. The corpse is to remain here tell the Master. Cover him up and turn down the gas."

Bagehot scrubbed his hands in the bucket of dilute carbolic acid that had been provided and dried them on the towel on the shelf close by.

"Goodnight Matt. And get back into the warm as soon as you can. Go and spend a couple of hours in the boiler house by the furnace till you sweat."

Bagehot walked down the road that was silent in the moonlight. An almost full moon had risen over the hills and woods where Tinker had made his camp. Already Orion was dimmed by the light. Bagehot was puzzled by the snake bites. Frith was a man who knew nature, and as Bagehot knew from talking to him, was unlikely to be bitten by one snake let alone twelve. Being bitten by twelve vipers was beyond comprehension.

Bagehot looked at the moonlight on the river for a moment, where the coots were still settling down with tiny trumpets of communication to each other. Even twelve doses of adder venom would not have been enough to engorge the brain and liver or blister the mouth and gut . . . Surely that was a stronger toxin that did that . . .

Then there was a blow to the head. And the marks of a kicking or beating over a length of time. Had Frith been under attack for some days? God knows, thought Bagehot as he crossed the Bridge, how I am going to make this into a report that makes some kind of sense. He must make sure the report goes straight to Lomas and not that arch-buffoon Glorey. And even Lomas and Hope, the two most intelligent men in the police, would have trouble sorting this out.

"Winny, I'm back!" roared the Doctor. "Bring me a bottle of claret with my dinner when you're ready!"

Bagehot dined alone on oxtail and dumplings followed by an egg custard and read an article from The Lancet as he did so. He kept his mind free of the torturous complexities of Frith's autopsy report. Winny came in to clear the dining room and table.

"That was excellent Winny. Excellent. I'll take some black coffee and a brandy in the sitting room and then you must get to bed. I'll be up and about for some time."

After Winny had brought him the brandy and coffee Bagehot piled the fire high with wood and coal till the room glowed with light and heat. Then he drew back the curtains and opened the French doors wide. This was a habit of the Doctor that infuriated Winny, for it let in condensation that dulled the brass fittings in the room. Bagehot arranged an armchair where he could feel the heat of the blaze and see the moon and stars. Then he began to turn over the puzzle of Frith's death. He lit a cigar and sipped brandy. He watched a tawny owl alight on the moon silvered bough of the horse chestnut and he saw its luminous eyes survey his garden, before it rent the air with its chilling cry. Bagehot pictured the field mice in the garden frozen into paralysed fear by the shriek. His mind wandered for a moment on to the evolution of the eye. From reptiles such as the vipers the eye had not changed much by the time mice had evolved. And yet in the owl the evolution had been specialised and rapid. He tried to visualise the eye of an adder as he had seen them on the rocks that autumn afternoon when he had seen Frith and the young farmer Gratton. He suddenly started up from his chair.

He closed the doors in case Winny should come in and chastise him, and went out of the room and crossed the dark hall to his surgery. There he lit the gas and took down a ledger from the shelf that contained details of his patients' visits. Turning to the back he ran his finger down the index till he found GRATTON John.

Fetching a pair of spectacles from his desk he turned to August 1902 and found, as he suspected, a reference to treating the young Gratton for an anal tear. Bagehot saw he had written 'Gratton says he has constipation and has strained himself. Weak laxative given.' Bagehot recalled the visit. The boy had been bleeding and was terrified. Bagehot had been suspicious but the boy had been embarrassed and Bagehot had merely given him soothing ointment and the laxative. He closed the book and replaced it. He turned out the gas.

This time he returned to the sitting room but he did not sit down. He stood by the window and looked out.

The anal fissure could well have been caused by buggery. Annie

Harryson had told Bagehot many times of the crimes she knew Frith had committed and women had told her in confidence and she had been unable to tell the police. Bagehot thought of the sack of adders that John Gratton had collected. Bagehot lit a cigar.

He thought of the report he must make to the Coroner. He thought of the police inquiry. He thought of the adder bites and the blow to the head he must include in his report.

He thought of the way the Police would think. Everyone knew Gratton collected the adders that were a menace in that part of the countryside. Twelve bites . . . He imagined the police investigation, the arrest of John Gratton. He saw him in Derby Assizes with an impatient Judge and with no decent counsel. The boy would be hanged. And he deserved better.

A rich man with a good barrister could make use of all the anomalies in Bagehot's report but it would be a struggle. Gratton would be seen to have attacked Frith with a stone and emptied a sack of adders over the unconscious man. Bagehot sighed deeply and clouded the moonlight with cigar smoke. Gratton was damned and it was a crying shame.

Bagehot put on his greatcoat and let himself out of the door into the quiet of the moonlit street. He made his way back over the Bridge and set off again for the Workhouse. The road was striped as starkly with the moon shadows of the elms, as Frith's back was striped with bruises. Bagehot strode along under the moon's noonday, his shadow as short as it was from the midsummer sun.

The gates to the Workhouse were shut and chained and the implacable iron was already furred with frost as Bagehot yanked at the night bell. He waited for the duty porter to arrive. He heard the ash leaves falling from a tree behind him as the frost bit the stems off, and smiled as he saw Edmund, an inmate, racing over the lawns. Edmund, labelled a 'benign lunatic', escaped Matron around the time of full moon and spent as much time as he could running round the grounds under the light of the moon.

"Take your time Fred!" said Bagehot as he heard the sound of

Fred Bailey's wooden leg tapping towards him. Fred had an accident on the railway and a leg amputated. His wife had died and Fred had no alternative but the Workhouse where he was employed as the Night Porter and Watchman. He undid the chains of the Gates.

"I need the keys to the Mortuary Fred. No! I'll come to your lodge and get them." He followed Fred into the lodge where a bright fire burned and Fred was frying sausages.

"They smell good Fred!" said Bagehot sitting on the bench and accepting Fred's invitation to have a sausage and a cup of cocoa. Fred produced two enamel mugs with the Workhouse crest on, full of hot frothing cocoa. Bagehot delved into an inner pocket and brought out a heavy silver flask full of whisky and poured generous measures into the cocoa for himself and Fred. He sat and talked for an hour with the porter.

"Well Fred, I've work to do in the Mortuary. And I'll tell you this Fred, I've never had a better supper than that!"

He took the bunch of keys Fred offered him and crossed the moonlit yard and made his way to the Mortuary. Behind him he was aware of the flash of linen as two nurses chased the lunatic.

Inside Bagehot lit the gas and surveyed the outline of Frith, still as a miniature alpine range under its sheet. Then he strode over to the roll top desk and pulled up a stool. He took out his glasses from his pocket and put them on. His glasses case gaped open, its red velvet interior grinning wide, the only colour in the whitewash and tiled chill.

Bagehot took a form and dipped the pen in the ink and began to write in the box designated as CAUSE(S) of DEATH

Haemmorrhage of brain caused by heavy fall after toxic ingestion and inhalation of alcohol mixed with self-administered herbs. Secondary causes due to liver failure and swelling of the brain. Arthur G. Bagehot MD (Glasgow)

Then he took out an envelope from a pigeon hole and his hand trembled slightly as he did so.

If Bagehot was troubled with the way he had presented the facts, so Hope had been troubled earlier. At the end of his beat he had gone to the tobacconist for his supplies and had been warmly thanked for ridding the town of Tinker. It dawned on him that the town thought he was responsible. Returning to his digs he found a cold ox tongue and the crisp heart of a celery and a warm loaf, pats of pale autumn salted butter, but no Mrs. Harryson. After a quantity of Derbyshire cheese and bread and butter and his usual ale, Hope got to his feet. He must make sure that everything was in perfect order. He put his uniform back on and went out into the moonlight and walked briskly to Bert Frith's cottage.

In his own mind Hope suspected young Gratton's involvement in the death of Tinker Frith. Walton had told Hope that there had been a vicious argument and Gratton had threatened the old man. And Hope had seen Gratton rushing away from the direction of Tinker's camp. It made sense to Hope that Gratton was implicated somehow, but he wanted first to see what Bert Frith had been up to on the Station. After all, Hope knew Bert Frith would have been as likely as anybody to kill his father. The Friths had no family loyalties or feelings, he had seen that with the conviction of the hapless Horace.

Hope discounted Maisie Frith. He knew she had been scrubbing for four hours; the Bakers were well known in the town for their penny pinching. Mrs. Baker would have stood over Maisie as she toiled. And Hope did not wish to think about Maisie. He did not want to think of the fact he had seen what they called in the town 'T'Owd Woman'. It contradicted a masculine pride in himself and his Christian upbringing. He put Maisie out of his mind as he trod the moonlit streets and where a fur of white frost was beginning to coat the cobbles. He knocked on Bert Frith's door.

It was unbolted and Frith stared at him with that Frith stare, so alike in each other and yet so different individually. Gerald's was enigmatic, Maisie's appealing and sexually inviting, Bert's was challenging. All were penetrating.

"Your father, Mr. Frith, died in the Infirmary of the Workhouse in the late afternoon. I need to ask you a few questions."

Bert Frith turned his head and shouted coarsely to his wife.

"Vi, the Old Sod's snuffed it. Gerrus a bucket, wilt? I shall be weepin' into it all neet for me feyther." he still said nothing to Hope.

"Why were you on the railway station this morning? What time did you arrive and did you remain on the station all the time?"

Frith laughed. "So you think I murdered that filthy old bugger. I wouldna mucky my hands wi' im. I went to the Station, Constable, (heavy sarcasm), because I were meeting my sister Molly. It were a family matter. I knew she were coming back on a train but I didna know which one."

This was so singularly unhelpful that Hope suspected Frith may be innocent of anything. He was taunting Hope. A little girl with blond curls and rosy cheeks came to the door and wrapped her arms round Frith's legs. Hope was astonished at the transformation in Frith's features.

"Ye'll get cold, love. Come, back to my knee by the fire."

He spoke to Hope with all aggression drained from his voice. "Go and see our Molly. She'll tell ye." Then with a flash of his earlier venom, "you're wasting your time, Constable. Annie Harryson could be on your knee in front of the fire instead of yo' traipsing the streets."

Hope ignored this and made his way almost at a run to Castle Street before Bert Frith could get to Molly. He knocked on the front door and was admitted by Molly. At once his suspicions returned that the Friths were somehow involved in their father's death. Molly's face was radiant.

The previous night had been a bad one for Miss B. Alarming nightmares about her distant relative the Duke had troubled her. His Grace kept appearing in his nightshirt, holding a pick and shovel, through the floorboards. At five in the morning Miss B. had developed palpitations that Molly could feel shaking the old woman's body and was screaming to the hallucination "Don't threaten me with your lantern! Please do not, I beg of you dear boy!" Molly had knocked up Dr. Bagehot.

Dr. Bagehot had been reading in an Austrian journal about sedation in patients with 'brain softening', and had been particularly impressed by a formula, that seemed both to sedate and stimulate, the decaying brain in such patients. He was eager to try it out on Miss Bentinck, but doubted if James the town Chemist stocked certain drugs. Seeing the state Miss Bentinck presented, he wrote a prescription out, and urged Molly to catch the early train to Millers Dale Junction, and then the Buxton train. There was an excellent Pharmacy in The Quadrant, that stocked all the drugs that may be needed for wealthy continental visitors to the Spa. Bagehot knew that German doctors often prescribed several of the drugs in his prescription. Leaving Winny in charge of a snoring Miss B., now in the arms of an opiated sleep, Molly spent a pleasant morning in Buxton. The prescription was dispensed by a young French chemist, who obviously liked the look of Molly. Before the return train to connect at Millers Dale Junction, Molly had time for an excellent coffee and ice and gateau in Collinsons in Spring Gardens. The whole outing cheered her up.

She was astonished to see Bert on the platform when the train stopped.

Like Miss B. Phyllis had had a bad night. Bert had seen tiny tadpoles of scarlet in the white handkerchief the little girl had been coughing into.

"Wouldst ye like anything for a treat?" Bert had asked his daughter before he left for his shop. Phyllis turned her own blue Frith gaze on her father.

"I'd like Aunty Molly to tell me a story with voices while I eat her chips," she had told him. Bert said nothing but gave her a kiss and went.

An hour later while cutting and stitching on his cobblers' bench Bert suddenly put down his awl and thread. He stared out of his shop window into the mist, motionless in thought, his daughter being the chief preoccupation. Then he suddenly got to his feet and closed the shop and went straight to Castle Street where he was told that Molly had gone to Buxton but would return as soon as she could. Bert had walked to the Station and waited. When the slow train from Millers Dale arrived Bert saw Molly alight. He did not waste words.

"Sis, I were a bit hasty when I told ye were not welcome. Our Phyllis keeps asking for her Aunty Moll . . ."

Bert Frith did not meet his sister's eyes. He kept them downcast and traced a pattern known only to him on the surface of the platform with his boot.

Molly knew Bert well enough to know that was as good an apology as she would get. She stood on tiptoe and gave him a quick kiss on his cheek.

"I'll try and get up for an hour later," she said

Returning hastily at six, after leaving Winny for an hour with Miss B. she had seen Ellie Slater.

"That big bobby's finished your feyther off for good!"

So Molly had been reconciled with Bert, cooked some chips for Phyllis in the finest beef dripping from Miss B.'s kitchen, taken her a stuffed rabbit bought months earlier in Matlock, told her the story of Thorn Rose with voices and heard her father was dead.

How she did not care. He was gone for ever and she hoped he would burn in deepest Hell. Her face was rejuvenated as she explained why Bert was on the Station and why she was there.

Hope went straight round to Dr. Bagehot to corroborate this. Bagehot was at this moment carving up Tinker but Winny, who knew everything that went off next door and in the Doctor's establishment ascertained everything.

Satisfied, and his mind on John Gratton, Hope went back for his bath and the notes that would cast a shadow of suspicion on John Gratton.

John Hope and Annie Harryson had been talking together since Hope had fetched his notebooks to write down the report of that momentous day. Annie had casually asked what he intended to report and as he often did, he told her.

A fierce discussion had ensued which had shaken Hope to his philosophical foundations and his understanding of the law and his job. They had talked it over for five hours now.

"Let's clear our minds Mr. Hope," said she. "You wanted to write that you heard a loud cry and you made your way quickly down the lane. You saw John Gratton hurrying to his farmhouse, despite the fog, you are certain of that. You found that old bugger Tinker, half dead with a head wound, and an empty canvas bag that you presume was Tinker's property that had been emptied and stolen. You only noticed it when you returned with the porter to carry the old devil down to the station."

She smiled her smile. "You also saw plants in the lane, the type I harvest, as though they had been dropped in a hurry. And you saw Bert Frith washing his hands in the urinal of the second class waiting room."

Hope was silent. And exhausted by her persistence.

"So, Mr. Hope, you write this down and that prize clown Glorey sees it, or even your much admired Superintendent Lomas. And what do they think? They think that John Gratton had murdered that stinking rat Tinker. Why, nobody will care. The law just wants a solution. You had it from Sam Walton they were on bad terms, John and Tinker, and John wanted him off his land and had threatened him. So John Gratton will be hanged. And Tinker will lie under the nettles and rot. I would hope that the Devil is roasting his bollocks in hell, but my religious certainties are not as secure as yours. And I say to you again. I have it in confidence that Tinker raped and buggered his way through life tho' nobody dares say so. Or are too ashamed and humiliated to do so. They certainly would not in court. So Tinker has been killed. He should have been executed by the law but he has escaped the law and somebody has done it instead. I ask you, Mr. Hope, what good will it do putting in this report, and putting John in Derby gaol, when the real criminal has been executed for us, and the world is well rid. I ask you again, Mr. Hope. What is the purpose of your report? What is the purpose in hanging John Gratton? Why are you going to write it thus?"

"The law and justice of the land," said Hope in a low voice, avoiding her flushed face with her furious eyes. He was shocked by a woman using such language and blasphemies. Annie Harryson's turn of phrase still stunned him.

"Law and justice my arse!" said Annie. He thought she was going to attack him.

"I'll begin again Mr. Hope. Tinker Frith, child molester, a practicer of incest and buggery, a rapist, has been executed, possibly by one of his victims. He is dead. The world is well rid. The town thinks you may have had a hand in it. You are the hero. The town is a safer place. Criminals will think twice before they do what they may because Constable Hope has eyes in his arse that miss nothing as well as a pair of handsome blue eyes of the normal variety. The world is a better place."

She hurled more pine cones on the blaze that burned jewel bright with the frost outside.

"And what will you do? You will have John Gratton arrested and hanged. That boy has worked to keep his mother and that farm and has harmed nobody. He was possibly harmed by that old bugger Frith. So Gratton is hanged. His mother cannot cope with the farm. She will pine away, end up in the damned workhouse, die from shame and grief. Because you have this crazy need to serve law and justice to the bitter end. What is the point Mr. Hope?"

"It is my duty as an officer of the Crown to uphold the laws of the land," said Hope feebly, but obstinate.

There was a long silence. The single silver chime announced the half hour after one.

"Then I shall tell you what I will do Mr. Hope. I shall go to Sergeant Glorey and say I did it. He will see in your notes I dropped the plants and his tiny male mind will think I dropped them as I fled the murder. He would love to arrest me, finger me as he shoved me into his cell before I went to Derby. And I shall say I saw Bert Frith in the woods. He will be in Court. And somehow he has the money for a good lawyer. You saw how he manipulated the evidence against poor old Horace. Just imagine what he would do in Court... I shall employ the best barrister I can get my hands on and I know a few in London. As you know, Mr. Hope, money is of no importance to me. I could pay a thousand pounds for the very best and not notice it has gone. English Law is the best money can buy Mr. Hope. Did you know that? I shall have the Court in uproar. I will make a fool of the law and you, I can think of one K.C. who will make mincemeat of your evidence because of the fog, because of Bert Frith washing his hands, because of the scattered plants. I could say I was attacked and dropped the plants, I could say Bert Frith helped me, because Mr. Hope I could get him to say that. He loathed his father. The Case will be thrown out. Hundreds of pounds wasted. Time wasted. The Crown's time that you revere so much! So much for your precious law. Not even your hero Lomas will be able to sort out the tangled web that my K.C and I will weave."

Another silence until the clock chimed two. Hope, drained and fatigued, suddenly saw his mother's image in his mind, frail and skeletal as she had been before she died, looking into his face as he sat by her bedside, proud of the fact he was in a police uniform, full of love and confidence despite her pain and misery. Memory of his mother had faded since that first day of Queen Victoria's death, when he began his duties and he thought of Mrs. Gratton, with her pinched and anxious face, hurrying through the town trying to make the best of her son's life and her own.

He said nothing.

He reached for his official notebook. He sharpened his pencil.

Proceeding down the lane to the Station I decided to warn Roland Frith about his language and threatening behaviour. I found he had sealed himself in his tent. On entering I found him unconscious, his head bleeding, possibly from a fall. I fetched aid and a stretcher from the railway station and we took Frith to the workhouse infirmary.

He showed the book by holding it up. He looked at Annie Harryson and saw her eyes full of tears.

"Constable Hope you are a fine man. And please. My name is Annie. And I would like to call you John."

She placed a warm and surprisingly soft hand over his and Hope suddenly realised he had never felt so happy.

Superintendent Lomas had spent the day of Tinker's murder in Derby in various meetings. Lomas had expected this and knew he would be unable to catch the last train back to the town. He hated staying in commercial hotels and had taken his pony and trap to

Matlock, left the pony in the Matlock police stables. He caught the late express from St. Pancras to Manchester that stopped at Derby and Matlock. He was in his pony and trap trotting the nine miles to the town on a deserted moon white turnpike road.

At Rowsley he discerned a syncopation in the usual rhythm of his pony May's hooves on the road. It sounded as if one of her hooves was troubling her. Lomas, who had an exhaustive knowledge of everybody, knew the night porter at Rowsley had been at one time a farrier in the Army in India. Lomas drove into the station yard. The porter, bored with the long night was only too glad to remove a sharp pebble from May's shoe.

"You won't have heard the news Superintendent. That old bugger Roland Frith has had his chips. They say that new man of yours, Hope is it, sorted the old devil out. Not before time either."

Lomas let the man rattle on for ten minutes. Then he resumed his way.

When the pony and trap came out into the lakes of moonlight on the tree lined road it was possible to see a hair line crease on Lomas' face that had not been there before. It was hard to classify this as anger, disappointment or great concern.

After only three hours of sleep Lomas walked to the Workhouse and presented himself to the Master. It was hardly five in the morning and the sky was jewelled with constellations above an autumnal chill mist on the river. The Workhouse was already stirring and the air redolent with the smell of porridge that had a taint of old cloth in it, carbolic and misery. Lomas was shown into the Master's Parlour where a bright new fire flamed, tended by an inmate.

Lomas requested a copy of the Report on Roland Frith and the Master obliged.

Lomas asked if he may make a copy and pen and ink and paper were supplied.

At six o' clock Lomas was at the Police Station.

He summoned Hope to his room straight after Glorey's dyspeptic parade inspection.

"Your notebook Constable," he said. While Hope undid his tunic pocket he made one of his rapid assessments. He noticed that Hope had dark circles under his eyes as though he had slept badly. He also noticed the young Constable avoided eye contact. He took the notebook and read it. He returned it to Hope and stared at him for several seconds in which time Hope made no attempt to make eye contact.

"Do you wish to say anything Constable?"

Was there the slightest hesitation? Did the lips move? Was there the hint of a shuffle? Lomas' expert eye took all of this in.

"Return to your duties Constable. I expect the Sergeant has put much thought into planning today's work for you after he has heard what the town is saying."

He watched the retreating Hope turn and go. Not once had Hope given him that open gaze that had so impressed the Superintendent over the last five years.

Although Lomas still took Hope out from time to time it was noticeable that the tours and lectures became less and less, despite the fact Lomas' annual report always painted Hope's achievements in glowing colours.

It was noticed by John and Annie that instead of taking Hope out with him, the Superintendent altered his routine.

At least once a month, on foot, he made the same walk. Up past the Station and on the old abandoned causeway to Walton's farm where he stopped for a chat. Always welcomed by Sam. Then back down to Gratton's farm where he had a chat with John and Mrs. Gratton. Mrs. Gratton was always welcoming, but he noted that John was reserved, avoided his eyes, a bit like Constable Hope on the morning after Tinker's death. Then Lomas went down to the Station and chatted to Baker the Station Master.

The Superintendent let them all do the talking; it was his way of discovering facts.

One spring morning six months later, Lomas stood on the Bridge, pausing a while after returning from one of these walks. Annie Harryson greeted him.

"Good morning Superintendent. Looking for something fishy?"

"No Mrs. Harryson. But I think I may smell a rat."

"Well, good luck to you, Superintendent. And good luck in your sniffing out."

"Good day to you, Mrs. Harryson."

Lomas walked this route until the outbreak of the Great War in 1914, when another murder concerning military men finally destroyed his faith in mankind and finished his life and career. And he never discovered the rat he thought he smelled.

Ten years later and Private Gratton stared through the mist beyond the trench and suddenly felt a nettle sting in his eyes and throat. Seconds later he was writhing on the ground as the chlorine gas attack clawed its way into his lungs. He felt as though red hot sticks were now being rammed down into his windpipe or the farm cat Tissy was clawing his lungs out.

As he fought to breathe with his dissolving lungs his dying brain flipped back to a struggle he had never forgotten, his fight with Tinker Frith. He had crept up on the old devil and brought down a boulder on his head. Frith had not gone easily into his death. There had been a struggle before John had pulled down the skin trousers of Frith and released the adders. His dying brain omitted the wait outside the tent while the adders did their work and he returned to the tent to restore Frith's breeches. Instead John saw his mother smile at him in the kitchen as he hurried in.

Turning at the door he saw the woods as vivid and green as May, green light was everywhere, bright as the angels of green that Dr. Ball believed, in the manner of Dante, flew round All Saints' Spire. And coming swiftly towards him was the Old Woman in White his grandmother had told him collected the souls of the dead.

Then death released John from the torment of his dissolving lungs.

So. His wife Annie, had been right. John Gratton had had nine years of farming on one of the loveliest farms in the township, sun and fresh air and a year with his new wife Doris and their baby son. Annie had wanted that, a normal happy life for the young man. And now John had repaid his debt for breaking the law. Or was it a debt? Hope had never come to terms with what he had done. And yet he knew his wife Annie was right. And yet . . .

He looked up for a moment. The golden arrow on the church spire was swinging in doubt and there was a drop of rain on his cheek. He stared at the clouds building from Buxton. There would be storms. Then his thoughts were back in 1905. For 1905 had been the real beginning of understanding life and law and compromise, just as that fearful discovery of corpses in 1907 had been the beginning of true understanding of life, death and sex and that had emphatically been learned in 1908. And the criminal incidents with Major Bunyan in 1914 that had, in Hope's own opinion killed Lomas and made Bert Frith the leader of a different kind of crime. Life went on, crime went on and there was much still to learn about it all. He was aware of the flash of a rainbow over Sam Walton's Bow Cross Farm and a sweep of low golden sunlight.

"Sir . . . the Reverend Jones has arrived and is waiting to begin praying for them dead soldiers." Sergeant Feares tapped Hope's arm.

“Thank you Sergeant,” said Hope. “They need our prayers.”

Made in the USA
Lexington, KY
03 July 2018